W9-BHI-958

Chopping
Spree

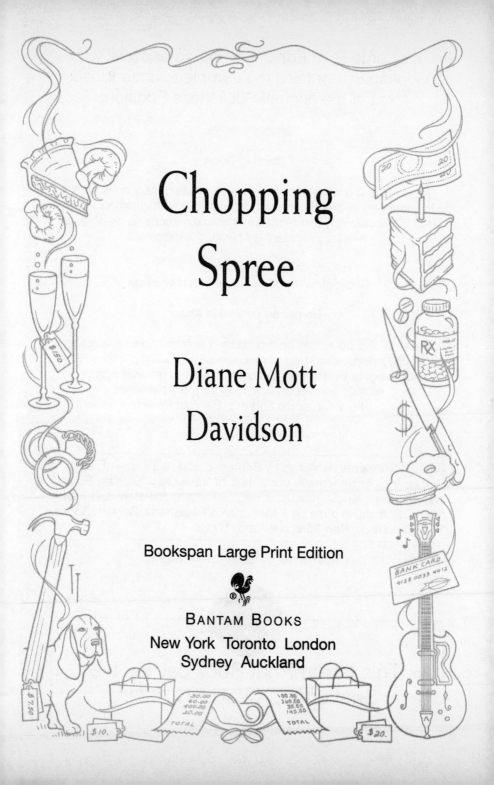

Chopping Spree

Diane Mott Davidson

Bookspan Large Print Edition

BANTAM BOOKS

**New York Toronto London
Sydney Auckland**

This Large Print Edition, prepared especially for Bookspan, contains the complete, unabridged text of the original Publisher's Eddition.

CHOPPING SPREE

A Bantam Book

ISBN 0-7394-2766-0

Bantam Books are published by Bantam Books, a division of Random House, Inc. Its trademark, consisting of the words "Bantam Books" and the portrayal of a rooster, is Registered in U.S. Patent and Trademark Office and in other countries. Marca Registrada. Bantam Books, 1540 Broadway, New York, New York 10036.

PRINTED IN THE UNITED STATES OF AMERICA

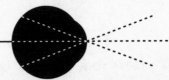

This Large Print Book carries the Seal of Approval of N.A.V.H.

To Julie Wallin Kaewert,
a black-belt shopper, brilliant writer,
and invaluable friend

ACKNOWLEDGMENTS

I wish to acknowledge the assistance of the following people: Jim, J.Z., and Joe Davidson; Jeff and Rosa Davidson; Kate Miciak, an insightful editor; Sandra Dijkstra, an enthusiastic agent with a superb staff; and Susan Corcoran and Sharon Propson, wonderful publicists.

For help with legal insights, I am indebted to Hal Warren, Assistant County Attorney, Adams County, Colorado, for answering questions about building procedures; and Natalie Frei, attorney-at-law, for insights into criminal law procedures.

In addition, I am thankful to Liz Hudd, biology teacher, Evergreen High School, Evergreen, Colorado, whose anatomy class performs the same tasks as the one described in this book (but Liz's students behave much better); Katherine Goodwin Saideman and Shirley Carnahan, Ph.D., instructor in Humanities at the University of Colorado, for their close readings of the manuscript; Lee Karr and the group that assembled at her home, for support and advice; Julie Wallin Kaewert, Ann Wallin Harrington, Carol Devine Rusley, and Cheryl McGonigle, for more support and advice; Triena Harper, Chief Deputy Coroner, Jefferson County Coroner's Office, Jefferson County, Colorado, for information on cadavers; Julie Brown, Office Manager, Elk Ridge Family Physicians; John William Schenk and Karen Schenk, JKS, for their freely shared culinary expertise; Nick LeMasters, General Manager, Cherry Creek Shopping Center, Denver, for insights into mall management; and as usual, for insights into law enforcement, Sergeant Richard Millsapps, Jefferson County Sheriff's Department, Golden, Colorado. For insights into the psychology of compulsive buying, I am indebted to the book *I Shop, Therefore I Am: Compulsive Buying and the Search for Self*, edited by April Lane Benson, Ph.D., published by Jason Aronson Inc., Northvale, New Jersey.

Finally, this book could not have been written without the knowledge and insights of my wonderful brother, William C. Mott, Jr., Vice President, Investment Banking, Goldman Sachs and Company, New York, New York. Bill's training as an architect and his business expertise in the area of mall management were invaluable at every stage of the book. Along with all of my family, I am exceedingly grateful not only for him, but for the fact that he was safely evacuated from the World Trade Center on September 11, 2001, by the New York Police Department. Thank you.

Getting and spending, we lay waste our powers:
Little we see in Nature that is ours;
We have given our hearts away, a sordid boon!

—William Wordsworth,
"The World Is Too Much with Us"

PRINCESS WITHOUT THE PRICE TAG
JEWELRY-LEASING EXTRAVAGANZA

Elite Shoppers' Lounge - Westside Mall
Monday, April 11
6 to 8 in the evening

Hors d'Oeuvre Buffet

*Crown of Cheeses: Brie, Gorgonzola, Gruyère,
Sharp English Cheddar, Camembert*

◆

*Herb Brioche, Crostini, Homemade Crackers
and Corn Chips*

◆

*Tiaras of Strawberries, Raspberries, Blueberries,
and Star Fruit with Creamy Fruit Dressing*

◆

*Empress Empanadas with Guacamole
and Sour Cream*

◆

*Sweethearts' Swedish Meatballs
in Burgundy Sauce*

◆

Golden Shrimp Rolls with Spicy Sauce

◆

Diamond Lovers' Hot Crab Dip

Shoppers' Chocolate Truffles

◆

Cocktails, Premium Wines and Beers

◆

Coffee, Tea, Chai, and Espresso Drinks

CHAPTER 1

Success can kill you.

So my best friend had been telling me, anyway. Too much success is like arsenic in chocolate cake. Eat a slice a *day,* Marla announced with a sweep of her plump, be-jeweled fingers, and you'll get cancer. Gob-ble the whole *cake?* You'll keel over and die on the spot.

These observations, made over the course of a snowy March, had not cheered me. Besides, I'd have thought that Marla, with her inherited wealth and passion for shopping, would *applaud* the upward leap of my catering business. But she said she was worried about me.

Frankly, I was worried about me, too.

In mid-March I'd invited Marla over to taste cookies. Despite a sudden but typical Colorado blizzard, she'd roared over to our small house off Aspen Meadow's Main Street in her shiny new BMW four-wheel drive. Sitting in our commercial kitchen, she'd munched on ginger snaps and spice cookies, and harped on the fact that the newly frantic pace of my work had coincided with my fourteen-year-old son Arch's increasingly rotten behavior. I knew Marla doted on Arch.

But in this, too, she was right.

Arch's foray into athletics, begun that winter with snowboarding and a stint on his school's fencing team, had ended with a trophy, a sprained ankle, and an unprecedented burst of physical self-confidence. He'd been eager to plunge into spring sports. When he'd decided on lacrosse, I'd been happy for him. That changed when I attended the first game. Watching my son forcefully shove an opponent aside and steal the ball, I'd felt queasy. With Arch's father—a rich doctor

who'd had many violent episodes himself—
now serving time for parole violation, all
that slashing and hitting was more than I
could take.

But even more worrisome than the
sport itself, Marla and I agreed, were Arch's
new teammates: an unrepentant gang of
spoiled, acquisitive brats. Unfortunately,
Arch thought the lacrosse guys were beyond cool. He spent hours with them,
claiming that he "forgot" to tell us where he
was going after practice. We could have
sent him an *e-mail* telling him to call, Arch
protested, if he only had what all his pals
had, to wit, Internet-access watches. *Your
own watch could have told you what time it
was,* I'd told him, when I picked him up
from the country-club estate where the
senior who was supposed to drive him
home had left him off.

Arch ignored me. These new friends,
he'd announced glumly, also had Global
Positioning System calculators, Model
Bezillion Palm pilots, and electric-acoustic
guitars that cost eight hundred dollars—
and up. These litanies were always accompanied with not-so-tactful reminders that
his fifteenth birthday was right around the

corner. He wanted everything on his list, he announced as he tucked a scroll of paper into my purse. After all, with all the parties I'd booked, I could finally afford to get him some really good stuff.

And no telling what'll happen if I don't get what I want, he'd added darkly. (Marla informed me that he'd already given *her* a list.) I'd shrugged as Arch clopped into the house ahead of me. I'd started stuffing sautéed chicken breasts with wild rice and spinach. The next day, Tom had picked up Arch at another friend's house. When my son waltzed into the kitchen, I almost didn't recognize him.

His head was shaved.

"They Bic'd me," he declared, tossing a lime into the air and catching it in the net of his lacrosse stick.

"They *bicked* you?" I exclaimed incredulously.

"*Bic*, Mom. Like the razor." He rubbed his bare scalp, then flipped the lime again. "And I *would* have been home on time, if you'd bought me the Palm, to remind me to tell the guy shaving my head that I had to go."

I snagged the lime in midair. "Go start

on your homework, buster. You got a C on the last anatomy test. And from now on, either Tom or I will pick you up right from practice."

On his way out of the kitchen, he whacked his lacrosse stick on the floor. I called after him please not to do that. I got no reply. The next day, much to Arch's sulking chagrin, Tom had picked him up directly from practice. *If being athletic is what success at that school looks like*, Tom told me, *then maybe Arch should take up painting*. I kept mum. The next day, I was ashamed to admit, I'd pulled out Arch's birthday list and bought him the Palm pilot.

Call it working mom's guilt, I'd thought, as I stuffed tiny cream puffs with shrimp salad. Still, I was not sorry I was making more money than ever before. I did not regret that *Goldilocks' Catering, Where Everything Is Just Right!* had gone from booked to overbooked. Finally, I was giving those caterers in Denver, forty miles to the east, a run for their shrimp rolls. This was what I'd always wanted, right?

Take my best upcoming week, I'd explained to Marla as she moved on to test my cheesecake bars and raspberry brownies. The second week of April, I would make close to ten thousand dollars—a record. I'd booked an upscale cocktail party at Westside Mall, a wedding reception, and two big luncheons. Once I survived all that, Friday, April the fifteenth, was Arch's birthday. By then, I'd finally have the cash to buy him something, as Arch himself had said, *really* good.

"Goldy, don't do all that," Marla warned as she downed one of my new Spice-of-Life Cookies. The buttery cookies featured large amounts of ginger, cinnamon, and freshly grated nutmeg, and were as comforting as anything from Grandma's kitchen. "You'll be too exhausted even to make a birthday cake. Listen to me, now. You need to decrease your bookings, hire some help, be stricter with Arch, and take care of yourself for a change. If you don't, you're going to *die*."

Marla was always one for the insightful observation.

I didn't listen. At least, not soon enough. The time leading up to that lucrative week in April became even busier and more frenetic. Arch occasionally slipped away from practice before Tom, coming up from his investigative work at the sheriff's department, could snag him. I was unable to remember the last time I'd had a decent night's sleep. So I suppose it was inevitable that, at ten-twenty on the morning of April eleventh, I had what's known in the shrink business as a *crisis*. At least, that's what they'd called it years ago, during my pursuit of a singularly unhelpful degree in psychology.

I was inside our walk-in refrigerator when I blacked out. Just before hitting the walk-in's cold floor, I grabbed a metal shelf. Plastic bags of tomatoes, scallions, celery, shallots, and gingerroot spewed in every direction, and my bottom thumped the floor. I thought, *I don't have time for this*.

I struggled to get up, and belatedly realized this meltdown wasn't that hard to figure out. I'd been up since five A.M. With one of the luncheon preps done, I was focusing on the mall cocktail party that evening. Or at least I had been focusing on it, before my eyes, legs, and back gave out.

I groaned and quickly gathered the plastic bags. My back ached. My mind threw out the realization that I *still* did not know where Arch had been for three hours the previous afternoon, when lacrosse practice had been canceled. Neither Tom nor I had been aware of the calendar change. Tom had finally collected Arch from a seedy section of Denver's Colfax Avenue. So what had this about-to-turn-fifteen-year-old been up to this time? Arch had refused to say.

"Just do the catering," I announced to the empty refrigerator. I replaced the plastic bags and asked the Almighty for perspective. Arch would get the third degree when he came down for breakfast. Meanwhile, I had work to do.

Before falling on my behind, I'd been working on a concoction I'd dubbed Shoppers' Chocolate Truffles. These rich goodies featured a dense, smooth chocolate interior coated with more satiny chocolate. So what had I been looking for in the refrigerator? I had no idea. I stomped out and slammed the door.

I sagged against the counter and told myself the problem was fatigue. Or maybe my age—thirty-four—was kicking in. What would Marla say? She'd waggle a fork in my face and preach about the wages of success.

I brushed myself off and quick-stepped to the sink. As water gushed over my hands, I remembered I'd been searching for the scoops of ganache, that sinfully rich mélange of melted bittersweet chocolate, heavy cream, and liqueur that made up the heart of the truffles.

I dried my hands and resolved to concentrate on dark chocolate, not the darker side of success. After all, I had followed one of Marla's suggestions: I *had* hired help. But I had not cut back on parties. I'd forgotten what taking care of myself even felt like. And I seemed incapable of being stricter with Arch.

I scanned the kitchen. The ganache balls, still wrapped, sat pristinely on the marble counter. Next to it, my double boiler steamed on the stovetop. OK, so I'd already taken them out. I'd simply forgotten.

I hustled over to my new kitchen computer and booted it up, intent on checking that evening's assignment. Soon my new printer was spitting out lists of needed foodstuffs, floor plans, and scheduled setup. I may have lost my mind, but I'd picked it right up again.

"This is what happens when you give up caffeine!" I snarled at the ganache balls. Oops—that was twice I'd talked to myself in the last five minutes. Marla would not approve.

I tugged the plastic wrap off the globes of ganache and spooned up a sample to check the consistency. The smooth, intense dark chocolate sent a zing of pleasure up my back. I moved to the stovetop, stirred the luxurious pool of melting chocolate, and took a whiff of the intoxicatingly rich scent. I told myself—silently—that everything was going to be all right. The party-goers were going to *love* me.

The client for that night's cocktail party was Barry Dean, an old friend who was now manager of Westside Mall, an upscale shopping center abutting the foothills west of Denver. I'd previously put on successful catered parties at Westside. Each time, the store owners had raved. But Barry Dean, who'd only been managing the mall for six months, had seemed worried about the party's dessert offering. I'd promised him his high-end spenders, for whom the party was geared, would *flip* over the truffles.

Maybe I'd even get a big tip, I thought as I scraped down the sides of the double boiler. I could spend it on a new mattress. On it, I might eventually get some sleep.

I stopped and took three deep breaths. My system craved coffee. Of course, I hadn't given up espresso *entirely*. I was just trying to cut back from nine shots a day to two. Too much caffeine was causing my sleeplessness, Marla had declared. Of course, since we'd both been married to the same doctor—consecutively, not concurrently—she and I were self-proclaimed experts on all physical ailments. (Med Wives 101, we called it.) So I'd actually heeded her advice. My plan had been to have one shot at eight in the morning (a distant memory), another at four in the afternoon (too far in the future). Now my resolve was melting faster than the dark chocolate.

I fired up the espresso machine and wondered how I'd gotten into such a mental and physical mess.

Innocently enough, my mind replied. Without warning, right after Valentine's Day, my catering business had taken off. An influx of ultrawealthy folks to Denver and the mountain area west of the Mile High City had translated into massive construction of trophy homes, purchases of multiple upscale cars, and doubling of prices for just about everything. Most important from my viewpoint, the demand for big-ticket catered events had skyrocketed. From mid-February to the beginning of April, a normally slow season, my assignments had exploded. I'd thought I'd entered a zone, as they say in Boulder, of *bliss*.

I pulled a double shot of espresso, then took a sip and felt infinitely better.

I rolled the first silky scoop of ganache into a ball, and set it aside. What had I been thinking about? Ah, yes. Success.

I downed more coffee and set aside the porcelain bought-on-clearance cup, a remnant of my financial dark days. Those days had lasted a long time, a fact that Arch seemed to block out.

When I began divorce proceedings against the ultracute, ultra-vicious Doctor John Richard Korman, I'd been so determined that he would support our son well that I'd become an Official Nosy Person.

Files, tax returns, credit card receipts, check stubs, bank deposits—I'd found and studied them all. My zealous curiosity had metamorphosed into a decent settlement. Wasn't it Benjamin Franklin who'd said, *God helps those who help themselves*? Old Ben had been right.

I bathed the first dark ganache globe in chocolate. OK, I'd replaced marital bitterness with bittersweet chocolate and bitter orange marmalade, right? And my life had turned around. Two years ago, I'd married Tom Schulz. As unreal as my newly minted financial success might seem, I did not doubt the miracle of my relationship with Tom, whose work as a police investigator had actually brought us together in the first place. Tom was bighearted and open-armed toward both Arch and me. So far, Tom and I had passed the tests that had been flung our way, and emerged still together. In this day and age, I thought, such commitment was commendable.

And yet, I reflected as I placed the sumptuous truffle on a rack to dry, one of the reasons I'd been so happy about my sudden financial success was that I'd vowed never to depend on Tom's income.

My earnings were now on a par with Tom's. After the money battles with The Jerk, financial independence was a phenomenon I'd sworn to attain and keep. Unfortunately, before marrying Tom, my profits had stayed in a zone between *Can feed Arch and keep gas in van* to *Going down fast; write for law school catalogs.*

I rolled ganache balls, bathed them in chocolate, and set them aside to dry. Scoop, bathe, set aside. Marla could grouse all she wanted; I savored my new success. I was even considering purchasing a new set of springform pans, since I'd already bought a new computer, printer, and copier, not to mention new tableware, flatware, and knives—a shining set of silver Henckels. I *relished* no longer renting plates, silverware, and linens! I laughed aloud when I finished the twentieth truffle, and made myself another espresso. The dark drink tasted divine. No wonder they called financial solvency *liquidity*.

I rewarded myself with a forkful of ganache, which sparked more fireworks of chocolate ecstasy. I did a little two-step and thanked the Almighty for chocolate, coffee, and business growth.

Roll, bathe, set aside. I was appreciative that I had scads of new clients. In hiring me, they offered testimonies from friends (Marla in particular), or claimed they'd caught the reruns of my short-lived PBS cooking show. Some even said they just *had* to hire this caterer they'd read about, the one who helped her husband solve the occasional murder case. Well, why they hired me didn't matter. New clients were new clients, and glitzy parties paid the bills. It had been stupendous.

For a while.

Now I looked and felt like zabaglione, frothy after being beaten too hard. And I was unsure of what was going on with my son. I rolled, bathed, and set aside more truffles, all the while avoiding my reflection in the kitchen window. I knew what I'd see there: a haggard face with licorice-black bags under bloodshot eyes, not to mention a fretwork of worry-wrinkles. My freshly shampooed, too-busy-to-get-a-cut blond hair, which people had always likened to Shirley Temple's corkscrew curls, now gave me the look of a soaked poodle.

You're obsessing again, I scolded myself as I set the thirtieth truffle on the rack. *You'll just make things worse.*

I focused on the ganache. As if to prove my truffles were indeed worthy of Westside's best-heeled shoppers, I'd offered one from an earlier batch to handsome, brown-haired Barry Dean, who, years ago, had taken a psych class with me at the University of Colorado. Back then, he'd flirted with me, he'd given me notes when I missed a lecture, he'd taken me out in his Mercedes for coffee after class. I'd patted his basset hound, Honey, who lay in regal repose on a blanket in the backseat. Tucking into our cappuccinos, lattes, and espressos con panna, Barry and I prided ourselves on being the only two coffee connoisseurs on the Boulder campus. I'd enjoyed our outings immensely.

The previous week, I'd given him the chocolate during our second meeting in Westside's new shoppers' lounge. Quickly downing three truffles, Barry had vented his frustration over the chronic delays in Westside's second remodeling in five years. His construction manager had quit in a huff and moved to Arizona; his volatile excavator promised one thing, then did another.

Since I'd had my own remodeling disaster, I'd murmured sympathetically.

Barry had eaten six more truffles—the man was *stressed out*—as we hammered out the party details. He offered to drive me back to my van. On the way, he promised, as he downed his tenth truffle, he'd take me out for coffee. *Just like the old days.*

At the espresso drive-through known as The Westside Buzz, the *barista* had recognized Barry. A Denver newspaper had just named him *The Mile High City's Most Eligible Bachelor,* and the *barista* went nuts. After she got over squealing, making change, and handing us our drinks, Barry had demonstrated the turbo on his new Saab (bought because someone had crashed into his Mercedes) to zoom away. At a red light, he'd shown me the car's stereo, CD player, fan ventilation of perforated leather seats, and other bells and whistles. The man loved cars, no question about it. I'd laughed and asked if he wanted another truffle. He'd placed his drink into the retractable cup holder, mouthed a drumroll, and popped another truffle—his eleventh—into his mouth. To my delight, he'd opened his gorgeous brown eyes wide and yodeled as he soared into a state of chocolate euphoria. Upon recovering, he'd ordered sixty. He feigned amnesia and panted, *Construction? What construction?*

I smiled, remembering. I bathed the fortieth ganache ball in dark chocolate, set it on the rack, and gave it a stiff appraisal. I had to admit, it had amnesia potential.

I took a deep breath and ordered myself not to indulge in another taste until *all sixty* of the chocolates were made. Instead, I *had* to start planning Arch's birthday.

At the moment, Arch was still asleep, as the Elk Park Prep teachers were meeting for an in-service. School that day didn't start till noon, my son had announced the previous night, and could we spend the morning shopping? I'd said no, I had to *work*. And besides, where had he been the previous day? He'd sighed. Then he'd pushed his glasses up his nose so he could give me the full benefit of his pleading eyes, which seemed huge against the background of his shaved head. Had I started purchasing *any* items on his birthday list? he asked.

I swallowed. I'd only bought the Palm; I hadn't had time for anything else. Arch had hoisted his bookbag and stalked out of the kitchen. I yelled after him that no matter how much money you had, it was never enough. He'd called back something unintelligible.

I rolled another ball of ganache and longed to stuff it into my mouth. Instead, I dipped it into the dark chocolate. Marla's warnings haunted me. What, exactly, was *enough*? On our day of planning, Barry Dean had told me about the jewelry-event-cum-cocktail-party guests, members of Westside's Elite Shoppers Club. The "Elites," as Barry called them, spent a minimum of a thousand dollars a *week* at the mall. Membership in the group guaranteed special coupons, special sales, valet parking, and events like the jewelry-leasing extravaganza I was catering that night. One thing I had asked Barry: Where did the Elites *put* all the stuff they bought? He'd winked, done his endearing-bachelor shrug, and said usually they rented storage sheds.

Perhaps buying wasn't the future of retail, Barry had added. Take jewelry leasing, for example, for which there was no need to store anything permanently. *You, too,*

Goldy, for two thousand, four thousand, or six thousand bucks a month, could wear a different piece of ultraglam jewelry every thirty days. Twenty percent off the cost of the yearly lease for all mall employees! I'd laughed and told him that none of the pieces I'd glimpsed—diamond, emerald, ruby, and sapphire necklaces—matched a single one of my aprons.

My business line rang. I put down the truffle, wiped my fingers on my stained apron, and actually prayed that this was *not* another new client.

"Goldilocks' Catering—"

"You're working," Marla accused.

"No, really, I was sleeping in. Then my best friend called and woke me up."

"Yeah, sure." She swallowed something. I guessed it was her latest version of hot chocolate, which consisted of hot cream, cocoa, and low-cal sweetener. Even though Marla had had a heart attack almost two years before, she'd had little luck losing weight on a low-fat, high-carb, low-protein diet. So now she was trying a some-fat, some-carb, high-protein diet. She claimed she'd lost six pounds and felt much better. When I'd asked what her cardiologist thought of the new regimen, she'd hung up on me. You had to be careful with Marla.

Now I said, "OK, I *was* trying to roll truffles, until my best friend called and forced me to smear chocolate all over my new apron."

"Quit bellyaching." She started munching on something, I didn't want to imagine what. "Yesterday I gave Arch a package for you. It's in your freezer. I want you to open it." I sighed, thinking of all the work I had to do. "While I'm *talking* to you, if you don't mind."

I knew my life would be much easier if I just tucked the phone against my shoulder, wrenched open the freezer door of the walk-in, and did as bidden. So I did. After a moment of groping, I pulled a very cold brown paper bag from a shelf. The bag contained—oh, joy—a pint of Häagen-Dazs coffee ice cream, hand-labeled "A," and a brown bottle of time-release vitamins, marked "B."

"OK, get a spoon and a glass of water," Marla commanded when she heard the paper rustling. "Take a spoonful of A, then a capsule of B. *Now*."

I again followed orders. The ice cream improved my mood, no question. But when I tried to swallow the vitamin, I choked.

"I can't believe you're doing the event tonight," Marla cried, not heeding my wheezing gasps. "You'll wreck *my* shopping experience, and everyone else's. You think people want a caterer who looks half dead? Shoppers want to *escape* reality, Goldy. They want to feel *rich*. They want to feel *young*. They'll take one look at you and say, *Why should I shop? She's gonna die and so am I.*"

I finally swallowed the vitamin and croaked, "Are you done talking about me kicking the bucket? 'Cuz I've got truffles to coat."

"No!" Marla wailed. "I need to bitch some more, and you're the only one who's home."

I refired the espresso machine, tucked the phone against my ear, and resumed work on the truffles.

Marla went on, her husky voice laced with anger: "I *was* going to lease the double strand of diamonds for the first month. They're *perfect* for the March of Dimes luncheon. But six thou a month? What'll I have left to give the March of Dimes?" She paused to devour more food. One of the whole-grain muffins I'd made her? Unlikely. "Then I heard that Page Stockham, also an Elite Shopper, wanted the same necklace. So now I'm trying to decide between a ruby chain and an emerald set in three rows of diamonds, in case Page gets it first. Oh, Page Stockham just makes me so *angry*. And to think I asked her to go with me to tonight's event."

"To *think*," I murmured sympathetically.

She ignored me. "Making matters even worse, Ellie McNeely wants the double pearl strand with the aquamarine, which I've had my eye on forever to go with a dinner I'm giving in May that I was hoping you'd cater, if you're not dead. Wait a minute, there's someone at the door."

I *mm-hmm*ed and continued dipping. Ellie McNeely, whom I'd done fund-raising with over a decade ago in the Episcopal Church Women, was an old friend from my rich-doctor's-wife years, one of the few old friends who'd remained a pal in my postdivorce, service-industry years. Page Stockham was the wife of Shane Stockham, Arch's lacrosse coach, and I knew her not at all. But the key fact from a caterer's perspective was that Page, Ellie, and Marla all had money to burn.

Waiting for Marla to return to the phone, I kept on with the truffles. Six to go. Roll, bathe, set aside. What had I been thinking about? Oh, yes, money to burn. I wasn't resentful, though, because moneyed folks were my best clients. And anyway, who was I to judge anyone else's *shopping*?

My eyes traveled to the carved wooden cupboard hanging over our kitchen table. I truly did *not* want to look down on folks who engaged in retail therapy. The reason was that during my divorce from The Jerk, and despite near-dire financial straits, I'd been a shop-to-feel-better gal myself. On weekends when it was John Richard's turn to have Arch, I'd visited every shopping center I could find. I'd strolled through perfume-scented air, by gorgeously stacked goods, past gaggle after gaggle of smiling, prosperous people. I'd loitered in front of brightly lit displays of embroidered baby clothes, rainbow-hued designer sheets, sleek copper pots and pans, even sugared, sparkling cinnamon rolls. I'd allowed myself to feel rich, even if my bank account said otherwise.

Come to think of it, maybe that was what Arch had been doing the previous day: shopping. Still, there weren't any luxury shops on East Colfax.

I retucked the silent phone against my ear, rolled another truffle, but stopped again to ponder the cupboard shelves. On each of those long-ago shopping trips, I'd bought myself a little something from the "Drastically Reduced" tables. My white porcelain demitasse cup and saucer, a tiny crystal mouse, a miniature wooden car laden with painted wooden gifts—all these had made me uncommonly happy. At home, I'd placed my minuscule treasures on the old cupboard's shelves. Without the stores' strong overhead lights, the little crystal mouse had not looked quite so brilliant; the cheap china cup had lost its translucence. But I'd never cared. Each piece had been *mine,* something for *me,* a small token of an inner voice, too long silenced, saying, "I love you." So who was I to judge Marla or her friends, Page Stockham and Ellie McNeely? They all wanted someone, even if it was themselves, to say,

I really, really care about you! And to prove it, have this!

Marla came back to the phone and said Ellie had arrived, and she had to go. Before the event, she, Ellie, and Page, who was driving down separately with husband Shane, would be getting the mud soak, the coconut-milk bath, and the vegetable-and-fruit wrap at Westside Spa.

"I'll watch for a moving luau."

"I'll catch you at the party," Marla retorted, undaunted, and signed off.

I rolled the fifty-eighth truffle. Then, lowering the scoop of ganache into the melted chocolate and setting it aside to dry, I made another espresso. To the far west, just visible out our back windows, a bright mist cloaked the mountains of the Aspen Meadow Wildlife Preserve. On the nearer hills, white-barked aspens nestled between dark expanses of fir, spruce, and pine. I peered at our thermometer. The red line was stubbornly stuck at twenty-nine degrees. *So this is Springtime in the Rockies?* newcomers always asked. *This is it,* I invariably replied. In June, you can take off your snow tires.

I slugged down what I vowed would be

my last coffee. Once again, worry surfaced. Where *had* Arch been yesterday? The rumor was that the rookies on the lacrosse team had been told their initiation would not be complete until they shoplifted something worth more than fifty dollars. Thinking about that possibility, my heart plummeted.

I disciplined myself to roll the next-to-last truffle. It broke into two pieces when I dunked it in the dark chocolate. Oh, darn! Guess I'll have to eat it, maybe with a fifth espresso! I pulled out the chocolate chunks swimming in the dark coating, placed them on the rack, then refilled the espresso doser. I rinsed the old porcelain demitasse cup and closed my eyes. Worry for Arch nagged at me. I balanced on one foot. I was *so* tired. . . . And then my much-loved cup slipped from my fingers. It shattered on the floor with a heartbreaking crash. Shards raced across the wood; bits of china smashed into the molding and sent reverberating tinkles throughout the kitchen.

My best shopping treasure was gone. Later, I tried not to think of it as an omen.

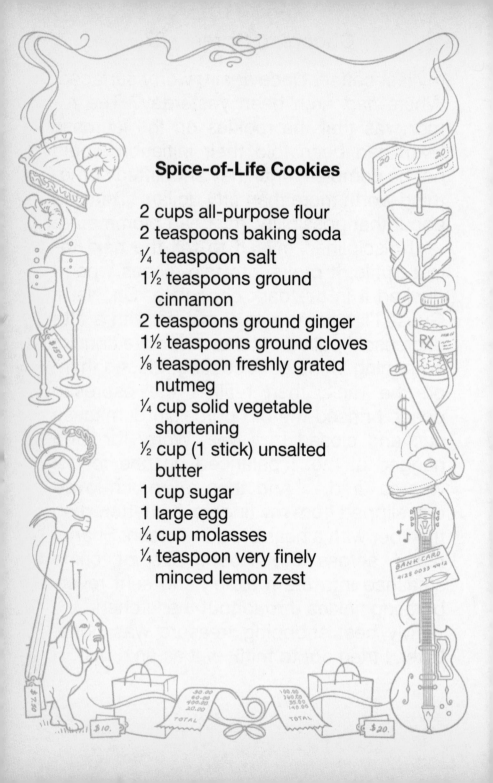

Spice-of-Life Cookies

2 cups all-purpose flour
2 teaspoons baking soda
¼ teaspoon salt
1½ teaspoons ground
  cinnamon
2 teaspoons ground ginger
1½ teaspoons ground cloves
⅛ teaspoon freshly grated
  nutmeg
¼ cup solid vegetable
  shortening
½ cup (1 stick) unsalted
  butter
1 cup sugar
1 large egg
¼ cup molasses
¼ teaspoon very finely
  minced lemon zest

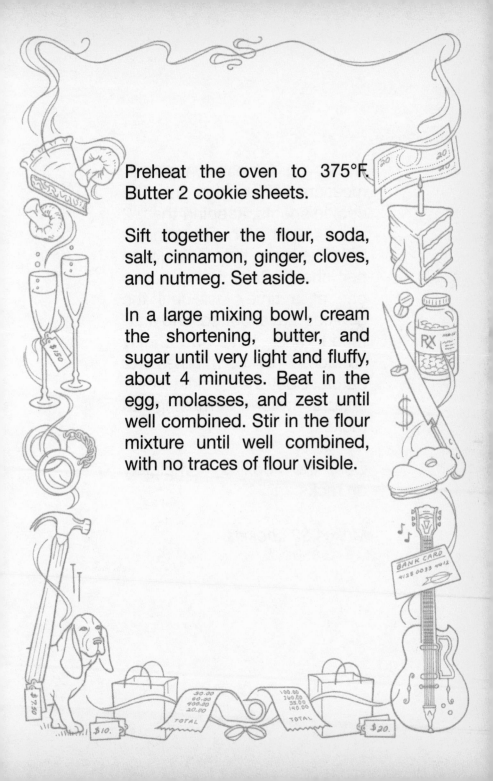

Preheat the oven to 375°F. Butter 2 cookie sheets.

Sift together the flour, soda, salt, cinnamon, ginger, cloves, and nutmeg. Set aside.

In a large mixing bowl, cream the shortening, butter, and sugar until very light and fluffy, about 4 minutes. Beat in the egg, molasses, and zest until well combined. Stir in the flour mixture until well combined, with no traces of flour visible.

Using a 1 tablespoon scoop, measure the cookies onto the cookie sheets, keeping them 2 inches apart. Do not attempt to make more than one dozen per sheet. Bake the batches one at a time, *just* until the cookies have puffed and flattened and have a crinkly surface, 9 to 12 minutes per batch. Cool the cookies for 1 minute before removing to racks.

Cool the cookies completely on racks.

Makes 32 cookies

Shoppers' Chocolate Truffles

Ganache:

½ cup heavy cream
1 tablespoon Grand Marnier liqueur
¼ teaspoon vanilla extract
11 ounces best-quality bittersweet chocolate, very finely chopped (recommended brand: Valrhona)
2 tablespoons (¼ stick) unsalted butter, softened
Cocoa powder for rolling (recommended brand: Hershey's Premium European-Style)

Coating:

6 ounces best-quality
bittersweet chocolate
(recommended brand:
Godiva Dark)
1 to 2 tablespoons clarified
butter or solid vegetable
shortening

Pour the cream into a heavy
1-quart or larger saucepan.
Add the liqueur and vanilla and
heat over medium to medium-
high heat until the mixture
reaches 190°F. Remove the
mixture from the heat, add the
chopped chocolate, and stir
vigorously until the chocolate

melts and the mixture is shiny. If all the chocolate does not-melt, you can *briefly* return the pan to the burner over low heat, stirring constantly just until the chocolate melts, when the pan needs to be immediately removed from the heat. Scrape the ganache into a bowl and allow it to cool at room temperature. (Do not attempt to hasten the cooling in any way.) When the ganache reaches 90°F, beat in the butter. Allow the ganache to cool until it is firm.

Using a 1 tablespoon ice-cream scoop, measure out the firm ganache into balls and place them on a cookie sheet lined with a silicone (Sil-Pat) sheet. Cover loosely with plastic wrap. Chill overnight in the refrigerator.

Remove the chocolate from the refrigerator and dust your hands with cocoa powder. Roll each mound into a smooth ball, then place it back on the cookie sheet. When all the ganache mounds have been rolled, return the cookie sheet to the refrigerator.

In a double boiler, melt the chocolate used for the coating with a tablespoon of the clarified butter or shortening.

Whisk it well until thoroughly combined and melted. Line another cookie sheet with aluminum foil. Working one at a time, drop a chilled ball of ganache into the coating chocolate, roll it around gently with a fork until it is completely covered, then lift it out of the pan, scrape off the excess chocolate on the side of the pan, and place the truffle on the aluminum foil. Work in this way until all the truffles are coated. If the coating chocolate begins to seize and become recalcitrant, add a bit more clarified butter to it and stir and melt as before. Work until all the truffles are coated.

Allow the coating to set up and cool on the truffles. (This usually takes over an hour.) Serve.

Makes between 12 and 15 truffles
(The recipe can be doubled, if desired.)

CHAPTER 2

I swept up the mess and went back to work. I was cloaking the final ganache globe with chocolate when Tom and Arch banged into the kitchen. Arch was clutching his usual sixty-five pounds of books, electronic gadgets, and athletic equipment. Lots and lots of athletic equipment.

At the second lacrosse game, I'd watched in horror as a forward had come barreling down the field, bearing down on Arch. My formerly little, formerly passive son set himself into a tough-gladiator defensive stance. When Arch pushed his weight into the forward's chest, the kid went flying. The team wildly applauded *my son*. I'd thought I was going to be ill.

The lacrosse players weren't the only thing that upset me about Elk Park Prep. The majority of EPP students were rich, undisciplined, and self-centered. A minority wreaked true havoc. Unfortunately, most of this contingent's bad behavior—throwing acid on kids in chem lab, drinking to the point of oblivion at football games, stealing liquor for house parties when parents were absent—went unpunished. I'd longed to call our local rag, the *Mountain Journal,* to report these incidents, after hearing about them at parties I catered. But Arch had made me swear not to.

I often worried about where all the misbehavior would lead. Unfortunately, the EPP teachers and administrators kissed the feet of the biggest donors. But besides the killer lacrosse and lack of consequences for big-time mischief, what bothered me most these days was EPP's free-wheeling curriculum. Take that anatomy class. On second thought, don't. This week, I was driving a contingent of Arch's classmates to Lutheran Hospital, where they would dissect . . . a cadaver.

I sighed. *Get used to it,* I always told myself. With the Furman County public school student-teacher ratio at fifty to one, and with Elk Park's hefty tuition coming out of The Jerk's hoard of cash, getting used to it was exactly what I needed to do.

I set the last truffle aside to dry and glanced at Tom. He looked dashing in a white shirt, gray pants, and my favorite wool sweater, a crewneck pullover the color of oatmeal. His brown hair was combed up at a jaunty angle, and his spicy aftershave wafted my way. I hurried over and kissed him on the cheek. He smooched my forehead and asked if I'd like more coffee. Dear Tom. He'd known my attempt to cut back on caffeine would be short-lived.

I said yes, then patted Arch on the shoulder, which was all the maternal affection he'd allow these days. My son—now surpassing me in height (not hard, since I'm five feet two inches)—slid away hastily and adjusted his new John Lennon–style wire-rimmed glasses. The previous month, I'd offered to buy him contacts. He'd replied that what he *really* wanted was laser surgery. He'd need eight thousand bucks, though, to get the great surgeon the Elk Park kids used.

I'd bought him new glasses.

Checking his reflection in the window, Arch ducked his chin to assess the new tobacco-brown fuzz on his scalp. He then checked his choker of shell bits, smoothed the oversized khakis and rumpled plaid shirt that were the school's unofficial uniform, and frowned. Something was bothering him.

"Uh, Arch?" I ventured rashly. "Where were you yesterday afternoon?"

"What's it to you?"

"Is that polite?" I asked.

"Is it polite to be nosy?"

I gave up. Tom offered me a cream-laced espresso. It was my sixth of the morning . . . amazing how these things add up. I slurped the fragrant drink—blissfully similar to hot coffee ice cream—and faced my next task: breakfast for Arch. Lacrosse players, I was always telling him, needed a large morning meal so they could build the strength to pound on each other.

I retrieved English muffins, eggs, butter, and jam, and tried to ignore the fact that Arch was guzzling an energy drink. When

I'd said I was giving up caffeine, he'd advised me to switch to the bottled concoction known as Virtuous Vigor. I'd tried one swig, and choked.

"Tom? Arch? In ten minutes, I can give you a late breakfast or an early lunch... your choice."

"No time, Mom," Arch replied as he simultaneously tossed the energy drink bottle into the trash and snagged another one. "Ready to go, Tom?" When Tom replied that he was, Arch said, "Oops, I need to get my spare long stick."

The long stick, I'd learned, is what the lacrosse defenseman uses to scoop up the ball—after he sends a forward into the air or onto the ground. As Arch galloped back up the stairs, I banged the eggs back onto the fridge shelf and slammed the door closed.

"He'll be fine," Tom murmured as he hugged me. "After I pick him up at practice, we'll make your favorite beef stew, ready when you get home from the mall. Arch gets plenty of good nutrition. Frankly, in the health department, it's *you* I worry about, Miss G."

"I'm *fine*."

"No," my husband countered. "You're not. You need to cut back, Goldy. You're exhausted."

"Would *you* like something to eat?"

He kissed me again, then stepped back. "When I get down to the sheriff's department, they'll have doughnuts waiting." He smiled. "Just kidding. Listen. After I leave Arch off, why don't you let me pick up some sandwiches...for you and Liz?" Liz Fury was the assistant I'd hired at Marla's behest. Liz had been a godsend. Tom concluded, "I can be back in an hour. Interested?"

I shook my head as unexpected tears pricked my eyes. When you endure seven years of being belted around by a Jerk, kindness comes as a shock. Guess I was more tired than I thought.

"Thanks, but no," I said hastily. "If Liz and I can get all our work done, we'll grab a bite at the mall. Then—"

Arch banged back into the room. He was now toting the long stick in one hand, the second energy drink in the other. "*Westside* Mall?" he interrupted. I nodded; his eyes brightened. "Westside Music *just* put the fifteen-hundred-buck Epiphone on sale for seven hundred. It's the *exact* guitar I need, Mom, and they only have *one*. And The Gadget Guy is having a *mega* sale, so everything is fifty percent—"

"Stop!" I said, too loudly. At least I didn't scream, *Seven hundred dollars!*

"Westside Music has *one* guitar on sale, Mom. By tonight it'll be gone."

I swore I'd check it out, then gave each of them a wrapped truffle for a mid-afternoon snack. With an air of being put-upon, Arch tucked the truffle into his bookbag, pawed through his athletic car-rier, and announced he was missing his Palm pilot and cell phone, and did I know where they were.

I did not. Arch banged back up the stairs, and I gave Tom a look. "My son has become a materialist."

"It's the age, Goldy."

"But where was he yesterday? What if he ends up shoplifting like those other Elk Park Prep kids?"

"Goldy, come on. Only one of those kids we caught was from Elk Park Prep, and he was carrying goods from a pen store, a leather boutique, and Victoria's Se-cret." Tom slipped into his jacket. "Plus, your pal Barry Dean, whose stores buy more advertising than God, has installed a new state-of-the-art security system at Westside. He's even threatened to bar certain kids from the mall."

I shook my head. I thought of my broken cup shards in the trash, and shuddered.

Tom jangled his keys. With shaking hands, I picked up the foodstuffs list to begin my check-off. Finally, Arch slammed back into the kitchen. He slipped a handful of electronic accoutrements into his backpack, then yanked up the bag in a practiced motion. In so doing, his untucked shirt revealed the skin of his back. I gasped.

The bottom fourth of Arch's back was inked with a tattoo of a lacrosse stick.

"Mother of God!" I exclaimed.

"What's the matter?" Tom demanded, startled.

"I...he..." I croaked. "So that's where you were yesterday, at a, at a, tattoo..." I couldn't finish.

"Back off, Mom!" Arch yelled.

"I, I—"

"May I see it, Arch?" Tom interposed

quietly. Eyeing me furiously, Arch faced me and lifted his shirt so Tom could inspect his back.

"Well, well," said Tom. "A tattoo. Had any bleeding or swelling?"

"*No.*" Arch flipped down his shirt, tucked it in, and announced he'd forgotten one more thing upstairs: his anatomy class assignment.

I sank into a chair. "I'm losing my grip," I moaned.

"Hate to tell you, Miss G., but that's what you're supposed to do with an almost-fifteen-year-old." He stroked my cheek and kissed me again. "Just concentrate on the cooking. Julian's helping you today?" he asked. "Along with Liz?"

I took two deep, yoga-style breaths. Liz Fury was good, but twenty-two-year-old Julian Teller, our one-time boarder and close family friend, was, in my opinion, the best young gourmet cook in Colorado. "They're both helping," I answered. Plus, I added mentally, Julian was close to Arch, and might have some ideas about dealing with adolescence. Maybe Julian had tattoos, too.

"You're *sure* you're going to be all right, Miss G.?"

I opened my eyes wide. I wasn't sure of anything. "Tom, I'll be *fine*. Julian's leaving Boulder at one, meeting us at the mall at two."

"OK, listen," Arch interjected as he traipsed back into the kitchen and deftly nabbed a third energy drink. "Could you tell Julian I need a chocolate cake with vanilla frosting? For my birthday? You'll probably be too busy to do anything, and Julian always makes me a *terrific* cake," he added.

"Arch!"

"One Epiphone on sale, Mom. *One*."

Tom winked at me and waved. The back door banged behind them. A moment later, Tom's engine growled in the driveway. My heart ached. Was I a failure as a mother? If I bought the expensive guitar, would I be succumbing to acquisitiveness? If I didn't buy it, would Arch get more tattoos?

Before I could answer these questions, however, there was a frenzied knocking at the front door. My peephole revealed Liz Fury.

"Where's your husband going this time of day? Is everything OK?" Liz demanded.

I stepped out onto the porch. "He's just taking Arch to school. Late start."

"Oh."

Liz, an early-forties single mom, was gifted with food and efficient at catering. With her tall, slender figure, attractive face set off by sapphire eyes and chopped silver-blond hair, she even looked the part. Or at least, she looked the way most people visualize an upscale caterer. She didn't look chic just at that moment, though. In the cold April wind, her hair had all blown to one side. Her cheeks and nose were red, and she looked less like a hip caterer than a silver-haired doll with a punk haircut.

Tom and Arch zoomed away. Liz, clutching a bag, hastened past me toward the kitchen. Under her coat, it looked as if she was wearing dressier-than-usual clothes. Hmm. I'd seen Liz talking earnestly with Barry Dean while we did the lounge measurements. Maybe she was trying to impress the most eligible bachelor.

And maybe I was becoming too obsessed with other folks' issues. I marched into the kitchen.

"What are we doing first?" Liz asked as

her eyes swept the room. "Why were Tom and Arch in such a hurry?"

"Ah...I don't know." I truly did not know what Tom was doing today, but I'd finally learned a thing or two as a cop's wife, among them: *Regarding police work, keep your mouth shut.* And anyway, I'd forgotten to ask what Tom's plans were; I'd been sidetracked by Arch's tattoo.

"I got that expensive Burgundy. You're right, though, it *will* make a difference." Liz banged bottles onto the counter, then hung up her coat and washed her hands. I complimented her on her outfit—shimmery white silk shirt, spotless black silk sweater, and wrinkled-silk gray pants—undoubtedly remnants of her high-flying days as a party planner and caterer for a high-flying corporation that had gone under. When her employer had declared bankruptcy, she'd tried to find work with other big-spending companies. But the new big guns in town had brought their own party planners. With no savings, Liz had ended up begging for food stamps. If I were in her position, I'd chat up single guys, too.

Without thinking, I asked, "Going somewhere after we finish tonight?"

"Well," she replied with a smile as she tied her apron over her beautiful clothes, "maybe." She lowered velvety lashes over her dark blue eyes. "Not that I'd ever tell my *boss* about my social life."

"Sorry," I mumbled.

A grin flitted across Liz's heart-shaped mouth as she retrieved a wide frying pan and containers of reserved beef drippings and clarified butter. I packed up the first container of truffles while she whisked flour into the melted fat, set the heat to low, and pulled out the beef stock. As I covered layer after layer of chocolate, Liz slowly stirred the stock into the roux until it thickened. Leaving it to heat, she went back to the refrigerator and perused the contents.

"Goldy, what else do we have left to do?"

"Shrimp rolls. You can check the crab dip. I've got two pages of printout over there. Could you, ah, bring me the grilled shrimp?"

Liz brought out the vat of shrimp, then perused the printout. A moment later she dove back into the depths of the refrigerator.

She bumped around for a bit, then called, "What'd you do, work all night on the Stockham lunch?"

"Just trying to get ahead. We've got that party plus Barry's lessee lunch the following day."

"What else are we doing for Shane? Calculators from sardines? Whole mushrooms in the shape of digital cameras?"

"Just finish the meatballs, would you, Liz?"

She emerged with the metal container that held our meticulously rolled and browned mixture of lean ground beef, heavy cream, freshly grated nutmeg, and other goodies. While she stirred the high-priced Burgundy into the meatball sauce, I arranged fat shrimp, thin noodles, fragrant chopped cilantro, and shredded carrot, broccolini, and black mushrooms into the shrimp rolls. Before we started on our last dishes—the crab dip and cheese trays—we treated ourselves to eight leftover shrimp and the last four leftover truffles. It wasn't a meal Elk Park Prep would highlight in their nutrition class. But so what? We were caterers.

An hour later, we entered the last stage

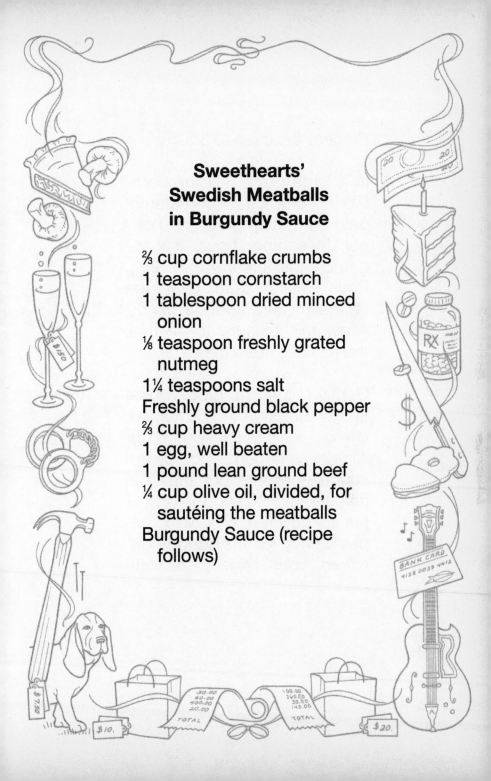

Sweethearts' Swedish Meatballs in Burgundy Sauce

⅔ cup cornflake crumbs
1 teaspoon cornstarch
1 tablespoon dried minced onion
⅛ teaspoon freshly grated nutmeg
1¼ teaspoons salt
Freshly ground black pepper
⅔ cup heavy cream
1 egg, well beaten
1 pound lean ground beef
¼ cup olive oil, divided, for sautéing the meatballs
Burgundy Sauce (recipe follows)

Preheat the oven to 300°F.

In a large bowl, mix the corn-flake crumbs, cornstarch, onion, nutmeg, salt, and pepper. In another bowl, mix together the cream and egg. Pour this mixture over the crumb mixture and stir gently. Allow this mixture to sit until the liquid is absorbed.

Gently mix in the ground beef until thoroughly combined. Using a 1 tablespoon (or slightly larger) ice-cream scoop, measure out the beef mixture into 36 scoops onto 2 plates covered with wax paper. Gently roll the scoops between your fingers to form balls. In a large frying pan, heat 2 tablespoons oil over medium-high heat until the oil shimmers. Carefully place the balls into the hot oil and sauté, turning once, until the outside is browned. (Do not cook the meatballs all the way through; they will be finished in the oven.) Using tongs, place the browned meatballs onto a rimmed, buttered baking sheet, or better yet, a baking sheet that has been lined with a silicone (Sil-Pat) sheet. (Do not discard the drippings in the pan.)

Place the meatballs in the oven while you make the sauce. (If the sauce is to be prepared later, bake the meatballs for about 10 minutes, or until just cooked through and no longer pink. Cool them and place them in a container that can be covered.)

After 10 minutes, test the doneness of the meatballs by slicing one in half. The interior should no longer be pink. *Do not overbake the meatballs*. Remove the meatballs from the oven as soon as they are done and set them aside until you are ready to reheat them in the reserved sauce. (Do not heat the meatballs in the sauce until you are ready to serve the dish. The meatballs are delicate and will fall apart if cooked too long in the sauce.)

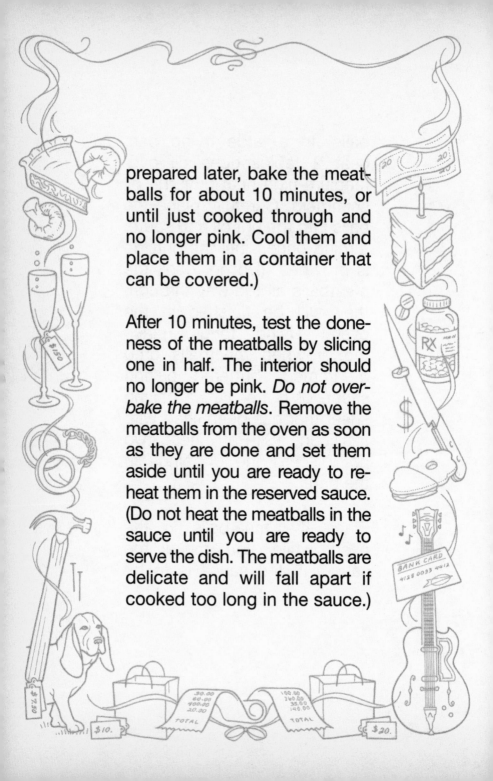

Burgundy Sauce:

¼ cup melted fat (strained pan drippings plus enough melted unsalted butter to make ¼ cup)
¼ cup all-purpose flour
1½ teaspoons sugar, or to taste
Freshly ground black pepper
2 cups homemade beef stock or 1 tablespoon beef bouillon powder dissolved in 2 cups hot water
1 cup high-quality Burgundy wine

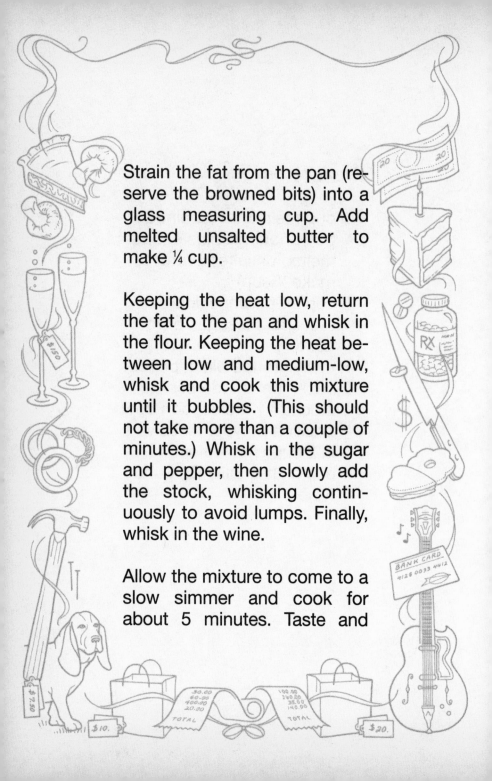

Strain the fat from the pan (reserve the browned bits) into a glass measuring cup. Add melted unsalted butter to make ¼ cup.

Keeping the heat low, return the fat to the pan and whisk in the flour. Keeping the heat between low and medium-low, whisk and cook this mixture until it bubbles. (This should not take more than a couple of minutes.) Whisk in the sugar and pepper, then slowly add the stock, whisking continuously to avoid lumps. Finally, whisk in the wine.

Allow the mixture to come to a slow simmer and cook for about 5 minutes. Taste and correct the seasoning. If the sauce tastes bitter, add a bit more sugar and allow the sauce to simmer another 10 minutes. If the dish is not to be served immediately, cool the sauce and chill, covered, until ready to heat and serve.

Just before serving, lower the meatballs into the hot sauce and bring the mixture to a simmer. Taste a meatball with sauce to be sure the dish is heated all the way through. If the dish is to be served as an appetizer, provide small bowls or dishes and spoons. If the dish is to be served as a main course, serve over hot egg noodles.

Makes 36 meatballs in sauce

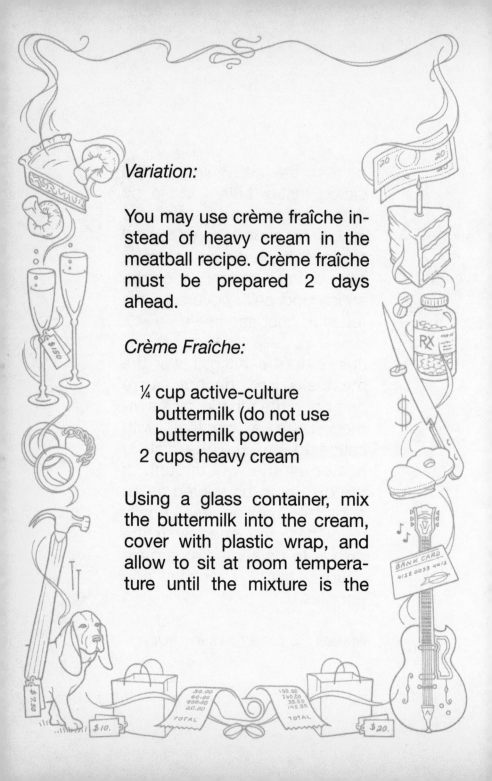

Variation:

You may use crème fraîche in-stead of heavy cream in the meatball recipe. Crème fraîche must be prepared 2 days ahead.

Crème Fraîche:

¼ cup active-culture buttermilk (do not use buttermilk powder)
2 cups heavy cream

Using a glass container, mix the buttermilk into the cream, cover with plastic wrap, and allow to sit at room tempera-ture until the mixture is the thickness of commercial sour cream, usually about 2 days. It can be refrigerated, covered, for up to 3 days. Since the recipe only calls for ⅔ cup, the rest of the crème fraîche can be used for dips and sauces.

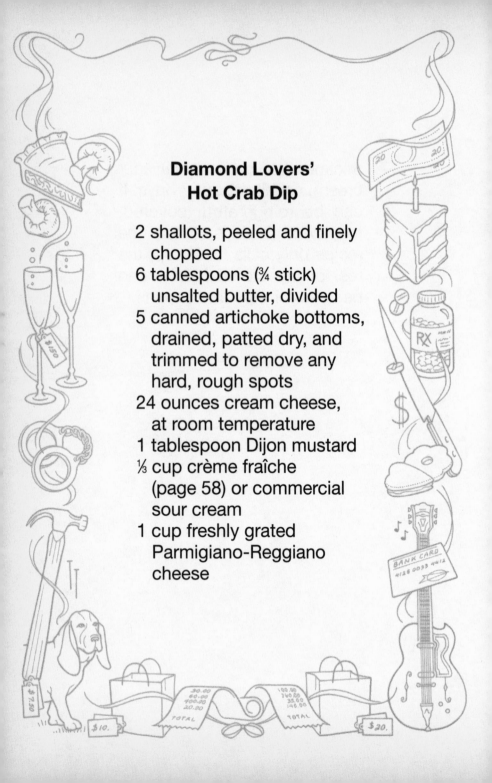

Diamond Lovers' Hot Crab Dip

2 shallots, peeled and finely
  chopped
6 tablespoons (¾ stick)
  unsalted butter, divided
5 canned artichoke bottoms,
  drained, patted dry, and
  trimmed to remove any
  hard, rough spots
24 ounces cream cheese,
  at room temperature
1 tablespoon Dijon mustard
⅓ cup crème fraîche
  (page 58) or commercial
  sour cream
1 cup freshly grated
  Parmigiano-Reggiano
  cheese

1 pound pasteurized crab, flaked and picked over to remove any stray bits of cartilage

2 cups fresh bread crumbs, preferably made from homemade bread (brioche is best)

½ cup finely chopped fresh parsley

Corn chips and crackers

Preheat the oven to 350°F. Butter an attractive 2-quart au gratin dish, preferably a dark-colored one. Set aside.

Place the shallots in a miniature food processor and blend until juicy, less than a minute. Over medium-low heat, melt 1 tablespoon butter, add the shallots, and sauté just until the shallots begin to turn golden brown. Remove from the heat and set aside.

Chop the artichoke bottoms into ½-inch dice. Set aside until you are ready to assemble the dip.

In the large bowl of an electric mixer, beat the cream cheese until very smooth. Add the mustard, crème fraîche, and cheese and beat on low speed just until combined. Stir in the crab, shallots, and artichoke bottoms until well combined. Turn the crab mixture into the prepared au gratin dish.

In a medium-sized sauté pan, melt the remaining 5 tablespoons butter and stir in the bread crumbs. Cook and stir just until the butter is absorbed and the crumbs are beginning to turn golden. Remove from the heat, stir in the chopped parsley, and distribute this mixture over the top of the crab dip.

Place the dip in the oven and bake for about 30 minutes, until the topping is golden brown and a small spoonful of dip scooped up from the center tastes very hot. Serve immediately with a choice of chips and crackers.

Makes 24 or more servings

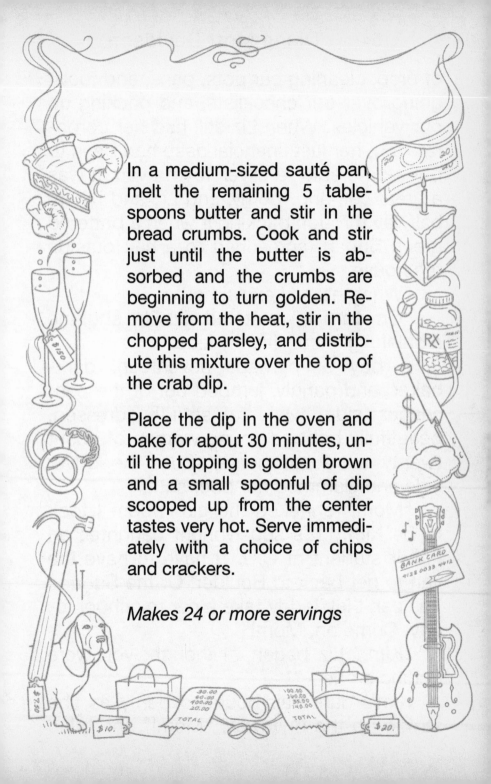

of prep: cleaning our pots, pans, and tools, going over our checklists, and packing up our vehicles. When Liz still had her corporate job, her last financial gasp had been to buy—on credit—a silver Toyota van. It was a great car, and roomy, and Liz and I were halfway through packing it when a battered green Subaru screeched to a halt outside the house.

"What the—" I exclaimed.

"Oh, darn it," muttered Liz. She shot me a baleful glance. "It's my kids."

A boy of perhaps seventeen, dark-haired and gangly, jumped out of the passenger side while a smartly dressed, beautifully bobbed young woman of about twenty extracted herself from the driver side and slammed her door shut.

"Mom!" shrieked the girl, whom I took to be Kim, Liz's super-bright daughter, an honor student at C.U. "I have to have the van to get back to Boulder! Or the Subaru! You can't let Teddy take a car to school today! Come on, Mom!"

"Kim," Liz began, "I thought you were getting a ride—"

Kim's dark hair bounced pertly as she strode up the driveway. "Mom!" she cried again. "You know *perfectly* well I can't get all my stuff into a friend's car! Why do you always side with Teddy? He's a terrible driver, anyway. And he's in trouble. You said so yourself. He shouldn't be going *shopping* after school, when I need to get back."

"Kim," Liz tried again, her voice low, "please stop shouting in front of Goldy's neighbors."

"Mom!" Teddy pleaded, his shoulders slumped, his face screwed into a look of anxiety. Teddy, I knew, was something of a screwup, although I was not aware of the details. "I don't have a ride to school today, and I've got stuff to do later, and I'm really, really late as it is—"

"Teddy, you're not supposed to—"

"Please let me have the Subaru," Teddy begged, "because I know it needs an oil change. Give Kim the van, let me have the Subaru until tonight. I'll get the oil changed, then pick you up at the mall. What time will you be finished? I can meet you at the—"

"Mom!" Kim was livid. "Why are you listening to him and not listening to *me*? I need the van! *Now!*"

Liz's blue eyes shot me a look of such hopelessness that my heart twisted in my chest. "Is there any way we can get everything into your van?" Liz beseeched me.

"Of course!" I said without hesitation. "Besides, I'd love your company."

She blushed, then asked if she and her kids could move the stuff over, so I wouldn't be bothered. I took this as a signal that she couldn't stand being embarrassed another moment. I nodded and mumbled that I had work to do inside.

Poor Liz, I thought, as I packed up the last boxes in the kitchen. She'd had her kids early, then been deserted by her husband. After the corporate job crashed and burned, she'd been left without resources. *I'd kill to get this job with you,* she'd told me two weeks ago, as her long, slender hands had offered me a foil cup of her signature Grand Marnier crème brûlée. I'd taken only one bite and informed her that she was *hired*! She'd managed to balance her schedule, money, and offspring problems—until today.

But we worked things out. Kim took the van; Teddy roared away triumphantly in the

Subaru. An hour later, crisis over, Liz and I were on our way.

My van zipped up Aspen Meadow's Main Street and around the curve of the lake, where ruffled dark water skirted a membrane of ice. April in the high country brings freezing temperatures, lots of snow, and only an occasional glimpse of the warmth to come. Chugging toward the interstate, we passed snowy meadows pocked with dun-colored grass. Stands of white-barked aspen looked as if they were wrapped in green mist, the first sign of emerging lime-colored leaves.

Driving by Flicker Ridge, I was forced to slow by the entries to two new upscale housing developments. Trucks, tractors, and front-end loaders rumbled across denuded meadows, where a sign now screamed that there were ONLY 3 SITES LEFT!, next to a handpainted offer, *Topsoil $70/load,* which lay beside a large, beautifully lettered sign announcing the presence of Ace Custom Construction. Trucks labeled *Ace* and *We Got Dirt* hauled loads of soil in and out of a fenced-off area. Melting snow still chilled the air, but the building of the new crop of trophy homes, each set on a mere quarter of an acre, was clearly well under way. I turned up the van's heat.

As we descended to the Mile High City, the air turned soft and warm. At my request, Liz cracked a window. Our winter in Aspen Meadow began in October and ended in May, two months longer than Denver and environs. By the time we arrived at the turnoff for Westside Mall, forty miles east of home, we had emerged into a gentle spring.

Not that arriving at the shopping center gave you a prospect of flowers, shrubs, or leafy trees. If anything, the mall's grand new stone entrance, flanked with sloping hillocks of dirt, gave the place the look of a military outpost. Barry had told me the mall landscaping had been postponed because of the construction delays.

As I slowed to make the turn onto Doughnut Drive, the road that encircled the mall, I remembered something else Barry had told me: *We're giving shoppers entertainment and discounts these days, to make up for the mess.* Tonight's Red Tag Shoe Sale at Prince & Grogan was the discount magnet. The catered jewelry-leasing party was the entertainment. The mess was just the mess.

I slowed the van and glanced in the direction of the construction, where a line of workers were putting in a winding sidewalk that would soon be dotted with inviting benches, restaurants, boutiques, and coffee kiosks. All this, Barry had told me, was *more* entertainment. *Shoppers want picturesque spots to sit, watch the folks go by, and eat food samples,* he'd said. *Shoppers don't live in a storybook village. But they want to pretend they do.*

And, he'd added, they were under severe pressure from the mall owner, Pennybaker International, to get the new village done. *Malls Are Getting Mauled* was the message from industry insiders. Suburban folks with money in their pockets were tired of concrete parking lots leading to blank walls enclosing identical sets of stores. They wanted to see and be seen as they strolled past trees, bushes, and sculptures. They wanted to go to the bank, the dry cleaner, and the bookstore, and then have lunch at an Italian restaurant overlooking a fountain. This was exactly what all the mall owners and execs, including Barry, were trying to offer. And at some point, all those shoppers would *also* need to purchase dresses, cosmetics, pots, pans, and shoes, which they could do inside the mall itself, a mere fifty steps away. The best way to promote Westside, Barry had told me, was to tack a fairy-tale village onto its back end.

At least Barry wasn't bringing in Snow White and the Dwarfs, I reflected, as my van chugged along Doughnut Drive. The new road was perfectly named. A twelve-foot-high berm of unlandscaped soil circled the outer perimeter. At the eight-foot chain-link fence surrounding the construction area, I slowed again, then stopped at the gate. Barry was not there to meet us. Liz gave me a questioning look.

Beyond the fence, acres of flattened dirt—what would eventually become the mall's new parking lot—sloped down to the roped-off area. There, a worker wearing a bright orange hard hat chugged around in a front-end loader, moving rocks from one enormous pile to another. The rest of the crew, clad in yellow hard hats, were clustered next to a hot dog vendor by the construction company trailer.

My eyes swept left and I barely escaped cursing aloud. The restyled back entrance to the mall—the one that led up to the Elite Shoppers' Lounge—was surrounded by a lake of muddy drainage water. At the edge of this brown pond, an imposing line of enormous dump trucks obscured any view to that rear entry. Worse, the water came up to the trucks' wheel wells. How were we supposed to transport boxes into the mall? By boat?

As if he'd heard my worries, the man driving the loader halted abruptly and hopped onto the rocks. This had to be Victor Wilson, the excavator Barry had mentioned, who'd been promoted recently to be the new construction manager. Victor was short and chunky, with a reddish brown ponytail sticking out from his orange hard hat. He shouted in the direction of the crew, who responded by tossing their trash and slowly moving back to the equipment on the sidewalk. I was impressed. After all the delays, it looked as if Victor was really cracking the whip.

"How are we going to unpack?" Liz asked me. "Where's Barry? Where's Julian?"

I scanned the drainage lake and spied a narrow wooden walkway spanning the water, curving around the row of trucks. Maybe we wouldn't have to don hip boots, after all.

I pointed. "See that plankway in front of the trucks? If you can open the gate to the construction area, I'll drive us as close as possible. With any luck, Julian will see the van."

"Why did Barry even say he'd *meet* us at the gate?" Liz asked. "That's not normal, is it? For a mall manager to help the catering team?"

"He's an old friend." I thought again of the flirtatious way she and Barry had seemed to be acting when we'd done our measuring. Then again, I'd learned in college that Barry was a seductive kind of guy. "Anyway, Liz," I added mischievously, "maybe Barry wanted to see *you*."

"Did Barry...?" Flustered, she ran her fingers through her silver-blond hair. "Did he mention my name? The fact that I was... helping you?"

"Liz, stop worrying. Everything will be fine. Just get the gate, OK?"

She hopped out, swung open the construction gate, and waved me through. Once the gate was shut and she was back inside, we bumped over deep ruts to get as close as possible to the big puddle. We ended up parking fifty yards from the wooden walkway. I still couldn't get a good view of the mall's rear entrance. Were the trucks parked flush against the shopping center wall? Hopefully, some kind of dike had been erected behind them, providing walking space that led to the mall's entrance.

If Julian and Barry didn't show up to help, and Liz and I had to skirt the truck-and-water mess to get to the lounge, we were going to have a devil of a time. I mentally calculated an hour and a half to haul everything in, another ninety minutes to set up and decorate the tables, another forty-five to do the last-minute prep on the food and set out the platters. Since my watch now said two o'clock, that schedule would put us right up against six o'clock—party time.

Liz and I heaved up the first boxes. We decided to trek down around the ruts to a foot-wide dirt path that seemed to run along the edge of the lake. The crow may fly as he may, but a smooth, longer way to the wooden plankway had to be better than negotiating hard waves of dirt. As we trod carefully on the springy plank boards, I spotted a foot-high wooden wall behind the trucks. So there was a seawall, thank goodness. Beyond it, a cement sidewalk looked dry enough for us to make it to the just-completed glass doors of the entrance. Despite the fact that I was lugging two boxes, I felt relief. Then Liz let out a little gasp.

Barry Dean had pushed through the glass doors and was striding along the sidewalk. Liz and I stepped off the end of the plankway spanning the drainage lake and started up the sidewalk toward him. Clad in a bright green sport shirt, khaki pants, and loafers, Barry acknowledged us with a hearty wave. Tripping along behind him was a young woman wearing a black halter top, white short-shorts, and chartreuse-green platform sandals. The woman was slender-hipped and big-busted. About thirty platinum ponytails stuck out from her head. She looked like a blond plant that had sprouted.

The young woman laid her hand on

Barry's arm to slow him. When he turned to face her, she did a little wiggle. Showing off her outfit? Demonstrating how all the pony-tails could jiggle at once? I groaned, shifted my load, and turned to check on Liz. She had stopped dead in her tracks. Luckily, she recovered quickly enough to grab her boxes before they fell.

Plenty of fish in the sea, I wanted to tell her.

"Honestly," Liz murmured. She rebal-anced her cargo, moved forward, and made her tone light. "That man would hit on my daughter."

Enthusiastic honking kept me from hav-ing to reply. From between the trucks, I could see a white Range Rover rocketing over the dirt ruts: Julian. He swung in next to my van, hopped out with a bag in his hands, and hightailed it toward the plankway. Meanwhile, Barry and the blond bombshell conversed in low tones.

"Hiya," Julian said, once he'd caught up to us. He put down the bag and expertly pulled off one of the boxes I was carrying. He'd cut his dark hair quite close to the scalp. (Not *bicked,* I wanted to tell Arch.) Julian was also clean-shaven and as handsome as ever. Plus, he was compact and muscled, dressed in balloon olive pants and a black T-shirt, and as usual, had come to *work*. Seeing Liz and her load, he immediately rejuggled my box so he could take one of hers. The kid was great: mature, bighearted, talented, and kind. I thought of Arch with a pang.

Julian swung the two boxes to one side as if they were nothing. "Hey, Goldy, I brought you one of those hot lattes made with cream from The Westside Buzz. You know, that drive-through place? I figured you'd be pretty tired by now, and since you gave up coffee, well—" He blushed and turned to Liz. "Sorry. We just met that once. I'm Julian Teller. Actually, I brought two lattes. One's for you, Liz."

"Thanks, Julian, but no," Liz told him. "You have it. And it's good to see you again, too."

"I'm so bad!" Julian enthused, as he proffered me the bag. "I've already had two of those things, and each Buzz latte has *four* shots. I'm pretty wired, I can tell you that."

"We can always use your energy," Liz

said, warming to him with a smile. Julian had that effect on people.

"Is that the Barry guy?" Julian asked. He lifted his chin at Barry and the blonde. "Down there?"

Barry Dean tilted his head toward the blonde, roared with laughter, then sauntered toward us. The young woman teetered along behind him.

"Hey!" Barry called. His grin flashed as he winked at me and opened his arms in greeting. "Speak of the devil!"

"I certainly hope not," Julian muttered.

I introduced Julian to Barry, who in turn presented us to his "dear friend," Pam Disharoon.

Pam *Disharoon*? I thought. Was that a combination of *dish* and *macaroon*? *I'm a cute dish; my hair's a macaroon?*

"I'm Liz," my new assistant politely announced to Pam. But Barry Dean could have introduced her, couldn't he? Instead, he squinted at Liz and pressed his lips together.

"Hello, catering team!" Pam's tone was bright. She lifted her pointed chin, sending the ponytails a-wiggle. "I'm sure you'll make great chow for our jewelry event!"

Liz Fury, master of cuttlefish pasta, flourless chocolate cake, and *salade composée*, turned green around the gills. *Chow,* indeed.

"Pam is the star seller in Prince and Grogan's lingerie department," Barry announced with pride. "She's the top saleswoman at the mall."

Liz made her voice falsely cheerful as she reshifted her box. "Goldy? Julian? I'm taking this up. See you all in the lounge." And before I could say anything, she took off.

"Well," said Pam into the awkward silence that followed. She gave Julian the once-over. In a coy, seductive tone, she addressed him: "So you're a *caterer*?"

"Pam," said Barry, "these people are here to work—"

"Caterer's assistant," said Julian, not fooled by Pam's attempt to flirt. "Goldy, give me your other box. I'll take this load up and come right back."

Pam took a sashaying two-step toward Julian, extended her red-nailed hands, and cupped his cheeks and chin. "Want some help?"

The well-coordinated Julian slid away

from her. "I'll meet you at your van, boss," he told me cheerfully, and headed toward the doors.

I hastened back to my van, eager to retrieve the refrigerator-bound supplies. Through the windshield, I could see Barry and Pam walking across the plankway over the water. Without warning, Barry whirled and held up his index finger, as if to correct her. Suddenly, their conversation *didn't* look friendly. Guess that meant Barry wasn't going to help with the boxes, after all. Thank God for Julian—although maybe Barry Dean felt differently.

By the time I'd unloaded the shrimp-roll and crab-dip boxes from the van, Julian had returned from the mall. "Liz is guarding the food in the lounge. The jewelry people are already there."

I nodded. On the list of catering rules you shouldn't break was *Never leave food where it can be swiped*. Sadly, half a dozen of my beef tenderloins had disappeared before I'd learned this.

"Oh," Julian went on, "and Barry and what's-her-name are having a lovers' spat."

"Let's avoid them."

Hoisting our loads, Julian and I avoided the ruts and hurried down the dirt path that led to the plankway. Ahead of us, Pam was stomping away from Barry. Her barely covered rump bounced as she tried to trot in the silly sandals. The plankway jiggled with each of her steps. The construction workers stopped and gaped. So did Barry Dean. Then he turned and again marched toward us. He looked as if he'd swallowed a frog.

"Goldy," he said once he'd met up with us on the dirt path, "could you and I have a talk?" Barry's endearingly handsome face and brown eyes, changed so little from our time together at C.U., beseeched me. "The mall has been turned upside down lately—"

"Can we just talk *upstairs*?" I suggested, panting. "I really need to get this food inside."

"I'd rather visit *now,*" Barry insisted firmly, "if you don't mind. I'll take one of those boxes." Julian, who was now halfway across the plankway, turned back and lifted his eyebrows. *Want me to rescue you from that guy?* Probably sensing my reluctance,

Barry implored, "Goldy, please. This is important—"

He was interrupted by the sound of a revving engine. It was loud, then very loud, like an airplane being warmed up. A short distance away, one of the dump trucks rolled away from the neat line of vehicles. The sun winked off the windshield as the truck plowed through the water. I couldn't see the driver.

"Oh, no, I knew it!" Barry cried. "No!"

"What?" I called to him. He knew a truck was going to start up? "Barry, what's the matter?" But he'd dropped his box and started running toward the construction gate. Where was he going? Was he going to try to outrun the truck?

My heart plunged. The truck roared and spewed exhaust. I glanced at Julian. The truck was headed right toward him.

"Julian!" I screamed. "Look out!"

Julian reared back and dropped his load. He sprang away from the path of the vehicle, lost his balance, and splashed face forward into the muddy water. The truck charged past him. I watched in horror until Julian's mud-drenched head, followed by his body, emerged from the water. I looked for Barry. He had stopped running and seemed frozen, watching Julian slosh through the puddle.

The truck was barreling toward us. Julian, sopping wet and shouting, was running raggedly along behind it.

I dropped my box, raced toward Barry, and grabbed his shirt. As I yanked him fiercely sideways, the huge, noisy truck swerved toward us.

"Barry, run with me, dammit!" I hollered. My old friend looked at me, his face stricken. He tried to hurry, but tangled his feet and stumbled to his knees.

The truck was thirty feet away and closing. With all my strength, I wrenched Barry's arm and body upward. His legs moved spastically as I pulled him over row after row of ruts. Finally, I tripped on one of the hard ridges and we were both airborne. We hit the dirt hard.

A foot down in a wide ditch, I could hear but not see the bellowing truck. It, too, seemed to be plowing up and down the ridges. I tugged on Barry, who was groaning as he tried to scoot along beside me. Hopefully, we were also headed away from the path the truck had been taking...a path straight at us. If I could not see the truck driver, I reasoned, then hopefully, he could not see Barry or me. The way it had been bearing down on us, I did not think that enormous dump truck was just a runaway vehicle.

The truck noise rose to deafening proportions. When our ditch narrowed, Barry and I stopped crawling. I eased up to have a peek. Fifteen feet from us, exactly where we had been when we hit the dirt, the truck vaulted the ditch where we now lay panting. All I could see of the driver was the shadowy reflection of a face behind a mud-splattered window.

Panting, Barry and I rose up on our elbows. I didn't think the truck driver had actually seen us. Once past the ruts, the truck picked up speed. It crashed through the construction fence with a fearsome clanking of metal. Then it hurtled across Doughnut Drive. With a deafening boom, it slammed into the embankment. The berm exploded. Dirt erupted over the truck. Clouds of dust mushroomed upward as an avalanche of soil poured onto the road. A person wearing a baseball cap and baggy overalls jumped out of the cab, clambered

clumsily over the embankment, then disappeared.

What was that about?

Beside me, Barry gasped and cursed. "I knew this would happen!" He was covered with mud. "I just *knew* it!"

CHAPTER 3

I coughed, spit out grit, and coughed again. Then I inhaled dust, coughed, and inhaled some more. I had the keen sense of having lost moments, maybe even hours— as if there'd been a period of blackness of indeterminate length. Maybe I had passed out.

I eased back onto the dirt and tried to clear the mental fog. My body lay crumpled between two dirt ridges. A severe aching sensation swept from my shoulders to my legs, slowly at first, then with more depth and speed. I groaned and elbowed up again to a half-sitting position. I gazed vacantly at the nearly lethal path the truck had taken. What had that been about? I had no idea.

Doing my best to ignore the pain, I took stock of myself. Not only were my legs, arms, and face filthy, my caterer's outfit was streaked beyond recognition. The remains of several shrimp rolls clung to my jacket. Looking around, I realized that the truck had squashed my box and sent the contents flying.

How much food had been lost? Would we be able to do the event?

Why had Barry yelled *I knew it*?

I brushed off my formerly white, formerly crisp caterer's jacket. Shimmering dust rose from the jacket as food strands showered the dirt. I sneezed violently.

Two yards away, Barry rubbed his face and hacked for breath. He had landed in a deep puddle, and his once-khaki pants were now the color of café au lait. His formerly green shirt clung to his torso like a mossy towel. Julian, his wet clothes stuck to his body, trotted toward us. He was shouting again, this time at the construction crew, something along the lines of getting their asses up here so they could help us.

Barry looked at me and blinked, then blinked again. He slid sideways in the puddle and reached in my direction.

"Goldy! Did you see the driver?"

"No. Whoever it was ran away." I didn't state the obvious: that whoever the driver was, he'd seemed intent on mowing us down.

"Do *you* know who it was?" I tried but didn't succeed in keeping the accusatory tone from my voice.

Barry shook his head and turned away from me. Why was his muttered "No" so unconvincing?

I studied the dump truck wedged in the embankment. Along Doughnut Drive, lines of cars had stopped. Honking and yelling rose above the throngs of curious drivers who'd left their vehicles and were hustling rapidly along the road. Why else? They were trying to get a better look at the accident.

We needed state patrol and the sheriff's department, I decided, and quick. With any luck, one of those drivers was using a cell phone to call for help right now.

And speaking of cell phones...I usually kept mine in my apron pocket. But I hadn't yet put on my apron, so I didn't have it. I sighed.

I was having a great day.

Barry was staring at the errant truck. There was blood on his forehead. Julian's words were finally discernible: *Are you all right?* I yelled back that we were fine. *How are you doing?* I wanted to know. Julian hollered that he was fine, then raced down to the construction area and called to more workers. Oh, to be young and able to run around in wet clothes.

I hauled myself to my feet, then offered a hand to Barry, still stuck in the puddle. He groaned and splattered mud as he righted himself. His hands were icy, his face pale. Once free of the ditch water, he shivered, grasped the back of his left thigh, and cried out in pain.

Victor Wilson, still wearing his orange hat, raced up the parking lot. Five workers jogged along behind him. The crew did not appear to be paying much attention to Victor's bellowed orders, commands that were liberally sprinkled with curses. With his red ponytail flapping, Victor swerved away from Barry and me and toward the truck, but not before I'd squinted at the boldly printed words on his sweatshirt. *We Got Dirt.* No kidding, I thought. Lots and lots of dirt.

Barry hobbled up beside me and we both spoke at once. *What happened, Who could have done such a thing, Are you badly hurt, Do you have a cell phone?* Without waiting for my reply, Barry wiped the trickle of blood from his scraped forehead and gazed at Victor, who was now climbing into the truck.

"No, no!" I yelled. "You shouldn't be doing that!" Ten minutes ago, the crazed driver of that vehicle had tried to kill us. Or at least it sure had seemed that way. Nobody should be touching anything until the cops arrived.

Disregarding my protest, Victor tried to start the truck anyway. The engine groaned, clicked, and refused to turn over. With another cascade of curses, he finally got the engine going. The behemoth truck revved and erupted into an insistent *beep beep beep* as it growled back from the embankment and swerved to miss the mountains of displaced berm dirt. The gaggle of spectators standing on Doughnut Drive moved aside en masse.

Julian, still sopping, sprinted over to us. He assessed me, then Barry, and asked if we needed to go to the hospital. We both said no. Just call the cops, I told him. Julian replied that he was calling the cops *and* an ambulance to have us looked at.

"No!" screamed Barry. "No cops! They'll drive away shoppers." He looked at me and swallowed. "Important saying in our business, Goldy. *Nothing clears a mall like a security threat*. We simply cannot afford to lose shoppers."

"Look, Barry." I raised my voice to match his. "More shoppers would *avoid* this place if somebody actually had been killed a few moments ago."

Barry groaned as he watched the line of cars along Doughnut Drive grow. The honking and shouting intensified.

Julian tersely ordered us to stay put. He was going to the Rover for some supplies. When I asked if he'd been able to make out who was driving the truck—man, woman, race, build—he shook his head. The first thing he'd seen was the truck's backside as

it catapulted out of the muddy lake and careened toward us.

When Julian roared up in the Rover a
few minutes later, he had already changed
into a spare sweatshirt and pants. He
leaped out and retrieved a battered first-aid
kit, a roll of paper towels, and his own cell
phone. I noted the smooth, peculiar-to-
Julian ability to do two things at once with
complete calm. He punched in 911, cra-
dled the phone between his ear and shoulder, and pumped disinfectant onto his
hands. Then he instructed Barry—in the
low, soothing voice Julian always assumed
in a crisis—to lie down. He had to get off
his injured leg, Julian explained.

Barry protested. He'd be just fine if he
could get into some clean clothes and
make a few calls. "And you, Goldy," Barry
said, his scraped face wracked with pain.
"I'm hoping you can just go inside and get
going. The mall really, really needs to have
this event go off smoothly."

"Mr. Dean, please." Julian spoke in a
low voice. "You'll be much better off if you
just let me help you. For a few minutes.
Come on."

Barry's insistence that we all needed to

get the hell out of here subsided. Groaning, the mall manager lay down as bidden.

Julian smoothed disinfectant onto Barry's face and arms, wiped away blood and muck with clean towels, and gently touched Barry's injured thigh. All the while, he murmured into his cell phone, telling the emergency operator what he'd seen happen. When Julian told the operator where in Westside Mall's parking lot we were, Barry abruptly wrenched away from my assistant's ministering hands. He struggled to a standing position, snarling that he didn't *want* any help from the cops, he just needed to get back to his office.

What *was* it with Barry Dean? First he wanted to talk to me privately and urgently. Then, after we'd nearly been run down by a truck, he'd submitted reluctantly to Julian's care, and told me to go inside and work on the event. Now he was back to yelping that he needed to get back to work.

While Julian walked after the hobbling Barry, trying to convince him not to leave, that he needed to be seen by a medic, I took stock of my own injuries. I'd had the misfortune to land on my kneecaps, which burned when I whisked off the tiny stones that had embedded themselves there. Blood spurted through a network of dirty scratches. My support hose, of course, were ripped and filthy. Other than my knees, I seemed to have emerged with some arm pain that would no doubt turn into a disgusting bruise. Still, no matter what the intentions of the truck driver, I had survived.

So now, I thought as I continued to massage my kneecaps, I only had to clean up, change outfits, figure out how much food we'd lost, and get on with the event. I knew the party would take place; Barry was determined. Thank God I had learned to keep an emergency pack of catering clothes in my van. I tentatively put one foot in front of the other, immediately registered acute pain in my back and hips, and sternly ordered myself to block it out. I had work to do.

Apparently Barry had again changed his mind about rushing to his office. He limped back to my side. Julian spoke earnestly into his cell phone. No, no ambulance after all, the injuries were slight. Police, yes. Yes, he went on, the attack had looked intentional, please send both state patrol and the sheriff's department. Yes, he would wait for them to arrive.

Barry's skin was ashen. He squinted, clearly miserable.

I asked, "You still want to talk? You want to tell me how you knew that was going to happen?"

Once again I got the beseeching brown eyes. "I do, Goldy." His voice cracked. "Just not right now." He rummaged in his pocket and held out a small keychain. "I left the lounge kitchen open for you, but you might want to lock it behind you, to protect the food while you're setting up, the way you said you needed to."

I frowned, but took the key.

"Could we . . . Goldy, you're an old friend of mine." His mouth twisted in a half-smile. Were those tears in his eyes? "Could we have our little chat later at the party? I have some things I absolutely have to do right now."

"Not a good idea, Barry. Come on. At least tell *me* how you knew that truck was aiming for us."

He blushed. "I didn't say that." I glared at him. Barry shook his head. "I really don't know who the driver was. I thought I did, but . . . Look, I really need to go." He started limping down to the mall.

"Barry!" I yelled sternly. "You can't leave before the cops get here!"

Barry stopped moving. His eyes slid to the offending truck, now moving slowly back toward the construction site. The vehicle's yellow auxiliary lights blinked as it lumbered downward. Back on Doughnut Drive, the crew waved traffic around the hills of dirt.

"Hey, old coffee buddy, I have a job to do." His voice had become testy. "That mess and the traffic jam need to be cleaned up before the Elite Shoppers arrive. The only thing I have to do is to make sure the shoppers can enter freely. That's how the mall makes money, remember?" I shook my head. He put his hands into his wet pockets and made his tone charming. "I'll talk to the cops, don't fret. I'll see you up at the lounge. Say, half an hour? Forty-five minutes, at the latest." He managed a wink before turning away. Good old Barry.

"But Barry—" I protested.

He moved forward, determined. After a moment he yelled over his shoulder, "Mall security will investigate this incident! They'll be my first call." He gave me a backhanded wave. "The shoppers' lounge, Goldy. Thirty minutes." He staggered away, *step,* hobble, *step,* hobble, *step,* hobble. Captain Ahab, managing a mall.

I shivered and clasped my arms around my ruined jacket. What was going on? It was clear I wasn't going to find out standing in the parking lot. Would the cops need me, if they already had Julian? Trying to ignore the pain, I walked over to him. Julian was closing his cell phone and shaking his head.

"Look, Julian, thanks for your help. I... need to get back to work. Barry's expecting the event to go off on time, I'm sorry to say."

Julian grinned ruefully. "I'll make your excuses to the cops, don't worry. But I swore on my mother's Bible that I'd stay here until state patrol and the sheriff's department arrive. One handles traffic accidents, the other...Oh, hey, we got company."

Victor Wilson was hustling toward us. He carried another first-aid box and a wrapped packet that I recognized as my emergency apparel kit. His wide, dirty face

I studied my layout design, placed the dishes on the buffet, then hurried back to the kitchen. There I opened the box with all the cheeses, crackers, and breads. But I needed a pop of energy. To heck with my cut-back-on-caffeine resolution: I needed to make some coffee, even if it was instant. In the back of a cabinet, I finally unearthed a jar of instant Folger's. Within moments, I was sipping a cup of the dark stuff.

Liz and I finished organizing the food and supplies by placing all the equipment we weren't using in a coat closet outside the kitchenette. Then we hurried back out to the buffet, where we placed the serving pieces at strategic intervals before setting the tableware, plates, napkins, and glasses. When Julian raced in at four o'clock, I was dying to ask him how things had gone with the cops. But that would have to wait. From the bottom of one box, we pulled out plain white tablecloths and lofted them over the eating accoutrements set out on the buffet table—the best way to protect the flatware from sticky fingers. We agreed to finish our food prep before taking a dinner break at four-thirty. At five-fifteen, we would reconvene to check the cold dishes, heat up the meatballs and empanadas, and do our final setup.

In the kitchen, Julian washed the berries, then brandished my new paring knife to trim the strawberries and slice the star fruit. I worked on the cheese platter while Liz started arranging the crackers and breads.

"I'm not taking a dinner break, Goldy," Julian announced, "until I hear how you met this Barry guy."

I sliced into a hunk of Gorgonzola and gave him a look. Liz giggled.

I said, "OK, nosy crew. It started with a puzzle. Actually, it started with an exam review class, some class notes, and a fight with The Jerk."

Julian raised a questioning eyebrow. "Go on."

I moved on to a slab of fragrant Cheddar, and thought back. "In *my* college days, there was a single place close to campus where you could get espresso drinks: The Hilltop Café. I practically lived there. Clutching a foam cup of cappuccino, I'd quick-step down the Hill to Group Psych class. Barry Dean sat next to me in class, but since I had just become engaged to

John Richard, I didn't really notice him. Didn't notice him, that is, until he asked me where I got that luscious-smelling coffee."

Liz tossed her head of silver hair. "Goodness. That's the best pickup line I've ever heard."

"Yeah, well," I said drily, as the two of them grinned. "On the last day of class before the final, the professor was doing one of those you-need-to-come-if-you-plan-to-pass reviews. The night before, John Richard and I had our first fight."

"Was this a fight of the physical variety?" Julian demanded, as he expertly moved aside a mountain of trimmed strawberries.

"No, all that came later." I peeled the wrapper off the Camembert. "This particular time, John Richard barged into my dorm room. I'd left a message saying I couldn't go to a med-school party with him because I was preparing for the Group Psych review and studying for the exam. He shouted and carried on and threw my books, mugs, shoes, and clothes all over the place. When he stomped out, I started crying and couldn't stop. My eyes got so red and puffy that I couldn't see well enough to go to the review class. I was sure I'd end up bombing on the exam."

Julian and Liz had stopped working and were leaning against the counters, all ears.

"I cast my swollen eyes over the class list," I said dramatically, "and who should be listed after yours truly but *Barry Dean*. It's really not that big a deal, guys."

"Wait a minute," Julian said, snapping his fingers. "I know that name! Barry Dean had a TV show out in Longmont, right? Not long ago, he was the answer to a trivia question in *The Camera. What C.U. alum ran a short-lived quiz show in a nearby town?*"

"Yup. Only it wasn't a quiz show, it was a scavenger hunt. Follow the clues around Longmont, learn about the city." I shook my head. "Barry used to love puzzles. Anyway, I stopped sniffling, called Barry's room, and left a message with his roommate asking if I could borrow the review-class notes. Next morning, someone slipped an index card under my door. It said: '*You can run but you can't hide; don't let your life go down the* BLANK.' And then he'd written HINT at the bottom of the page: *'Check the field-house.'* "

"Oh, I wish I'd had a boyfriend like that," Liz said with a sigh.

"He wasn't my boyfriend!"

"Go on," urged Julian.

"So. I went to the C.U. fieldhouse, and found a penciled sign with the Greek letter *psyche* on the door to the ladies' room. I was afraid I'd find the notes in a *toilet,* of course, but taped on the other side of the ladies' room door was a manila envelope. Writing on it said, let's see, *'First third of notes, Goldy. Everything will be just ducky if you* BLANK.' I thought for a few minutes, then zipped over to the campus duck pond, where another letter *psyche* was taped to the bridge, along with a second manila envelope that contained the second third of the class notes. This envelope's message read, *'Will just wake up and smell the . . .'* So of course I dashed to The Hilltop Café, where Barry was sitting at a corner table and smiling like the proverbial Cheshire."

"You can run but you can't hide," Liz repeated thoughtfully. "Don't let your life go down the toilet. Everything will be just

ducky if you wake up and smell the coffee?"

"Yeah," I said with resignation, as I
started on the last cheese. "Barry looked at
my mottled cheeks and puffed eyes, then
glanced at my engagement ring. He said, 'I
see your ring, and I see your face, and I
say, don't marry this guy.' Which unfortunately brought a fresh outburst of tears
from yours truly. And that's how Barry Dean
and I became coffee buddies, driving all
over the Boulder-Denver area in his Mercedes with the basset hound in the back,
looking for good coffee before I ignored
Barry's advice and married the doctor from
hell."

Both Julian's and Liz's faces looked
sad, even stricken.

"Come on, guys, it's not that bad. The
Jerk is history, and now we've got a big gig,
thanks to the Quiz King of Longmont Ca-
ble. So let's do it."

We finished at precisely four-thirty.
Barry had not yet shown up. I figured that
he must have decided after all to talk to the
cops, instead of to me. Fine. That was what
he needed to do. Right before my eyes,

Denver's Most Eligible Bachelor had become its Most Eligible Basket Case.

Liz gave me the kitchenette key, then offered to treat Julian to dinner at the mall's new gourmet sandwich shop. Julian arched an eyebrow in my direction. I shrugged and told them to go on. If I planned to follow through on my new resolve to keep better track of Arch, then I needed to give him a call.

I locked the kitchenette and dropped the key into my apron pocket next to my cellular. Amazingly, I'd remembered to bring the phone from the van. For the first time, I was glad I'd finally given in to Arch's everyone's-got-one-but-me cell-phone demand, even though I knew he'd resent what he called my "checking on him." Tough tacks.

"Yeah." This was his new cool-guy greeting.

"It's Mom. I'm down at Westside—"

"Did you get my guitar yet? Did Marla find the new Palm pilot? How about the Internet watch?"

"I haven't had time to do anything besides work. I don't know about Marla. What are you doing?"

"Changing my clothes after *lacrosse* practice, Mom, what do you think I'm doing?"

"I was just worried—"

He groaned. "Mom, I have to *go.* Lacrosse practice is *over,* I'm *cold,* and Tom is *waiting* for me." He paused. "Does this mean you won't be buying my guitar today?"

"I just...well. Maybe we should talk later."

He hung up, and I scolded myself for expecting meaningful communication at this stage of Arch's life. My stomach growled. I popped out of the lounge and wandered past the mall's alluring window displays and two huge common areas, one a coffee shop, the other an enormous play area where kids whooped it up as they leaped on and off hard rubber play sculptures in the shapes of fried eggs, toast, bacon, and pancakes. At length I came to a franchise restaurant where I wolfed down a depressingly cold steak sandwich, which tasted more of grease than beef. I had fifteen minutes before I needed to be back in the lounge. I tossed my trash, steeled myself, and went looking for Westside Music.

It was not until five-twenty that I scooted back out of the store. I was now the irritated, humbled owner of a seven-hundred-dollar electric guitar. Needless to say, the purchase had *not* proved to be as joyful as I had visualized. For some mysterious reason, my credit card company had balked at the purchase, despite the twenty-thousand-dollar limit they had recently bestowed on me. After running my card, the salesclerk had frowned, looked me over suspiciously, and announced in a loud voice, to me and all the people in line, that the sale had been *denied*. Did I, he asked loudly, want to pay by *check,* or not make the purchase? I blushed and meekly wrote out a check. Unfortunately, my card denial had rung alarms at Westside Music. While the people behind me groaned and muttered, I was forced to undergo a check-approval process that rivaled entering Pakistan without a passport.

Hauling the bulky guitar, I trotted past the breakfast sculptures—still filled with screeching kids—and past window displays that I willed myself to ignore. When I reached the steak place, I realized I'd walked the wrong way and was at the opposite end of the mall from the lounge. If I tried to stash the instrument in the van, I wouldn't get back to the lounge until after the jewelry event began. . . .

I gritted my teeth and raced back toward Westside Music. It was hard to ignore the curious stares from adults and children alike. *A singing caterer works both ends of the mall?* I ignored their gapes and tried to imagine Arch looking happy when he opened his gift. That happiness might last less than an hour, but so what? Besides, I had something else to look forward to: *canceling that damn credit card.*

I arrived, breathless, at the Westside Music counter. I paid no attention to the salespeople, whom I'd mentally dubbed the Smirking Clerks. I announced to the salesman who'd handled the botched card sale that I needed him to keep the guitar for me, please, until later in the evening. He informed me icily that they closed at nine. I'd be back by then, I vowed, and took off.

I stopped running only when I arrived at the lounge entrance. It now boasted two beefy security guards. Swirling around them was a chattering group of beautifully dressed women. They seemed to be milling about with the sole purpose of assessing one another's outfits, makeup, jewelry, and shoes. Putting my sweat-drenched and rumpled caterer's garb out of my head, I ducked past the women, then rummaged through my tote for ID. I flashed it at one of the guards, who nodded. Then I pushed through the service entrance to the kitchenette, washed my hands, and sped out to the main room.

To my surprise, the jewelry cases had also been covered with white damask cloths. I sprinted to the tables and about fainted with relief. Julian and Liz had set out everything. The food-laden buffet looked stunning.

"Hey, Ms. Punctuality," Julian said, straight-faced. "Aren't you glad Barry had a spare key to the kitchenette?"

"Sorry, really, both of you. And . . . what? Barry opened up for you?"

Julian nodded at the stage, where Barry, in fresh clothes and moving as if he, too, had downed a few painkillers, stood holding court with the band.

"He was looking for you," Julian told me. "Oh, but you should know that he only opened the kitchen when we promised him we'd give him something to drink. Something alcoholic. He wanted it from *us* instead of the bartenders, because he didn't want any of the salespeople to see him taking a nip. Several large nips, if the truth be told. So much for him being a caffeine guy."

Liz giggled. Julian grinned broadly, happy to entertain.

"So," I asked as we sauntered back to the kitchen, "did Barry ever talk to the cops?" They both shrugged. "How did you do with them, Big J?"

"State patrol just asked me the basics—you know, what happened and when. I told them you'd seen the accident, too, but they said they had plenty of witnesses, and since nobody had been hurt, they didn't need to talk to you. Anyway, state patrol and the sheriff's department officers told Victor to take them down to the truck. They told me to come, so I did. Get this. They found a pair of *cuff links* on the cab floor. Did we know whose they were, they asked. Victor said no, and so did I. So the cops put 'em in one of those brown paper bags. You know, the kind Tom uses for evidence."

I stopped and arched an eyebrow at

him. He grinned. "They were *gold* cuff links, Miss Nosy. They had two sets of initials on 'em and some writing on the back."

"Whose initials? What did the writing say?"

"I don't remember all of the initials," Julian replied. "The writing said something about making money. I don't really remember what."

"Julian."

"OK, OK, I remember one set of initials was B. D. So maybe they were Barry's."

I thought again of Barry's paranoia, how he'd wanted to talk to me, how he'd freaked out over the truck incident, how he'd then decided not to chat with me, but hustled back to his office.

"Go figure," I murmured.

Liz shook her head. "All Barry Dean could think about was getting a drink. He slugged that expensive Burgundy straight from the bottle. Said he couldn't take much more for one day."

Julian added, "He said you were his *old buddy* and it would be OK—"

"Don't worry," Liz told me, "I threw away the rest of that bottle. Thirty-four bucks a pop, though. We should charge him extra."

I made for the stage. Barry was plugging in his microphone. No question about it, the man cleaned up well. In fact, he looked downright spiffy in his tuxedo. As I got closer, though, I noticed his face was red and sweaty. Worse, he was a bit too obviously chewing on a mouthful of breath mints.

"We've got a videographer here," he began, once he'd swallowed the candy. He pointed to another tuxedo-clad fellow clutching a camera. "Every woman attending gets a video of the event," Barry went on, "so she can see herself in her chosen necklace or earrings. You're not camera-shy, are you?" I groaned. "Don't be nervous, we'll cut any food accidents."

"Actually, *old buddy,* what makes me nervous is you drinking wine straight from the bottle."

"Oh, sorry about that." He paused and gave me the full benefit of his seductive brown eyes. He seemed to be struggling with words, thoughts, something. "Goldy, about that truck—"

"Did you talk to Colorado State Patrol?"

"Er, no, but I wondered if—"

Whatever he was wondering was cut short by the band striking up "Diamonds Are a Girl's Best Friend." Barry muttered something that sounded like "Holy Moly" as the lounge doors opened.

The Army of Gorgeous Women streamed in. Clad in bright-hued silk, satin, and taffeta, they hiked up their skirts and flew to the shrouded jewelry cases. Exclamations of *Damn!* and *What's going on?* rose above the music. Barry grabbed the microphone.

"Ladies," he announced, "and gentlemen," he added, acknowledging the sprinkling of men, "before we start with our serious business tonight, please help yourselves to drinks and hors d'oeuvres! Then I will explain how our event is going to work!"

I made my way to the kitchen while Barry flattered the women and charmingly described how *easily* and *effortlessly* they could wear these hundred-thousand-dollar pieces they needed and *owed* to themselves, for mere *pennies* per month. Julian and Liz hauled loaded appetizer trays out to the guests. I snagged a platter of empanadas and sailed after them.

"...And for those of you who are *still* in need of a bargain for that next big party," Barry was announcing fervently, "look for the *perfect* pair of shoes at Prince and Grogan's Red Tag Sale! Tonight, you Elite Shoppers are entitled to an additional fifteen percent off...."

"Barry Dean is *so* charming," Marla said as she sidled up next to me. She winked and dunked an empanada into guacamole. She was wearing a stunning royal blue dress with a matching cape. Without her usual array of glittering jewelry, she looked different. She'd informed me she wanted to come to the event as a clean canvas. "I'd love to listen to Barry Dean all the time. In my car, in the bathroom, in bed...while looking at his picture."

"How was the spa?"

"Fabulous! Plus, I have so much to ask you, especially about—"

"Marla, I have to—"

"Calm down, I'm having a couple of empanadas." She grabbed her cape and folded it over her arm, then nabbed two more empanadas, downing one and then the other, while four other women helped themselves to my tray.

"Tell me about the truck," Marla whispered conspiratorially, once the women had moved on. With a paper napkin, she wiped creamy green stuff from her upper lip.

"You heard about that already?" I asked, stunned. Marla opened her eyes wide, a picture of offended innocence. Of course the Queen of Gossip knew about everything. Why was I surprised? "Well," I began, "somebody got into a truck, slammed down the accelerator, barely missed Barry the Charming, not to mention yours truly. Then whoever was driving crashed the truck into the berm. Trying to get out of the way, Julian, Barry, and I all got soaked with mud and grime. I lost a whole box of shrimp rolls, not to mention a big chunk of setup time."

"How'd you ever get the food done, then?" she mumbled through another empanada.

"The excavator and his crew helped. They brought in almost every box. Actually, I guess he's the construction manager for the mall addition. He said he felt responsible for one of his trucks almost killing us."

"That's not Victor Wilson, is it?"

I sighed. And here I thought Marla only knew folks with incomes of a million and up. "How can you possibly know..."

Marla looked sideways, taking in the fact that Julian and Liz were bringing out the first plates of truffles. "I don't know *him*. I went out with his brothers. Don't give me that look. Consecutively, not simultaneously. First was Bachman. Bachman's a surgeon, a friend of The Jerk's. Well, sort of a friend. John Richard couldn't stand that Bachman gave better parties than he did, which is why I went out with him." She frowned at the empanadas, as if unsure whether to have another one. "Victor's other brother is an attorney, has a big place in Aspen, built for him by Victor, he said."

"Nice. Now if you don't mind—"

"Julian told me they found some cuff links inside the truck." Marla finally decided to tuck into another empanada, her fifth. "Do you have any idea whose they were?"

"No. I don't suppose *you* know whose they were."

"Not yet. But I will. Here's a juicy tidbit for you, though. Shane Stockham has just lost his lease at The Gadget Guy. He's trying to placate dear wife Page, who told us at the spa that she heard this morning about his cash *dam,* which is the opposite of cash *flow*. Page wants a bauble from the diamond people, and Shane's stretched thinner than gold plate. Brace yourself: You might see fireworks."

I glanced at the Stockhams, whom I was doing lunch for later in the week. Had I received the final payment for their event? I couldn't remember. As I watched, Shane reached for his wife's shoulder. She moved out of his reach. I groaned. After I refilled the platter, I took up a plate of truffles and headed for some hungry-looking ladies who were drooling over the handsome twenty-something guys in the band. Barry, who'd just finished a glass of water (at least, I hoped it was water) stepped back up to the microphone.

"I truly can't believe how gorgeous you all are! You look as if . . . well, as if you were going out for a fancy dinner with your husband's new boss!" This was met with squeals of laughter. "But ladies . . . would you feel completely confident if you weren't wearing some very *special* jewelry, the kind that indicated how *important* you *really* are? What if your husband's new boss happens to be a twenty-eight-year-old woman who wears skimpy dresses from Escada and diamond necklaces from Tiffany's?"

The women glanced uneasily at one another. Clearly, Barry's attempt to make them feel insecure was hitting home.

"Wouldn't you want to be certain you looked your best?" Barry crooned. "But you wouldn't want to wear a piece that could *bore* you in a year, would you?" There was a ripple of edgy laughter. "That's why we're here! We'll get you to *elegant* at a fraction of the cost...and next month you could start wearing something *completely* different!"

As he launched into an explanation of leasing, I glanced around and saw Julian chatting with Liz and, of all people, her son, Teddy. Dressed in faded jeans and a tattered red sweatshirt, Teddy looked as gangly and insecure as he had that morning. But I had thought Teddy wasn't picking Liz up until later....I certainly couldn't afford for her to leave now.

Barry finished his speech to frenzied clapping, squeals of pleasure, and the band's enthusiastic rendition of "Ruby, Ruby." The empanada and truffle platters were again almost empty. On either side of the room, the jewelry salespeople whipped the damask cloths from the jewelry displays. And then something bizarre seemed to be happening. There was noise, scuffling, muffled epithets, and struggling.

People were fighting.

I turned in time to see two security guards grabbing Teddy Fury by his elbows. Then the meaty guards picked Teddy up under his arms and began dragging him from the lounge. Liz, up next to the guards' impassive faces, was scolding them—to no avail.

Dumbfounded, I scanned the crowd for Julian. Oh, Lord. He'd abandoned his catering tasks and was standing at the corner of the stage, engaged in a heated, fist-shaking argument with Barry Dean. Barry, his arms crossed, was shaking his head.

"This isn't happening," I whispered in horror to no one in particular. One thing I knew from long food-service experience: If there's a fight at a party, everyone will blame the caterer.

"Oooh, I just love being waited on," cooed a woman at my elbow as she reached for an appetizer. I whirled.

It was Pam Disharoon. The blonde wore a skimpy hot pink dress that showed lots of cleavage and even more leg. "How do you like my outfit?" she demanded, wiggling her hips the same way I'd already seen her do with Barry.

I said, "Fabulous. Is it a nightgown or a dress?"

Pam pouted. "Both." She grabbed the last empanada and scampered away.

I put down the tray and moved quickly behind the jewelry salespeople to get to the stage. Up there, Liz had joined the Barry-Julian squabble. The guards reached the doors, wrenched them open, and hauled Teddy out. The band kicked up the music a few notches, but the noise of Barry, Liz, and Julian arguing was still clear.

I hopped onto the stage and approached the three of them, looking as stern as possible. They formed a tight clutch of hostility.

"He's a child—" Liz exclaimed, her

voice just below a shout. Her silver hair shone in the spotlights.

"He's a *thief*!" Barry retorted, his face flushed, his chin pointing defiantly at Liz.

"You just cannot *do* that to a kid," Julian cried angrily. "You're going to ruin his—"

"Excuse me," I said with as much authority as I could muster. "This argument needs to be put on hold, and I mean, *right* now. Liz and Julian, go back to work right away. Barry," I said sternly, "you hired me. There are two hundred potential clients out there who will remember this party for this altercation, unless you stop this minute. We can talk *later*. Understand?"

All three mumbled OK, yes, sorry. Julian and Liz hastened down the steps at the side of the stage. Barry opened his mouth to say something, but he couldn't get the words out before another volcano of yelling erupted.

By one of the two cash registers—set up to handle the leasing arrangements—a man and woman were arguing. They were young, they were attractive...they were Page Stockham and...Shane Stockham.

"A thousand dollars a month!" Page shrieked. With her blond hair done up in a fancy French twist, and her slender body sheathed in white silk, she looked like a latter-day Audrey Hepburn. But her demeanor was the opposite of the gracious, softspoken Hepburn's. She screeched at her husband: "You cheap bastard!"

"Don't talk to me like that," Shane bellowed, using the same tone of voice I'd heard so many times when he disagreed with lacrosse referees. "You're lucky you get anything!"

"You tightfisted asshole!"

"You *bitch*!"

Shane lunged forward and slapped Page in the face. My stomach turned over. Page responded by kneeing her husband in the groin. When the two backed away from each other, the crowd parted to give them space.

At that moment, the security guards reentered the lounge. Dumbfounded, they looked to see what the new disruption was about.

I knew what it was about, having had lots of experience in the domestic violence department. I jumped off the stage and pushed through the throng toward the warring partners. The Stockhams had stopped screaming obscenities. Shane was trying to slap Page again. She was fending him off. I tensed my biceps, stepped up next to them, and grabbed the right arm of Page and the left arm of Shane. Using all my strength, I pulled them apart.

"Guards!" I yelled. "Come here now, please! Come take Mrs. Stockham *out,* now! *Now! Please!*" I glared at Shane Stockham and said tersely, "You need to back off, Shane. Right now." I continued to grip his left forearm. Shane was a well-muscled man, with slicked- back brown hair and a handsome baby face. He had that young, all-powerful movie star look. "Stop this," I said in a low voice. "A piece of jewelry isn't worth a fight."

The security guards reached for Page. She yanked herself away from me, then hopped quickly behind one of the jewelry display cases. Shane, meanwhile, also pulled out of my grasp. He turned his back and walked toward the stage, away from the exit doors.

"Hey, Shane! Cheap bastard!" Page taunted. "Business failure! Come get me now!"

The guards, upset at being foiled, lumbered a bit more quickly on either side of the case, trying to apprehend Page. Again she was too quick for them. With a few agile steps, Page danced back out by the buffet table, not far from me, but probably twenty yards from where Shane was walking away.

Shane turned slowly. His furious eyes fixed on his wife.

Page hissed something incomprehensible. Shane, in turn, raced back in her direction. Page neighed in triumph.

Shane was charging toward his wife. There was just one thing in his way: me. A warning chill raced down my spine.

"Security!" I squealed.

Shane kept coming. My mind conjured up Shane as the hot-tempered lacrosse coach and Arch, my little Arch, who was trying so hard to become a tough athlete. If I just stepped out of Shane's way, he'd hit Page. *Do what Arch does,* I thought. *Pronto.*

I'd seen it over and over. Arch set his position against the attack man, then used his body weight to send the attacker in the opposite direction. When Shane was a yard from me, I placed my shoulder at right angles to his chest. Then, just as he was about to slam into me, I jerked up and under his chest, and whacked him with such force that he reeled upward. The muscled poundage of Shane Stockham went airborne. I staggered backward. Outstretched hands couldn't prevent me from falling. I thudded to the floor, landing with a jolt of pain on my shoulder.

The security guys, who'd called for help, finally forced their way forward. Two of them manhandled a shrieking Page toward the exit. Three guards seized Shane and pulled him upright. When they tried to march him out behind his wife, I noticed that he was limping slightly.

"You nosy bitch!" Shane yelled at me, his face scarlet with fury. "What do you know about anything?"

I rubbed my shoulder. For the second time that day, I wondered if it was broken.

CHAPTER 5

"That was pretty awful," Marla commented as she escorted me to the kitchen to tend to my shoulder. "Is somebody going to call the cops? The guards shouldn't be the only ones dealing with Shane."

"I'll call the cops," Julian assured us. He asked if he could check my shoulder; I said yes. "It's not broken," he reported, after gently poking the shoulder blade and asking me to move it in a circle. He frowned, pulled out his cell phone, and punched buttons. "I'm going to run down to the parking lot, see if I can snag a cop who might still be there. I'll let the sheriff's department dispatcher know what's what, too. Where would those guards have taken Shane, the mall security office?"

"Probably," I replied weakly. What *was* going on with Shane Stockham? Did he dare think that I'd still be putting on a lunch for him day after next? At that moment, I couldn't ponder anything that was two days away. I *did* want to know the reason for the fight among Liz, Barry, and Julian. Julian had taken off, which only left one person to ask.

"Liz," I began, "I need to know why you and Julian—"

"Please," she said in a low voice, as she bent over the sink, where she was washing platters. She would not meet my eyes. Marla, all interest, leaned in. Liz said stiffly, "I promise to tell you later, Goldy. My son should call me soon. Then I'll know more." She turned the water off and lifted her chin. Tears spilled as she faced me. "Look, I'm sorry I argued with Barry, but he started it. If you could just trust me to help us get through this party, I promise I'll tell you the whole story later."

I gnawed my lip. Liz had become invaluable to my catering business. I simply could not, *would* not force her to explain herself in front of Marla. Teddy had been hauled out; the Stockham crisis had erupted right after that. And Liz had apologized. I murmured that it was fine for us to talk at her convenience.

Liz nodded her thanks, then worked silently drying the platters and assembling new trays. Marla filled a dishtowel with ice and lightly pressed it into my shoulder. The events of the day filled my mind. First the truck had almost mowed me down, then Shane Stockham had almost mowed me down. And, as Liz had reminded me, we were in the middle of an event. . . .

Marla murmured in my ear, "You should have stayed in bed."

The band burst into "The Emerald Isle." After a few moments, against Marla's stern advice, I tentatively lifted a tray. I ignored stares as I transported it out to the buffet. Marla bustled along beside me, tossing smiles at the gawkers. When the guests realized no new crisis was brewing, they turned their attention back to the jewelry cases and continued trying on glittering necklaces, earrings, and bracelets. The videographer slithered through the crowd, occasionally asking women to pose for him. When Marla insisted he follow her to a jewelry case, I wondered fleetingly if the videographer had caught the Stockhams' conflict on tape.

A few moments later, Marla magically reappeared at my side. She stepped back for me to admire her newly rented double strand of pearls with diamonds. Brilliant matching earrings and tiny barrettes wreathed her pretty, plump face in twinkles. I gave her a thumbs-up.

She said, "You don't want to know what these cost."

"You're right." I straightened platters and stirred the meatballs in the sauce. "So," I asked her, "do *you* have any idea what Barry and Liz and Julian were fighting about?"

"I can guess," she said. "You don't need Liz to tell you the whole story; I can fill you in on most of it. Don't you know that little Teddy's had a few shoplifting incidents here at Westside? More than a few, if my sources are correct. Julian must know about Teddy's problems, because he was in on the argument. When he comes back, I can cross-examine him."

I groaned. "Well, then, what was Shane and Page's fight about? Do their spending disagreements often turn violent?"

"I've heard stories," Marla replied knowingly. Three beautifully outfitted women sidled up to the table. Marla's eyes glided over to them. "I can't talk about the Stockhams out here, Goldy," she announced in a stage whisper, "with people eavesdropping. You know, I *tried* to warn you—"

I interrupted Marla by asking her to come back to the kitchenette after a few minutes. I picked up the empty chafer of meatballs and hightailed it back there myself.

When she pushed through the door, I was ladling meatballs into a sauté pan to heat them up. The rich smell of Burgundy sauce steamed through the small cooking space.

"If Shane is hell-bent on doing harm to his wife, then I'm not going to cater a party at his place on Wednesday or any other day," I said. My voice sounded a tad more rancorous than I intended.

Marla shrugged. "Shane and Page have one of those love-you-one-minute, hate-you-the-next relationships. You watch, tomorrow he'll buy her a ruby bracelet, or a round trip ticket to Paris, or maybe both. That's the glory of numerous credit cards, yes?" Actually, I did not know, having limited myself to one about-to-be-canceled card. "Shane *just* received that eviction notice from Barry, although I think it's been coming for some time now. You should have heard Page's reaction, like a rich kid who's been denied Christmas. By the way, she told me that they added folks to the guest list for the lunch you're doing for them. Shane wants to include a group of potential investors to underwrite his moving the business on-line."

I peered at her in disbelief. "He's added to the guest list? Does he have some new caterer in mind?"

Marla popped a piece of Gorgonzola into her mouth. "Mm-mm." She moved her hips in time with her chewing, then said, "Shane still thinks *you're* his caterer, doll."

"That son of a bitch told me the lunch was for his best customers."

"Yeah, well, he told Page the eviction was just a tiny setback, and that he'd lease her something really *gorgeous* today." Marla nabbed a morsel of Camembert.

"You'd think losing your livelihood would mean cutting back on expenses. You can imagine how well Page would react, in fact, *is* reacting to *that* idea."

As Marla bustled behind me on my way back to the buffet table, I recalled those long months when The Jerk had refused to pay the full amount he'd been ordered to give Arch and me. There'd been weeks of peanut butter, homemade bread, nonfat dry milk, chunk tuna, and noodles. When I was strung out beyond my ability to cope, our priest had come to visit. He only came once, admitting he didn't want to jeopardize John Richard's continued financial support of the parish by appearing to take sides. I was tempted to bring up John Richard's current fling with a woman in the choir, but did not. In any event, the priest informed me that the most desperate folks he counseled were ones who went from having money to suddenly *not* having money. Most of them, he added, lived in denial for at least a year, unable to give up the high life. So they racked up debt that took decades to repay. And he certainly hoped, he concluded as he chomped into his sixth peanut butter cookie that I had made especially for his visit, that I would not bury myself in debt! I'd sat in silence as he swallowed the last of the cookie, then asked him to leave.

Well. Mustn't grumble, as the Brits are wont to say.

I assessed the buffet table. If Shane and Page wanted to live in denial, that was their problem, not mine. At the moment, we needed still more refilled trays. I headed back to the kitchen. Marla made a wide U-turn and followed.

"OK," she began as I pulled a new tray of beautifully arranged, succulent fruit from the refrigerator. "Here's the scoop on why Barry kicked Shane out of Westside. First, are you aware of how they figure rents in a mall?"

I frowned at the fruit tray. *How mall rents were figured*. Wait—I did know this. "Yes, Barry told me. It's a base figure plus extra for the—what's it called?...CAM. Common area management," I added, as I scoured the refrigerator for our Creamy Fruit Dressing.

"Very good," said Marla.

I carefully placed dollops of the dress-ing—equal parts sour cream and mayonnaise—into a crystal bowl that fit in the center of the tray.

"That's not quite all—"

"Hold on." I paused before covering the large jar of dressing, long enough for Marla to grab a spoon and help herself to a large mouthful. I instantly prayed for the county health inspector to be a thousand miles away. "Rents," I said, as I stored the jar. "OK. If a store is doing well enough, it's supposed to pay a percentage of its sales to the mall. But The Gadget Guy shouldn't have had a problem with that. That place is always mobbed!" I shouldered the fruit tray. "*Was* always mobbed."

"The Gadget Guy was a huge success," Marla agreed, as she followed me out of the kitchen. "The place did so well that they should have been paying *extra* to the mall owners, but Shane cried poor. So Barry had his accounts audited, and guess what? The Gadget Guy owed the mall owner, what's their name?"

"Pennybaker International."

"Owed Pennybaker over a million dollars. Pay up in thirty days, Pennybaker said, or you're out of here, forever. Shane didn't even have a hundred thou, much less a mil. The eviction notice was delivered yesterday afternoon."

I set my tray on the buffet, where women dripping with leased jewels dug in for second, third, or—was it possible?—fourth helpings of truffles. They squealed and wiggled and raved about the rich chocolate. Curse of the cocktail buffet: People eat too much, because it's all right there in front of them. When I'd retrieved a load of glasses and plates, I stopped to scan the lounge. Barry was nowhere in sight.

Marla moved away. I unloaded the dirty dishes and glasses, then began a lap around the lounge to retrieve more of them. Liz and Julian, I noted thankfully, were bent on the same task at the room's opposite end. The dregs of the buzzing crowd clustered around the jewelry display cases, doing last-minute deals. Marla waved at friends, pointed to her new necklace, earrings, and barrettes, and then nipped back toward me. She must have gleaned a final tidbit of gossip.

"More news," she said eagerly. "Shane's future is looking even dimmer."

"Financially?" I replied. "Or legally, after

he gets through with the cops for coming at his wife?"

"In the money department, Barry's not backing off on demanding the mall's million." Marla's voice was hoarse. "*Shane* claims he wants more time to bring together the cash. That party you, uh, *may* be doing at his house? He's hoping these potential investors will write him checks to bail him out of everything. So. How's your shoulder?"

"It's fine," I lied, realizing my best friend wanted to get back to shopping and talking, not necessarily in that order. "Thanks for your company. And all the good info," I added with a wink.

Marla nodded, gave me a huge smile, and skittered away to coo over someone's diamond necklace.

It was almost seven-thirty, and the lounge was finally emptying. At least the platters had held up to the end. Liz and Julian appeared and also asked about my shoulder. I told them it was fine. Liz wondered if she and Julian could grab a quick cup of coffee, as they needed to talk. Then they would come back to do cleanup. I nodded. She didn't mention the argument with Barry. I certainly hoped she didn't want to visit with Julian so they could agree on a story.

Stop being paranoid, I ordered myself.

Marla swooped back and signaled that we go into the kitchenette. "I've got a flask in my purse," she whispered. "This was supposed to be a *cocktail* party, and all Barry Dean managed to offer was *wine*. Disgusting. I've got some sherry in here, Dry Sack, your favorite. Why don't you have some?"

I politely declined her offer, which brought on a why-can't-you-ever-relax harangue that I ignored.

"OK," I said, after Marla took a sip of her sherry. "What else have you got?"

Marla leaned forward, eager to share. "Shane and Page fought because he didn't lease her a piece from the six-thou-a-month category. Page is a compulsive shopper, like her sister. The woman is crazed, I'm telling you. Maybe they both are. Anyway, Page wants everything her sister has, and the sister got a piece from that six-thou-a-month case."

"Her sister?"

"Pam Disharoon. Goldy, where have you *been*?"

I wrinkled my nose at her. "The blond lingerie saleslady? She has so much stuff that Page Stockham is jealous of *her*?"

"Word is that Pam is *loaded* with goodies, all gifts from boyfriends. She doesn't have to work in sales, but she does for the thrill of it. Apparently, she's a whiz at both selling stuff and *getting* stuff. Free stuff. She goes to a guy's house. She and the guy have a wild lovemaking session on his Oriental rug, all while the guy's wife is away, of course. Pam says, *Oh, if only I had a rug like this, I could think of us on it.* Next thing you know, a Kirman's delivered to Pam's front door. I'm telling you, the woman is infamous. I can't believe you haven't heard about her."

"I've been *working*. Too hard, according to you. What about Page?"

Marla sniffed. "Page is *insanely* jealous of Pam. Page watches her sister like a hawk, to see what she gets. Then Page goes out and buys the same thing, only bigger. It's like a game between them."

"And Shane fits in how?"

Marla sipped more sherry. "Well, I just

heard Shane and Page are in counseling, individually and together. Last month Page spent fifteen thousand dollars just on *stuff.* That woman can't walk past a store without buying something that she thinks Pam *might* have. Page just bought a new white Audi, because one of Pam's boyfriends gave *her* one. Page can't *stand* the fact that Pam's Audi license plate says 'GOGIRL.' She thinks it means *go get more stuff.* "

I stacked the last of the dirty platters in a cardboard box. "So Page bought one because Pam had one? *There's* a great motivation for purchasing a luxury vehicle."

Marla put down her glass and obligingly scraped a platter into the new trash bag. She hesitated, as if trying to remember something. "And that's not all," she added. "Before she was kicked out of tonight's party, Page told a friend of mine that Shane had told *her* that ninety percent of the *new stuff* Page just bought has to go back. Page was upset, whoo! The last ten percent, she stowed in a storage shed—her fourth. But it's not as if she isn't trying to change. I hear she's on an antidepressant that's supposed to help with compulsive spending. Plus, she's in individual counseling, as well as a support group for over-spenders. Anonymous, of course."

"For crying out loud—" I couldn't imagine keeping *any* secrets from Marla. The woman was a bloodhound.

"You haven't heard the worst of it. The reason Shane had to come with her here? As part of their counseling deal, Page gets no credit cards, no checkbook. So if she wants something, Shane has to be there to get it for her."

"How'd she get the fifteen thou worth of *stuff* this month, then?"

Marla raised an eyebrow. "Ellie McNeely called and left a message for Shane. He'd applied for a loan and it had come through. The minute Page heard it, she raced down to the bank and talked the clerk into letting her get the dough. Bye-bye loan."

We were interrupted by Liz and Julian entering the kitchenette. Julian told me Barry had given us the go-ahead to pack up the buffet.

"Would it be possible for me to leave early?" Liz asked. "I need to go find Teddy—"

I held up a finger for her to wait. "Marla?

If you don't mind, I need to visit with my staff."

Marla assumed an attitude of peevishness, then winked at Julian and flounced out.

To Liz and Julian, I said gently, "You realize how arguing with a client during an event can wreck everything." Liz opened her mouth to protest, then stopped when she saw my face. "This is not nosiness, Liz. This is your boss needing to know why you were fighting with the client . . . especially," I added with a smile, "when we haven't received the staff gratuity."

They both hesitated. Then Julian said to Liz, "You'd better just tell her."

Liz's thin, pretty face was tense. "Teddy's had trouble here at the mall—"

"Trouble?" I interjected, remembering what Marla had told me. "What kind of trouble?"

Outside the kitchenette, Barry was making an announcement that customers only had five minutes to complete their leases . . . and they might want to stow their pieces in their cars, if they were moving on to make great shoe deals at Prince & Grogan!

"My son had a theft problem," Liz said huskily. "You probably read about it in the paper, they just couldn't release his name because he's a juvenile."

"I actually heard about his... problem from a friend. What does that have to do with Barry?"

Reluctantly, Liz continued: "Teddy... used to wait in that eggs-and-bacon area, where parents let their kids play. Sometimes people sit at tables around the edge of the play area, to drink coffee or tea. You know it?" I nodded. "Teddy would... watch, until the parents or the coffee drinkers were distracted. Then he'd walk off with their bags. Their purses, too." She ran her fingers through her short silver hair. "Their wallets. That's why I wanted to talk to Julian. I just keep thinking if Teddy could have a role model—"

"Liz. The fight with Barry? Why did the security guys haul Teddy out of the lounge?"

"Law enforcement has talked and talked to Teddy, and he's doing so much better. But then Barry Dean," Liz began savagely, "*barred* him from Westside. Technically, it's called *being trespassed*. He's not allowed into the mall for any reason. If mall security catches him, they automatically call the cops and have him transported away—"

"This *sucks!*" Julian interjected angrily. "Here's this seventeen-year-old kid, who's just trying to find his mom so he can give her a ride home, and then that creep gets him dragged off—"

"Sounds like Barry was just trying to do his job," I pointed out gently.

"Oh, puh-leeze," Liz scoffed. "Barry didn't have to have Teddy humiliated. There were enough guards holding on to him to stop an army, for God's sake. And I'd like to know why my son was immediately hauled away in front of everybody when he didn't even do anything, and Barry stood still while Shane Stockham tried to beat up his wife and whacked into you instead. Hello?"

"Well, uh," I said, but couldn't finish. Liz had a point.

"Anyway, why am I talking to you?" Liz's voice was defiant. "I need to go find out where my son is." She tugged off her chef's jacket and tossed it onto the counter. "If you don't want to pay me for my work today, that's fine. Good-bye."

With this, she stomped away.

"That went well," Julian commented.

"Look, I'm sorry," I retorted. "But why didn't they just agree to meet outside the mall? If the kid knows he's not supposed to come into the mall, why would he do it?" I let out a breath. "This was a Goldilocks' Catering *party*. And we saw not one, but *two* fights." I slumped against the counter, exhausted and in pain. Worse, I felt defeated.

Julian's dark eyebrows knit into a straight line. "Let me help you with the cleanup and packing. I'll stay as late as you want. And...I know a catering staff shouldn't argue with anyone. So you don't have to pay *me,* either." He paused. "Teddy just felt *so* awful when I talked to him tonight."

I resisted commenting on how awful the people Teddy stole from undoubtedly felt when their packages and purses disappeared. Instead, I thanked Julian for staying to help. And of course I would pay him, and Liz, too. Talking about her brought up a fresh worry. She and I had come down from Aspen Meadow together....What if she couldn't *find* Teddy? How would she get home? Did she have a cell phone? When I voiced this worry to Julian, he said Liz had his cell number. If she got stranded, she'd be sure to call.

By the time Julian and I had cleaned the kitchen—to make way for more mess—and reentered the lounge, the crowd had vanished. At my suggestion, Julian offered the remains of the buffet platters to the band and the jewelry salespeople. They pounced as if they hadn't eaten for months. I smiled. "Free food" is always great publicity for my business. And after the evening's crises, I needed all the help I could get.

I stacked more empty trays and carried them to the kitchen. As usual, Barry had done another of his disappearing acts. Stockham conflict or no, if Barry thought I was going to leave without my check for the staff gratuity, he was wrong.

After twenty minutes of washing platters and shuffling them to the van, we were almost done. Still no Barry. After all my admonitions about staying cool, I was starting to simmer.

"One of the musicians gave me a note the last time you were out at the van," Julian said as he brought the last of the platters into the kitchen. "I thought it was for me, but it was for you. From Barry Dean."

"A note? Or a check?"

Julian wordlessly handed me a single piece of paper.

Hey Goldy! it read. *Great event, despite the problems. I have your check, and a tip for you, too. Meet me at the Prince & Grogan shoe sale at 8:30. Your buddy, B.*

It sure didn't *feel* as if Barry Dean was my buddy anymore. I glanced at my watch: quarter to nine. Great.

"Look, Julian, Barry's being elusive. I've got to find him in Prince and Grogan to get our gratuity. And I need to pick up Arch's guitar, too, before I get there."

"You bought Arch a guitar?" Julian asked, his eyes brightening. "Why don't you let me pick it up? It'll save us some time."

"You don't know Westside Music. I'm not even sure they'll let *me* have it, and I just paid them hundreds of dollars for the damn thing."

When we hurried back out to the lounge, the lights were blinking. A bored voice from an unseen loudspeaker announced that the mall was closing in fifteen minutes. I looked around in dismay. Julian and I had done quite a bit, but at least twenty more minutes of cleanup awaited us.

"Look," Julian said, aware of my problem. "I'll finish the cleanup extra fast while you nab the guitar and the check. Then I'll meet you back here, say, no later than ten after nine. They won't lock us in, I'm sure. Plus, that'll give Liz time to call if she doesn't find Teddy. Then we can drive in convoy out of the lot. I *don't* want you all driving out of here on your own, what with killer truckers on the loose. You'd better leave now, though, in case Westside Music closes early. You can always get the staff gratuity check later, you know."

In the catering biz, "getting the check later" was not something you should *ever* do. Food is perishable; events get messed up; people decide not to give you your money. But I had no time to remind Julian of all that. I needed to get Arch's guitar. I thanked Julian and dashed out of the lounge.

The mall was finally emptying. Rolling metal gates had been drawn halfway down most stores' entrances. Shoppers, weighed down with bags, straggled toward the exits. Strobe lights flashed overhead, and unseen speakers warned customers to shove off. Only one family remained at the bacon-and-eggs area. Their young son, perhaps four years of age, was clinging to an oversized piece of toast.

"I can't leave the bwed alone tonight," he howled. "The bwed will be lonely!"

I walked faster and prayed that Tom and Arch had arrived home safely from lacrosse practice. Had Shane left his mild-mannered assistant in charge of the usual carnage at practice, I wondered, while he came here to the mall to threaten his wife and me?

At Westside Music, a much-body-pierced young woman was guarding the front doors. When I arrived, she lifted her metal-dotted chin and announced in a chilly voice that the store was closed. But I could see a clerk at the register, the same fellow who'd waited on me in the first place. I said I'd only be a minute, pushed past the sparkly gatekeeper, and scurried over to the salesclerk. Deep in thought, he was counting the contents of the cash register, one bill at a time, very slowly,

mouthing   *twenty-two,*   *twenty-three,*
twenty-four, twenty-five....

"I need my guitar, please," I said
sweetly.

The guy shook his head without looking
up and kept counting. I could see the guitar
leaning against a CD case behind him. I
rummaged through my pockets and pulled
out the crumpled receipt.

"*Please,* sir. I'm not here to cause you
trouble. Just keep counting and hand me
that guitar I've already bought—"

Again, the clerk shook his head. Overhead, the lights in the store dimmed. Once
more, I asked him to hand me the guitar;
the fellow acted as if he had not heard a
word I'd said. One more reason to discour-
age Arch from joining a garage band: *Musicians go deaf fast.*

"Well," I persisted, keeping my tone
light, "since it's *clear* you don't give a *fig*
about customer service, I'm just going to
take matters into my own hands." The clerk
wrinkled his brow but did not cease counting. I moved closer to the cash register.

"We're closed!" bellowed Body-Pierce
Gal from the entrance.

Startled, the deaf cash-counter glanced

up as I sidled in behind him and grabbed Arch's guitar. Tucking it under my arm, I waved the receipt at him. He peered at it, then frowned and nodded. I raced toward the exit. Mission accomplished, I thought. I sprinted past the startled gatekeeper and headed for Prince & Grogan, Barry Dean, and the money Liz and Julian seemed so intent on refusing.

At the entrance to Prince & Grogan, I pulled the guitar to my chest and zipped inside. The P & G employees were busying themselves with their tallies. Where had Barry's note said he'd be? Ah yes, the shoe sale. In the far right corner of the main floor, I spied an enormous banner: *Red Tag Shoe Sale!!!* Clutching the guitar, I sped toward it.

Making a straight path to shoes proved a challenge, however. Scented air seduced my nose to the perfume counter. Brightly colored spring outfits on impossibly slender mannequins made me wonder if I'd ever again have a slim figure. Probably not. My cross-store hike was slowed by the dimming of lights and relentless announcements that the store was closing.

I skittered around departments and displays until I finally landed at a large area denoted by a fancy-script sign: *Ladies' Shoes*. In the plush P & G redo of two years ago, the shoe department had been outfitted with thick beige carpet, beige-striped loveseats, and brown-patterned chairs. Artfully placed among the furniture were glass-topped tables that probably had been neatly stacked with shoes before the Tornado of Shoppers blew through. On either side of the sign, two tall, deep cabinets held only a few sandals teetering from shelves. Unfortunately, the department held no *Barry*.

A couple of salespeople were picking their way through piles and piles and *piles* of shoes. Their probing gait, as they sorted and boxed footwear, reminded me of beachcombers'. Another salesperson was frowning at the only open cash register. I held the guitar high as I wended my way toward her, dodging picked-over pumps, boots, sandals, slippers, and loafers, all of which lay higgledy-piggledy across the floor. Perhaps Barry had been here, and given the saleslady our check. Or, following his usual style, maybe he'd written another note about where to go for payment. If this was going to be like the hunt for the psych classnotes, it was going to be a *very* long night.

"Excuse me, but have you seen Barry Dean, the mall manager?" I asked politely.

The clerk gently closed the cash register and gave me a sympathetic look. "I sure haven't. Sorry."

"I was the caterer for the Elite Shoppers party," I attempted again, still hopeful. "I'm just trying to get our final check. Could he have left a note for me?"

She gestured to the beachcombers. "They might know. They've been working here longer than I have."

I thanked her and looked around. To avoid the mountains of shoes, I decided to backtrack to the edge of the department, then make a straight shot past the cabinets to the workers. Another overhead announcement reminded customers that the store was *closed,* and that all salespeople needed to check out immediately.

So: I hurried. Fearful that I'd miss talking to the sorting salespeople, I lofted the guitar and began to pick my way around the piles of shoes. Ignorant of my presence, the workers called to each other, something about the *cleaning crew,* and *just finishing this last bit.* I glanced back at the cash register. The helpful saleslady was already walking toward the escalator.

"Crap, crap, crap," I muttered, as I teetered at the edge of a pile of leather pumps with cutout designs around the toes. When I began to lose my balance, I overcompensated by yanking the guitar sideways. I wobbled over the shoes and staggered like a drunk. When I tried to get a foothold, I reeled forward, let go of the guitar, and fell onto the shoes.

My head hit the side of the cabinet hard. The low doors swung open, and I saw stars. *I can't believe this is happening again,* I thought, as I lay on the pile of shoes. *This is the third time I've fallen down today!*

The overhead lights in the department began to click out in a methodical manner. I groaned and turned over. The salespeople had vacated the department. No help was forthcoming. I registered another groan nearby.

It was not my voice. Fear snaked up my back. I peered around.

The open cabinet doors had dislodged a stash of shoes and a mannequin. Could the frenzied shoppers have pulled down a mannequin?

I was startled by another groan. It came from the mannequin, which had on black dress shoes and black socks.

The shoe with a sock was attached to a leg, and then there was another shoe, and another leg...

Oh, Lord.

The legs were attached to a torso. To a body. A still warm, unmoving body.

Fighting off nausea, I pawed frantically over the shoes. Didn't I recognize those striped tuxedo pants, those shiny black shoes? *Please, God, no,* I prayed, as I ignored my pain and burrowed through pumps with cutout toes, sandals, loafers, and platform shoes, to pull out this ... person, who was groaning. This ... person who was clearly not supposed to be here.

Finally I got to the body's face. It was twisted to one side.

The body was Barry Dean's.

A pulse, I told myself, as I groped. It was faint. Weak. With some effort, I managed to turn Barry partway onto his side. He groaned again, but kept his eyes closed.

There was a knife in his stomach. Blood poured onto the scattered shoes and beige rug.

"Barry!" Was I yelling? It came out as a croak. "Barry! What happened to you?"

The air behind me swished. I stiffened and tried to scramble off the shoes. A warning voice echoed inside my head. What was—?

Swoosh. I grabbed for my pocket, for my cell phone. *Crack.* Something struck my head, very hard. Everything faded to darkness, but not before I could ask the question that had haunted me since I reached Westside Mall, an eternity ago.

What the *hell* was going on?

CHAPTER 6

From the distant reaches of my cerebral cortex, I heard Marla's voice. *You should have stayed in bed.* Then her reproving voice morphed into Julian's. *You need to peel the potatoes.* Was he making potato appetizers? Wait, I was lying on the potatoes. Is that what Julian was calling to me about?

Why couldn't I move?

I tried to wiggle my arms and legs. My head throbbed. Every effort at motion brought stabs of pain. I opened one eye to get a look at the hard, bumpy potatoes on which I appeared to be lying.

Not potatoes. Shoes.

"Julian," I mouthed. "Help him."

Hey, Goldy! Julian cried, much closer now. *How did your . . . What happened to . . . I can't . . .* He tried to move me off the shoes. Then he cried out. I registered him stumbling toward Barry. A second later, a woman's scream split the air.

Suddenly, a rumbly voice, one I didn't recognize, spoke sharply. Julian protested. I mustered up strength to inch forward, but couldn't go far. Unconsciousness claimed me the way bullies used to push me down the school slide—before I was ready.

A scent assaulted my nose. I jerked upward. My brain seemed to be cracking, splintering like glass. The stink of ammonia again hit my nostrils and I yelped. Something bad had happened, was happening, was about to happen again. What? Why?

"Mrs. Schulz," came the deep, unfamiliar voice, much closer than before. "Wake up. We've called the medics and the police. They're on their way."

A large, rough-skinned hand grabbed my wrist. The same powerful hand pressed my wrist veins. For a pulse? When I tried to twist my neck to see who was talking, nausea steamrolled over me.

"Julian," I moaned. "Where's Julian?"

I opened my eyes.

A wide, pasty male face loomed in front of mine. The man was wearing a security guard uniform. "Just don't worry about your guy Julian," his slanted mouth announced. "We've got him. He's on the other side of—"

"But—" I struggled to remember what had brought me to this pile of shoes. A shaft of memory intruded. "Where's... Barry?" I struggled upward. I was half sitting, half lying on the bed of shoes. Barry had been right over...there.

And then I saw him. A silver knife handle protruded from his stomach. His head lay at an impossible angle. His hands were limp. He, too, lay on the pile of shoes. Blood had drenched the leather and pooled on the carpet. He wasn't groaning anymore.

I couldn't look at the blade's silver handle. Or at the blood. *Oh, please, no.* Tears welled up in my eyes. And all I could think was: *That's one of my new knives.*

• • •

Loud voices, heavy footsteps, and more clammy hands feeling for my pulse signaled the arrival of cops and medics. An eternity had passed since the pasty-faced man had waved an ampule of ammonia under my nose. Now a second dose of stink smacked my nostrils. Was I seeing two fellows in white uniforms, or was I seeing double?

"Mrs. Schulz," said one of the white uniforms, "your husband is here." He reached behind my head and began touching it. When his fingers pressed onto an unexpectedly painful spot, I gasped.

"How about if you *don't* poke me with an ice pick?" I squealed. I was vaguely aware of not being very nice.

"Mrs. Schulz," said the other uniform. There *were* two of them. This second medic's soothing voice was a tad higher than his comrade's. "Please cooperate."

Now the first medic probed my neck. "Does it feel as if anything is broken?" I tried to shake my head, which was a mistake. When I whispered no, he said, "Your husband will meet you at the sheriff's department. We're taking you to the hospital. OK?"

"No, *not* OK." My voice sounded like razor blades. "I need to go with my husband. Please, let me be with Tom."

With stubborn resolve, I pulled myself to my knees. The medics grabbed my arms. I stood up, wobbled, and would have fallen if the two of them had not tightened their grip. "Thanks. Really, I just need to go with my family. Now, please."

The EMS fellows murmured that I could not. They helped me off the shoe mountain and onto the solid floor of Prince & Grogan. Then they declared that the coroner was on his way, and I could not talk to *anyone* until I'd gone to the hospital, and then to the Furman County Sheriff's Department. This did not sound right, but my head was too fuzzy to pull up the legalities of the situation. Especially since I did not know what that situation was, exactly.

Barry must be dead, I thought, and fought back tears.

The department store had an eerie, darkened look. As the medics led me toward an exit, I squinted and tried to make things out. Several salespeople—at least, they looked like salespeople—sat in chairs dispersed around the floor. Each one was talking to a uniformed cop who either knelt or sat nearby, notebook in hand. Finally I spotted Julian. He was slumped in a chair in the men's shoe department. Three cops clustered around him. All looked grim.

Then I saw Tom. A sob convulsed my body. My husband's somber expression spoke of something else I couldn't face.

Despair.

"Tom!" I cried. "Come with me!"

He brought a finger to his lips and shook his head.

Black spots clouded my vision as I stumbled up the ambulance steps. One medic got behind the wheel and the other insisted I lie down—but not before I'd registered a dark, seated presence behind the stretcher.

"Please," I said as I tried to focus on the ambulance ceiling instead of my pain, "what happened to Barry?"

There was a silence. Then, "That's what you need to tell us," announced the man behind the stretcher.

Overhead, a light came on. A headache gripped my skull. I blinked and clung to the side of the stretcher as the ambulance began to move. I said, "I don't understand. Who are you?"

"Did you kill Barry Dean?" asked the voice.

More pain stabbed the back of my head as I jerked around. The dark presence was a bulky man in a slate-gray suit. He had salt-and-pepper hair and a ruddy face. His dark eyes locked on to mine.

"No, of *course* I didn't!" I protested, astonished. "Barry was my friend. He was an *old* friend," I added weakly, as black clouds again loomed behind my eyes. "And whatever happened to my Miranda rights?"

The cop wrote something in a notebook, then frowned at his pen. Finally he looked up and introduced himself. He was Detective Sawyer. "How about your assistant, Julian Teller?" Detective Sawyer asked. "Did *he* kill Dean?"

"Look, Detective, *neither* of us stabbed Barry Dean. Julian is the kindest, most helpful—"

"How does your head feel?" Detective Sawyer interrupted.

The ambulance swayed as it pelted forward. Belatedly, I registered the siren. It felt as if it, too, was right behind my eyes.

"My head hurts," I replied. "And you're making it worse, Detective Sawyer. But listen...this is important...."

The ambulance slowed unexpectedly. I turned around and lifted my chin—which sent daggers slicing down my neck—and peered out at blinking sawhorses. A large yellow arrow indicated a detour around the dirt mess from the dump truck accident.

"Something important," I tried again with the cop. The words eluded me as I twisted back to look at him. "Did you know that tonight...in Prince and Grogan? That was the second time today that somebody tried to kill Barry. Tried to hurt Barry and me. Julian was there, too—"

"When was the first time?" The detective looked bored.

"This afternoon. A truck almost mowed us down—" I said urgently. If only he understood...

"Julian Teller called in that accident," Sawyer announced, unperturbed. "He wasn't a victim of it."

My hands clenched into fists. "Will you *shut up*? Will you let me explain?"

"When did you go into Prince and Gro-gan tonight?"

"Do you know who my husband is?"

"Yes indeedy. When did you enter Prince and Grogan?"

I struggled to think back. When did I en-ter the department store? I'd picked up Arch's guitar at Westside Music, but that had taken longer than I'd expected.

"Oh, my God, the guitar!" I cried. "Where is it?"

"You were hit with it, Mrs. Schulz. It was badly dented, and now it's being held by the police to be checked for prints. Please try to think when you entered the store."

That new guitar was dented? It was be-ing held by the police? What was I sup-posed to give Arch for his birthday? My head ached.

What was the detective's question? Oh, yes, when had I entered the department store. Let's see. After leaving the music store, I'd scuttled into P & G and made my way through the departments looking for Barry. . . .

"I went into Prince and Grogan around five to nine, maybe a little after, I'm pretty sure—"

"And you discovered Dean when?"

Effort at thought worsened my headache. "Around nine, I guess, but—"

"Can you explain why we got a nine-one-one call, at exactly nine o'clock, with someone saying Dean was dead? Which would be just as you came into the store?"

"Nine o'clock? Well, maybe I'm wrong about those times. But you see, when I found Barry, he wasn't dead...he was groaning. Then someone hit me, maybe because they wanted to finish Barry off—" Something was bothering me. What? I tried to review Sawyer's last set of questions. "Am I, uh, a suspect in this, Detective? Because I sure don't like your tone of voice. Not to mention that you seem to have forgotten my Miranda rights?"

This, too, he ignored. "Was Julian Teller with you at that time? When you entered the store?"

At five to nine? I wondered fuzzily. *Why would he do that?* This detective was being too damn aggressive, I thought angrily. I lay still and prayed *Lord, help me*. Over and over. It helped.

"Know what?" I murmured after a few minutes. "I have a head injury. And I know a bit about your line of work, Detective Sawyer. Law enforcement isn't supposed to question someone with a fresh head injury and no hint of Miranda. So I'm just going to wait." My head spun. I tried to clear it, but my brain was fogged in. "I'm not going to answer a single one of your questions. And since I'm not under arrest, I'm going to call my lawyer at the hospital."

Detective Sawyer expelled breath and slapped his notebook closed. Actually, I desperately wanted to call Tom. And if he for some reason couldn't advise me, I would have to call Marla, not a lawyer. My own lawyer was pretty good at getting The Jerk to pay child support, but that was it. Marla, on the other hand, had the inside scoop on the moneyed and powerful in Denver, and her circle of acquaintances would surely yield connections to some of Denver's hotshot criminal defense attorneys. On the other hand, when she heard the department was trying to nail me, or Julian, or both of us, for murder, I would have to make my next call to her cardiologist.

The ambulance pulled to a stop. What had felt like an hour in the vehicle had only been a few minutes, as Southwest Hospital was near Westside Mall.

I couldn't read the clock inside the Emergency Room, no matter how hard I tried. A headache raged in my skull like a thunderstorm, complete with flashes of lightning. How long had I been out? I did not know. What I did know was that every muscle and bone in my body cried out with pain and fatigue. I cursed my helplessness. I balked when a nurse poked, prodded, and questioned me. While waiting for the doctor, I disobeyed orders to stay put. Instead, I hobbled out to the reception area and called Tom's cell. No answer. Fearful the nurse would come out and claim me, I put in a call to Marla.

There was no answer at her home. I tried her cellular.

"You're not going to believe—" I began.

"Oh, yes I am!" Her dear, husky voice crackled. "I just talked to Julian. I'm on my way to the department. The *sheriff's* department."

I held the phone away from my ear. "I'm at the hospital—"

"What?" she squawked.

"I need you to help Julian—"

"What do you think I'm doing? I've got an associate of Steve Hulsey's on his way to the department to meet Julian. Hulsey himself is coming to help you."

I shuddered. "No-Holds-Barred Hulsey?" The Denver papers were invariably filled with tales of criminal defense lawyer Steven Hulsey, of Hulsey, Jones, Macauley & Wilson. Recently, Hulsey had defended a drug dealer who'd murdered a rival in front of three witnesses, all of whom, apparently, had serious vision problems.

"That's the one," Marla said proudly. "Did you hear how he got Stafford Roosevelt off? It was in the papers last year. Big Bucks Roosevelt, serial rapist, supposedly. But we'll never know, since Hulsey got him off on a technicality. And just last month, the associate who's coming down to help Julian, Cleve Jackson, convinced a jury not to convict a fellow lawyer of bank fraud."

"Yes," I said weakly, "I heard about that one." In the fraud case, Cleve Jackson had repeatedly asserted that the police had mishandled crucial evidence. For their part,

Tom and the department despised any and all from Hulsey's office.

"I'm paying the legal bills, don't worry," Marla yelled. "I am *so* pissed off. And I can't believe what Julian...!" Her voice cracked, disappeared, came back. "He didn't even *call* me until the cops had questioned him for an hour, and now he's consented to a damn polygraph! Julian said he didn't *do* anything! He wants to prove it with a lie detector test! Cleve Jackson should already be there. Julian should wait—"

"Listen," I said desperately as the nurse signaled that the ER doc was ready to see me. "I need to go..."

Marla grumbled words unfit for Sunday school, declared that she'd bring Julian back to her place when the cops and Cleve Jackson had finished with him, and signed off.

I endured the next hour in as good a humor as possible. Detective Sawyer hovered doggedly at the edge of my vision. When the ER doc said it looked as if I had a mild concussion, I asked to see my husband. Detective Sawyer, looming, announced grimly that Tom had gone down to the department and would meet me there.

Sometime after midnight, the ambulance that had brought me to the hospital from Westside Mall arrived at the Furman County Sheriff's Department. I had been up since dawn, I had escaped a truck accident, I had catered an event, I'd found my client dead, I'd been whacked on the head, I'd awakened in pain. And now, it seemed, I was in the thick of a criminal investigation. I was beyond exhausted, beyond wounded and bewildered. I was numb.

Mutely, I allowed myself to be escorted to one of the interrogation rooms. It was graced with a single table and four chairs, one of which held Detective Sawyer. The instant I entered the room, Sawyer flipped open his notebook.

A microphone stood like a wired totem in the middle of the table. The right-hand wall boasted a one-way mirror. Unlike what you see in movies, Tom had told me, there was no one actually *behind* the one-way glass, no sharp-eyed team gauging my reactions, no sharp-tongued cop asserting that I'd just told a basket of lies. According to Tom, an unmanned videocamera recorded the whole interview. I hugged myself. More than the cop's notebook or the microphone, the image of that solitary camera rolling tape made me dizzy.

A tall, wide-bodied man swept in. I recognized Steve Hulsey from his TV interviews. The nightly talk shows loved having him on, as he put it, "to tell people the inside story of law enforcement." Hulsey had a dark face featuring deeply grooved cheeks and thick dark eyebrows that sprouted like sails over shrewd, assessing eyes. He'd slicked his black hair into place with a glistening substance that made the strands resemble porcupine quills. His hastily donned power suit, a severe charcoal pin-striped silk, was only slightly rumpled. His voice rumbled like an approaching storm.

"I'd like this woman to step into the hall, please," he announced to the two detectives. It was not a request. It was a command. The detectives nodded and I walked slowly into the hall.

The famous attorney introduced himself, then crushed my hand when he shook it. In somber tones, Hulsey advised me to *wait* after each question from the detectives. I was not to answer a single query until he gave me permission. If he didn't like the way things were going, he would say so. Meanwhile, if he objected to anything, I was to keep my mouth shut. When I begged him for news of Julian, his face turned even more formidable. We would have to talk about that later, he concluded, and turned back to the interrogation room door.

"What about my husband?" I asked. "Have you talked to Tom?"

"Tom Schulz is off this case. His family members are involved." Hulsey's voice came out like a growl. "Your son is at your house. A friend is with him. Listen to me, Mrs. Schulz. If I'm going to help you, I need you *not to worry* about anybody but *yourself*. We need to focus on getting you out of this."

"I just...OK, look," I said with sudden clarity. "Our first problem is with the detective in there, a creep named Sawyer. He was obnoxious in the ambulance and didn't Mirandize me—"

"A detective questioned you *before* you were examined by a doctor?" From down the hall, an authoritative-looking, red-haired man with a clipboard strode rapidly toward us. Seeing him, Hulsey lifted his chin and sucked in his breath, like the wolf about to blow down a little pig's house. Then he turned back to me. His beetlelike eyes bored into mine. Forget lie detectors; this guy was the genuine article. "A policeman asked you questions *before* or *after* you were seen in the ER?"

"Uh, before. I told him I wouldn't answer his questions."

"Mrs. Schulz," said Hulsey. His voice melted to chocolate, which scared me even more. "Do not fret about Sawyer. *I* am here. *They* are going to fret about *us*. *Are* we *clear* on this?"

Whether from fatigue, physical pain, or stress, I did not know, but I suddenly laughed and kept laughing. *Were we clear?* I said, "You bet. Ice-crystal clear. High-country spring-water clear." I was grinning like a madwoman, but Hulsey ignored me. No doubt he'd seen his share of lunatics.

The clipboard-toter passed us and opened the door to the interrogation room. Hulsey and I followed.

"Gentlemen," declared Hulsey, "my client is fatigued and injured. So let's make this quick, OK? And," he said with grim finality, "there will be *no* polygraph."

Sawyer tapped his open notebook and gave us a blank look. The other fellow, whose few strands of red hair had been pulled across his balding head, did not acknowledge Hulsey's request, but merely gave a brusque nod. He informed us he was Detective Collins and his associate was Detective Sawyer, and that this interview was being recorded.

I stated my name and address into the microphone, glanced nervously at the mirrored glass hiding the videocamera, and tucked my cold, trembling hands inside the big pocket of my apron.

Come to think of it, why was I still wearing the apron? I felt for my cell phone: still there. The note from Barry: also still there. But...what in the world was the small plastic jar my right hand suddenly closed over? I swallowed hard and cautiously moved the jar lower into my pocket, as deep as it would go. Unless I was very much mistaken, I was gripping a prescription bottle full of pills. Where had it come from?

Unobtrusively, I pulled out my hand and

placed it in my lap. There was no way I was going to show these cops what I'd just discovered, thank you very much. Every now and then, it's important to be smart. Which is what I wish I had been while hunting for Barry Dean in the Prince & Grogan shoe department... at least to the extent of jumping up and screaming for help when I'd first found Barry in the cabinet.

"Take us back," droned Detective Collins. "Begin with the jewelry party. That was the last time you saw Mr. Dean alive, yes?"

"Yes." Barry'd been quite visible at the party, I told them. There were security tapes, as well as a professional videotape, of the event. I told them the *very* last time I'd seen Barry alive had been toward the end of the event. No, I had not actually *seen* him leave. I told them about Barry's uncharacteristic wine-guzzling. I started to describe the forcible expulsion of Teddy Fury, and Barry's heated argument with Liz Fury and Julian, but I hadn't even completed three sentences before Hulsey shook his head.

Had I received my check, the cops wanted to know. Barry had the final payment, I replied, which was our agreed-in-advance gratuity.

"Is that a set amount?" Collins asked.

"It's usually twenty percent of the bill. If things go well and the client is feeling generous, sometimes we'll receive up to thirty percent. But Barry left without giving us anything, which I was certain was an oversight—"

"We found a check to your firm in his pocket. Sorry, we need to keep it for a while. Why were you certain this was an oversight?"

"Barry and I . . . were old friends."

"How were you old friends?"

Hulsey glared at me in warning.

"We went to C.U. together," I answered tentatively. What could be incriminating about that? "He studied architecture. I was a psychology major. He sat next to me in a psych class, shared his notes with me, and asked me out for coffee. We drank a lot of cappuccino together. He called me his coffee buddy." Collins raised an eyebrow. "We were *not* romantically involved. Barry told me I shouldn't marry my first husband, and he turned out to be right."

"How about lately?" asked Collins, uninterested in the criminal doings of Doctor John Richard Korman, my ex. "Maybe you weren't involved with Dean in school, but lately, did things change?"

"Don't be ridiculous." Both cops gave me practiced blank expressions. "No, Detectives, we were not *ever* romantically involved. *Never*."

"Why did Barry Dean hire an old college friend to do mall catering?"

"Because a mutual friend, Ellie McNeely, recommended me. Plus, I think he might have seen my picture in the paper."

"Which picture was that? The one from a couple of years ago, when you found *another* body in Prince and Grogan?"

"No," I said stiffly. "It was from this February, when I finished a job in Aspen Meadow. Catering for the Hydes. Heard of them?"

Collins's lips twitched in a distinctly ghoulish grin. "You mean," he asked, "that photo in the Suburban section, showing you all wet? After you fell into the moat at Hyde Castle?"

"I didn't *fall* into the moat, I *jumped* into it. And that was to get away from someone who was chasing me."

Hulsey cleared his throat. His eyes drilled into me: *SHUT. UP.*

Collins shifted in his chair. "But you didn't get away from someone who hit you with a guitar. Was that because tonight, you recognized the person who was chasing you?"

"Nobody was chasing me, that I know of. I didn't even hear the person come up behind me. If I had, I might have avoided getting whacked with a guitar."

"Was that person Julian Teller?"

"No."

Collins shook his head disbelievingly. "The catered event ended. You and Julian Teller made trips to take your equipment back to your van, yes?"

"Yes. And then I came back and Julian—who is one of my *assistants*—told me..." I could feel my anger rising. Why had they asked if Julian had hit me? "Actually, Julian handed me a note that Barry had given one of the musicians. It said he—Barry—had my gratuity for me."

There was a silence. "We need to see that note," decreed Sawyer.

I fished into my apron pocket, careful not to disturb the prescription bottle

tucked there, then pulled out the crumpled note and slapped it on the table. So
much for fingerprints, I thought belatedly.

Hulsey asked permission to see the
note and to have a photocopy made as
soon as possible. The cops nodded yes.
My lawyer bent over the paper, pulled out a
tiny brushed-gold notebook, and wrote in
it. The cops announced that they were going to have the handwriting analyzed. In-
wardly, I groaned. Did Barry's script look
like Julian's?

Collins gave me a puzzled look. "*I have
your check, and a tip for you*? You called it
a *gratuity*."

My frustration clouded to confusion. *A
tip for you*. A *tip* like a *police tip*? And earlier, after the truck accident: *Goldy, could
we have our little chat later, at the party?*

"I *did* think the check was our gratuity.
Barry had wanted to talk to me. Earlier in
the day, he had said he wanted to have a
chat."

"Wanted to chat with you about what,
exactly?" Collins rasped.

"Excuse me." Steve Hulsey's deep rum-
ble made me jump. "I won't allow my client

to be taken out in a boat to go fishing with you guys. Finish this up."

Collins's glum expression did not change. "So you went to the Prince and Grogan shoe department, in search of this *tip*. Any idea why he wanted to meet you in Shoes?"

"I'm warning you again, Detective," interjected Hulsey, who moved impatiently in his chair. "Fish again, and I'm reeling in the line."

"Mrs. Schulz," said Collins, unperturbed and persistent. "After you received this note, did you go directly to Prince and Grogan to rendezvous with Mr. Dean?"

I had never realized how ugly the word *rendezvous* could sound. "No. I already told you, I had to pick up my son's guitar at Westside Music. That took," I added, before he could ask, "about five, ten minutes at most. After I picked up the guitar, I headed into Prince and Grogan, again, as I told you before. The store was closing and people were cleaning up, counting the contents of cash registers, like that."

"Who knew you had to get the guitar first?"

"Well, my two assistants. Liz Fury had

asked to take off early, because her son had been forced out of the mall, as I told you. She wanted to find him." Another glare from Hulsey stopped me from elaborating. "And of course Julian Teller knew I had to go back to the music store. He stayed in the lounge and promised to finish packing up. He's very good that way. Hardworking. Caring. And *honest*," I added, pointedly.

"Then what?"

"Well, if you read the note, you'll see Barry was expecting me about half past eight. But it was quarter to nine by the time I received his message, and I still had to pick up the guitar for my son's birthday." I waited for them to ask me how old Arch was or when his birthday was, but they were silent. "So I was running late when I arrived in Shoes. Barry wasn't there. I asked the cash register lady if she'd seen him. She hadn't, so I thought I'd try the two salespeople who were cleaning up. But I slipped on the shoes—"

"You slipped on them," commented Sawyer, ever the skeptic.

"Yes. I was carrying the guitar, and it was heavy, and the women had dumped the shoes in piles all over the place.

Leather is slippery," I said fiercely, giving them a glare of my own. "I stumbled, fell, and hit one of those big cabinets. One of the doors came open, and I saw what I thought was a mannequin in a tuxedo, but ... it groaned. I ... It was Barry. I tried to pull him out, and he groaned again, and then I saw all the blood. I took his pulse. It was weak. And then I guess I was going to do a compression—"

"You didn't call for help?" Sawyer again.

I took a shaky breath. After a moment, I said, "No. I didn't. I should have, in retrospect. But my theory now is that whoever was trying to kill him was right behind the cabinet, waiting to finish the job. As soon as the salespeople left, after I'd pulled Barry out of the cabinet and checked for his pulse, the killer whacked me with the guitar. He or she wanted to get me out of the way and finish the job—"

Collins held up a hand, then spoke slowly. "Did you see who hit you?"

"No, I didn't see a thing. I didn't hear anybody's voice, either. One minute I had Barry's wrist in my hand, the next my head was smashed and I saw nothing but black. After a bit, I heard Julian calling me, and someone waved ammonia in my face. Then you guys showed up, and I was carted to the hospital. And now we're here."

Collins said, "Did you see the weapon used to kill Barry Dean?"

There was a silence. I had not told Hulsey about this; now I wondered what in the world to say. The last thing I wanted to do was implicate Julian, Liz, or myself any further. But refusing to answer would look worse. And lying...what would that do?

"Yes," I said quietly. "I saw it. It was... one of my knives. From a new set I bought recently."

Collins opened his mouth to ask another question, but Steve Hulsey was too quick for him.

"That does it, gentlemen. Thank you." He stood and motioned for me to do the same. I got to my feet too quickly and swayed, suddenly dizzy. I blinked, saw my chair, and grabbed the metal back.

"Mrs. Schulz, please don't leave town," intoned Sawyer, as he slapped his notebook closed. My kick-ass lawyer held the door open for me and I walked through.

"I need you to visit my office," Hulsey told me. "Will tomorrow morning work?"

His office, as it turned out, was half a mile from Westside Mall. What catered event did I have the next day, or rather, that very day, since it was now well past midnight? My beaten-up, woozy mind drew a blank. When do you need me there? I asked Hulsey. Ten A.M. sharp, Hulsey replied. And in the meantime, talk to no one.

Tom, oh dear God, *Tom*, was waiting for me on a plastic chair in the lobby. He walked toward me swiftly, arms out-stretched. Hulsey vanished.

Enfolded in my husband's arms, my body shook uncontrollably. I swallowed and tried to pull myself together. There was *no way* I was going to fall apart in the lobby of the sheriff's department.

"Let's go," Tom whispered.

He gently helped me into his Chrysler, and murmured that he'd arrange for my van to be brought back to the house early the next morning. I leaned my head back and inhaled the comforting scent of Tom's car. I wanted so badly to be in bed, to be asleep. But something was gnawing at me.

"Where's Marla?" I asked as Tom started the engine. "Did she and Julian take both of their cars back to her house in

Aspen Meadow? Or did he go back to Boulder?"

Tom let the engine idle, his hands on the steering wheel. Illuminated by the lot's pink streetlights, his face was luminescent. Ominous. "Do you know how many cups of coffee Julian drank today? Yesterday, that is. Monday. While he was working with you."

"What?"

"Miss G., it's a simple question."

"I don't understand..."

"Just think. *How many cups?*"

I took a deep breath. "OK. He mentioned he'd had two four-shot lattes before he arrived. He brought two more, one for Liz and one for me." I tried to dive back into the muck of the day's events. "Liz didn't want hers, so...I think Julian drank it. Then we made coffee in the kitchen, and he had dinner with Liz, so it's probably safe to say he had about...oh, the equivalent of fifteen or sixteen cups of coffee over the course of the day. Why?"

Tom pressed his lips into a thin line and shook his head. Then he clasped my hands in his. "Julian drank a ton of caffeine. Then he found you in the department store, unconscious. He also found Barry, with *your* knife in him. Julian's a good kid, he was terrified, he tried to pull the knife out of Barry Dean. Then the *one* security cop on duty at Prince and Grogan spotted him, and yelled at him to back off. Julian freaked out, and when the cops heard he'd had his hands on the knife, they said he had to come in for questioning. When they brought him into the department, he didn't wait for a lawyer. He insisted on submitting to the polygraph. To prove his innocence."

My own voice felt as brittle as cracking ice. "What are you telling me?"

"Too much caffeine can screw up a polygraph, Miss G. Julian was found with his hand on the murder weapon. Just as damning, he has no alibi for the time he was loading your van by himself, which was when you were picking up Arch's guitar. When Julian took the lie detector test, he flunked it."

"No."

Tom squeezed my hands harder. "Goldy, Julian's been arrested for murder."

CHAPTER 7

We made it up the interstate in silence. The going was slow, as a light snow was falling. At home, our hall clock donged lightly for half past one. I checked our pets—Jake the bloodhound and Scout the cat—who were slumbering peacefully in their separate housing area. Then I stumbled upstairs. I creaked open Arch's door. He was snoring. So was his pal, Todd Druckman. Just recently, Arch had outgrown his bunk bed, so Todd was curled inside a sleeping bag on the floor.

With a husband in law enforcement and an ex-husband behind bars, our little family had dealt with criminal activity more than most. Still, I was worried about how Arch would deal with the arrest of Julian, our cherished family friend. I also wondered if heart-attack-prone Marla would stay calm. Several years ago, in a bizarre discovery of adoption documents, we'd learned that Julian's birth mother had been Marla's dead sister. My old friend had passionately embraced the role of being Julian's aunt. Would she be able to cope with his arrest?

Would I?

I brushed my teeth, shucked my clothes, and pulled on pajamas. I fell into bed, certain I'd start fretting and never fall asleep.

But I did sleep, so soundly that the creep of daylight into the bedroom, the early shriek of crows, the drone of traffic from Aspen Meadow's Main Street—not one of these registered. At nine-thirty, Tom tiptoed in to wake me.

He sat on the edge of our bed and asked me how I was feeling. I realized I had a headache, a shoulder ache, and nausea. I assured him I felt fine.

"I took Arch and Todd to school. Oh, and I canceled you out of that wedding re-

You probably won't have it until well after Arch's birthday. Sorry."

The morning felt unreal. I was still in bed at nine-thirty. I didn't know what was going on with Julian, and I wasn't racing to a catering assignment.

Outside, it was still Aspen Meadow in April. Our front yard pines, laden with new snow, trembled in the cold breeze. Thick white clouds chugged through an expanse of sky, dollops of meringue on a blue plate.

And Barry Dean was dead. My old coffee buddy. I saw his smiling face, heard his teasing. *This* could *not* be real.

And yet it was.

"Come on," said Tom, mustering some cheer. "Can you manage a shower on your own?" When I nodded, he said, "I'll meet you in the kitchen. I'm making you a Dutch pancake. Oh, forgot to tell you. Two friends of mine from the department stopped by real early. I gave them your keys, and they brought up your van. I've already cleaned all your dishes and platters and whatnot."

"What would I do without you?" I murmured.

Twenty minutes later, after I'd managed only two yoga asanas and a quick shower, I dug into Tom's warm, light Dutch pancake. It dripped with golden melted butter and genuine maple syrup from Maine. I began to feel a bit more optimistic. Tom had also fried an entire pound of bacon. The salty crunch of meat perfectly complemented the delicate pancake. I told him it was the best breakfast ever. He beamed.

"I need to take off," he said. "Do you want me to do anything for you? Did they give you a prescription for a painkiller?"

"I've got both aspirin and ibuprofen," I replied. "But thanks for worrying."

He donned his jacket but seemed reluctant to leave. "Sure you're OK to drive to Hulsey's office?"

"Absolutely." I stood to fire up the espresso machine. "I'm going to putter around here before stopping at Hulsey's. I'll be done in time to pick up Arch at lacrosse practice."

"Can I bring home dinner?"

"Tom. If you don't let me cook, I'll go nuts."

He kissed me and took off. As the house fell silent, I booted my computer, popped two aspirin, and pulled myself a double shot of rich, dark espresso. Be-

cause I needed to take care of myself—
didn't everyone say so?—I topped the coffee with a mountainous glob of whipped
cream.

And then I thought of Julian, in jail, with
no espresso and a bunch of criminals as
his new roommates. Tom was off the case.
Would Hulsey wait for a new polygraph before he moved forward with his own team
of investigators? Probably not. But meanwhile, Julian, with no alibi, was stuck in jail.
It would take a few days for the lab work to
come back, but trying to pull my knife out
of Barry meant, of course, that Julian's fingerprints were on the murder weapon.

If I don't help him, who will?

I swallowed more espresso, then
tapped computer keys to open a new file:
BARRY DEAN.

Tom had told me a hundred times: *You
have to figure out what you know before
you can concentrate on what you don't
know.*

I typed in everything I knew about Barry.
His background at C.U. His deep affection
for basset hounds. His brief work with the
Longmont TV show. Business school. Marketing. His job managing Westside Mall.

His status: Most Eligible Bachelor. And then I looked down at my espresso cup. *He loved coffee,* I typed numbly.

Both his old classic Mercedes and his rarely used BMW racing car had boasted leather coffee-compartment caddies that fit over the hump between the front seats. Dear old Honey the Hound had presided over our outings, her mournful eyes regarding us from the rear seat. When we'd met the previous week, Barry had said that Honey had passed away, but that he still loved bassets and had just gotten a new one. He'd been so full of enthusiasm for canines, I'd told him about our own hound, Jake. He'd laughed and wanted to know more. Did he howl? His new dog did.

Who was taking care of his new dog now? The cops? The pound?

I veered away from that thought and forced myself to concentrate.

Love interests, I typed. Let's see. He'd gone out with all kinds of girls at school, but wasn't as enthusiastic about them as he was about dogs, coffee, or cars. I knew he'd been seeing Ellie McNeely, and that she had recommended my catering company to him. Possibly, he'd also been seeing Pam Disharoon. I'd suspected he'd been seeing Liz, but realized now that their familiarity was probably based on Liz's nervousness about catering for a fellow who'd barred her son from the mall. The rest was a blank.

Find out what BD was up to with women, I typed. *Jealousy there?*

My head throbbed and I pulled another espresso. Did I dare to take another couple of aspirin? No. Tom's words came back to me: *Did they give you a prescription for painkillers?* My apron, I thought. What was in that prescription bottle?

I sprinted up the stairs. My head felt as if I were balancing a pine log on top of my cranium. Balancing a *large* pine log. Balancing a large pine log with a guy teetering on *each end.*

I groped in my apron pocket and pulled out a brown bottle from Westside Pharmacy. *March 22,* the tidy label read. *Rx No. 2880. Dr. Louis Maxwell. Barry Dean. Take 1 as needed for headache. Vicodin ES tablet.*

How on earth had the bottle gotten into my apron pocket? It had to have fallen out of Barry's pocket, I reasoned. When I scooted forward to check his pulse, I must have inadvertently picked it up.

Vicodin was a narcotic painkiller. Barry had to have had some monster headaches. Was something worrying Barry to cause him crippling headaches? I typed a new question into the file: *What caused BD's headaches?*

OK, let's see... there were a few more random facts I knew about Barry. He'd just bought an older house far out Upper Cottonwood Creek, an Austrian-chalet-style dwelling with gingerbread trim à la Hansel and Gretel. A detached garage held his cars—I thought he'd told me that at one point he'd had three vehicles—the old BMW racing car, a new white Audi, and the classic Mercedes, which had been wrecked, only to be replaced by the new Saab. Behind the garage, there was a large paved area where he kept his pontoon boat. Without kids and a wife to support, Barry could afford expensive toys.

I fingered the prescription bottle. Would the cops allow me inside Barry's house? Probably not. *I need to help Julian,* I thought. *I need to find out what Barry was up to. I need to discover what whoever killed Barry was up to.* Back in the dark divorce days, I'd become an expert at ferreting out incriminating evidence. It's important to use your talents, right?

Speaking of John Richard, for better or worse, he had been temporarily moved to a less crowded jail in Colorado Springs. We made the two-and-a-half-hour trip on a weekly basis, so Arch could visit his father. But at least The Jerk would not be in the Furman County lockup to hassle or intimidate Julian.

Julian. My heart ached. He'd been a part of our family for only a few years, but it felt like forever. He worried incessantly about Arch and me. He helped Arch with homework and visits to museums; he even corrected Arch's drafts of English papers, something I was forbidden upon pain of *death* to do. Julian brought over his signature chocolate croissants whenever he visited. And he always, always helped me out at catered events when I needed him.

If I told Tom about Barry's pills, he'd make me turn them over to the cops. So I was tampering with evidence. But I wasn't ready to give up Barry's prescription bottle just yet, at least not until I ferreted out the reason for the painkillers. After frowning at the little brown bottle for a minute, I wrapped it in plastic, opened the freezer side of the walk-in, and stashed it in a place I doubted Tom or Arch would ever look: a plastic tub half full of frozen clarified butter.

I was going to help Julian, I resolved. He possessed a keen intelligence, a great willingness to help out, a love for our family, and unfortunately, a quick temper. And now his desire to help others had landed him in a load of trouble.

So, Tom had relieved me of my catering assignments for that day. Until I could gather more supplies, there was little I could do to work on other events for later in the week. Meanwhile, my psyche needed to cook.

I washed my hands, tore the leftover bacon into bits, then washed my hands again. My whisk clicked the side of the bowl as I violently beat together a salad dressing. Finally, I washed and dried head after head of tender baby lettuces.

Despite my frenzied activity, my mind kept circling back to Julian. I'd introduced him to Liz, who had introduced him to her son Teddy, whose plight had touched Julian. His sense of justice had propelled him to confront Barry Dean. Julian always tried to do the right thing. Of course, this had also included trying to pull the knife out of Barry's stomach.

I quickly stored all the food. Even if Hulsey forbade me, I was going to go down to the jail. I was going to demand that Julian Teller be released.

Fat chance of that, I thought. I groped again in the freezer, tried to avoid the tub of butter (the hidden prescription seemed to scream at me), and clattered ice cubes into a glass. I poured heavy cream into the glass, then put that into the freezer while I searched the refrigerator side of the walk-in for something luscious. Aha—a last piece of flourless chocolate cake topped with raspberries and strawberries. I whipped some more of the cream, ladled it on top of the cake, then pulled four shots of espresso and poured it into the glass over the chilled cream and ice cubes. I took a delicate mouthful of the chocolate cake, then sipped the creamy coffee. The dark, rich chocolate melted in my mouth and sent a flash of pleasure up my back. Forget aspirin—this was a real painkiller! Then I allowed the luscious coffee to roll over my tongue. My brain felt sharper, no question.

I frowned at my computer's blank screen, then looked outside. The sky was turning. The brilliant white clouds had darkened, which promised more snow. I turned my back on that particular gloomy prospect, took another large bite of chocolate, cream, and berries, and washed it down with the rich coffee. Think, I ordered myself, as I surveyed the kitchen and my cooking equipment.

Which reminded me. What about my missing *knife*? Somehow, one of my new Henckels knives had ended up in Barry Dean's gut.

I set aside my snack and typed, *Who stole the knife? How? When?*

But I knew the answer almost as soon as I typed it. Anyone could have slipped into the kitchenette while Julian, Liz, and I were busy with the crowd. Sneaking in through the service entrance, once the main doors were opened, shouldn't have been too hard either, because at that point the security guards were inside the lounge.

There ought to be some way to determine...Wait. The lounge had boasted a multitude of cameras, all poised on the party. Cameras on the walls; cameras overhead. Plus, there'd been that videographer. Surely, one of those cameras had captured the knife thief sneaking into or out of the kitchen. Or had the knife made it to the buffet, say on one of the platters, and been snitched from there? When I visited the jail, I'd have to ask Julian if he'd spotted anything suspicious. And getting back to cameras, there should have been some hidden ones focused on the Prince & Grogan shoe department, right? Wouldn't *those* videos show how Barry had died?

I finished the cake and put in a quick call to Tom. Hopefully, he'd sniffed out news of the investigation. Did being off the case mean being excluded from the progress of the investigation?

"Tom," I said to his voice mail, "could you see if the cops got hold of the security-camera videos from the lounge, and from the P and G shoe department? Oh, and if you find out anything else about Julian's case, would you please call?"

As soon as I hung up, the phone rang. I pounced on it. It was Marla.

"Goldy, what the *hell* is going on? Julian didn't even *know* Barry Dean. I say the hell with waiting for another polygraph. I told Hulsey to get his investigators on this *right away*. I'm not pleased that Hulsey's not dealing with Julian himself. He should have given *you* to Jackson."

"I—"

"And what is it with you and Julian, guzzling all that caffeine? Don't you know better than to drink *so* much of it?"

"Well, I'll have to *remember* that," I replied huffily, "the next time I cater a buffet for fifty on less than five hours of sleep, and can peer into one of my crystal balls to see that Julian will face a polygraph for a murder investigation that *very* day. Oh, and since you didn't ask, I'm feeling just fine after being hit over the head."

Marla rattled ice cubes, then gulped down something. It wasn't even noon yet. I hoped whatever she was drinking was non-alcoholic.

She took a deep breath. "Sorry I yelled at you. You know how fond I am of Julian— I'm just scared, that's all. Tell me what they've got on him, would you please?"

So I told her the little I did know, much

of which she probably already had weaseled out of Julian or his lawyer. In addition to failing the polygraph, Julian had no alibi for the time Barry was murdered. He had also been accused—by whom, I still did not know—of being behind the wheel of the truck that had very nearly mowed Barry and me down. And worst of all, his fingerprints would no doubt show up on the murder weapon.

"No alibi? *I'll* say I was with him."

I shook my head. "No, I'm sure he was loading supplies and dirty dishes into my van, the way he said he would." And speaking of vehicles, I wondered, where were Barry's Saab and Julian's Range Rover? Had the police impounded both vehicles?

"But," Marla protested, "if I say he was with me, will they let him out of jail?"

"Funny thing about cops, girlfriend. They're interested in the *truth*."

"But we ought to be able to do *something!*"

"You could call Detective Sawyer, to see if they've impounded Julian's car or Barry's Saab. If not, get a couple of friends to take you to Westside, then find the Rover and drive it up to your place. Could you do that? Do you have keys to the Rover?"

"Absolutely. It was my sister's car, remember? And I never throw anything away. How about Tom? Can he help?"

I retrieved a pie crust from the freezer side of the walk-in. I needed to keep cooking if I was going to stay even remotely rational. "They've taken Tom off the case, because there's family involvement. Look, Marla, I'm going to look into this—"

"Well, thank God for something!"

"—but you can't tell *anyone* what I'm doing. You can't spill any details to your pals. If you do, Hulsey, the cops, and Tom will all have a fit. Now, tell me everything you know about Barry's social life. Was there a Significant Other in the picture?"

She blew out air. "Of *course*. Barry was seeing Ellie McNeely, didn't I tell you? Ellie hooked up with him the second she got that bank job. I heard it had become *très, très* serious. But Ellie had this suspicion that Barry was seeing somebody *else* on the side. According to her, Barry would go places and not tell her where he'd been. He wouldn't show up when he promised. She'd see him at the doctor's when he said he was skiing. She spotted him at the bank when he'd said he had an all-day meeting in Vail. And he skipped a dinner they were supposed to attend, claiming he'd been caught in a traffic jam west of the Eisenhower Tunnel. So *I* told her to hire a private investigator—"

"You did *what*?" Sometimes Marla's meddling knew no bounds.

"Not too long ago, Ellie's purse was stolen at the mall. Louis Vuitton, of course. It had her car keys in it. In her wallet, there was a picture of Ellie's daughter, Cameron, standing beside the rear of their silver Lexus. The photo included the Lexus license plate, sorry to say. The thief found the car in the mall parking lot and tried to steal it, but instead rammed it into Barry Dean's gorgeous old Mercedes. Totaled it, too. The Mercedes, not the Lexus."

"What?"

"Is there an echo on this phone line? Didn't Barry tell you why he had to buy that new Saab?"

"Not really," I mumbled. Barry had mentioned his beloved old Mercedes had been wrecked. That was all. And I considered Ellie a friend. Why hadn't I heard about all this? But I knew the answer, as usual. I'd been too busy catering. Finally, I said, "Sorry to be so skeptical, but if Ellie was mad enough to hire a private investigator to follow Barry because she suspected him of dallying, isn't it possible that she faked the theft and drove her Lexus into his Mercedes herself?"

"Well," Marla shot back, in the tone she used when the gossip became especially juicy, "there's all kinds of speculation, of course. Maybe her bag was never stolen, but I wouldn't sacrifice a Louis Vuitton *anything* to fake a theft. I'd claim someone had stolen some tote I got free with a perfume purchase. But the most prevalent theory is that that brat Teddy Fury swiped Ellie's bag. Everyone knows that kid's a klepto. The cops didn't find Ellie's LV purse when they discovered what was left of his stash of stolen goodies, though."

"How do you *know* all these things?" I demanded, exasperated.

"Well, unlike you, I'm not spending all my time cooking. I'm eating lunch *out* and hearing all the *latest*. Or I'm hustling out for a bite after the midweek church service, where people go when they just can't wait until Sunday for news. I go to the athletic club every day and wave my arms around, so I can please my cardiologist and catch up on more news that I missed at lunch or church. And when I'm not on the phone with you, I'm on with someone else, finding out stuff to *share* with you."

I didn't reply. I was still recovering from Marla's revelations.

"So did Ellie's P.I. find out damaging stuff?"

"Goldy, all I did was recommend that she *hire* someone. After all, Ellie's older than Barry is...was. Since she finally got her divorce settlement, she has money, lots and lots more than Barry. So she *had* to find out if he was getting serious so he could get his hands on her money. She also wanted to know why he was lying to her about being in Vail and whatnot." She paused and crunched on something, probably a cookie. "So. You want to call Rufus Investigations?"

After I jotted down the number, I signed off. I washed my hands and reflected a bit, then fluted, pricked, and baked the pie crust. I would make a quiche, I decided, and use up this morning's leftover bacon.

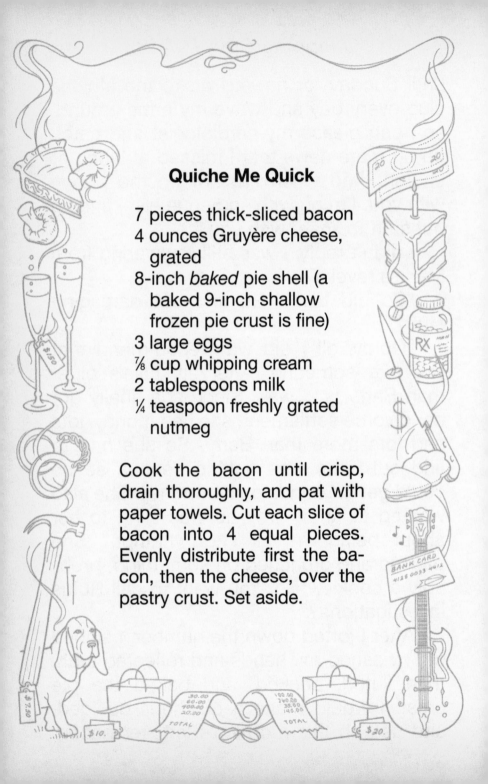

Quiche Me Quick

7 pieces thick-sliced bacon

4 ounces Gruyère cheese, grated

8-inch *baked* pie shell (a baked 9-inch shallow frozen pie crust is fine)

3 large eggs

⅞ cup whipping cream

2 tablespoons milk

¼ teaspoon freshly grated nutmeg

Cook the bacon until crisp, drain thoroughly, and pat with paper towels. Cut each slice of bacon into 4 equal pieces. Evenly distribute first the bacon, then the cheese, over the pastry crust. Set aside.

Preheat the oven to 350°F.

In a large mixing bowl, beat the eggs until they are thoroughly combined. Beat in the cream and milk, then sprinkle on the nutmeg and stir until combined. Pour over the bacon and cheese, and set carefully in the preheated oven.

Bake for 30 to 40 minutes, or until the quiche has puffed and browned slightly and is set in the middle. (Check with a spoon to make sure there is no uncooked liquid in the center of the quiche.)

Serve immediately.

Makes 6 servings

The pie would be rich, creamy, and soothing, and would go perfectly with a field
green salad dressed with raspberry
vinaigrette and defrosted homemade
baguettes. Goodness, but I was glad Liz
was doing that wedding reception this
afternoon.

No one can recover from a head injury—much less investigate—on an empty
stomach, I reminded myself. I would have a
salad, baguette, and slice of quiche before
donating the rest to the neighbors, since it
wouldn't keep for Tom and Arch. The
neighbors would be thrilled.

I tucked the phone beneath my ear,
started grating Gruyère, and put in a call to
Rufus Investigations. I was told that John
Rufus had left that morning for Africa, on
an extended assignment. I swallowed hard
and begged his secretary to look up something about a client of theirs. Ellie McNeely
had hired Mr. Rufus to have somebody sur-
veilled, and now that person has been murdered. The secretary let out an exasperated
breath.

"Let me have the name of the victim,
then," she said, as if my call were ruining
her day. Which it probably was.

I gave her Barry's name, then testily explained that a young friend of mine had been arrested for the murder, and whatever Mr. Rufus had discovered would help this innocent young man get out of jail....At that point, the secretary interrupted me and brusquely read the tenets of Rufus Investigations' confidentiality policy. When law enforcement contacts us, we will be sharing information with *them and them only*—

I thanked her and said good-bye before slamming the phone down. Then I cracked three eggs, whacked on my big mixer, and beat the eggs with almost a cup of whipping cream. Whipping cream, so aptly named. In cooking, you could take out your frustrations by *whipping, folding, beating,* and *smothering*.

And here folks thought the home cook was so *docile*.

I piled the chopped bacon and grated Gruyère into the cooled crust, sloshed the eggs and cream over all, then artfully grated nutmeg on top. After sliding the luxurious concoction into the oven, I phoned Ellie McNeely.

"It's Goldy," I began. "Please don't hang up. I *really* need to talk to you—"

"I can't talk." She was whispering. "There are two men here from the sheriff's department, and they want me to come in for questioning. You see, this private investigator I hired called them from the airport when he saw the headlines this morning. The headlines about *Barry*." Her voice trembled. "That *bastard* private eye, Rufus, told the cops I was having Barry followed. He told them all about Barry and me, and why I was having him tailed, and now Barry, the man I thought was going to marry me, has been killed—"

The line went dead. I imagined Detective Sawyer, hovering like Uriah Heep, pressing the dial-tone button while poor, wretched Ellie sought comfort from a friend. Doggone it.

John Rufus had called the sheriff's department from the airport? I imagined a man in a trenchcoat, reading the newspaper while waiting for his jet to Capetown, then making a beeline for a pay phone. Probably private investigators were like doctors and shrinks, that is, if they had information that might shed light on a crime, they had to share it. But why couldn't he stay in this country and help out a bit? Yet another question occurred to me. Was it possible John Rufus had been in Prince & Grogan last night, and seen who stabbed Barry? If so, would he have told the cops *that*? I grabbed the phone and left another message for Tom.

I cleaned up the kitchen. Then I went back to my file.

Find out if Private Investigator Rufus was in the department store, I typed. *Find out what Ellie knows. Find out if Rufus told the cops anything that could help Julian. Did B.D. have another girlfriend, say, Pam Disharoon? If so, how jealous was she? For that matter, just how jealous was Ellie? Why did Barry lie about a meeting, and go to the bank instead? Why did he say he was skiing, and then hustle off to the doctor?*

And most importantly: *Is there any information that can clear Julian?*

The quiche emerged puffed and golden brown. I cut myself an enormous slice and smiled after the first bite. The bacon gave the pie a lovely crunch, the Gruyère added tang and substance, and the eggs and cream gave the whole mélange a texture like velvet. I awarded myself points for concocting such a dish in the midst of stress. Next time, I would omit the bacon, and make one for vegetarian Julian when he got out of jail. With remarkable discipline, I dutifully carried a newly tossed salad, warmed baguettes, and the rest of the quiche to my next-door neighbor, Trudy. She swooned with joy and complimented me extravagantly. I actually felt happy for the first time in twelve hours.

Back at home, my answering machine was blinking. I had three messages. Murphy's law of answering machines: Leave the house for less than ten minutes? You're going to miss your calls.

The first was from Tom. His reassuring voice warmed me, but what he had to say turned my blood to ice. The cameras in the lounge had recorded Barry schmoozing with a number of guests, first Ellie, then several others, including Pam Disharoon. Unfortunately, the tapes also showed that Julian had had not one, but two squabbles with Barry. And by the way, none of the cameras captured my knife being transported in or out of the kitchenette. Except for the eight cameras focused on the display cases, there had been only two others, and they had recorded nothing regarding the murder weapon. The only tape the cops hadn't checked was the one from the roving videographer; the detectives were tracking that fellow down now.

The cameras on either end of the P & G shoe department, Tom went on, were focused on the cash registers to keep tabs on the employees, and the chairs and couches, where women might be tempted to slip a pair of shoes into another shopping bag. No camera had been focused on the cabinets by the wall. Moreover, with the way the cabinets had been placed, there had been enough room behind them for a person to hide while I was struggling to help Barry. In any event, no videotape showed the murder, me coming in, or Julian finding us.

Tom concluded by saying he was hoping that his friends in the department would continue to share information with him. That data-sharing would dry up instantly, however, if Julian flunked the second lie-detector test.

The next message was short and bitter-sweet. It was from Liz Fury.

"Goldy, I'm hoping you're OK. The Grigsons just started their wedding ceremony. Everything looks good for the setup, food, service. I added six dozen frozen spinach appetizers, by the way, from my freezer. Don't know if Tom told you I got two of my former staffers to help." She paused. *"I, um, really hope you're feeling better."* Her voice became apologetic. *"Goldy, I'm sorry I ever introduced Teddy to Julian. I just thought if Teddy could have a role model, a strong kid like Julian, that he might want to try to turn his life around. I had no idea that Julian would turn violent toward Barry."*

"Oh, shut up," I muttered.

"And," Liz went on, *"I certainly didn't think that with all those people there, Barry would order Teddy to be escorted from the mall, especially since he was just looking for me."* She let out a harsh laugh. *"If you can imagine, the cops wanted to know where I was while Barry was getting himself stabbed. I told them I was looking for my son. After being dragged forcibly out of the mall, he'd gone to his usual haunt, the nearest McDonald's. That's where I found him. Look, I have to go. Let's talk when you feel better."*

Or even sooner, I thought grimly, as I pressed the button for the final message. Lo and behold, the husky voice of Ellie Mc-Neely burned through the wire. Her tone was of someone trying to get a grip on a situation spiraling out of control, and failing.

"Goldy. I'm...at the sheriff's department. Sorry we were interrupted. Do you... did you know...is it true that Julian saw..." She snuffled. *"Did you know anything about what the cops found in that runaway dump truck? They were...They were supposed to be a gift...besides, I was having a facial wrap, and I don't even know how to* drive *a damn* truck! *I—"*

And then the message ended.

Had Ellie once again been cut off? Or had she lost her nerve? No matter what, I now knew another data nugget: That Ellie McNeely had knowledge of the cuff links. So Ellie and I needed to have an extended chat.

It was almost one o'clock. I typed the contents of all three messages into my new "Barry Dean" file, reread the entire file, and created a list of places I wanted to visit or call, with questions. *Rufus Investigations, or somebody who has access to their data. Ellie McNeely. Westside Mall—Barry's office. Barry's coworkers.* Would Barry's colleagues be helpful, or as difficult to deal with as everyone else in this case? I knew there was an assistant manager for the mall, but I had no idea what his name was. *Find out what Barry was being so secretive about. Why had he wanted to talk to me right away, then changed his mind after the truck incident? And why was he taking painkillers?*

I imagined Hulsey reading this file, and becoming apopleptic.

I thought of the Vicodin in the freezer and frowned. Not only was I, by keeping something from the crime scene, engaging in evidence-tampering, I was also guilty of possession of a controlled substance without a prescription. There seemed to be many things I needed to avoid telling Hulsey, as well as Tom. My breaking the law would make them *both* apopleptic. I wondered if the medical examiner would find narcotics in Barry's bloodstream.

I had too many questions, and very few answers. I glanced all around the kitchen, as if any of my fancy new paraphernalia—

laser printer, copier for menus, plain-paper fax, new standing mixer, new multibladed food processor—could help. My equipment was mute. That's the problem with technology. The ads promise you'll be able to improve your life with complicated new machines. But if *improved life* looked like figuring something out, you were in trouble. Marketing claims to the contrary, machines couldn't come up with good ideas.

Still, there were possibilities. Our new printer could create logos, spreadsheets, and all kinds of cool stuff. To find out about Barry's health problems, I reasoned, I would have to have a logo, an address, and a fax number.

From my files, I dug out my contract for the Westside Mall events. I always keep a photocopy of the initial check, including the client's driver's license number, and—key for my developing investigation—Barry Dean's Social Security number. Although the client for the Westside events was the mall *owner,* Barry Dean had been their representative. In the remote event of a bounced check, a collection service tracked the check-writer through the SSN. Sheesh! I'd learned from Tom that there were lots of uses for that good old Social Security number.

I switched computer programs and began to play. Ten technology-packed minutes later, I was ready. I didn't want to imagine what Hulsey or Tom would think of what I was up to. If I ended up getting caught, the consequences would probably involve prison garb.

Once more I reached for the phone.

"This is Doctor Gertrude Shoemaker," I announced firmly and matter-of-factly to the receptionist at Dr. Louis Maxwell's practice of general medicine. Although I'd hated filling in for secretaries who'd walked out on The Jerk, I'd at least learned how doctors who wanted information behaved. *Brusquely*. "I'm with Aspen Meadow Neurology. A patient of yours is here. He's paying for his own CAT scan. Diagnosis is chronic headache. I'm not sure he's telling me the truth as to how and when he first contracted symptoms, and I need a copy of his records. The patient has authorized the release."

"Fine, Doctor," Maxwell's receptionist replied. "Fax us the standard release form on your letterhead, and we'll fax his records back to you as soon as possible."

"When would that be?"

"No later than four o'clock today, Doctor."

I hung up and prayed that Maxwell's receptionist had not read the morning paper, which would have told her that Barry Dean was not sitting in my fictitious doctor's office, but lying in the morgue.

I quickly put together a standard release form, then wrote a cover letter on my new fake letterhead for Aspen Meadow Neurology. (As if backwater Aspen Meadow would even *have* a neurologist! But we did boast nine chiropractors.) I entered Barry's Social Security number, stared hard at the contract Barry had signed with me, and then carefully forged his signature. Then I faxed the whole thing off to Dr. Maxwell's office. This was a very long shot, and the diagnosis would probably come back, "Patient claims headaches are stress-related." Still, if you were going to let no stone go unturned, you had to start upending every rock ... and hope there wasn't a rattlesnake under one of them. And, hope that all the laws you were breaking didn't come back to bite you.

And speaking of laws, it was time for me to visit the jail. After that, I would stop by the office of my own criminal defense attorney! Life's little ironies.

I stopped first at our town's drive-through Espresso Place, and ordered and paid for a four-shot latte. Of course I wanted to bring Julian one, but I knew from experience that there would be glass between us, and we'd have to speak to each other via phone. Plus, I didn't want him to screw up *another* polygraph. The attendant handed me the drink, and my skin turned cold. Latte had been one of Barry's favorites.

Overhead, fast-moving, dark clouds thickened and roiled. An ominous gray nimbus stretched eastward from the Continental Divide. As my window hummed closed, the unmistakable smell of snow drifted into the van. Would I still be catering the next day's luncheon for the Stockhams? There had been no message, no apology from them for their eruption at the mall. I wasn't going anywhere close to their huge house near the Aspen Meadow Wildlife Preserve without working things out.

Despite the rising storm, or maybe because of it, the number of tractors moving dirt around in the new section of Flicker Ridge had doubled since I'd noticed the area the previous morning. The trucks and tractors chugging hither and yon looked like a military operation. Two We Got Dirt trucks rumbled past the *Topsoil $70/load* sign, which now stood next to a revised sign: *Only 2 home sites left! First come, first served!* The price had been crossed out, and a new sign taped over it: *Open to bidding.* Uh-oh. If they'd written *Make offer,* that would have meant sales were slow. *Open to bidding* meant folks were scrambling to buy the sites, perhaps because the developer had priced them too low. The trucks growled and swooped over the mounds of dirt. Nothing like avarice to get a job done.

Half an hour later I was gripping a phone and staring at Julian through a scratched Plexiglas panel. His handsome face looked haggard and weary, and his unshaven cheeks gave him a grizzled appearance. The too-large orange prison suit did not flatter his muscled body. Worst of all, he looked as if he'd neither slept nor showered since the arrest.

"This is crap!" he exploded into the phone. "I don't belong here! It's crap! Can't Tom help me? I came looking for you, and the next thing I knew, some cop was slapping handcuffs on me. And now this lawyer says—"

"Julian, please," I urged. "I've got a lawyer, too, an associate of the guy who's helping you. My guy will probably tell me not to come talk to you, because it would look bad. But I'm here to support you. So, please, please don't be angry with me. I know you didn't kill Barry."

Julian's shoulders slumped in dejection. "I was trying to help him."

"Begin at the beginning and take me through the time after I left the lounge. Minute by minute. I especially need to know if you saw anyone—*anyone*—with one of the new Henckels knives."

And so Julian took me through it. It was almost exactly as I'd thought. I was disappointed, but not surprised, that he hadn't seen the knife disappear. After I'd left with Barry Dean's note—the one Barry had handed off to a musician, the note Julian had read—Julian had finished packing up the dirty dishes and equipment. He had been surprised that I hadn't shown up by the time he'd completed the loading and cleanup. The security and jewelry people were gone, and the mall was closing. He'd locked the lounge and come looking for me.

"I wonder why Barry didn't have one of his security guys lock up the lounge, and take the key."

Julian rolled his eyes. "I wish I knew, because then I wouldn't have had to say *I don't know* fifty times to the cops. When they asked me and asked me about the kitchenette key, I kept telling them that clients often ask us to lock up when we leave. And no one's been robbed or murdered yet. Or at least, not until last night." He groaned.

"It's OK," I murmured. People who aren't caterers have a very romantic view of what we do. They think it's all intriguing recipes, chic food, and glam presentation. They have no clue about, and certainly don't want to hear about, the ordering, prepping, dealing with clients, dishwashing, cleaning, locking up, and other drudge jobs associated with food service.

"OK, let's get through this," Julian said wearily. "I forgot to tell you that when I finished, about five after nine, I made myself another cup of coffee in that kitchen. Everybody was gone. The coffee was instant, but I didn't care. I knew I had to drive back to Boulder, and I was afraid I'd fall asleep at the wheel. When I finished it and you still hadn't come back, I started to get worried. I went to the mall office and no one was there. So I went looking for you."

"You remembered from the note to come to Ladies' Shoes?"

"Yeah." His voice was morose. "I saw the store was closing fast, so I hurried over to Shoes. And there you were on the floor. Barry, too. I didn't think. I turned him over, and when I saw the knife, I just pulled on it. How could I be so dumb?"

I tapped on the scratched plastic shelf in front of me. "So, no one saw you during the last ten, fifteen minutes before you came into the shoe department?"

He sighed in despair. "Nope. I saw a few cashiers inside the stores that were closing, but nobody looked out at me, 'cuz they were all busy counting the cash in their tills." He rubbed his bloodshot eyes. "Anyway, I had just tugged once on the knife, when this department store security guy started hollering at me to move away. He called the cops and eventually I was hauled off. Of course I wanted to take the polygraph, why wouldn't I? I didn't *do* anything! I had no idea Marla was calling a lawyer, and he didn't show up until the cops were through with me and it was too late. Now I'm behind bars on suspicion of murder. I was advised of the charges today. And—ready for this—even if I pass another polygraph, it might not help, 'cuz polygraphs are *inadmissible*. Those cops are gathering evidence to charge me with murder. Unless something turns up, they're going to hold me until the next regular arraignment day. My damn prints on the weapon are the worst...."

I shook my head, mute. The unreality of it all was dizzying. Julian had Cleve Jackson plus a team of Hulsey's investigators working to clear him. But somehow I didn't trust Hulsey's people to find out who had really killed Barry Dean.

I'd known Barry. I'd taken the job he offered me. I was the one who'd found him after he was stabbed. At that unforgettable moment, Barry had uttered a deep, shattering groan. Then the real killer had whacked me with the guitar and, presumably, finished the job on Barry. Not only had I not been able to help my old coffee buddy, I was wondering what in the world I would be able to do for poor Julian.

Not for the first time, my mind hollered at me that *I had to do something*. My heart agreed.

CHAPTER 8

I promised Julian that Tom, Marla, and I were working hard to get him out. Marla would be coming to see him later in the day. But Julian, his skin grayed by the fluorescent lights, appeared even more discouraged and disheartened. He asked about Arch. I put effort into sounding enthusiastic, but I knew it didn't ring true. Arch was doing well, I related, forcing a smile. As usual, my son was keeping mum in the social department. He enjoyed lacrosse and was impatient for Julian to come home. After all, Julian needed to bake his fifteenth birthday cake! The family party was set for this Friday!

"That's the arraignment day," Julian said joylessly.

I swallowed and reassured him again that this nightmare would be over soon and that everything would turn out fine.

"Yeah, yeah," Julian said, as if he had not heard me. "Look, please don't call my parents, OK?"

I looked at him in surprise. Julian adored his adoptive parents, and trekked down to Bluff, Utah, a couple of times a year to visit them. "Don't you want them to know—"

"No, I don't," he interrupted me. "It'll give my dad a heart attack. If it goes to trial and all that, I'll call their neighbors and have them go over and break things to them gently."

"Well—"

Julian shrugged, offered a dispirited wave, and got up to leave. I plastered a grin on my face and gave him a thumbs-up.

On the inside, of course, my frustration was reaching fury level. I left the jail and raced to Hulsey's office, frantic for good news. Funny thing about good news. You shouldn't go to a criminal-defense attorney looking for any.

Steve Hulsey's office was decorated in a palette of oxblood leather, ultradark mahogany, cranberry glass, and maroon wool. Maybe this was some deranged decorator's vision of a bloodbath. Hulsey sat, statuelike, behind the vast mahogany desk, which was the size of a ten-person life raft. And oh boy, I could just imagine desperate clients clinging to it. Hulsey would be telling them what he could and couldn't do for his fee, which a former client had informed me was a twenty-thousand-dollar retainer, plus eight hundred bucks an hour after that. Hulsey, the very image of a westernized Buddha, was wearing another silk suit, a shimmery silver-gray pinstripe. I wondered if he also wore silk underpants à la Al Capone. One fact was clear: Steve Hulsey might represent desperate hooligans, but they were desperate *rich* hooligans.

His terse greeting was followed by: "You said you wanted to talk to me about your innocence, Mrs. Schulz."

"Absolutely." But where to begin? Not at the end, for I knew the Buddha would berate me if I told him I'd just visited Julian in jail. I fidgeted while reminding myself that Barry Dean's Vicodin and all my machinations over the prescription also needed to go into the don't-tell-your-lawyer category. *Eight hundred bucks an hour!* my conscience screamed. At least tell him *something*!

Hulsey's eyes were piercing. I was sure he was reading my thoughts. His face turned thunderous; one of the black eyebrows rose. *Will I ever be able to put this guilty-looking woman on the stand?* he seemed to be asking himself. *Probably not.*

I took a deep breath, then told Hulsey I'd first met Barry in school, where we'd had a class together. I'd lost touch with him after I got married and he graduated. He'd called me this March, though, to book a couple of parties. Hulsey frowned. I explained that Barry had heard about me from a mutual friend, Ellie McNeely, whom he had either proposed to or was about to. So he'd hired Goldilocks' Catering to do the cocktail party accompanying the jewelry-leasing event. I was doing another event for him, or at least I was supposed

to, this Thursday, a lunch for potential tenants in the mall's addition...I faltered.

"Did Dean talk to you about his business? Mall business?"

"He told me he'd been working at
Westside Mall for the last six months.
He'd always been...My suspicion is—" I
hesitated.

"Go on."

"Well, I just thought that if I were the
person hiring Barry, it would be not so
much for his expertise, even though he
might have been super at what he did. But
his real assets were his charm and...en-
thusiasm. They were contagious."

Hulsey's brow furrowed, so I plowed on:
"Barry was trying hard to jump-start sales
and establish shopper loyalty to Westside
before any more new malls opened in the
Denver area. He loved to talk about shopping, about all the goodies that were available, especially at Westside. He was
frustrated that the new mall addition was
taking so long, but he perked up when I
gave him some chocolate." Hulsey's scowl
deepened. I was obviously blathering.
"Look—Barry really didn't share very much

with me about his job... or his personal life. I'm sorry."

"Tell me everything about the hours leading up to his death."

And so I did: Barry asking to chat with me, the truck incident, Barry's unwillingness to stay and talk to the cops, Barry craving a drink, the jewelry-leasing party with its bewildering conflicts—Liz, her son, Barry, Shane and Page Stockham—and through it all, the hectic catering. Barry had left without saying good-bye, I told Hulsey, then returned and dropped off the note about the gratuity. Or at least I thought it was about the gratuity, but maybe that word *tip* had meant something else. The next thing I knew, I was slipping on a pile of shoes in Prince & Grogan. When I tried to regain my balance, I fell onto a cabinet. The doors swung open, and I saw a man's legs, shoes, tuxedo... it was Barry. He groaned, I tried to pull him out, and then something struck me—

"So he wasn't dead at that point?" Hulsey interrupted. "Before you were hit?"

"No. I thought I felt a weak pulse."

Hulsey scribbled a few notes, then locked those impenetrable eyes on me once more. "You know the police have arrested Julian Teller. But I've got to warn you. From the way the detectives were questioning you, they're obviously considering you a viable suspect—"

"*Me?* Why?"

"Because you found the corpse. Because your knife was in Barry Dean's gut. And that's just the beginning. The cops say they wanted that note so they could analyze the handwriting and compare it to Julian's. But they'll compare it to yours, too."

"Barry gave the note about the tip to a musician," I protested. "Julian only read it before he gave it to me."

Hulsey waved this off. "Here are the charges they might be thinking of making against you: First-degree murder. Conspiracy to commit murder. Accessory to murder, or accessory after the fact—say if you asked Julian to pull the knife out of Dean. And then there's tampering with evidence, in case there's something from that scene that you're hiding from them." He lifted both eyebrows.

I was right. Hulsey *could* read minds, after all. I shrugged and lifted my hands in a helpless gesture.

"Mrs. Schulz, you're my client. I don't want you talking to anyone about this case. Do not see or speak to Julian Teller. Doing so would strengthen the DA's conspiracy case, if he has one. Do not go to that mall and start asking questions about Barry Dean—"

"As I told you, Mr. Hulsey." It was my turn to interrupt. "I *have* to go to the mall on Thursday. I've signed a contract and I've been paid. The food supplies have been ordered. I have a catering commitment to honor, and my reputation depends on not backing out of events."

"What kind of party is this, exactly?" His voice had turned patronizing.

"Westside Mall is running scared at the prospect of new Denver malls wiping them out. Or undercutting them. This second event Barry hired me to do is a gourmet lunch for potential tenants in the mall addition."

Hulsey gave me that get-to-the-facts expression again. So I got to them.

"The owner of Westside, Pennybaker International, is sending out a high-powered team to secure leases for the vacant portion of the new addition. On Thursday, they've invited twelve of the hottest companies in the Westside area to hear the official pitch on why any retailer who wants to make *big* money needs to have a store in the mall addition."

"What are you serving?" Hulsey said unexpectedly.

"He-man food," I replied with what I hoped was a high-class sniff. "Oriental dumpling soup. Prime rib. Mashed russet and sweet potatoes. Strawberry-rhubarb cobbler. Barry ordered that food hoping that once they ate it, all the retailers would feel rich enough to afford Westside."

Hulsey sighed. "If you do the event, I want you to concentrate on *food*. Not *crime*. Understand?"

I nodded. He told me that he would get in touch with me if he needed to, and I should do the same. I took my leave, and noted we'd been together half an hour. For Marla's four hundred bucks, I'd been told stuff I either didn't want to hear or was planning to ignore. If Julian was still in jail on Thursday, did Attorney Hulsey *really* think I'd concentrate on food and not crime?

If so, he was sadly mistaken.

Since Hulsey's office wasn't far from Westside Mall, I drove over there. If anyone asked, I'd say I was looking for Julian's Range Rover, which was sort of true. In any event, as long as I was going to violate Hulsey's instructions, there were two people I wanted to talk to: Pam Disharoon and Ellie McNeely, the two purported girlfriends of the deceased Barry Dean. I knew Ellie had been taken to police headquarters. Now she was probably back at work at the bank. But Pam worked for Prince & Grogan, in the lingerie department. I could always use a new nightie, couldn't I?

I followed the route Liz and I had taken just the previous day—which seemed an eternity ago—along Doughnut Drive. Where yesterday only a handful of workers had been visible, now there was activity everywhere. I passed a crew raking and smoothing the cavernous hole in the berm made by the errant dump truck. Near them, another gang of laborers dug holes in the topsoil. Flats of spruce bushes stood nearby, ready to be planted. Did the crews work alternate days, or had someone lit a fire under them? Had Barry's murder somehow accelerated the slow-as-molasses construction of the new addition? Hmm.

To my further surprise, the construction lot was more than half-full of trucks ranging from tractor-trailers to pickups. Workers diligently transported sheets of plywood, spray-painted drywall, or pointed high-powered hoses at freshly laid concrete pavers. Diesel-powered cranes lofted yet more workers onto the roofs of almost-finished stores. Those guys scampered up and over the pitched surfaces as if they were playground equipment. A newly painted banner floated overhead: *Boutiques Opening Soon!*

Oh, yeah? When?

Another surprise: The construction gate was open and unattended. Management must have decided that sparing a worker to be gatekeeper was not possible, especially with the heightened level of construction bustle. Still, in light of the truck incident, you'd think they'd at least be a bit more careful.

I ignored the new *No Trespassing* sign and sailed the van into the construction lot. The drainage pond, now with chunks of ice floating in it, was slick with oil. Workers driving Caterpillars were digging and smoothing the layer of rutted dirt over which the dump truck had lurched toward us. Which one of those workers had claimed he'd seen Julian piloting that truck? I wondered.

I slowed and surveyed Westside Mall's main parking area. Compared to the usual crowd of vehicles, the number of cars was anemic, no more than a third of the previous day's. Apparently, the newspaper articles on Barry's death had discouraged shoppers. For those who hadn't caught the news and had ventured out, driving past the yellow police ribbons surrounding Prince & Grogan would have sent them packing.

What had Barry said? *Nothing clears a mall like a security threat.* Or a murder, apparently.

I parked near one of the Skytrack cranes. Victor Wilson, excavator-turned-construction-manager, was nowhere in sight. I headed toward a cluster of workers standing near a Dumpster. They were leaning over a drop cloth dense with paint cans. Something must have been wrong with the paint, because the workers were having a heated discussion.

I sauntered up and asked them where their boss-guy was. The painters exchanged guarded looks.

"I've just got a quick question for Victor," I improvised hastily, "about the construction. I'm the caterer for the tenants' lunch later in the week, and they asked me to find out when Victor was going to give the go-ahead to occupy the new stores."

Several workers shook their heads and backed away. It was clear they weren't going to help me. I turned to the remaining workmen.

"Anybody know when the new stores are going to be ready?"

Silence. A short, heavyset Hispanic man carrying two paint cans ambled up. I smiled at him and he grinned back, more than I could say for any of the other fellows. Before I could repeat my request for info, a long, lanky crew member, perched on one of the ladders by the new Il Fornaio, yelled in a Southern accent that Victor wasn't coming in that day. I exhaled and told myself to be patient.

I lowered my voice and addressed the remaining workers. Had anybody seen the accident with the truck yesterday? One or two nodded. That was going to set back the construction schedule for sure, I said, shaking my head. Ah, I asked, had anyone seen who was *driving* that truck? No, no, they shook their heads and avoided my eyes. *We didn't see. Not a thing. Uh-uh*.

The workers began to disperse around the Dumpster. I felt suddenly desperate. "Do any of you know who told the police that my assistant was driving the truck?"

The heavyset fellow grinned. The name *Raoul* was embroidered on his workshirt.

"Yeah," said Raoul, "I know who told 'em and—" Raoul registered that the few remaining workers were staring at him. Abruptly, he closed his mouth.

"Who *was* he, though? *Who* told them?" I demanded. My voice had become shrill.

"He weren't nobody, lady," said the lanky fellow, as he stepped down the ladder. He had sand-colored hair and skin the color of a pecan shell. He moved in my direction and spoke like someone in authority. "He was a temporary worker. He just quit." *He jest quee-at.*

"But who *was* he?" I persisted. "He told the police that lie, and now a friend of mine is in jail."

"Lady, that guy is *gone*. Does anybody remember his name?" Pecan-shell turned to the remaining workers.

No, no, no, came the chorus of denials. *No lo conosco. Don't know him.*

What was going on? Were these guys covering for a buddy who stole big trucks and tried to mow people down with them? They clearly had lots of sympathy for him, even if his quitting had left them a worker short.

This project is cursed, I asserted silently. The workers, avoiding my eyes, picked up their cans and walked away. *These guys,* I decided, *are not happy campers*. First their construction manager walks out, then one of their trucks is swiped and run into a fresh berm, then a worker lies and vanishes, and now nobody knows the whereabouts of the boss-guy who is supposed to be running things. Emphasis on the *supposed to.* Maybe some answers would be forthcoming if the Furman County attorney could get here and serve a handful of subpoenas, but it was unlikely that *I* would be able to extract any more information.

I reached into my purse, pulled out a handful of cards, and handed them to Raoul. At least he'd graced me with some kind of answer. His paint-stained fingers closed around my offering.

"Look, Raoul," I implored, "if you do happen to remember the name of the guy who told the cops who drove the truck, I'd really appreciate a call. Please—it's very important."

I made my way across the rickety makeshift bridge that spanned the icy drainage puddle. At the glass-prismed doors, I glanced back at the construction crew. To the amusement of his coworkers, Raoul was flinging my cards one by one into the Dumpster.

Furious, I marched into the mall. My injured right side rebelled and shot an arrow of pain into my lower abdomen. I clutched my side, leaned against one of the marble walls, and took a hacking, uneven breath. The few beautiful people shopping that day passed me by.

What was I doing here? I was supposed to be resting; I'd promised the doctor and Tom that I would. Worse, I was at one of the two places—the other being the jail—that Counselor Hulsey had ordered me *not* to go. Could my lawyer refuse to represent me if I didn't do what he said? Might the construction workers call the cops and say the caterer from Monday was bothering them with her nosy questions? Didn't she have enough catering work to keep her busy?

I gripped my side and soldiered on, trying not to think of the wedding reception I'd been booked to do that day, trying not to think of Liz and her crew working while I was here at the mall. I also veered away from reflecting on the work-intensive events I was scheduled to cater over the next two days.

And then, suddenly, I was trying not to think of Julian. Someone had set up our old family friend, of that I was sure. But who? And why? This person was violent, no question about it. Paranoid, I looked all around. Nobody appeared to be following me. I limped forward and tried to ignore the image of Shane Stockham's enraged face as he'd rushed forward in attack mode.

Oh, my God. *Shane Stockham*. He was Elk Park Prep's lacrosse coach. *Arch's* lacrosse coach. As I hobbled along, I punched in the numbers for my son's cell phone.

"It's Mom," I said into his voice mail. "Don't go to lacrosse if Shane is there. Call Tom or me instead. This is very important. One of us will come and get you. Call me on the cell. Arch, this is *important*." I blocked out an image of my son making a disgusted face when he listened to the message.

My first stop was the Prince & Grogan lingerie department. No, Pam Disharoon was not working that day, a scarlet-haired clerk informed me. Pam's only in on Wednesdays, Thursdays, Fridays, and Saturdays, or I could leave a message.... On another one of my business cards, I scribbled a note asking Pam to call. I hoped *this* card wouldn't get tossed, but with my luck ... No, better not reflect on that, either.

I pushed past an exit sign and headed down the narrow hall that led to the mall manager's office. If I couldn't get any answers there, this trip was going to be a complete bust.

I spotted Westside's assistant manager, whose name I now remembered was Rob Eakin. He was behind the glass surrounding his office by the tiny reception area. I'd met Eakin once. He was a short, wide fellow whom I judged to be in his forties. Now, his brow glistened with sweat as he listened to two people whose raised voices penetrated the glass separating them from me. With Barry gone, Rob Eakin must have been named acting mall manager. He didn't look too good.

I nodded to the receptionist and moved to the chair closest to Eakin's office. Right before I filed for divorce, I'd overheard The Jerk boinking a nurse in an empty hospital room. After that, no amount of righteous eavesdropping bothered me. Still, try as I might, I couldn't quite make out what the people in the office were squabbling about.

I sighed in frustration.

The plumply padded receptionist—whose name I struggled to recall—watched me intently. Her cheeks were puffy and mottled, her eyes bloodshot. Her French-twisted blond hair resembled an unkempt haystack. Crumpled tissues lay scattered across her desk. A multibuttoned phone blinked and buzzed. She ignored it.

"I remember...you," she told me. Her wobbly voice indicated she'd been weeping. "You're the...caterer. The one who solves crimes."

"The very one," I replied amiably. "How's it going?"

"Awful." It came out like a sob.

"It's terrible, isn't it? Poor Barry. Um, why didn't you take today off?"

She pressed a tissue to her eyes, unable to respond. Two of the blinking phone lines went dark.

"Sorry," I said gently, "but I do have a catering question that needs an answer. It's about the lunch event Barry hired me for, this Thursday, the one for the potential tenants."

The receptionist—her name was Heather, I finally remembered—stifled another sob. "I wish you could find out what happened to him!"

"I do, too," I said softly. "I...I miss him. Barry and I used to be friends, back in our college days."

"Really? Way back then? That's sweet."

I bit down on telling her that less than two decades—not glacier-forming epochs—separated me from my college days. Instead, I waited while she reached daintily for more tissues. Truth to tell, Barry's and my friendship had lasted only a semester, which was four months. Then, after years of silence, he'd hired me to cater at the mall. We had been friends; then we'd gone our separate ways.

So, I thought suddenly, why the great push to be friendly again?

Heather blew into one tissue, then dabbed her eyes with another. I realized I was staring at her. Something was bothering me.

"Uh, Heather? How do *you* happen to know I've been involved in crime investigations? From that article in the paper about Hyde Castle? Did Barry show that to you? He told me my friend Mrs. McNeely had urged him to hire me. How does the article fit in?"

"Oh, yeah, Barry told me all about it." She pulled a miniature compact from her bag and patted powder on her nose. "He told me how you dived into this pond to look for a murderer—"

"It was a moat—"

"—and how you always were able to find out what a criminal had done, and how good you were, and stuff like that. He was looking at you and about four other caterers, and then he read the article and told me to call you! To see if you could do the jewelry party and the potential tenants' lunch."

The phone buzzed again; this time Heather decided to answer it. I rubbed my temples. This was not what Barry had told me when he'd called. While Heather talked into the phone, I closed my eyes and tried to reconstruct.

In March, Barry had phoned me out of the blue. He'd been brimming with the charisma and gusto that had made him, well, Barry Dean. We had a friend in common! he exclaimed. His dear friend Ellie McNeely, who knew me so well from our church work together, had recommended Goldilocks' Catering to him! Where had I been all these years? Why hadn't I called him? I'd been astonished to hear from my old coffee buddy. I'd offered a précis of Life

paper and swore she'd deliver it as soon as possible. Seeing my worried look, she told me that if Mr. Eakin couldn't handle my request, she'd let me know herself about the Thursday lunch. Meanwhile, from the glassed-in office, the raised voices were suddenly audible.

"You need to do some damage control, Eakin! We don't figure this thing out, we're going to lose half our tenants!" howled a male voice.

"I've got two-thirds of them *already* screaming!" shrieked a young woman in a white shirt, black blazer, and black bow tie. Her face had turned scarlet; her brown hair, pulled into a tight bun, strained at its riggings. "They want twice as many security guys as we've already got!"

Eakin closed his eyes and rubbed his temples.

Heather's eyes widened. "Look, I *promise* I'll call you if I find anything Barry left you," she stage-whispered. I nodded, not hopeful. If the cops had been through everything, it was unlikely there'd be anything left for Heather to find.

I thanked her and started to leave. Then I turned back. "Where is Victor Wilson today? I went out to the site. I had something to ask him, but he's not there."

Heather clucked disapprovingly. "Not a clue. Not that I would care about that asshole," she added.

"You don't get along with Victor? How come?"

Once again we were interrupted by arguing from the inner office.

"You've got to get the cops out of here!" the bunned bow tie lady squealed. "They're driving customers away!"

"They can't leave until they figure out what happened!" Rob Eakin yelled back.

Heather waved her hand. "Victor Wilson orders me around like I'm his secretary, not Barry's. He hires and fires workers whenever he feels like it, which gets us into a real mess with the worker-comp people and the unemployment-benefits people. And the Civil Liberties guys claim he treats Hispanic workers badly and pays them less than we do the other workers. For our office, the worst thing is that he keeps everyone dangling about when these stores are going to be finished. Victor's a *major-league* asshole."

"Did Barry get along with him?"

"Well," Heather said with a sniff, "would you, if you were mall manager? Victor makes fourteen tons of paperwork for us, gives us a bad name in the Hispanic community, and won't tell us when the damn stores are going to be done."

"Were he and Barry enemies, then?"

Heather snorted a laugh, the first time she'd looked amused all morning. "You are *bad*, girl. Is this how you get crimes solved?" She giggled some more, then slid her eyes over to the contentious meeting. "The cops asked me about *each and every person* who worked closely with Barry. I looked up everyone's schedule, even the security guys'. For Victor, I called Westside Community College. He teaches a class there on building your own house addition. Every Monday. Last night, Victor was giving a test." She giggled again, unable to control herself. I began to worry about the hysterical tone creeping into her voice. "I tried to take that class and gave up. Victor said, 'While the little woman's making you an apple pie, you can be the big man building her a brand-new kitchen.' So I said, 'I am *so* out of here.'"

My eyes strayed to the glassed-in office, where all of the participants in the altercation were talking into cell phones.

"Did, uh, Victor try to order the previous construction manager around?"

"Lucas Holden? Noto? He was the last construction manager."

"Was that his name?" I asked. "Lucas? Who's Noto?"

"That's just what we called old Lucas. No-toe. On account of a girder that fell on his big toe once, so he lost it. I'm like, Call a toe truck, yo! But nobody thought that was funny."

I sighed. Heather definitely needed some time off.

"So what happened to this Lucas Holden?" I asked resolutely.

"He *quit*. Another asshole," she declared vehemently.

"And where did Lucas go?"

"Oh, the letter he wrote us said he was going to Arizona someplace. Nobody ever called him Lucas, though. Strictly No-toe."

"Do you have an address for... Holden?"

Heather swiveled in her chair toward her files. "I'll look, if you'd like. But you don't want to get mixed up with No-toe, trust me. He's the reason we're in the mess we're in, with the new stores not ready, construction loans to pay, a drainage mess to clean up, a shortage of workers, blah, blah, blah. Don't get me started on *No-toe.*"

I didn't, even though I was increasingly eager to find out if Lucas Holden, aka No-toe Holden, had gotten along with Barry and everyone else at the mall.

Heather frowned over one file, then stuffed it back in the drawer when she read the concern in my face. "Look," she said. "I'll try to get No-toe's phone number for you. If I can't find it, I'll ask Victor if he has it somewhere." She grabbed for her tissue box and muttered, "Victor. What an asshole."

Since we'd already traveled that particular loop, I nodded a good-bye. From the inner office, the voices rose again.

"If you can't hire more security, then maybe we need a new acting manager!" the first man howled at Rob Eakin.

"Great idea!" screamed Eakin.

"Find out who killed Barry, would you?" Heather implored, as she crumpled her latest tissue and dabbed her eyes.

"I'm trying," I said gently, over the noise of the office fight. "Take care of yourself, Heather."

Then I backed out the door.

CHAPTER 9

As I gunned the van toward Aspen Meadow, Julian's face stayed in my thoughts. He was emotionally and physically strong; anyone who knew him knew that. Surely he'd be able to handle whatever the jail experience offered, from bad cellmates to horrid food. When Julian *did* get out of jail, he'd probably start a campaign to bring fresh vegetables to inmates.

I tried to smile, but couldn't. The memory of Julian's haggard face and downcast spirits was too strong.

Barry, I reminded myself, as I raced onto the interstate. *Barry is the key.* My thinking was getting clearer in this department. My assumptions began with the theory that Barry had gotten himself into some kind of trouble. Ellie McNeely and I had been friends for a long time. When Barry was looking for a caterer, Ellie had told her boyfriend-who-hadn't-given-her-a-ring-yet about me. But Barry hadn't decided on a caterer until he'd read the article about the debacle at Hyde Castle. Somehow, that article had clinched it. Barry'd figured if he hired his old pal, amateur crime-solver Goldy Schulz, she could straighten things out. But his attempt to fill me in on his dilemma—or even tell me what the dilemma was—had gone terribly awry.

The snow-capped peaks and plum-purple shadows of the Continental Divide came into view. I pressed on the accelerator.

Barry's dying and Julian's arrest were not my fault. Still, I felt responsible. If only I had tried harder to make Barry talk to me... If only I had been less obsessed with my catering event....

Barry had tried to reach out to me. But he had been too proud, too scared, too *something* to just blurt out what was bothering him. And now he was gone.

Ringing from my cell phone made my heart jump. It was Alicia, my supplier. Was I ready to receive this week's food order? Yep, I replied, you bet. Alicia promised to be at our house in thirty minutes. So much for stopping by the Bank of Aspen Meadow to see if Ellie could visit. I called the bank to try to set up an appointment with her, but was told she was being questioned *again* by someone from the sheriff's department. A detective had taken Ellie to the bank's conference room, and had asked not to be disturbed. Yes, I was told, a message would be left for Mrs. McNeely, asking her to return my call.

Barry might have thought I was an ace amateur sleuth, but it looked now as if my reputation was becoming a drawback. Maybe I was paranoid, but Pam Disharoon wouldn't or couldn't see me; ditto Rob Eakin, Ellie McNeely, and Capetown-bound John Rufus. Well. No matter what, I was going to find a way to get Julian out of jail.

And then—*surprise!*—my cell phone rang again.

"Goldy, it's Page Stockham."

"Uh, well. Yeah." I couldn't even stammer out a proper greeting. "What's up?" I asked feebly. "How are you and Shane, uh, doing?"

"I really, really want to apologize to you." Her breathy voice cracked. "So does Shane. He's going to call you later. Look, it's all my fault. I started the fight at the party. I'm sorry. Oh, God. Please, please say you'll cater for us Wednesday. We need this lunch *wicked* bad."

"I don't know what to say. Maybe we should think it over," I murmured. Excuse me, but it was *Shane* who'd started to attack his wife. Page had prodded and ridiculed him, yes. But instead of charging her, Shane could have walked away. In fact, they both could have. But Page hadn't rung me up for marital advice.

"Don't abandon us," she pleaded. "Marla told me you'd probably cancel, and I needed to call you and eat dirt. Please, please don't cancel on us. We're under terrible stress financially, and we're going to a counselor, because money is, the lack of money is, well, killing us."

I turned off on the Aspen Meadow exit and tried to think of what to say.

"Let me think about it," I said to Page.

"Please, Goldy. I'm really, really sorry. We both are."

"We'll talk later," I promised. We signed off.

The first thing I did when I slammed into the kitchen at home was check the fax machine. Empty. The voice mail, though, announced that five folks had called.

The first message was from Tom. He was swamped, so could I pick up Arch today after all? Please call him if I could not, and he'd shuffle things around. I smiled. Of course I would get Arch. By the way, Tom added, Marla called and demanded that he look into Shane Stockham, to see if Stockham had any reports of, or arrests for, domestic or any other kind of violence. No, Tom said. Shane was clean.

The second message was from Arch, who'd checked his cell phone voice mail between classes—strictly forbidden at Elk Park Prep—and was calling from the boys' bathroom. Flushing sounds punctuated the static as Arch sullenly announced that Mr. Stockham was *not* coaching lacrosse anymore, and had I gotten him fired? My son went on to say that he would be going to practice no matter what, and Tom wasn't coming to pick him up, so he needed me to be there *right* at five o'clock. And please don't tell him when to go to practice and when not to go. I sighed as his phone slammed shut.

The third call was in a husky voice. *"Find out why Barry Dean had headaches, lady. Then you'll get all your answers."* I sat up straight, taken aback. The caller had hung up without leaving a name. I played the message four times, but could not recognize the voice. My caller ID said the number was unavailable. I saved the message and moved on.

Shane Stockham's contrite tone was next. *"I am so sorry we had a problem yesterday, Goldy. It was all my fault. And by the way, I'm quitting coaching at Elk Park Prep. We're just having too many problems. Anyway, I hope you won't press charges against me for coming at you yesterday."* He paused, and I almost felt sorry for him. Almost. *"If you're not too mad at me, Page and I are still hoping to have this party tomorrow. At our place, at noon. Come by whenever you need to set up. Goldy...I hope you can forgive me."* He signed off.

Shane Stockham was doing *really badly*. Well, this I knew from Marla, Page, and now him. But he had quit coaching? Just because he and his wife had had a tiff at the jewelry event?

The final call was from Pam Disharoon. *"My friend phoned and said you wanted me to call, so here I am. But you're not there. I'll be at P and G tomorrow, Wednesday, from ten to six. Same on Thursday and Friday, and ten to ten on Saturday. OK?"* She didn't sound pleased, and she didn't bother to say good-bye.

I put on my apron and reflected. Arch was mad at me, Shane was sorry as hell, and Pam was miffed. And I wasn't sure why any of them were feeling the way they were. But it was the third call I'd received that had me the most bewildered. *Find out why Barry Dean had headaches.* Well, I was trying to find out. And who had made that call? Raoul, the construction worker? Rob Eakin, the mall's acting manager? Victor Wilson? The caller had been a male, I was pretty sure, and not like anyone I'd heard before.

A knock on the front door derailed that particular train of thought. My peephole revealed strawberry-blond Alicia, my supplier since I'd opened Goldilocks' Catering. She hauled in baskets of fresh wild mushrooms—stunning arrays of everything from chanterelles to Portobellos—plus marbled slabs of standing rib roast, lusciously flavorful greenhouse-grown strawberries and rhubarb, and the rest of the supplies for the next two days' parties. As she was leaving, she handed me a brightly wrapped compact disc.

"It's for your kid. I can't understand this music," she said with a wink, "but the guy at the store told me this is what they're listening to these days. Tell Arch happy birthday from me."

I thanked Alicia profusely, gave her a check for the supplies, and got to work storing the food. Once done, I stood immobilized in the middle of our kitchen. Frustration gnawed at my brain. I needed to cook. Working with food always helped put things in perspective.

On my new computer, I pulled up the menu for Shane's luncheon party. Yes, I was going to do it. He had apologized; his wife had apologized. Besides, he was the one who'd flown through the air and landed on the lounge floor. Maybe he was quitting coaching lacrosse because he was black-and-blue. Maybe he was quitting because he'd been thrashed by a *mom*.

I felt my mouth curl into a smile. Finally, *finally,* I was beginning to look forward to doing the Stockhams' lunch. I tried to recall the layout of their place. The house itself was a gorgeous log dwelling in a stunning development of executive homes near the entrance to the Aspen Meadow Wildlife Preserve. As my printer spat out the menu, recipes, and schedule, I called Shane back and left a message thanking him for his apology. All was forgiven, I said, while making a serious mental note to bring a can of Mace to the party, just in case he lost it again. In my message, I enthusiastically concluded that my crew and I would start setting up around ten tomorrow.

I searched for and found my Mace, then slipped it into my purse. As I scanned the menus, I tried to recall everything I'd heard from Marla about Shane and Page. According to Marla, Shane's store, The Gadget Guy, had received an eviction notice from Westside Mall. This notice had to have come from Barry. Complicating Shane's problems were 1) Westside wanted a million bucks' worth of back rent from him, and 2) his wife Page had a compulsive shopping problem, an addiction severe enough to warrant antidepressants and group therapy. Moreover, Page was locked in a to-the-death competition with her sister Pam, for *stuff*.

But how had Shane and Page Stockham felt about Barry? If either one of them had been on bad terms with him, why had they come to the jewelry event? Ah...but I knew the answer to that. More than anything, Page craved whatever big-ticket items sister Pam managed to land. Apparently, Page hadn't gotten what she wanted. No doubt that was why she and her husband had fought. I'd have to ask Tom if the videotape had shown anything else about the whole Shane-Page-Pam-Barry situation.

I made myself a perfect cup of espresso to wash down a couple of aspirin and two homemade caramel brownies that Alicia had thoughtfully left on the kitchen table. Oh, boy, I thought, as warm fuzzies spiraled through my veins. Nothing like chocolate and coffee to kill pain.

I switched files and typed all I'd learned that day into the "Barry" file. Sipping the last of the coffee, I added my new crop of questions and licked my fingers. Then I read over the file. Why did the image of grasping at straws come to mind? I ignored the image, washed my hands, and rinsed the strawberries and rhubarb.

My fax rang. Since Arch's short-lived foray into quantum physics had taught me that, indeed, the watched pot never boils, I was sure the same principle applied to fax machines. So I trimmed and halved the juicy strawberries, cut the crunchy emerald-and-ruby rhubarb into tidy widths, and mixed both of them with a judicious combination of cornstarch and sugar. Yum.

I carefully set the bowls of glistening fruit aside, then grabbed the spill of faxed pages. The brief cover letter was followed by a photocopied page from Barry Dean's medical records. Ha!

I read the doctor's notes and then, stunned, sat down to read them again.

Pt. fought with a friend, who pushed him down. Pt. lost balance, fell into deep ditch, landed on back of head.

Headaches ever since. Pt. v. stressed. Thinks he may have tumor. Pain excruciating. Vicodin script, follow in 2w.

I swallowed hard. Dog*gone* it. If only, if *only*, Barry had told his doctor who this belligerent "friend" was. Finding out why Barry had headaches might be the key, but it looked as if I'd have to wait for Mr. Anonymous Phone Call to elucidate that particular datum.

Then again, maybe Barry *had* told his doctor the identity of the pusher. *My girlfriend, who set a P.I. on my tail. My other girlfriend, the lingerie saleswoman. The owner of The Gadget Guy, after he slapped my face with his eviction notice. The construction manager, before he suddenly quit.* And those were only the folks who immediately came to mind. Poor Barry.

I nibbled on the brownie crumbs and puzzled over the fax. This fight-with-a-friend tidbit had to get to the cops. Once they knew this, *they* could question Dr. Louis Maxwell. So how did I pop this information over to law enforcement without getting myself into big-time hot water?

I started working on the Stockham lunch. Shane and I had done the contract at the end of March, when he'd shown me his sumptuously furnished home, including a damask-and-chintz dining room and glassed-in garden room. Did he know back then that he was about to be evicted from the mall? I didn't have a clue.

I stared at the list of dishes.

Shane had wanted at least some of the food to be in the shape of electronic equipment, he'd told me. He'd shown me a few gadgets, and I of course knew what Arch's collection of electronic marvels looked like. No matter what the thing *did,* I decided, it either resembled a remote control or a pancake. For this reason, we'd decided on a first course of Asian dumpling soup, with the dumplings in the shape of portable compact disc players. As I was also set to serve wonderfully flavorful soup at the potential mall tenants' lunch on Thursday, I'd already made and frozen batches of the oddly shaped dumplings during one of my recent fits of insomnia. I would defrost them early tomorrow before floating them in the boiling broth. The broth, however, still needed to be made.

From the refrigerator side of the walk-in, I pulled out three vats of homemade chicken stock that I'd begun defrosting before starting on the jewelry event. As it heated, I sliced onion and gingerroot, packed fragrant Chinese parsley into measuring cups, and carefully added them to the steaming stock. Within ten minutes, rich scents of the Far East wafted through the kitchen.

Shane had also requested three gourmet salads, to be served *plated*. I groaned. I needed to talk to Liz Fury, to make sure she could work the lunch with me. As we worked, we could visit about all that had happened. Since I knew she would still be working the wedding reception, I put in a call to her home. *"Please give me a ring about the Stockham party,"* I implored.

While I was cooking the shrimp for the Today-Only Avocado-Shrimp Boats, Tom unexpectedly showed up.

"I thought you were swamped," I exclaimed with more surprise than I intended. I turned off the whirring food processor and gave him a hug. "It's only four o'clock."

He chortled. "Afraid I've been fired, Miss G.? And that's why I'm home? Actually, I . . . just decided to delegate that work. Anyway, I've been thinking about cutting back to half-time, since my wife is making so much dough with her catering business. And this way, I can go get Arch, if you want."

I smiled in spite of myself, pulled away, and poured the sweet-sour dressing for the shrimp into a large jar. "I . . . I went to see Julian," I confessed. "I know you and Hulsey both said not to. But I was too worried."

"See what I mean?" Tom replied, with a grim smile. "If you're not in a mess, you make one."

"He looks awful," I continued. "Plus, I was wondering if the lounge videotapes showed any conflict between Page Stockham and her sister, Pam Disharoon, or between Shane Stockham and Barry Dean . . ." I stopped talking, suddenly suspicious. "Tom, won't you please just tell me why you're home so early?"

"We-ell, since I shoved my work onto others, and since I'm not assigned to the Dean case, I got to worrying about my recently injured wife, and wanted to see if she needed help—"

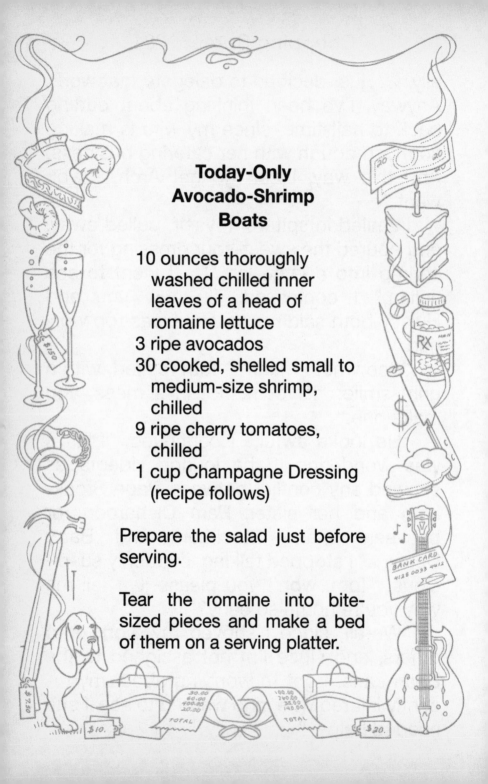

Today-Only Avocado-Shrimp Boats

10 ounces thoroughly washed chilled inner leaves of a head of romaine lettuce

3 ripe avocados

30 cooked, shelled small to medium-size shrimp, chilled

9 ripe cherry tomatoes, chilled

1 cup Champagne Dressing (recipe follows)

Prepare the salad just before serving.

Tear the romaine into bite-sized pieces and make a bed of them on a serving platter.

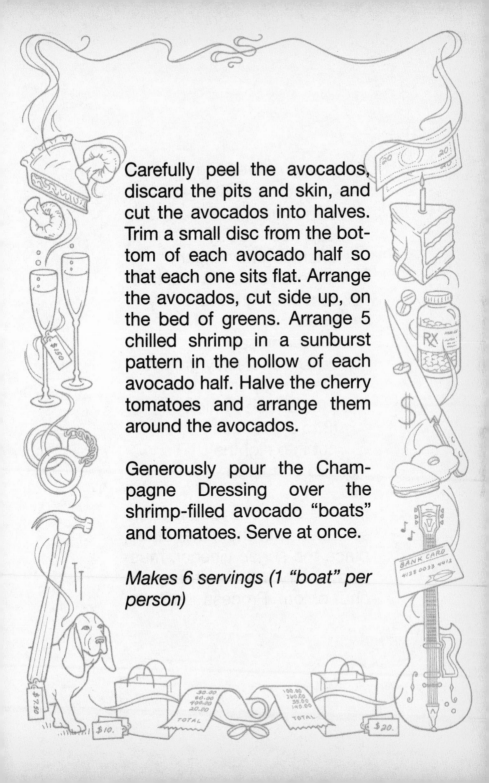

Carefully peel the avocados, discard the pits and skin, and cut the avocados into halves. Trim a small disc from the bottom of each avocado half so that each one sits flat. Arrange the avocados, cut side up, on the bed of greens. Arrange 5 chilled shrimp in a sunburst pattern in the hollow of each avocado half. Halve the cherry tomatoes and arrange them around the avocados.

Generously pour the Champagne Dressing over the shrimp-filled avocado "boats" and tomatoes. Serve at once.

Makes 6 servings (1 "boat" per person)

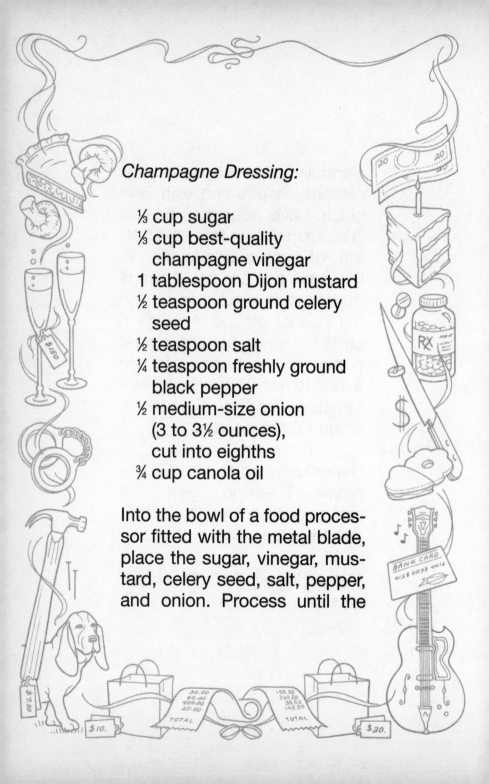

Champagne Dressing:

⅓ cup sugar
⅓ cup best-quality
  champagne vinegar
1 tablespoon Dijon mustard
½ teaspoon ground celery
  seed
½ teaspoon salt
¼ teaspoon freshly ground
  black pepper
½ medium-size onion
  (3 to 3½ ounces),
  cut into eighths
¾ cup canola oil

Into the bowl of a food processor fitted with the metal blade, place the sugar, vinegar, mustard, celery seed, salt, pepper, and onion. Process until the onion is completely pulverized, then slowly dribble in the oil, processing until thoroughly emulsified. The dressing should not be kept more than 3 days.

I turned back to the shrimp, now a tantalizing pink in their lemon-and-herb bath. "I'm fine."

"Touchy, touchy. Maybe you don't want to hear this, either, but I think that even though I'm home, you should still go pick up Arch today. He's worried about you."

"About his new guitar, you mean. Now wrecked and in police custody."

"Look, I called down to Westside Music, and they're going to phone their other stores to see if we can get another one."

"Uh-huh."

"Miss G., would you come back over here, please?"

I drained the first batch of shrimp, put down the sauté pan, and walked into his open arms. He gently held me as he asked, again, how I was doing.

"Not so hot."

"Explain."

"I feel responsible for Julian." My voice wobbled treacherously. "I feel—helpless, and you know how I *hate* that."

"Excuse me, Wife, but I've never seen *you* helpless."

"Thanks for the vote of confidence, Husband."

He glanced over my shoulder at the counter. "How about if I make us enchiladas? Would that make you feel better?"

I actually laughed, then pulled away from his embrace. "Sounds wonderful. But Tom, there's something I need to tell you first."

"You mean besides the fact that you visited Julian against orders? I don't think I should hear this."

I began shelling the shrimp while he washed up and readied the enchilada ingredients. Had I turned over the faxed pages so he wouldn't see them? I couldn't remember. "Well, it's like this. I've sort of been looking into this whole thing—"

"Yeah, so I gathered. Sounds more like you've been *snooping* around. Maybe I *don't* want to hear this—"

"Somebody called here a while ago, didn't leave a name. Said I needed to look into why Barry Dean had such terrible headaches. I saved the message. Anyway. Then I, uh, learned that a friend of Barry's pushed him down a while back. After the fall, he had such bad headaches that he had to take prescription painkillers."

Tom considered the pan in front of him.

288 Diane Mott Davidson

The corn oil he'd heated to soften the tortillas sputtered. He lowered the first golden disk into the pan, flipped it, and laid it in a nest of paper towels.

Finally he asked, "And a prescription for painkillers after having fallen during this fight with a friend is significant because...?"

"Well, I just thought if you cops could find who called here, or who the friend was that pushed Barry down, you might find out who killed Barry."

My ever-observant investigator-husband swept his eagle eyes over the kitchen. Then he washed his hands, moved down to my computer, and turned over the pile of faxed pages.

"Kee-rist. How in the hell did you get these from a—" he raised a bushy, sand-colored eyebrow at the letterhead, "from Barry Dean's *doctor*?"

"That's one thing you *really* don't want to know."

He groaned, then said, "OK, Miss G., I will pass this on to the guys working the case—"

"Please don't give them those other pages, OK?" I imagined Hulsey's furious face as he thrust the faxed report in my face, demanding to know how long I'd fraudulently worked under the alias of Dr. Shoemaker.

"Don't worry," Tom reassured me. "But I have to warn you, whoever shoved Barry down probably was not a 'friend.' People lie when they go to the doctor. 'How many cigarettes do you smoke a day?' 'Oh, doc,' says the pack-a-day smoker, 'maybe two or three.' 'Who pushed you down and caused these headaches?' 'A friend.' Yeah, right. And especially with our Mr. Dean being as secretive as he was, he'd lie more easily than he'd tell the truth."

"Oh-kay," I said, as I peeled fresh Bosc pears for the next salad. "I just thought knowing more about that fight and those headaches might help Julian."

Tom listened to the tape with the anonymous message several times. He did not tell me what he planned to do about it. After that, he and I worked side by side, but mostly in silence, for the next half-hour. When I finally asked if he had found out any more about the Dean case, he shook his head. He did remind me, however, that because Julian's fingerprints were on the

murder weapon, he would face arraignment no matter what.

"How can they charge him on so little
evidence? Who made that nine-one-one
call alerting the police to Barry's murder,
anyway?"

"They've listened to it a hundred times.
It was from a pay phone outside Prince and
Grogan. They can't even tell if it was a
high-voiced man or a low-voiced woman."
He shrugged. "If something comes along to
clear Julian, he'll be out."

"Somehow I don't feel reassured."

"Miss G. What we do know is that
someone tried to mow Barry Dean—and
you—down, and didn't succeed in killing
him, and then someone knifed him, and *did*
succeed in killing him. And that person left
evidence of himself or herself *somewhere*.
We just need to find it," he concluded. I
was thankful he hadn't added a comment
about needles or haystacks. "That's *we*
meaning the sheriff's department, Miss G.
Not *we* as in Goldy, Marla, and Tom. OK?"

"Of course," I replied sweetly. He
groaned again.

CHAPTER 10

I finished the pears, dropped them into a simmering, barely sugared syrup, and gave directions to Tom for the poaching and finishing. Then I grabbed my coat and announced I was off to pick up Arch. Tom grinned and swore he'd have dinner ready when we got back.

In the gathering twilight, I held my husband's smile in my mind as I zipped toward Elk Park. Maybe he wasn't too mad at Dr. Gertrude Shoemaker, impostor neurologist, after all. I knew it irked him when I tried to insert myself into his cases...but I never did it when I didn't have some kind of personal stake in solving the crime. Someone shoots out our window, poisons a client at an event I'm catering, or kills a fellow and exults when our family friend is arrested for the crime—yes, I was going to get involved. As they used to say in my native New Jersey, *Whaddayathink I'm gonna do?*

Darkness blew in along with charcoal clouds from the west. The high hills covered with pine trees turned to black velvet. A whirl of snow fogged the windshield; I flipped on the wipers. I thought of the scantily clad, hapless lacrosse players. *Welcome to springtime in the Rockies!*

I turned through the massive stone gates and gunned the van up the winding driveway that led to Elk Park Preparatory School. A caravan of four-wheel-drive vehicles, their lights on, sped down the driveway in the opposite direction. The kids must have been dismissed early. A lot of parents actually watched the practice, then called the coach later to offer unconstructive criticism. I wondered if *that* was why Shane had quit.

Snow swirled into the parking lot. Half a dozen Lexuses and BMW's, their engines running, clustered by the pathway that came down from the fields. High above the lot, by the portable toilet at the edge of the fields, a few camel's-hair-clad parents stamped their feet and clapped with mittened hands. Arch would die of embarrassment if I even showed my face at lacrosse practice, so I stayed put.

And that was how I saw Shane Stockham threaten a woman. Again.

The two figures first attracted my attention when they whacked open the thick wooden doors of the headmaster's house. They paid no attention to the resultant crash or echoing bang of hinges. Shane Stockham I recognized instantly: His stocky body, rigid stance, and distinctive gait were unmistakable. He wore a ten-gallon hat and a sheepskin jacket—de rigueur Colorado wear for the upscale wannabe cowboy. Raised voices indicated things weren't going well between him and his companion, a fashionable-looking woman wearing a mid-calf trench coat and leather boots. A twisted Burberry scarf held her blond-brown hair in place. She walked swiftly and gave off an assured, regal air. At one point, she stopped by an electric lantern to listen to Shane. After a moment, she reached out to touch his shoulder. He slapped her hand away and vigorously told her to shut *up*. The woman, momentarily thrown off balance, recovered and yelled at Shane to back off. I squinted to see her face in the gloom.

It was Ellie McNeely.

I groped through my bag for the Mace. I clutched it with my right hand and vaulted from the van. Shane might apologize on the phone all he wanted, but if he thought he was going to hurt my pal Ellie, he had, as my mother used to say, another think coming.

As I tore across the snow-dusted lot, I tried to imagine why those two had even been *in* the headmaster's house. Meetings of all kinds were held in the luxurious residence, with its real Oriental rugs and antique furnishings. But if they'd been at a meeting, where were the other folks? Ellie's daughter, after recovering from her parents' brutal divorce, was one of the handful of sophomores in the National Honor Society; Shane's airhead twin daughters were freshmen. I couldn't imagine that both parents had been called in by the headmaster because the girls had somehow gotten into an argument. When I was ten yards away from them, I ducked behind one of the Lexuses.

"... trying to tell you that circumstances have changed," Shane ranted, "and you're not *listening!*"

"I am," Ellie retorted, "but you know very well that all of the financial commitments of the school are made on the basis of those pledges. We offer teachers positions with fixed salaries... Oh, Goldy? What on earth are you doing here?"

The two of them stopped in their tracks. Both looked at me curiously as I stepped out from the shadow of the Lexus. As the snow drifted down, I tried to think of what to say. The freezing can of Mace was making my right hand ache.

"Uh," I said, "uh, I just saw you two..." I fumbled about for words and squeezed the Mace can. Shane had backed well away from Ellie, and I was unsure of what to say or do. At the far edge of the lot, someone in a silver SUV honked.

"Well!" said Ellie. "That's my daughter, honking *my* horn at *me*. I have to go. Talk to you later, Goldy." With that, she turned with a sweep of trench coat and walked delicately across the snow to her van.

"Ellie," Shane called after her, his tone suddenly apologetic—*hmm*—and calm, even cajoling. "Please, Ellie. Please think about what I'm saying—"

"No-o!" she called, making her voice sweet. She didn't turn back.

I tried to give Shane a look that was both punitive and sympathetic. I was itching to know about their conflict. Shane rubbed his eyes, tilted his head back, and groaned.

"Goldy, so, did you get my message about tomorrow?"

His question startled me. I shivered as if unexpectedly chilled, tucked my hands hastily into my pockets, and let go of the Mace. Only then did I give him a bright smile. Even if I did have more reason to be wary of him than ever, Shane, after all, was a client.

"Yes, and I left one for you. We'll be there at ten—" I stopped. My God, I'd forgotten something. In the bustle of last week's events and the commotion of the last twenty-four hours, I had neglected to obtain Shane's final payment for the lunch.

I emphatically had *not* received the last six hundred dollars he owed Goldilocks' Catering...which should have been paid five days ago, before he'd gone on a jewelry-leasing binge with his wife. This was not the gratuity, which I would be picking up after the event. This was the second payment for the food and service. It was just the sort of detail that I'd feared would slip between the cracks, now that I'd become so busy. My heart sank.

"But," I continued with another blinding smile, "I'll need the second installment before we can do the party. I've got all the food ready."

"Look, Goldy, I am *extremely* sorry for what happened yesterday. My wife is...on medication....Things just sort of fell apart. We're very enthusiastic about this luncheon party, believe me."

"I need the check, Shane."

"There are so many things I need to talk to you about," he countered nervously, cutting his eyes from side to side, as if looking for someone or something more important to do. "So many things that I don't know where to begin..."

My hand slipped back into my pocket

and I gripped the Mace. As Shane rattled on about how successful the luncheon was going to be, I wondered where he was going with this conversation. Make that, where Shane was going, period. Tonight he'd flailed at Ellie, then he'd asked me whether I'd received his message. Then he'd refused to address the nonpayment issue, and hopped back to yesterday's event. My skin broke out in a chilled sweat. The only other person who jumped from topic to topic like that—to keep you off guard—was The Jerk, my ex. And he usually started leaping around verbally before he punched me in the face.

"I'm enthusiastic, too, Shane!" I said as I edged away. The last bunch of lacrosse players was straggling down the steep path from the now-deserted field. It was an idyllic scene. Street lamps brightened the parking lot. Slow-drifting snowflakes resembled feathers shaken from a pillow. Behind the gaggle of athletes stumbled Arch. He might be bigger and stronger than he'd been at eleven, but he hadn't given up his permanent place at the back of the line. "Gotta go, Shane. Remember the check tomorrow, OK? First thing, before we set up."

To my dismay, he bolted toward me. Should I shriek and make a run for it? I tightened my grip on the Mace.

"Look, Goldy. Don't run off, please. 'Cuz I... really want to talk to you. It's important, I promise."

If he was going to tell me that he didn't have the money for the party, that he'd pay me next week, next month, or next year, then I was going to punch him in the face, future clients be damned.

"It's about the mall, you see," Shane persisted. "You're such a great person, Goldy, I feel as if I really could tell you—" He hesitated.

"Shane, please. I'm getting cold. Tell me what?"

He lowered his voice. "It's about Barry Dean."

I stopped short. I had to restrain myself from grabbing Shane by his sheepskin lapels and shaking him.

"*What* about Barry Dean?"

"Well, it's just that... I don't know how much you know about the way a mall works—"

"Look, can you just get to the point? My son's waiting for me, Shane."

He gulped, then brushed melting snow off his handsome, square face. His brown eyes shone with worry. And guilt? I wasn't sure.

"I got into trouble. I... did a bad thing, but Barry made it much worse. I... cooked the books of The Gadget Guy. The reason I did it was that once we broke a certain level of sales, the amount of rent we owed Pennybaker International, according to the terms of our lease agreement, went way up. With... Page's shopping problem, and our current level of debt, we just couldn't pay more rent. Just could *not*. So... Barry, who had done next to nothing in terms of his promised promotion for mall tenants, offered to do a deal. He wouldn't evict me if I paid him fifty thou up front in cash, off the books, and another fifty thou at the end of the year. But... I couldn't. So he pulled the plug on me. There, I said it." He paused to take a raspy breath and fixed me with his sad stare. "I know you're going to ask me did I tell the police about this. The answer is no, I couldn't do that either. Risk going to jail for cooking my own books? Forget it. So I'm trying to get into on-line ordering now, out of our house. But if any of my potential backers—the people who are coming to lunch tomorrow—find out I messed with the figures at the store, they'll run away faster than a herd of elk. I didn't cheat anybody, Goldy, I just wouldn't pay that mall their extortionary demands. And I couldn't afford to pay Barry his bribe. I don't have that kind of money."

In the near distance, a car honked. This honk came from *my* van. *Arch* was honking at *me*.

"Shane, why are you telling me all this?"

He ran his fingers through his tousled hair. "Because I know your young friend has been accused of Barry's murder. I didn't want you to think I killed Barry, in case Barry had told you about our...conflict. I can't afford negative publicity at this point. And I've read how you sometimes get involved in these cases—"

"OK, OK. Is this accounting crime what you were just talking to Ellie about? Because she was close to Barry, too?"

Shane snorted. "No, we have an issue...with the school. But being in that mall, I saw the way things went. I mean, in addition to not doing the promotion he promised, Barry was not the most moral of

302 Diane Mott Davidson

guys, you know? He had a woman problem, and I think that's why he wanted the
payoff. To keep up his woman habit. Otherwise, he'd have to stay with old stick-
in-the-mud Ellie McNeely. For a while,
anyway."

"Mom!" Arch shrieked. "Come on! Let's
split! You've got a cell call! I'm starving! It's
cold! Mom!"

"I have to go." My thoughts were tangled from all the new information. Did I believe Shane, or not? I wasn't sure. "So you
think this fifty thou was for him, then, not
the mall?"

"Of course it was for him! What do you
think I've been trying to tell you here?"

"Shane, tell the cops all this."

"You mean your husband?"

"No, no, Tom's off the case. Anything
you can tell the cops about Barry will help
them get the big picture. If you have any
documentation of what . . . Barry did, show
it to them." I did not say, Documentation of
what you *say* Barry did. But I thought it.
"Maybe Barry pulled this blackmail stuff
with other store owners. Just call the department and get connected with the assigned investigators. Please? Believe me, it

will look much, much better for you if you tell the cops what happened. If they find out elsewhere, they'll come after you."

"*Mom!* Goldy Schulz! Come *on!*"

Shane pressed his lips together, then backed away. Somehow, I didn't think he was bolting to a phone.

My stiff, chilled fingers wrenched the driver door open, and I was confronted with my son's stiff, chilled face. His fingertips pressed hard on the mouthpiece of the cell phone.

"I am *so* mad at you!" he hissed furiously. "First you get my coach to quit. Then you come to pick me up, only you don't pick me up, because you get in a long conversation with my *former* coach. Which is what you *always* do. Talk, talk, talk. So I sit in here. Cold. Waiting. Starving. And now we won't be able to go home, because you're going to have to talk to *this* person." He thrust the phone at me.

I gritted my teeth. When Arch acted like this, I didn't know if he was showing the dark side of teenage temperament—which seemed to be *all* dark, come to think of it— or if he was following a more troublesome path on the way to behavior similar to that of his Jerk father. The amazing aspect of this little speech from Arch was how articulate he was when he was enraged. Since this was the opposite of his suave father, who became obscenely incoherent when he was angry, I fastened my seat belt and put the car into gear. I was not, I decided, going to respond to Arch.

"I'm so *hungry,*" Arch growled, as I put the phone to my ear.

I pressed the phone into the front of my jacket to cover the mouthpiece. "Tom is making enchiladas, and—"

"I don't *care!*"

Give up, my inner voice counseled, before I reminded him how much he loved Tom's cooking. So I did. I piloted the van toward the edge of the snow-frosted parking lot. Into the phone, I purred sweetly, "This is Goldy Schulz of Goldilocks' Catering. May I help you?"

"You must be making a lot of money, to put someone on hold on a cell phone for seven minutes!"

I sighed. Just what I needed today, one more crab. Tomorrow night I would make crab dip.

"How can I help you?" I suddenly remembered the anonymous call I'd received earlier. This voice was deep, too...but I was fairly sure I was being bawled out by a female. Still, you can't be too careful. "And who are you, if you don't mind my asking?"

"You can come pick up this puppy. Barry Dean's basset hound. He's late."

"He's dead," I countered bluntly.

"I'm looking right at him."

I paused. Maybe I needed yet more caffeine, even if it was almost dinnertime. "Who is calling, please?"

"Goldy, fer chrissakes," growled the husky voice. "It's Darlene Petrucchio. You useta come into my store, and that kid who useta live with you useta come in, too. Darlene's Antiques and Collectibles. And what do you mean, he's dead? He's sitting on my kitchen floor, drooling."

"Barry Dean is *dead,*" I said, speaking very slowly and distinctly.

"Well, I *know* that!" cried an exasperated Darlene Petrucchio. "Otherwise, why would I be calling you? Barry called yesterday and said he was leaving you his dog. He's *late.*"

OK. I was driving, one-handed, down the slick, snow-covered curves of the Elk

Park Prep driveway. I couldn't stop to talk sense with chain-smoking, raspy-voiced Darlene of Darlene's Antiques and Collectibles, or my son would explode. I needed a time-out. I needed to get out of this Abbott and Costello routine about dogs and dead guys.

"I can't take care of this hound another night!" Darlene shouted, coughing. "He howls and cries and he's driving Gus and me nuts! Come and get him, will you? He's *late*."

"*Who* is late?" I tried again, with deliberate loudness, like an American bellowing English at a European.

"Jesus H. Christ, Goldy! The *puppy* is late! That's his name! *Late!* How many times do I have to tell ya?"

"Thanks, Darlene!" I sang into the phone. Studiously avoiding the word *late* or its cognate, *later,* I said, "I'll be over ... after dinner ... say, half past seven. Where do you live?"

"Where do you think?" she shrieked, as a dog howled mournfully in the background. "Next door to Barry Dean, fer chrissakes!"

To save us further miscommunication,

she slammed the phone down and broke the connection.

Maybe I could bring Darlene and Gus a box of chamomile tea. She seemed to need it.

Regarding the central question now running my life, who murdered Barry Dean, I now had new input. Barry Dean had left me his *dog*. No question, that would really clarify my thinking on this case.

CHAPTER 11

I met Tom's hearty greeting at our front door by falling into his arms. "I need help!" I gargled. The reason I didn't add "My son's driving me crazy!" was that Arch was right behind me.

"I've got a glass of sherry waiting for you in the kitchen," Tom replied, without missing a beat. "Driving to Elk Park Prep can be awfully demanding."

Arch grunted before announcing: "I'm starving!"—in case I hadn't recalled that crucial information.

"Dinner'll be ready in less than five!" Tom replied, his voice jovial.

Arch hefted up his backpack, lacrosse stick, and bag, and vaulted up the steps two at a time. The door to his room slammed resoundingly.

"I can't drink sherry," I told Tom as I plodded into the kitchen. "I have to drive somewhere tonight."

"Tell me you didn't take on another catering job. Tell me you're going to stay and enjoy these enchiladas."

"After dinner, I have to go get a dog. His name is Late. Wait a second. I'll tell you all about it *later,* while we eat."

Tom smiled, winked, and wisely decided not to ask me how I'd become ensnared in canine rescue. Instead he peered into the oven, nodded approvingly, then removed a large pan of fat enchiladas. A thick layer of melted Cheddar cheese bubbled over the dark, pungent enchilada sauce that in turn smothered the rolled and stuffed tortillas. Tom called upstairs.

"Hey, Arch! The enchiladas are done! In fact, they're overdone! Next time don't let your mother take so long!"

Arch roared with rage.

When Tom turned back to the kitchen, chuckling, I said, "Don't start. He already blames me enough for...oh, *everything*. And please don't use the word *late*. It has to do with the dog that I need to go pick up."

Tom ignored me, which was a good thing. Two minutes later the three of us were digging into sour cream–topped enchiladas bursting with Tom's mélange of spicy beef, beans, onions, garlic, black olives, and picante. I moaned with pleasure. Arch shot me a disapproving look which said *Even at home, Mom can embarrass you!*

My mind returned to the parking-lot confrontation between Shane Stockham and Ellie McNeely. Later, when Arch had gone upstairs to do homework, I would tell Tom about it, to get his ideas. In any event, I was back to feeling uncomfortable about catering at Shane and Page's mini-mansion the next day. Maybe I'd feel better if I could talk to Ellie and find out why she'd argued with Shane.

When my inner mind shrieked, *You're so damn nosy,* I forked in another delectable bite.

"Anybody talk to Julian today?" Arch demanded.

I recounted the high points of my visit to the jail. Tom had also dropped in on Julian, but had left when the defense lawyer showed up. My son then asked when *he* could go see Julian, and I said probably this weekend. Arch's mood lightened a bit. This made me think that perhaps the cause for his anxiety had not been my usual mom-misbehavior, but his worry about Julian, who was like a big brother to him.

"I'm wondering," I ventured at length, "does anybody mind if we adopt another dog for a while?"

"Uh-oh," Tom groaned.

Arch, however, brightened. "Sure! I can help. What kind of dog is it?"

"It's a basset hound."

"Miss G.?"

"OK, it's Barry Dean's basset hound. Barry left it to me."

"He *left* it to you?" Tom echoed. "We're just now getting his lawyer to talk about the will. How could you know about what he left and to whom?"

"His neighbor called. Darlene, the woman who owns that used-stuff store on Main Street. Apparently Barry called her yesterday before he died. Said if anything happened to him, I was supposed to take care of his dog, who is really a puppy. Darlene's going to have a conniption fit if she has to have him another night."

Somehow, my wonderful husband absorbed and translated this. "Miss G., why do you think Barry would ask *you* to take care of his dog? Are you saying he had a premonition that he was going to get killed, and called his neighbors to make provisions for his puppy?" he asked mildly.

Arch, his curiosity piqued now that he'd chowed down five enchiladas, raised his eyebrows. He'd wanted a second dog ever since we acquired Jake, a bloodhound who'd been mistreated before we took him in. Now Arch saw his chance coming. I did not want to ponder what Scout the cat would think of another dog adoption, however. Things could get ugly.

"I don't know why Barry wanted me to have his puppy," I told my family truthfully. "But I really think I should go get him."

Tom mumbled something about letting the cops know what I was doing. Also, the department would need to find out if Barry had said anything *else* to Darlene. I told him the cops could talk all they wanted to

Darlene, to me, and what the heck, to the dog.

We finished our meal thrashing out logistics for the week, who would be where when, how the driving would work, and so on. Such are the joys of contemporary domestic life. Arch and I thanked Tom for the fabulous dinner. Tom offered to do the dishes, and I accepted with gratitude.

"I'll come with you, Mom," Arch piped up unexpectedly as he finished loading the silverware into the dishwasher, a job he had done without being asked. "I got most of my homework done in school. While you're driving, I'll take care of the dog."

"Why, thanks, Arch. I'd love your help."

And so off we went.

"You're *late*," Darlene announced ungraciously as she swung open the door of her log cabin. Short, slender, and about sixty, Darlene wore an emerald green turtleneck and a fashionable-ten-years-ago black velvet skirt and vest. Her salon-dyed light orange hair was meticulously arranged in an Annette Funicello bubble, and her impeccable-but-heavy makeup glowed in the light from an overhead chandelier made from antlers. She looked like a perfectly preserved dried apricot.

"Very late," she added, with the quirk of an arched, red-penciled eyebrow.

I took a deep breath and reminded myself to be pleasant. I smiled and said, "Let's not use the dog's name, OK? Darlene, you remember my son Arch? He loves dogs and will help me get Late home." From inside the cabin, Barry's hound howled so loudly I suspected he'd heard me.

O-woo! O-woo! Get me out of here!

"C'mon in, he's waiting for you!" Darlene closed the door behind us. She added, "He's in the kitchen. I had to pile some stuff by the door to keep him in." A prolonged crash preceded a spill of cardboard boxes out the kitchen door. A streak of black, gold, and white hurtled toward us. "Late!" Darlene shrieked, in a voice that would have started an avalanche.

Late paid no attention whatsoever. Arch had dropped to his knees as the dog rushed us. The bassett bounded up, tongue extended, slathering Arch's face with kisses. My son, overwhelmed, toppled back on his behind. Late howled with exultation. Darlene screeched a torrent of commands that the puppy ignored.

"Darlene!" I called over the general confusion. "Can you tell me exactly what Barry said? You know, when he called to tell you about his puppy?"

Darlene was headed toward the kitchen. I followed, and managed to trip over only one box upended by the puppy.

"Here's his food dish, water dish, and vitamins," she said, as she dumped mismatched plastic bowls and other canine paraphernalia into a grocery bag. "He was outa Puppy Chow." She whacked the bag down beside me on the counter. "All's Barry said to me was, 'If I have to go on a business trip allova sudden, I want Goldy Schulz t'have my dog.' Then he asked if I knew who you were, the caterer who helps her husband solve crimes, and I said yeah, and he asked me to go get the puppy right then. I said, 'So yer goin' on a business trip, then?' And he says, 'Maybe.' So I went and got the puppy. That was yesterday. I'm tellin' ya, I can't go through another night listening to him howl and whine. I mean, I used to watch Barry's house and the puppy when he had to be out of town for a coupla nights, but it's not like he left me any cash to take care of the hound for the rest of his *life*. I am sorry Barry died, though. He was a nice neighbor, if a little— Well, you know. Overdosing on the social life."

Out in the hallway, Late's piercing yip was giving me a headache. Arch was egging him on in Boy's Dog-Speak: *Yeah, boy, c'mon boy, sit, yeah, roll over, yeah! OK, I'll rub your tummy. Bet you're hungry, right, boy?*

Overdosing on the social life? "Did Barry have many girlfriends?" I ventured.

Darlene rolled her eyes, opened her refrigerator, and popped open a beer. She did not offer me one, which was probably just as well.

"Look, I already talked to that private dick—"

"John Rufus?"

Darlene slurped foam. "Yup, and I told him about the bra saleslady—"

"Pam?"

"Yup." Darlene tried unsuccessfully to suppress a belch. "That's what the cops called her when they showed me her picture. Blonde who wears her hair in sort of a pickaninny?"

"The very one."

"Well, she's been over there, too. Those two, Pam and Ellie. That's all I know about Barry's girlfriends. 'Cept he didn't leave either one of 'em his dog."

"Thanks."

Darlene put down the beer, picked up the grocery bag, and shoved it at me. Since she couldn't find any puppy food, she added, she'd given Late some chili last night. He'd seemed to like it.

"Chili?" I repeated, nonplussed. *No wonder you were up all night.*

When Darlene raised that thin eyebrow again, I hustled back to the foyer. Arch had thoughtfully brought along a leash and was clipping it to Late's collar. Late, panting, twisted his stubby, muscled neck to look me over. He was a hefty, short-haired black hound with a wide, white chest and magnificent gold streaks along his face. He did resemble Barry's old hound, Honey, especially with his red-rimmed eyelids around large woeful eyes. *I'm grieving,* his countenance seemed to say, *cheer me up.*

"He's just three months old," Darlene explained from behind me. She couldn't hide the joy in her voice at the prospect of ridding herself of the hound. "Oh, and he goes to High Country Vet, so you might want to check in over there, you know, see if he needs shots or worming or something."

I thanked Darlene and headed out after Arch and the puppy to the van. Late's enthusiasm for Arch did not extend to going in a car, however, and once we were all inside, the little dog started whining inconsolably. I started the engine. The dog wailed even louder.

"Let me try to calm him down, Mom, before you pull out. I brought him some smoked pigs' ears."

"Jake won't be happy you snitched from his store of treats."

At this, Arch launched into more Dog-Speak: *Don't worry, buddy, your new brother is going to love you, yeah, buddy, Jake's a big old bloodhound who shares everything,* et cetera, et cetera. I disconnected from Arch's reassuring chatter and Late's crying, and studied Barry's chalet-style house next door. Two sheriff's department cars were parked in the driveway. The red police tape that I knew was printed with the word *Evidence* had been strung around the house and yard. Hmm.

Barry's house stood out in this neighborhood because he'd taken great care to make it look handsome. While Darlene had continued to paint her home an opaque lime green—hip some decades ago in Aspen Meadow, like everything else about Darlene—Barry had painted the gingerbread trim of his dark brown wooden house a bright red. Now, the outside lights illuminated not only the Swiss-style abode, but the fresh fall of snow in the front yard. The curtains were pulled, but a lit interior told me the detectives were working.

Without thinking, I released the brake and allowed the van to roll down to Barry's driveway. Arch, preoccupied with calming the dog, did not notice. Nor, apparently, did anyone inside. I powered down my window and stared at the house. *Why did you leave me your dog, Barry?* I heard no answer to my question but puppy whining and the frigid night wind sweeping through the pines.

"Mom!" Arch whispered. "You're freezing me out! Late's shivering! Close the window, would you?" The dog threw back his head and began to howl. *"Mom!* What are you waiting for?"

We took off. Tom was not at home, which puzzled me, but Arch helped me get the separate "pet housing area," as we called it, ready for our latest guest. Because of the catering business, I had to be extra careful about keeping the animals out of the kitchen. I tried not to think of the unsuccessful box barricade Darlene had built for Late.

Late, meanwhile, was getting to know Jake out in our fenced backyard. Like Barry's yard, ours was blanketed with snow. Howls, yips, and growling let us know the two canines hadn't quite decided to be friends. When Arch opened the back door, Jake began to lumber in, but was impeded by Late streaking through his legs. Arch said he'd calm Jake if I could get hold of Late. I quick-stepped into the living room, where Late was avidly sniffing one of Tom's Oriental rugs.

"No you don't, buster." I scooped him up and hugged him to me, then lowered myself into one of the wingback chairs. To my surprise, Late turned, perused my face, and began to sniff my chin. My heart melted at the sight of those droopy brown eyes with their pink rims. The dog appeared worried. *You,* he seemed to be thinking, *definitely aren't Barry.*

"Why did your master leave you to me?" I asked him. "From the sound of it, he had two girlfriends. Why didn't he leave you with one of them? The only thing recommending me was that we already had a hound. Different kind, though."

In my lap, Late panted, but said nothing.

"Was it because of the truck accident?" I asked Late. "Barry was scared because that truck nearly killed him as well as me? So he called his neighbor and said, 'If I die before I get home, give my dog to the caterer'? "

Late still wasn't in a talkative mood, so I just patted him. Arch appeared, carrying a tray of homemade dog biscuits. Apparently, Late's olfactory glands worked as superbly as Jake's, because he whirled, jumped off my lap, and tore toward Arch. Arch, delighted to be once more the center of the basset's universe, started feeding him goodies from the plate. When the phone rang, I headed for it, mostly to prevent myself from mentioning crumbs and dog-mess to Arch.

"I had to finish up something at work," Tom reported from his cellular. "Apparently my delegating didn't work out as well as I'd hoped. Anyway, I didn't want you to worry. Did you get the dog?"

"Yeah, thanks for asking. Arch is spoiling him rotten even as we speak."

"Is he cute?"

"He's black streaked with gold and white, and he has a face frozen in the 'sad' setting."

Tom snorted. "Did Barry ever mention to you that he wanted you to take care of his hound? The detectives are still working at his house."

"Nope. I saw them there, by the way. Do you happen to know who's going to inherit the place? I don't think Barry has any kin."

"I don't know about kin. One of the guys mentioned that Barry had left his goods to the ASPCA. It'll be a while before they can get the transfer worked out, though. Why?"

I couldn't tell my husband *Because I'd like to be able to snoop around in my old friend's house, and figure out why somebody stuck a knife in his gut.* So I just said,

"Oh, I need to know what kind of food he was giving the dog, that's all."

"Uh-huh."

I always wondered why I bothered to lie to Tom, since he could invariably tell when I was skirting the truth. A fierce crackle broke our connection before I could protest, or even ask when he would be home.

Arch appeared in the hall holding the puppy in his arms. Could that be a smile on Late's face?

"I'm going up to finish the last bit of homework I've got," my son announced. "I'll take care of Late. What kind of dumb name is that for a dog, anyway?"

"I have no more idea about that than I do why Barry left him to me."

Arch turned and started up the staircase, his usual clomping replaced by gentle steps. Snug in Arch's arms, Late wagged his tail like a metronome.

In the kitchen, I started some milk heating for hot chocolate. While I stirred heavy cream and sugar into best-quality cocoa, I listened to the answering machine. There was only one message, and it was from Heather, the weeping mall office secretary.

Westside was in limbo over the lunch event I was supposed to be catering on Thursday. She just wanted to give me a heads-up. Super.

I whisked the steaming milk into the cocoa mixture and considered. I had not heard back from Ellie McNeely. The kitchen clock said it was almost nine. Ellie was a friend, so I sipped the cocoa and punched in her number. No answer. Either she wasn't at home or she wasn't picking up.

Arch appeared in the doorway and said he thought Late, who was whining again, might need to go out. Hearing Arch's voice and the whining puppy, Jake started scratching at the door to the pet area. I released Jake while Arch held on to the puppy with one hand and opened the back door with the other. Snuffling wildly at Late while giving me occasional confused looks, Jake seemed both curious about, and disheartened by, our canine orphan. Finally Jake loped through the back door. Late, howling, streaked after the bloodhound. I sensed imminent canine combat, although I was confident Jake could fend for himself. For the first time since we'd arrived home, I caught a glimpse of Scout. The cat's green eyes peered down at the dogs from his perch in a small pine tree.

I sipped more hot chocolate and tried to think. Since the previous night, I hadn't made it through a single hour without worrying about Julian. This hour was no exception, I thought, as I finished the chocolate. Just before ten, I washed my cup, let the dogs in, and settled them into their little room. A moment later, Scout scratched at the door, and I carefully placed him into his feline bed on a shelf above the hounds. Then I punched in the numbers for the St. Luke's recorded prayer list and added Julian's name.

I was starting up to bed when the dogs began to wail. I sighed. Was this what we were going to have to listen to all night, every night? Outside, someone killed a car engine. *Oh good,* I thought, my spirits rising. *Tom's back.*

But it was not Tom. A timid knock at the front door only intensified the dogs' howling. I checked the peephole, then opened the door.

Ellie McNeely, her trim figure still swathed in the trench coat and scarf in which I'd seen her earlier in the evening, gave me an apologetic look. Her hands fidgeted as she struggled for words. What was she sorry about? The unannounced visit? The late hour? The fact that she had not answered my calls?

Her hands finally came to rest on her lapels. She smoothed her coat and tossed her bangs off her forehead.

She said, "We need to talk."

"I've been *trying* to get hold of you."

"Please, Goldy. I need you to come with me. I feel...awful." A zigzag of emotional pain twisted her lovely face. "The cops suspect me. They told me not to leave town. They say I need to be clearer about my relationship with Barry. What about the cuff links? What about this? What about that? They want me to give a minute-by-minute accounting of where I was Monday night. I told them, I went home with a friend. Why don't they believe me? Are they going to let Julian out and send me to jail instead?" Her voice cracked. "If you don't help me, I don't know what I'll do."

CHAPTER 12

"Come with you where?" I asked, bewildered. If we needed to talk, why couldn't we do so in my snug kitchen?

"For a drive," she replied enigmatically. She looked up and down our street. A chilly whip of wind slashed through the evergreens. Ellie turned back to me, stamped her boots, and pulled her gloved hands into fists. "Please. It would help me so much to talk to you. But...it just has to be the two of us."

"It's almost ten o'clock, Ellie. And there's no one here but my son. Why don't you come inside? I'll make you some hot—"

"*Please,* Goldy!"

I pressed my lips together, then nodded. Ellie was my friend from both St. Luke's and Elk Park Prep. In fact, she was one of the only school parents who'd ever even been *nice* to me. Plus, she seemed distraught. And if I was going to help Julian, I needed to find out what Ellie knew. If that meant taking a drive, so be it.

"Let me run tell Arch I'm leaving."

I sprinted up the stairs and informed Arch that Ellie McNeely was here, and we were going out for a bit. I'd put the pets to bed, I assured him, and Tom would be home soon.

"I don't need a *baby*sitter, Mom."

OK, it was official. I had had enough. "You know, Arch, I wish you would try to be a *bit* nicer to me. Even a tiny bit would do."

"Sorry, Mom. But you are *always* bugging me."

How was telling him I was going out "bugging him"? I didn't know. Lately, it seemed as if there were lots of things I didn't know. I asked, "Do you want the animals up here with you?"

"I suppose." He threw off his quilt, revealing his standard nighttime wear of sweatshirt and sweatpants. "That way I can take care of the puppy, in case he gets scared." He swung his legs over the side of the bed and paused, hunched over. He struggled for words. "Good idea, Mom," he mumbled.

I'd had a *good idea*? Where were the Guinness people when you needed them?

While I donned my snow boots, mittens, down jacket, and scarf—with the temperature in the single digits, the wind chill was bound to be horrific—Arch shepherded the two dogs up to his room. Scout the cat, not surprisingly, decided to stay put.

Ellie sat waiting for me in her new SUV, a silver BMW that was the twin of Marla's. The car was lovely, but in its interior light, Ellie didn't look very good. Her expensively colored hair had turned waxy, probably from being repeatedly raked by her manicured nails. Her face, usually flawlessly made up, was puffy and still wrought with worry. The whites of her eyes were dark pink. From crying?

"I don't suppose you've heard how somebody or some*bodies* are trying to smear me?" she demanded as I slid into the cold leather passenger seat.

"I've heard some things. That's why I've been trying to call you."

She revved the engine that she'd kept running while I was getting ready. "I suppose you heard the story about my Lexus being stolen and rammed into Barry's car."

"Yeah. But that was a while ago, wasn't it? Barry took me out for espresso at The Westside Buzz in his new Saab. He loved having a fancy new car, and didn't seem too upset about losing his old Mercedes."

"Well, *somebody's* upset about it." She flipped on the overhead light and handed me a typescript clipped to several photographs. "I've got a friend who works on the *Mountain Journal*. She got her hands on copy they're planning to run tomorrow."

As she piloted her tanklike vehicle toward Main Street, I peered at four blown-up, grainy photos. The first featured Ellie, clad in a tailor-made suit, which made her look stern and manageresque. The second and third showed Barry. In one, he was smooching the cheek of a beaming Pam Disharoon, whose pigtails bobbed enthusiastically. The third photograph of the bunch showed Pam whispering in Barry's ear, while he sported an impish, cat-who-swallowed-the-canary grin. The fourth photo was a blurry shot of the county coroner's van. I turned back to the typescript. The caption read: *The Man Who Loved Too Much?*

How had the *Mountain Journal*, which demanded that I submit my ads two weeks in advance, put together a background article so quickly? But I knew the answer to that. Gossip, easily obtained in Aspen Meadow, sold copy. In our small town, it didn't take long to call dozens of sources and put together a smutty article—full of "alleged's"—that masqueraded as news. And with computers speeding up typesetting, you could gather enough garbage the day after a murder to put together a story and still meet press deadline.

I hastily skimmed the palaver, with its repeated references to a "love triangle." The fact that Julian had been arrested for Barry's murder was glossed over, and for this, at least, I was thankful. I guessed the *Mountain Journal* brains, such as they were, had figured a detained caterer's assistant wasn't as sexy as two women smitten with the same man.

In the *Man Who Loved Too Much* article-to-be, two incidents were detailed, beginning with: *"Last month, witnesses claimed an unidentified woman shoved Barry Dean into a ditch on the mall construction site,"* followed by *"Mrs. McNeely's allegedly stolen purse"* and her *"allegedly stolen Lexus keys,"* which had ended up with *"the Lexus belonging to Ellie McNeely somehow getting smashed into Barry Dean's classic Mercedes. The Mercedes was totaled."* The paper proceeded to have a field day with the cuff links ordered by Ellie to be engraved for Barry being found in the out-of-control truck that had almost killed him earlier the previous day, only hours before he was brutally murdered. Who had been their sources on this? How I wished I knew.

"It's unbelievable," Ellie said, her voice just above a whisper. Her tone was resigned, despondent. "My boyfriend-who-wasn't-quite-my-fiancé was infatuated with a lingerie lady. Now he's dead, and I'm implicated. I can't even grieve, because the cops are showing up on my doorstep, at my office, you name it. They ask things like, 'After you picked up the cuff links, Mrs. McNeely, how did you get them into the truck?' And worse, 'Have you had medical or military training, Mrs. McNeely? Did you learn how to stab someone so that they'd be certain to die?' "

"Oh, no."

"I'm going nuts! I think they're just holding Julian Teller until I crack! Then they'll arrest me!"

"OK, first of all," I said, shaking the typescript, "forget our local rag. People leak stuff to it all the time, their own version of how they want something to read. The staff never checks a single fact, because they don't have time once they round up their material. How come nobody calls them 'alleged reporters'?" I was hoping Ellie would laugh, but she didn't. I tossed the packet into the backseat and turned off the light. We were now chugging past the Bank of Aspen Meadow, where the thermometer read two below zero.

Hunched over the steering wheel, Ellie shook her head grimly. "Not to be materialistic," she went on woefully, "but the gold cuff links I bought for Barry are in police custody, and I *don't* have that engagement ring Barry promised me—"

"So you *were* engaged?"

She squirmed. "Well, not really. We'd been talking about it. He told me he had a big surprise for me, and he eventually said it was 'the ring I'd been hoping for.'"

"How long ago was this?"

She shrugged. "About a month? He gave me a riddle I couldn't understand, though. He promised to help me with it. I ordered him a pair of cuff links, and paid almost three thousand dollars for them. But then I saw him with Pam, in the mall, having lunch. He'd told me he had a meeting with the Pennybaker people, and there they were, acting like lovebirds. That's when I hired Rufus."

"Did you push Barry into a ditch?"

"No."

"Do you know why he had headaches?"

She sighed. "I only knew that he did have headaches. He told me he'd been fighting with someone who worked in the mall. I thought, a fight, like, argument. I didn't think he meant a real physical fight."

"You never picked up the cuff links?"

"My purse was stolen! My car was

stolen, then wrecked! I had no ID, no credit cards, no driver's license! Remembering the cuff links was way, way down on my list." She sighed, but it came out like a sob. "Now the cuff links are being held by the cops as evidence in a murder. It's like I tried to do something nice for a man I believed really cared about me, and the whole thing backfired. Backfired beyond belief."

I murmured, "Yeah, it sure did."

"Dammit, Goldy!" Ellie's voice turned strident. "Say something that's going to make me feel better! Why do you think I came over? I thought Barry Dean *loved* me! And now my life has gone to hell!"

"Well...," I ventured. "I don't know if this will make you feel better, but in the You're-Not-Alone Department, I was married to a man who, even though he was a well-paid doctor, gave me only two hundred dollars, in cash, to spend on Christmas. Because I wanted him to care about me—even though I knew on some deep level that he didn't—I spent a hundred and fifty dollars of that tiny hoard on a Seiko watch. I'd even felt lucky to find it on sale! But the Seiko wasn't a Rolex, and the day after Christmas, I found the watch in the trash."

Ellie managed a wry smile. Then the smile turned bitter. "What am I going to do? How can I keep little Cameron from being humiliated by all this?"

"Your daughter will be OK," I assured her. "She knows you're a good mom." I remembered Arch's brusque declaration: *I don't need a babysitter*. "Anyway, Ellie... Cameron's in tenth grade now. Maybe she's not so little anymore."

"And here I was thinking what a *loving* stepfather Barry would make." She sighed. "I'm just worried the other kids will read this trashy *Journal* article and make fun of Cameron. I hate to think of those Elk Park Prep bitches hurting her feelings."

We whizzed by the lake. Wind-blown pebbles of snow pelted the ice. Under the bright night lights, a few brave skaters were taking advantage of the late burst of freezing weather. Just the thought of skating made me shiver.

"Ellie, where are we going?"

"Well, if you don't mind, we're going to Elk Park Prep. I...I forgot something."

I knew she was lying. "The school will be locked up, Ellie."

She waved one hand. "Doesn't matter. I'll explain when we get there."

"Speaking of Elk Park Prep, can you ... explain to me why you were arguing with Shane there tonight?"

She exhaled and slowed around a curve. "Board business is supposed to be confidential."

"Ellie, I promise, I'm not going to get on the phone and call people about board business."

"Shane ... is having financial problems."

"I know about the eviction from Westside." I gnawed the inside of my cheek. *I know he was holding back on his rent. I know his wife has a bad spending problem. And worst of all: I know I haven't received final payment for this lunch I'm doing for him tomorrow.*

Ellie squinted into the darkness. "Shane's blaming his problems on Barry. I don't believe this story about Barry demanding a kickback for ignoring the rent issue, by the way. In any event, Shane's broke. And in debt. So ... he and Page are pulling their girls from Elk Park Prep.

They're demanding their two-thousand-dollar deposit for next year back. I tried to explain that we simply can't do that. The deposits are nonrefundable. But you saw how Shane was tonight; he wouldn't listen. If you heard about the car accident, you probably know how Page intercepted his loan money."

"I do."

"I can't bend school rules for him. I can't help him at the bank, either. But he just refused to believe that I can't."

We pulled through the school's massive stone gates. Elegant street lamps lit the drive like luminarias. The BMW rolled smoothly over the snow-rutted road.

"What's bothering you most, then?" I probed gently.

She exhaled again before replying. "Bothering me *most*? You mean apart from the fact that a man I loved and was hoping to marry might have been betraying me, but we'll never know because now he's dead?"

"Ellie—"

"Let's see. The cops aren't making my life easier. I've told them over and over, I hired Rufus because I thought Barry was cheating on me. Whether he was having a bona fide affair with Pam or was just infatuated, having a mental fling, Rufus never did find out. That's what's so funny! But those detectives are obsessed. I told them I was having a massage when somebody tried to drive over Barry. They don't listen. I swore Marla, Page, and I left Prince and Grogan just before nine, but they won't let go of it. I got a ride home with Elizabeth Harrington. So what? The cops just keep insisting and poking into my life. OK, here we are."

We drove into the parking lot we'd just left a few hours earlier. Lights rimmed the asphalt and lit the sidewalk angling steeply up to the lacrosse fields. The place looked desolate and forlorn. Ellie reached for the door handle, then hesitated.

"Ellie, where *are* we going? The headmaster will be fast asleep."

She gnawed her bottom lip and hesitated. "Apparently, there's some evidence that will clear me. Somebody called, said they'd leave it for me at the lacrosse field. And I don't know who it was, so don't ask."

"Said they'd leave evidence at the *lacrosse* field?" Was this like Barry leaving me his puppy? "Who left evidence at the lacrosse field?"

"I don't know."

My eyes followed the shadowy sidewalk up to the dark, bleak playing field. Under dimmed lights, the empty bleachers looked like the skeleton of some prehistoric beast. The portable toilet looked like a gloomy, abandoned outpost.

I asked, "Why not leave this evidence at some warm, populated place like the library, for crying out loud? Why not give it directly to the police?"

"Who knows? Look, you can see that there's nobody up there. We'll just run up and get it." Ellie popped open her glove compartment. I was thinking she'd be reaching for a flashlight, but no. Her hand emerged with a small twenty-two, a woman's gun.

"Oh, Ellie, no." As much as I was curious about what someone might have left for Ellie, I didn't want to be a part of anything involving a gun. "This is ridiculous. The sun will be up in, what? Six hours? Seven? We'll go get the 'evidence' then. Let's go home."

Ignoring me, she grabbed her cell

phone with her free hand and stuck it into her coat pocket. Still gripping the ugly little gun, she said, "I told you, Goldy, I'm desperate. Let's go before this wind blows whatever it is away." She inhaled, gripped the pistol, and slipped from the car.

Crap, crap, crap. Why had I come out with her in the first place? And why couldn't she be a liberal and believe in gun control? I powered up my own cell and hit the automatic dial for Tom's phone. If he was at the department or at home, it would be on. If he was between the two, we might be out of range. When the messaging service answered, I cursed silently. Then I announced that I was at Elk Park Prep with Ellie McNeely, and that if we weren't back by eleven, come get us. While Ellie stamped her boots and gestured impatiently to me with the pistol, I reached into my bag and pulled out the Mace. Did everyone in Aspen Meadow carry a weapon? I followed her, but didn't feel a bit comfortable.

The wind died for a bit as our feet crunched over the snow of the parking lot. Ellie glanced around; I kept my eyes on the field. On the bleachers, I could just make out a pile of lacrosse sticks, loaners the school kept on hand for practice. A crumpled athletic bag sat atop the players' bench, abandoned or forgotten. Then again, maybe it contained evidence that would clear Ellie of innuendo...or murder.

"Actually," Ellie said, with a nervous laugh, "this is sort of like one of Barry's little games. You know, follow the clues."

The wind picked up again, and I shivered inside my jacket. "Heather the receptionist told me you hadn't been able to find the engagement ring."

"*Heather* told you?" she asked, shaking her head. "What, was Barry so embarrassed by my stupidity that he laughed at me with his secretary?"

"I...I don't know." Actually, it did sound sort of smarmy, as if Barry not only had been playing games with Ellie, but looking down on her as well. He'd even made jokes about her behind her back.

We climbed over a plow-made drift at the edge of the lot. Ellie tried to make her voice cheery. A cover for fear?

"The clue for the ring went something like, '*When we fight, and then we...go to bed, that's how you'll find your ring.*' So I thought it had to do with sex or foreplay, and I ripped through sheets and box springs and pillows, with Barry laughing the whole time. I never found any ring."

I slipped on the ice, dropped the Mace, and grabbed for the handrail at the side of the walkway. I also cursed Barry Dean, because it looked as if he'd poked almost relentless fun at a woman he supposedly was committed to.

"You all right?" Ellie asked.

I grabbed the rail. "Let's rest for a sec."

"Sure. Anyway, I wanted to *believe* he was sincere," Ellie went on. Her breath was coming out in steaming gasps. "I *believed* I'd find the ring eventually. So that's why I bought him the gold cuff links and left them to be engraved."

"You left them to be engraved, and then what happened?"

She sighed. "I tucked the jeweler's receipt into my purse, bought a cup of coffee, and sat down by the tot lot. That was when the purse was ripped off. In the mess that followed, I spaced out about the receipt. Not very smart, huh?" She paused. All was silent, except for the wind rushing through the trees above the playing fields.

"Later, when the cops were trying to cut a deal with Teddy Fury, that teenage brat admitted he'd stolen my purse along with twenty or so others. He claimed he dumped it—he remembered the Louis Vuitton pattern, and was afraid of being caught with it—after taking the cash. According to Teddy, somebody *else* must have picked my purse out of the Dumpster, and lifted my car keys and the receipt. Just like later that same day, Teddy claims, somebody *else* crashed my car. Later in the week, Teddy also swears, somebody *else* used the receipt to pick up the cuff links. Then whoever did that conveniently placed the cuff links in that damn truck." Her eyes watered as she smiled at me. "Are you ready to go?"

We made our way slowly up the sidewalk. I had a new appreciation for all the walking Arch had to do in a day. And he carried a heavy bag.

"What do you think?" Ellie demanded, when we were halfway up the steep ascent to the field.

"I think my lungs are going to burst."

"What do you think about Teddy Fury's story?"

Ellie seemed determined to downplay the fact that we were out in the freezing wind, at night, chasing after elusive evidence on a deserted school field. Fine. We soldiered on.

"What about the jewelry clerk?" I asked. "Did he remember the person who picked up the cuff links?"

"Nope. And whoever it was didn't have to sign anything. The clerk who handed over the cuff links looked at a sheriff's department photo of Teddy Fury and said Teddy wasn't the one."

We were finally at the bleachers. Gusts of snow swirled up and around the field. Only two halide lights, one by each net, lit the shadows. Ellie traipsed in front of the bleachers, which held nothing but the sticks, and then over to the players' bench, where she set down her pistol and dumped out the contents of the bag. Socks, Gatorade bottles, a jersey, pads, and a book fell onto the snow. Ellie stooped and pawed through them, then straightened.

"Nothing!"

Surprise, surprise. "Let's go. We can—"

"Oh, wait." She picked up the gun and pointed it at the toilet. I peered at the battered metal door. A manila envelope had been taped to it. Manila envelopes, Barry's old trademark. Ellie quick-stepped toward it. Reluctantly, I followed.

"This says, *'Evidence is inside'*!" she cried in dismay, as she noisily ripped the packet off the door. "Dammit!" Wrenching the door open with her free hand, she stuck her head inside. A second later, she stepped closer to get a better look.

Then she shouted and disappeared.

"Ellie!" I cried, scrambling toward the toilet. "Ellie!"

"Goldy!" Was she struggling with somebody? My whole body was braced, hoping against hope not to hear a gunshot. "Goldy!" Her voice sounded as if she was at the bottom of a chasm. "There's no floor in here! Don't step inside! It's just all ... blech!"

"Ellie!" I was at the toilet door, which I swung open recklessly, concerned only about Ellie. I looked inside. The smell was unbelievable. I could not see her. "Ellie?" I wailed. "Where are you?"

"I'm waving at you."

I saw only blackness. I blinked and squinted. It didn't help.

Ellie's voice said, "I'd guess I'm about eight feet down. It's an extra large tank that the school bought to save money."

I didn't say, *But what happened to the damn toilet? What happened to the floor?* Instead, I told Ellie: "Wait. I'm going to go bang on the headmaster's door. He'll be able to call for help."

Before she could reply, I skidded back in the direction of the walkway. Five, ten minutes at the most, I would have her out of there.

Then I heard a car . . . but saw no headlights. The car sounded as if it was slowly winding up the school driveway, approaching the lot. Was it possible that it was Tom? Could he have received my message? I doubted it.

And where were the car's lights? Why would you drive around in the dark without lights?

"Somebody's coming!" I croaked.

"Oh, no! They said to come alone! They don't know you're here!" Her voice was getting hysterical. "Goldy!"

I watched carefully. I finally made out a vehicle that had almost reached the parking lot. One of the lights along the driveway briefly revealed it as a small four-wheel-drive vehicle. It was not Tom.

Ellie had been lured here, and she'd stepped into a trap. My instinct told me whoever this was approaching in that dark car wasn't here to help. I skittered back to the portable toilet and pulled the door completely open.

"OK, pay attention," I called into the darkness. "Do you have your cell phone?"

"Yeah." Her voice was hoarse. "And the pistol."

"Press a button on your cell phone so I can at least see a little light. I need to know where you are."

A tiny square of green glowed a foot out of reach. In the sickly light, I could just make out Ellie's face.

"Hand me the gun!" I commanded. Not that that would do much good. The two times I'd been with Tom at target practice, I'd completely missed the paper man with the concentric circles around his heart. But I knew how to ease off a safety. And I knew how to make a lot of noise.

I lowered myself to my knees, then lay flat. Ignoring the stench, I inched forward until my shoulders were over the pit. There

were sloshing sounds as Ellie moved below. The car roared into the lot.

The stench was horrific, the air frigid. I
took shallow breaths while reaching for the
pistol, which Ellie pressed into my hand.
Once I had it, I eased upright.

"Whoever got me to come here isn't expecting *you*," she warned desperately.

"Yeah, yeah," I said as I scrambled to
my feet. I hid most of my body around the
far corner of the portable toilet, and only
stuck my head out far enough to see the
parking lot. The small four-wheel-drive was
slowly circling Ellie's car. "I need you to yell
for help!" I commanded Ellie.

"Help!" Ellie shrieked obediently.
"Help!"

Far down in the lot, the vehicle stopped.
It idled by Ellie's car. Were any of its windows open? I couldn't tell.

"Again!" I whispered.

Ellie screamed, "Help! Come and get
me! *Help!*"

Moments later, the driver-side door of
the new SUV swung open. A figure in a
long, hooded coat emerged. Tall? Short?
Fat? Thin? Impossible to tell from way up
on the field. Whoever it was cast a glance

up at the portable toilet and headed across the lot toward the path.

"Do a man's voice," I urged, "like you're coming to help!"

"OK, Ellie," she bellowed in a surprisingly convincing bass, "I'll be right there!"

"Me, too!" I hollered. Then I held the gun out and fired. One, two, three shots exploded.

The figure froze and glanced up.

"I think I got him, Ellie!" Ellie's bass voice boomed out from the toilet tank like a whale's. "He's not going to bother you!"

I let out a high cackle and fired another shot. The figure trotted back to its car, hopped in, and gunned the motor to get away.

I put the safety back on the pistol and stood stock-still, shivering uncontrollably. It wasn't from the cold.

After a moment, I called down to Ellie, "Our visitor's gone." Ellie began to cry. "OK," I said, with a matter-of-factness I wasn't sure I was feeling. "Let's rescue you! How are you doing?"

"I don't know whether it's worse to freeze your butt off or be asphyxiated!" she sobbed. "Please, please, get me out of here!"

I peered into the darkness, and tried to come up with some idea of how to rescue Ellie. The wind had picked up again, and my eyes began to tear.

"OK!" I called. "I'm going to go get the headmaster!"

"No!" she yelled. "That'll take forever! You know that lacrosse bag? It had a pocket knife in it—"

I squinted at the upended athletic bag. OK, got it. I set the gun down, then moved quickly over the ice and snow. I rummaged through the bag's detritus, and finally closed my freezing fingers around a Swiss Army knife. I gasped out steam and moved to one of the lacrosse goals, where I sliced, chopped, and hacked to free the net from its moorings. Once I had an armful of netting, I closed the knife and hustled back to the portable toilet. There I twisted the white nylon into a makeshift rope and tossed one end down to Ellie.

Gripping the jerry-rigged line, she climbed up as I tugged with every iota of strength I possessed. I groaned and strained, but kept pulling until Ellie heaved herself up from the pit. Once out, she gasped for mouthfuls of clean air.

We hobbled back down to Ellie's car. Ellie's coat, clothes, and boots smelled terrible. She stripped down to her underwear in the bitter wind and jumped into one of her daughter's spare sweatsuits. Shivering and crying, she revved the engine to drive me home.

CHAPTER 13

On the way back to my house, Ellie calmed down, and we talked in earnest. Yes, someone had deliberately lured her to that field and that hole. Yes, she was in danger. When she left me off at home, she promised to take Cameron out of school and stay someplace safe, "until this whole thing blows over." She would call both Marla and me when she was settled, and give us her number. And yes, she had to let the cops know where she was, too.

"Thank you so much for coming tonight," she said. Her voice quavered, and her face was still pale with worry. "Oh, Goldy, I'm so sorry—"

"It's OK. Take care of yourself, Ellie. And don't forget to let me know where you and Cameron are."

Tom was putting on his boots when I stomped through the front door. "Miss G., I just got your message. What happened?"

I gave him an abbreviated version of the night's events, then begged to take a shower. He said he would call the sheriff's department to examine the toilet and lacrosse field. It might or might not be attempted murder, he added somberly, but we were definitely looking at criminal mischief. Technically, the lacrosse field was a crime scene. Great, I thought, as I stumbled up to steaming hot water and lots and lots of soap. Now Arch was *really* going to love me and be more polite.

Some time later, I snuggled up next to Tom's warm body. His smooth, pine-scented skin felt heavenly.

"The dogs are in with Arch," he whispered.

"I know. I told him it was OK. You know how he loves dogs. And at least Late isn't howling. He must feel protected by Arch

and Jake." Tom was silent. "Why am I talking about a basset hound?" I said. "I just
rescued a friend from a frozen toilet tank,
for crying out loud!"

Tom's laugh shook the bed. He en-
closed me in a bear hug, then planted a
passionate kiss on my neck. And that was
just the beginning.

Lovemaking, like food, can be wonderfully healing.

Wednesday morning, an even stronger
icy wind battered the house and shrieked
through the trees. Brilliant pink clouds
shone along the eastern horizon. I'd lived in
Colorado too long not to know this was a
winter storm front announcing itself. I made
French toast for Tom and Arch. While Tom
was rinsing the dishes, Arch offhandedly
lifted his shirt to show me his tattoo.

"All the lacrosse guys have 'em," he explained. "And sometimes they come in
handy in identifying corpses, Tom told me."

"Arch, *please*. A mom would like to start
the day knowing her son is focusing on
school, not corpses."

"Oh!" he said, brightening. "That re-
minds me. Todd is going to pierce my ear
so I can wear one gold earring."

My stomach turned over. "Please, Arch. Please don't pierce your ear." I was suddenly desperate for another espresso. "Isn't it time for you guys to take off?" I asked, trying not to sound exasperated.

"Yup!" Tom said with cheer, as he put on his jacket and Arch hoisted his backpack.

"Don't you want your lacrosse equipment, buddy?" I asked. Then I remembered that they'd be missing a goal, the one I'd hacked to pieces. Plus, the snow-covered field was about to be turned into a crime scene.

Arch sighed. "There's no lacrosse today. You're one of the moms taking us on the field trip to dissect a cadaver at Lutheran Hospital. Don't you remember?" I rubbed my forehead, baffled. "You were going to pick up Todd and me and a couple of other guys in the parking lot at four. Are you still going to be able to do it, or should Todd call his mom to take over?" His tone said that he suspected I would once again let him down.

"*I will be there,*" I promised through clenched teeth.

As Tom hustled Arch out the door, I

pulled myself a triple shot of espresso and took a long sip. Heavenly. Before starting to cook, though, I turned my attention to the animals. I brought Jake's and Scout's bowls in from the deck, filled them with food and water, and put the dishes back outside. On the deck, I stared down in confusion at two of my Minton bone china bowls, now crusted with dog food and ice. Arch had either ignored or forgotten the bag from Darlene, and had poured some of Jake's food into my expensive china bowls to feed the puppy. Shaking my head, I filled the china bowls with soapy water, then reached into the grocery bag from Darlene that held Late's dishes.

I pulled out one, then the other. When I felt tape on the dish bottoms, I casually turned each over, then gaped at them in disbelief. When I recovered, I put them down carefully and filled some old bowls of ours with more of Jake's food for Barry's puppy. When all the dishes were outside, I called the animals. Scout was, as usual, no place to be seen, but Jake and Late came bounding over and began gobbling.

Back inside, I put in a call to Darlene Petrucchio. I kept staring at the two dishes she'd given me. They both looked as if she'd hastily applied masking tape to them, then penned in the name.

"Darlene!" I said when she picked up. "It's Goldy Schulz—"

"It ain't even eight in the morning! I don't wanna hear what you gotta say! I ain't takin' that hound back!"

"Darlene, please. This is very important. Did Barry Dean tell you to write the puppy's name on the bottom of these two dishes?"

"What? Lemme get some coffee."

I waited, then asked her my question again.

"Yeah, yeah, he told me to write the name just the way he spelt it. He said tape it on the dishes before I gave you the puppy. I said, 'Why don't you do it yourself?' He just laughed. He said he couldn't spell. And I said, 'No kidding.' He also said you'd get a kick out of it."

"Hold on a sec. So has this *always* been the puppy's name?"

"No, no, no," Darlene corrected me. "Barry was going to call him Honey Boy or Honey Hound, something like that. But those sounded too girly, you know? Or maybe it reminded him of his old dogs, I

don't know. So we just called the puppy
Puppy. Until Monday afternoon when he
called. He said jes' to put that name on. He
said he knew the spelling was wrong. But I
should just write it the way he spelt it, and
tape it onto those bowls. So I did."

I thanked her and hung up, troubled.
The dogs had finished eating, and were eager to come in from the cold. I settled them
in their pet condo and washed and dried
their dishes. Then I studied Darlene's block
letters, penned in blue ballpoint on masking tape.

I thought Barry had named the hound
Late. But staring up at me from both dishes
was the word LATTE. *Latte,* the coffee drink.

So. Was this a joke? Or was this Barry's
little good-bye puzzle to me?

What had Barry and I had in common?
Psych class. A love of dogs. *Coffee*.

Barry hadn't been a very good
boyfriend to either Ellie or Pam—at least,
not in my opinion. But he'd been a regular
old *good friend* to me once, and we'd
drunk a *lot* of coffee together. So was Barry
saying, *Take care of my dog, and you'll love
him since he's named after a coffee drink*? I
supposed so.

It wasn't much, and it was sappy to boot. But it made me cry anyway.

At eight, the phone rang. To my surprise, it was Rob Eakin, now acting manager of Westside Mall.

"Sorry to be calling so early," he apologized. He sounded hurried. "I'm in early, trying to get a million things straightened out."

"What can I do for you?"

I heard him take a deep breath. "We're postponing the Prospective Tenants' Lunch," he said timidly. "Ah, indefinitely. When there's a crime in a mall, potential lessees get cold feet," he rushed on. "Half of the prospective tenants who were coming to the lunch have already canceled. We're expecting the rest to be no-shows. And with the drainage problem still delaying completion of the addition, we don't have much to show folks who might want to locate here. Frankly, we can't take the chance of turning them off permanently."

My heart plummeted. I tried to take a yoga cleansing breath and ended up gasping. The twenty pounds of aged prime rib in my side-by-side would last two, three days at the most. I could freeze it, of course. However, the chances of finding another client with the same menu were slim.

There was something that worried me more, however. With mall traffic down because of Barry's unsolved death, and with construction on the much-touted addition delayed, would Rob Eakin expect a refund for the Tenants' Lunch? By contract, of course, the money was mine, and we were talking over a thousand dollars. Despite my new prosperity, this was not a sum I could afford to see disappear, especially since I'd already spent most of it on Arch's trashed guitar.

"You're going to, I mean, do you have another date—"

Rob Eakin sniffed. "We're sorry to be canceling within twenty-four hours of the event. But you'll have all that food left over that you can use elsewhere, not to mention a whole day off, courtesy of the labor cost we've already paid for." He cleared his throat, and a voice in the back of my head snarled, *Hang up on this dolt right now*. But I didn't, and Rob Eakin raised his voice. "We'd like to rely on your *honor* and have you *refund* us seventy-five percent of our payment."

"Mr. Eakin. *I* have *also* paid for that food. In the labor department, my staff will expect to be paid, whether they show up or not." I inhaled to steady myself. "Goldilocks' Catering pays its bills for food and labor. *We* don't want to get a reputation for reneging on our commitments. In fact, we have an excellent reputation for servicing the best-heeled clients in both Furman County and Denver. Perhaps you've seen some of the articles about us in the *newspapers*." When all else fails, threaten media exposure. Especially in the *Mountain Journal*.

Rob Eakin hesitated. "Barry did tell me you'd been in the news. We ... don't want you to speak negatively of us." Bingo.

"Oh, no," I replied hastily. "Never."

"We're ... actually thinking of doing a big Fourth of July event. When the mall addition is finally open."

"Fourth of July?" Nobody wants prime rib on the Fourth; they want barbecue. Besides, a three-month stay in my freezer would burn that beef to toast. And did Westside's management really think the addition wouldn't be done until *summer*?

"Look, Mrs. Schulz." Eakin's voice indicated he was backtracking, hopefully the length of his entire frigging mall. "I...I promise you'll be the caterer for our next event."

That sounded fair to me, I said. I thanked Eakin and hung up.

I frowned at the marble counter, trying to think. Yes, the full payment from Westside had been deposited, and yes, I had all this food left over, but I didn't like having a big event canceled, even if the cancellation wasn't my fault. I wondered if it was possible that Westside had canceled for a reason other than the one Rob Eakin had given. Maybe the new mall management didn't want to have anything more to do with Goldilocks' Catering, what with my assistant jailed on suspicion of murdering their manager.

The phone rang again.

"It's Ellie," my friend announced.

"Are you OK?"

She sighed. "Cameron and I are at the Westside Suites. You know it?"

"Yes." The Westside Suites, not far from Westside Mall, were the closest thing to a luxury hotel that Furman County offered. "You called the police, I take it?"

She snorted. "I had to...I'm a suspect in a murder case, remember? Even though they have Julian in jail, somebody in the sheriff's department or county attorney's office thinks 'the cuff-link lady,' as they now refer to me, had *something* to do with Barry's death. In a couple of hours, they're coming over *here* to ask me some more questions."

"Better phone a lawyer."

"That's my next call."

"*Please* take care of yourself, Ellie."

"I'm trying." She hesitated. "Thanks for being such a great friend, Goldy."

"I'm trying to be just that," I told her firmly.

After we signed off, the phone rang yet again. I couldn't handle any more bad news, so I ignored it. The phone rang and rang. The sound reverberated dully in my head. Our machine finally picked up. The message was long. I couldn't face it just yet.

Time for some coffee and positive thoughts, I reflected resolutely. I pressed the buttons on two machines: the espresso

and answering ones. Dark, life-giving caffeine swirled into a green Italian demitasse
cup Tom had given me, while Liz Fury's
voice on my answering machine announced that the wedding reception had
gone well. Her daughter Kim had brought
her van back, and now she, Liz, had just
dropped Kim off with her new Boulder
housemates. If I needed any special food
supplies—Boulder was a mecca for gourmet goodies, and she was just leaving—I
could reach her on her cell phone. Otherwise, she'd be back by nine to help with
the Stockhams' lunch.

Just what I needed: more food! But it
was good of Liz to call. She and I needed
to have some face time, no question about
it. We'd had a bit of a spat at the end of the
mall event, and of *course* I was going to
pay her for her work that evening, plus
double her regular fee for bailing me out
with the wedding reception. But we had to
talk. Without implying anything, without being rude, I needed to know how my new
assistant—who'd appeared to be flirting
with Barry Dean in our final strategy meeting—really felt about the man who'd barred
and then forcibly evicted her shoplifting

son from the mall. Had she actually had a date after the event? Or had she canceled so she could go off to find Teddy? What had happened with Teddy? And how had Liz gotten home, since she had no vehicle at the mall?

Worst of all, I thought, as Liz's recorded voice continued to speak, was this question: Had Liz been so furious with Barry that she'd stabbed him to death? I shook my head. No way.

Still, there was lots to find out at a single catering event. I booted up the menu for Shane Stockham's capital investors' lunch. Liz's recorded voice kept droning on. It had been snowing in Golden to beat hell, she didn't think that would slow her up, we needed to think about Easter ham dinners to make in advance for big clients. . . .

She stopped talking for a moment. The recorded buzz of empty cell-phone communication filled my kitchen.

"Teddy's disappeared," Liz said abruptly. "Oh, Goldy, he took his mittens but not his damned boots!" Sobbing, she hung up.

I slammed down some of the espresso—hot, powerful, and just what I needed—then dialed Liz on her cell. She answered before the end of the first ring.

"Liz, it's Goldy, and you're going to be fine," I reassured her. "Your son is seventeen. He'll survive without boots."

"Goldy, you don't understand." Her voice cracked. "After I...found him Monday night at a fast food place, I called the cops, the way I'd promised back when he was...first trespassed from the mall. I said I'd keep track of where he was *every minute—*"

"Wait. You mean the security guys didn't call the cops to get him hauled off somewhere?"

"I guess they tried, but the sheriff's department told the security guys to release him outside the mall. I suppose they did that, because when I went into the security office to find Teddy, the guards told me my son had told them he'd go to McDonald's. And the cops would contact me later. Which they did, but not until late Monday night. They...came to see me about Barry, asked a bunch of questions about where I was when, where Teddy was when, that kind of thing. Before they left, they told me I had to keep track of Teddy all the time."

"Good Lord." Confused, I guzzled more espresso. "So. What *did* happen after you left us Monday evening?"

"I told you." A hint of exasperation wended into her voice. "I went to the security office, then walked to the McDonald's near Westside, and Teddy was there, chowing down. He had my little car, remember, and I drove him home. Yesterday, while I was doing the wedding reception, he snuck out! He didn't even have a *car*! I thought maybe he was with friends, but then he didn't come home." She stopped and gasped for breath. "Before he left, he ...he put on his ski mittens that he always leaves by the front door. Then he nabbed one of my ... of my carving knives. He proceeded to *pick-ax* his way into a batch of credit cards that I'd frozen in a plastic container of ice at the back of our freezer."

"Oh, no ..."

"He didn't take his boots, so he wasn't going snowboarding. I know where he was going," she continued, her voice bitter. "Shopping. And before you ask, yes, I canceled the cards. A couple of them, anyway. I think there were about eight in there, and all I could remember were the Visa and Saks Fifth Avenue—"

"You don't have to work today," I interjected. "I can manage, I promise." This wasn't true, of course. With Julian in jail and my body somewhat the worse for the nighttime excursion to the portable toilet, I really did need Liz. But she was hurtling over a much larger bump on the motherhood road than anything I'd been dealing with lately.

"No, I've *got* to work," she protested, her tone urgent. "I can't just wait for him to call, I'll go nuts. The cops have my cell phone number. They swore they'd call if Teddy showed up...or got caught. God, I feel awful!"

"As soon as you get here, I'll fix you some breakfast. I'll be fine on prepping the lunch." Better than fine, I thought. I'd just had an idea.

"Goldy, you're the best. And I haven't even asked how you're doing."

I thought I could say I'd been feeling pretty crappy, but that seemed tactless. "Everything's fine. Well, not really. Tom told you Julian's been arrested."

"And I told him how bad I felt. How's Julian doing?"

"Not too good. Liz... I thought you had a date or something with Barry after the party." When she snorted, I said, "Do you know anything about Barry's social life? I guess I mistook your... chat with him at our planning meeting as, I don't know, *interest*."

She guffawed. "No! I didn't have a date, although I thought a judge I'd gone out with might show up at the leasing event, so I dressed up. But he didn't show. Let's see, Barry's social life... well, I thought he was going out real seriously with Ellie McNeely. In case you wondered why I was being so nice to Barry at our meeting, I was trying to get on his good side, in case Teddy showed up again and made more trouble. Didn't work, though."

"Do the police... I mean, are they searching for Teddy because he's underage, or because he's missing, or—" I couldn't finish my own sentence, because I knew the answer.

"They don't look for anyone who's just missing until forty-eight hours have gone by." The line filled with static; Liz must have been driving by some high rocks. "They're searching for Teddy for the same reason they told me not to leave town. Even though Julian's been arrested, we're both still suspects in Barry's murder." She paused. "Goldy, you're one of the few friends I have."

The line went dead.

Well. I hadn't felt particularly good since the portable toilet ordeal, but now a warm glow suffused my senses. I had helped Ellie, after a fashion. And now I was helping Liz. Arch might think I was always bugging him or getting in the way, but at least my friends appreciated me. On this happy note, I put in a call to Marla, who was out. Well, Easter was right around the corner. Marla always spent enormous amounts of time and money finding clothes in the hues of dyed eggs. Then again, maybe she was hunting for more gossip that could help Julian—to her, this would be much more attractive than groping in ice-covered undergrowth for eggs.

And speaking of which...outside, a blinding curtain of snowflakes had begun to whirl down. Welcome to spring in Aspen Meadow. One year, it had snowed every day in May. I pitied Liz driving the narrow, winding foothills road between Boulder and Aspen Meadow.

I turned my attention back to the Stockhams' menu. The dishes Shane had ordered—primarily cold salads—were more suitable to the brief spell of unseasonably warm weather we'd had back in March than to what we were experiencing now, that is, the usual "Springtime in the Rockies," which was basically "Return to the Arctic." Plus, what about these extra people I'd heard about . . . not from the client?

I took all the food for the Prospective Tenants' Lunch out of the refrigerator and placed it on the counter. It was possible I had a way out of this food mess.

Making small last-minute changes to a menu was a prerogative I reserved. The proviso—always explained to clients—was that Goldilocks' Catering would make up the cost difference if the new dishes, necessitated by market, weather, or oversight-on-our-part situations, were more expensive than those originally ordered.

And speaking of expensive, I wanted to ask Shane about these possible extra guests, and remind him of his payment due. Yes, I had the money from Westside, but if I didn't hold Shane responsible for *his* bill, too, then word would get out, and all of my contracts would be undermined. I fully intended to give Westside a huge discount on their next catered event, anyway. I just could *not* start doing last-minute renegotiations for the number of guests and the financial terms of my contracts. If there was one thing I'd learned on the business side of catering, this was it.

Eight o'clock was a tad early to be calling a client, but Shane was pretty Type-A, so I figured he, too, could be on his third cup of coffee. I punched in the buttons for the Stockham house.

Shane answered on the first ring. "Oh, God, don't tell me you're canceling!" His voice shook with dismay. "Sorry! I have caller ID, Goldy. The snow's really coming down, but I *know* you'll be OK. Problem is, I'm worried now that a dozen deep-pocket investors won't want chilled food—"

"A dozen, Shane?"

He continued, oblivious. "Could you whip up another soup? Maybe a French onion, with cheese-slathered croutons? Page bought some Gruyère last week, I think it's still around. Omigod, look at this *snow*. Do you have four-wheel drive on your van?"

"Shane, hold on." I then reassured him that the snow was not an issue, except as it impacted the menu. "Remember, Shane, you booked for six people. Not twelve. Six."

"Oops! I've added half a dozen women, didn't I tell you?"

"You did not. Most caterers would say it was impossible."

"Oh, *please,* Goldy. I'll pay you *more* than double."

"You're in luck. I'll do it for one and a half times the first rate, provided I actually get the payment from you when we arrive." He moaned, but I went on: "How would you feel about a gorgeous prime rib of beef with red wine gravy?"

"Today? Really?"

"Yes. But Shane, remember your check? I need it before my assistant and I set up."

"Can we barter?" he whined. "I can get you some fabulous electronic equipment! Wholesale!"

"Shane!" I closed my eyes. *You may*

eventually want to work with this person again, I reminded myself. "I need a check from you for a thousand dollars before we start."

He lowered his voice. "I've got a perfectly nice ruby, sapphire, and diamond ring right here in front of me, Goldy," he whispered. "Over a half carat for each stone, flawless quality, great colors. The stones alone are worth twelve thousand bucks, and that's not even counting the fourteen-carat-gold setting. If I don't get a check from an investor today, you keep the ring."

I sighed. "Do you *own* the ring? Or did you lease it?"

He gulped. "It's...mostly paid for. We owe about another thousand for it on Visa. I promise, Goldy, that's the *truth*. I swear, if I don't pay up today, it's yours, and the Visa bill is ours. The ring's worth about fifteen thousand. Such a deal!"

I cast a glance along our counter, taking in the enormous rib roast, the bundles of endive and radicchio, the boxes of wild mushrooms, the bowls of fresh strawberries and rhubarb. I tried to imagine hauling all of it over to the Stockhams', along with a bald guy with a jewelers' loupe. Then if the gems weren't genuine, I could wring Shane's neck.

"When do I get the ring?" I heard myself say.

"I can bring it over now, or, or, I can give it to you when you arrive." He hesitated, and lowered his voice to a whisper. "Probably safer if we wait until you get here. I swear, Goldy. If I don't give it to you the second you walk in the door, you can dump the food in Cottonwood Creek. It runs right past our house." Before I could reply, he said, "Hey, that prime rib sounds *great*. Oh, and could you name one of the dishes after these women? I want to flatter them a bit. We all know gadgets are the wave of the future! But these females keep moaning about nest eggs. Help me placate them, will you? I tell them they need to 'Get wild!' I even call them my 'Wild Girls,' and they love that. See you at ten."

And then the slimeball hung up.

What would happen to the women's nest eggs if Shane's business failed again? Would they be offered emerald necklaces? In these situations, I always tried to think of what Tom, my wise husband, would say.

You're already driving yourself crazy trying to control your own burgeoning business, plus Arch, plus a police investigation involving Julian, my internalized Tom-voice reminded me. *You don't need to add taking care of Shane's investors to Goldy's List of Controllees.*

I checked our larder, fixed myself another coffee, and began to type.

*Investors' Lunch for Twelve——
Revised Menu
Wednesday, April 13
Steaming Gadget-Dumpling Soup
Wild Girls' Grilled Mushroom Salad
Ad Guys' Roast Beef and Gravy
Mashed Russet and Sweet Potatoes
Brioche Rolls
Super Spenders' Strawberry-Rhubarb
Cobbler with Vanilla Ice Cream*

First things first. I brought out cardboard boxes and packed in the vats of chilled, Asian-flavored stock I'd already made. After preheating the oven, I put in the roast. I would sear and roast it partway at home, then finish it at the Stockhams'.

Outside, the snow was thickening.

Looking down, I wondered how my raw-skinned, much-washed hands would look with a ruby, sapphire, and diamond ring glittering on one finger. It didn't matter. If we didn't get paid for this lunch, I was going to *sell* the damn ring.

I started water boiling for the potatoes. After trimming the enormous, firm Portobello mushrooms, I whisked together the luscious sherry and balsamic vinaigrette in which the mushrooms would be briefly bathed before I grilled them in the Stockhams' state-of-the-art kitchen. Food was great, I reflected, as I got swept up in the rhythm of cooking. It's dealing with *folks* that makes catering so challenging.

Liz arrived, her coat dusted with snow, her nose red. She proffered a bag of cinnamon and cheese Danish from the Aspen Meadow pastry shop.

"I didn't want you to fix anything for me," she protested sheepishly. "Anyway, I thought I wouldn't be hungry, what with my son on the loose, getting us into so much debt I won't be able to charge at the grocery store anymore. But I'm ravenous and out of cash...not a good time to run into the store clutching your credit card."

It turned out that I was ravenous, too. While the potatoes and roast cooked, we dug into the Danish and told credit card jokes. I wrote Liz a check for the Monday event, for which she was almost pathetically grateful. Then we rewashed our hands and quickly divvied up the tasks for the rest of the lunch. Liz, who had a remarkable knack for presentation, asked to be put in charge of piping side-by-side dollops of mashed sweet and russet potatoes in the potato skins.

"I'll make it look great," she promised. "A fat golden swirl of mashed russet next to a creamy orange swirl of sweet potato, both piping hot and crackling with melted butter. Trust me."

"Trust you? You're making me hungry all over again, and I just downed two Danish!"

We worked feverishly over the next hour. As I energetically mashed the white potatoes—Liz was working on the fleshy, orange sweet ones—I wondered how to broach the subject of Teddy. *Can anyone account for every movement of Teddy's, from the time he left the security office to the time you picked him up at McDonald's?*

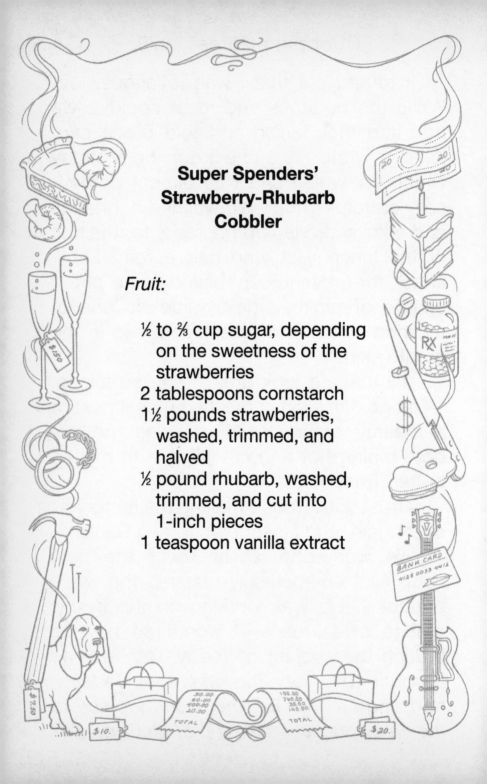

Super Spenders' Strawberry-Rhubarb Cobbler

Fruit:

½ to ⅔ cup sugar, depending on the sweetness of the strawberries
2 tablespoons cornstarch
1½ pounds strawberries, washed, trimmed, and halved
½ pound rhubarb, washed, trimmed, and cut into 1-inch pieces
1 teaspoon vanilla extract

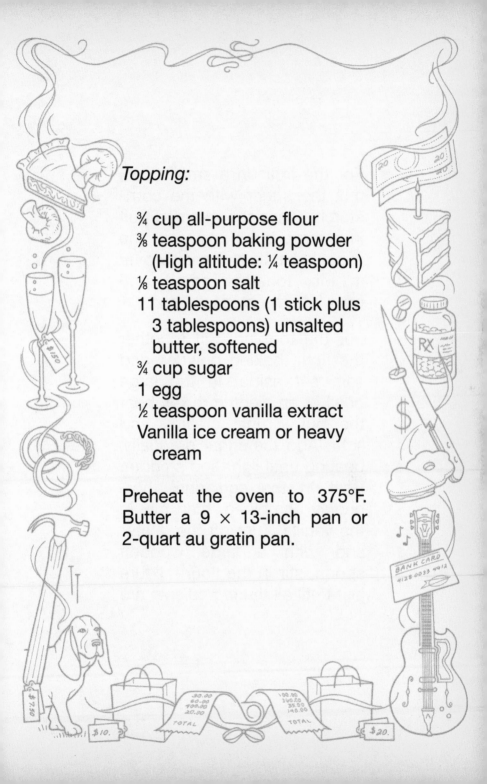

Topping:

> ¾ cup all-purpose flour
> ⅜ teaspoon baking powder
>   (High altitude: ¼ teaspoon)
> ⅛ teaspoon salt
> 11 tablespoons (1 stick plus
>   3 tablespoons) unsalted
>   butter, softened
> ¾ cup sugar
> 1 egg
> ½ teaspoon vanilla extract
> Vanilla ice cream or heavy
>   cream

Preheat the oven to 375°F. Butter a 9 × 13-inch pan or 2-quart au gratin pan.

For the fruit: In a small bowl, mix the sugar with the cornstarch. Place the trimmed fruit in a large bowl and pour the sugar mixture and vanilla over it. Mix together gently and pour into the prepared pan.

For the topping: Sift together the flour, baking powder, and salt; set aside. In the large bowl of an electric mixer, beat the butter until creamy and light. Add the sugar gradually, beating until light and smooth. Beat in the egg until thoroughly combined, then mix in the vanilla. Turn off the beater and with a large wooden spoon, stir in the flour mixture just until all the ingredients are

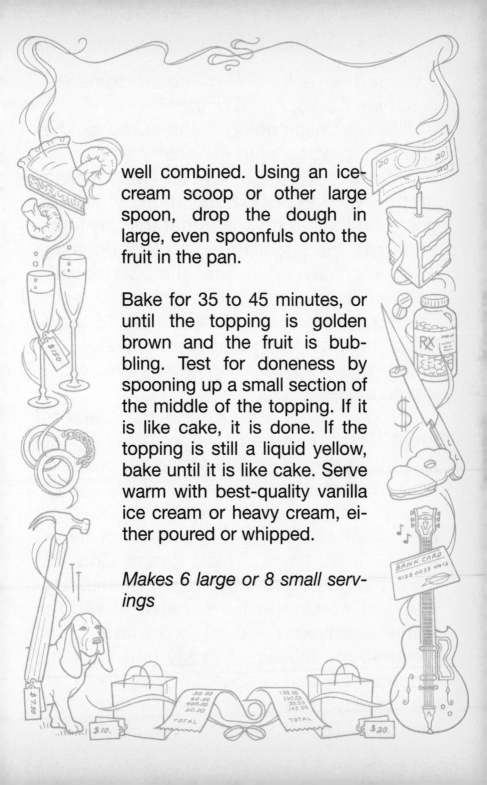

well combined. Using an ice-cream scoop or other large spoon, drop the dough in large, even spoonfuls onto the fruit in the pan.

Bake for 35 to 45 minutes, or until the topping is golden brown and the fruit is bubbling. Test for doneness by spooning up a small section of the middle of the topping. If it is like cake, it is done. If the topping is still a liquid yellow, bake until it is like cake. Serve warm with best-quality vanilla ice cream or heavy cream, either poured or whipped.

Makes 6 large or 8 small servings

I wanted to asked. *How about someone vouching for your own doings?*

"How's Julian doing?" she asked as she fitted a piping tip onto my pastry bag.

"I saw him yesterday. He was feeling pretty low, didn't talk much about what was going on there. I do know that the day after an arrest, the sheriff's department does an advisement by video from the courthouse. Lets you know what you're charged with. The arraignment comes a couple of days later. I'm just hoping that someone else will emerge as a suspect, someone, say, without an alibi—"

"Teddy and I are lucky in that department," Liz interjected, without looking at me. Instead, she concentrated on heaping scoops of mashed potatoes into the pastry bag. "I left you around quarter after eight, then went straight to Security. I left them around eight-thirty, which, thank God, is what the guards told the cops. Somebody was just coming in for his shift at McD's when I arrived there at eight-forty, and watched me talking to Teddy until we left, around nine-thirty." She finished the first four potatoes, and gave me a look. Triumphant? Defiant? I couldn't tell.

"Well," I said thoughtfully as I brought an oversized bag of field greens out of the walk-in. "Hmm. So...if Teddy's not a suspect, why would he take off? It's just going to make them come down harder on him when they do find him."

Liz filled another bag with snowy whipped potatoes. "Teddy took off because he was under stress. When he's under stress, he shops."

Or steals, I added silently, but said nothing. I rinsed the field greens and set them aside to drain. What else could I ask Liz before it was time to take off? "Know anybody who might have pushed Barry down, causing him headaches?"

Liz finished a creamy swirl of whipped white potato and smiled at me. "What *are* you talking about?"

Nothing, I said. After all, if she or Teddy had had enough physical strength to push Barry Dean down, I was pretty sure that she would have at least blushed when I mentioned it.

Two new inches of heavy, wet snow plastered the sidewalk, trees, and streets by the time Liz and I set out. My new van boasted not only four-wheel drive, but new snow tires, also taken care of by Tom. Gosh, but it was nice to have a husband who actually cared about me.

Liz told me that she, too, had new tires. But she wasn't nearly as gleeful about it. Teddy had had new radials put on her van right after he got out of jail for his latest shoplifting offense. It was to say he was sorry, Liz explained, as we trudged through the cementlike white stuff with our last boxes. Of course, he'd charged them.

I led the way to the Stockhams' place. The Aspen Ranch area was situated just at the foot of the Aspen Meadow Wildlife Preserve, a sprawling hundred-thousand-acre wooded refuge for elk, mountain lions, and all other manner of wildlife. Hunters, hikers, fishermen, Scouts, and nature lovers shared the Preserve and gloried in the Aspen Meadow itself, reputedly one of the largest living organisms on earth (a stand of aspens is actually one tree that has developed an extensive root system and become *many* trees). The Aspen Meadow was also the namesake for our town, which benefited from the tourism that the Meadow itself brought.

Four years ago, the sale of the ten-thousand-acre Burdock Ranch abutting the Preserve had provoked the usual hysterical conflict between Colorado's pro- and anti-growth folks. After two years of vicious wrangling, Aspen Ranch, a luxurious sub-division featuring five- to ten-thousand-square-foot homes on ten-acre lots, had been approved. The builders swore they were preserving the character of the Wildlife Preserve. *We could put up ticky-tacky condos,* they'd threatened the plan-ning commission, who eventually denied their application. But the county commis-sioners—all of whom had received huge campaign donations from the builders, it was later reported, and not just in the *Mountain Journal*—unanimously reversed the decision of their own planners and ap-proved the project.

Wending my way through the wide, snow-blanketed streets of Aspen Ranch, I quickly lost my way. Lots of snow-covered trees and meadows looked like lots of other snow-covered trees and meadows. Plus, for all their money, the builders had messed up pretty dramatically on the street signs. They were long, slender, wood-carved af-fairs now completely frosted with ice and snow. Unfortunately, the numbers for the houses were also carved in this same style, and despite their placement at the end of each driveway, were illegible. I wasn't having fun trying to find Thirty-two Aspen Ranch Lane, even though I'd been there before.

I finally got a clue from the mailboxes, grand wood-and-metal boxes painted with birds, pine branches, stagecoaches, and—thank you, Lord—*Dr. and Mrs. Turner Macalester, 18 Aspen Ranch Lane* lettered on the side. I slowly rumbled past Dr. and Mrs. William Knapp, Dr. and Mrs. Bachman Wilson, Dr. and Mrs. Paul Cardero...and wondered why the developers hadn't built a hospital at the entrance to the Wildlife Preserve. It would surely shorten up everybody's commute.

I slowed as we climbed Aspen Ranch Lane. I knew we were only about a mile from the Preserve, but the white expanse of trees did not look familiar. I'd visited the Stockham place when the ground had been clear and the wooden street signs legible.

Finally, I drew up to a long, gently ascending driveway that looked vaguely familiar, not because of the trees and rocks or snow-covered sign, but because a familiar vehicle was blocking the driveway.

Marla had told me at the jewelry party about Pam Disharoon's white Audi, with its license plate GOGIRL. I groaned.

I hadn't anticipated having to ask a *very* early guest to move her car, especially not a guest who reportedly had an unstable relationship with her sister, the volatile Page Stockham, my client. Still, would this give me a chance to question the elusive Pam on her relationship with the hapless Barry Dean?

Another question formed in my brain as Liz and I sat in our vans, plumes of exhaust spiraling upward through the cold, moist air. Was Pam here to attend her brother-in-law's cash-raising lunch?

Or was she here to disrupt it?

CHAPTER 14

"Are the keys in it?" Liz demanded, banging on my windshield. When I shrugged, she raked her hair with her gloved hands, traipsed through what must have been ten inches of snow—it always snowed more west of town, here by the Preserve—and peered into the Audi.

"Think you should call them on the cell phone?" she cried.

I shook my head and jumped out of my van. "By the time I reach them, and they argue and debate until somebody decides to get dressed and come down here, I could have made it up there and put pressure on

Shane to drive me back down." I arrived at her side. Despite the fact that I wore a wool jacket, I shivered in the biting cold.

"OK. While you go up, I'll stay and guard our stuff."

I began the long tramp up the driveway. There was only one set of footprints in the snow, undoubtedly Pam's. The uphill walk itself was actually very pretty, like being transported into a set for *The Nutcracker*. Trees high and low were hung with glittering ribbons of snow. The ground was thickly frosted, and was still a pristine, crystalline white. Sunbeams slanting through the pine and aspen branches winked off errant flakes. I would have had more inclination to appreciate all this if I hadn't been worrying about how we were going to do the lunch *without being able to drive up to the house*. We really needed someone to move Pam's damn car.

After what must have been a mile of trudging, the large log house came into view, a pretty-but-oversized two-story affair that Shane had smugly informed me was in the style of Swedish Country. By the time I arrived at the carved front door and rang the bell, I felt as if I'd traipsed across Sweden by way of the North Pole.

"Where have you been?" Shane demanded even before I began shaking off snow in his foyer. "I was expecting you twenty-two minutes ago." His face was flushed, his tone accusing. I told myself to count to ten. While silently ticking off numbers, I took in his outfit: cream-colored silk shirt, suede Western riding jacket, leather cowboy pants and boots, Stetson hat. Shane was apparently going to make his pitch costumed as a high-flying cowboy. Well, I'd seen weirder.

"There's an Audi blocking your driveway," I pointed out. "We can't get in. And I need payment before we start."

Shane heaved a sigh of exasperation. He mumbled, "The ring's coming, I promise." Then he hooked his thumb in the direction of female voices bubbling from the interior of the house. I tugged off my boots and shuffled past the dining room, which was beautifully done up with a lavish floral centerpiece, gleaming crystal, Imari-pattern china, and linens in rich red, navy, beige, and gold.

"Dining room looks good," I mumbled,

and forced a smile at Shane. I really didn't want to carry my bad mood into a confrontation with Pam Disharoon.

"Oh, I got the flowers and styling done in exchange for a Palm pilot," Shane replied. "And the china was one of Page's many, uh, extravagances."

The living room offered more Swedish Country stuff. This seemed to mean lots of tall white furniture, wood sculptures of forest nymphs, chunky tables, and etched portraits of Nobel prizewinners. A fire blazed and crackled in the moss-rock hearth. Still shivering from my trek up the driveway, I longed to warm myself in front of it. But I sensed that wouldn't go over very well.

Pam and Page, both lounging in tall, white corduroy wing-back chairs, registered my arrival. Why was I bothering *them,* their dismayed looks said.

"There's an Audi in our way," I announced to the two women. "We can't get the vans up the driveway."

"Oh, it's mine," Pam said offhandedly, reaching into a large Louis Vuitton purse. Was that purse the uniform tote of the yuppie set? And how had she avoided having it snatched by Teddy Fury? "I just *had* to take that nice long walk up the driveway. It was so...so *sensual*! Out here in the boon-docks, the snow is *seductively* pretty! Couldn't you just imagine *rolling* in it with someone you love?" She treated Shane and Page to a dazzling smile. Then she turned and tossed me an *LV* key ring, which only my best imitation of Arch snag-ging the lacrosse ball enabled me to catch. "Here. You can move it." So much for my hopes of Pam shrieking with embarrass-ment for causing so much trouble with her car, and then scrambling from the room to move it.

In my business, pots can boil over. The *caterer* can't. Not for the first time, I was having a hard time staying cool. I avoided a glance into the gilt-edged mirror over the mantel. If I did, I was sure to see steam whistling out my ears.

"I'll drive you back down," Shane inter-posed hastily. "Need me to preheat the oven or anything?"

I swallowed the words *What I need is for you to give me that damn ring this instant, or call Kentucky Fried Chicken for your lunch.* Instead, I nodded. "Four hundred degrees."

"Done."

A few ringless minutes later, we were bumping down Shane's driveway in his old truck. He had put on a navy cashmere coat to cover his invest-in-me outfit, and his nervousness was increasing to the point that he almost made me jittery.

"I'm going to get you the ring," he announced preemptively, "I just need to wait until Pam and Page have settled into one of their little squabbles. Then neither one of them will leave her seat to get wine or whatever, and we can do the deed."

"Shane—"

"I don't know why Pam's here," he interrupted me. "Page told her we were having investors over for lunch, and Pam decided to crash the party. Unless she has a wad of money somewhere that I don't know about, she's just another mouth to feed. At best. At worst, she and Page will have a fight." Slowing the truck, he shot me a worried look. "Do you sometimes have to break up arguments at catered events?"

You mean, I nearly said, *like the tussle between you and your wife just two days ago?* Instead, I answered, "It happens. Usually I can find a way to distract everybody's attention. Like inviting them to come eat dessert. Speaking of which, does that mean we'll now have thirteen for lunch?"

Shane blushed. "Well, yeah. I guess. Sorry. But don't worry, they always get into such a big fight that they miss dessert. I just wish they'd argue now, and Pam would stomp off before my investors arrive." He swerved to avoid a pine tree—his driveway *was* treacherous—and pulled up by Pam's Audi. From behind her frosted windshield, Liz beeped and waved.

"Just park the Audi on the far side of the garage, near the middle storage shed," Shane advised. "Then you all can get your vans next to the house."

I hopped out, mulling over the words *middle storage shed*. How much *stuff* could a couple with two ninth-graders *have*? Enough, apparently, to fill a house and several sheds. I started the Audi on only the second try. Pam wouldn't have won any awards in the Clean Car Competition, that was for sure. A cereal bowl with hardened flakes clanked back and forth on the carpet in front of the passenger seat; newspapers strewn across the backseat swished forward as I accelerated; a Starbucks cup of long-dead coffee sloshed in the container by the radio. Well, I now knew one thing for certain about Pam: She was a true slob. During the few minutes I let the Audi warm up, I pawed through everything within reach. With Julian in jail, I had no scruples left. Unfortunately, I found nothing about Barry's murder or anything else that might bear on the case.

I crept up the driveway and pulled Pam's car carefully to the right of the garage where there were indeed three lovely log storage sheds. Liz piloted my van behind me. Shane trucked her back to her own van while I began unloading supplies. After Liz roared up the driveway and parked beside me, Shane used the plow-blade on his truck to smooth out a parking area in front of the house. Meanwhile, Liz and I quickly trekked the last of our supplies into the kitchen.

One of the gold-and-white-granite countertops held *two* almost-empty wine bottles. The sisters' talking and laughing had ratcheted up several decibels. I began to worry. It was only 10:30 A.M. Forget dessert, how sloshed would Pam and Page be by *lunch*? I shoved this concern aside and relieved Liz of her last box. Within five minutes, we were working side by side in the kitchen.

"If this guy can't manage to keep a store going, where did he get the money to buy *this* place?" Liz whispered as we carefully heaved the twenty-plus-pound beef roast into the oven. It would be hot and perfect by the time lunch was ready.

"He inherited it, I think," I whispered back. "According to Marla, Shane's gone through a string of bad businesses. Page married him for his money, but the dough's leaking away. That's the main reason he's seeking investors to take his business online."

"Have you ever actually catered an event for Page Stockham?" Liz asked. Her tone indicated that *she* had, and had lived to tell the tale.

"I thought you didn't know them," I protested, still whispering. "I'm only vaguely acquainted with them, through Marla."

Liz rolled her eyes. "I don't *know* them.

But I had the misfortune of having to cater for her once." She hissed: "She is *impossible*."

I pressed the button on the nonstick spray can and lightly coated the Stockhams' indoor grill for the mushroom salad. "I thought you only catered for your corporation."

"I did," said Liz, as she organized thirteen soup bowls on large saucers. "But Page was chairing a fund-raising event that my company was hosting. She drove me nuts—nickel-and-diming my department to death, trying to get a more expensive menu for the amount contracted. She kept saying she'd talked to this or that catering company and they could do such-and-such for so much less! Finally I told her I didn't care, go ahead and hire somebody else. Just be sure to have it OK'd by the corporation. The corporation told her *I* was their in-house caterer, and she could *not* hire anyone else and expect them to pay the bills. Plus I was in charge of approving the guest list. I never saw it, and had a floating number of attendees from her, ranging from two to three hundred. In the end, Page invited all her friends, even though they didn't give a whit about the charity. She acted as if it was *her* party, thrown just for her and her pals, to whom she talked loudly while the director of the charity made his pitch. 'Try some of my caviar,' she urged her pals, once we broke for food. She kept telling them to load up on the barbecued prawns and roast suckling pig, they'd been so difficult for *her* to get! She used that party to pay off all her social debts, forever."

"For crying out loud." The themes of this marriage—of entitlement to money that belonged to others, of treating people who worked for you like slaves, of not paying for what you received—were becoming crystal clear. The Stockhams were arrogant, self-centered rule-breakers who blamed all their problems on others. Had Barry Dean threatened this selfish way of doing things? According to Marla, Barry had discovered The Gadget Guy's nonpayment of rent, and had demanded compensation. In the parent guidebooks, they call this *consequences*. Had Barry's insistence on consequences for the Stockhams cost him his life?

I couldn't concentrate on this question, because I had to plate up the greens that would form the base for the mushroom salad. Worse, Liz was still regaling me with her tale of Page Stockham.

"So at *that* point, Bitch Page went behind my back and complained to one of the vice presidents that I'd been uncooperative. She even advised him not to pay my food bills. She claimed I was jacking up the price! She is an *insufferable* bitch! I hope she doesn't recognize me today. Maybe my new haircut will help."

She advised him not to pay my bill. . . . Well, here we were setting up in the kitchen and *I still didn't have a ring*. I glanced around the kitchen: Liz was bringing the Asian stock up to the simmer and unwrapping the dumplings. I drizzled the glistening marinade over the wild mushrooms, and went to look for our host. By golly, I was going to pack everything up and skedaddle if he didn't *pay*.

Shane, his mouth drooping, sat in what I hoped was not a drunken stupor on a love seat across the living room from Page and Pam. The sisters' conversation seemed to be reaching the simmer much faster than our dumpling soup.

"*I* helped Aunt Linda find the new doctor who did her so much good," Page was insisting, gesticulating with her wineglass. "*I* fired that cardiologist who'd misdiagnosed her, and *I* was the one who ordered new tests and hired her a new cook. *You* couldn't be bothered, Pam, because *you* were too busy trying on nighties for men twenty years your senior—"

"Excuse me, but at least I have a *job,*" Pam retorted, then slugged down wine. "That's unlike *some* people, who live off others' unearned wealth."

"Oh, so you're a communist now?"

"Furthermore," Pam steamed on, "*I* didn't go rifling through Aunt Linda's cobalt stems until I found the goblet where she hid the diamond pendant—"

"That diamond pendant was *stolen!*"

"By whom?"

"The cook!"

"Would that be the same cook *you* hired?"

"I didn't *know* she was a thief!" Page screamed.

Pam took another noisy gulp of Burgundy. "Excuse *me,* but I think you know *all about* thieves!"

"Exactly what are you insinuating?"

"You've got that pendant and I want to know where it is!"

"Shane," I said in a low voice. "I'll need payment before we can proceed."

Shane's face was frozen in pain. While the two sisters screamed, he hauled himself out of the love seat and motioned for me to follow him down the hall. Intent on their argument, Pam and Page did not register our departure, which was probably for the best.

"These are the bathrooms, in case clients ask," he told me, pointing to each side of the hallway. I told him this was good to know. I reached in to flip on the lights of a black-and-silver rest room on one side, and a peach-papered and marble-countered one on the opposite wall. I never broke my stride. I didn't want to give Shane the chance to get distracted—again.

"OK, now we need to be quiet and quick," he warned, as he creaked open a door that bore a floral-bordered needle-point sign: *Page's Place*.

"You're going to take the ring out of your wife's room?" I asked, incredulous. I looked around the room. Page's Place was as disheveled as Pam's Audi. Clothes spilled out of drawers of white-and-gold French Provincial furniture; open closet doors revealed a heap of discarded coats next to a heap of shoes; the plush cream-and-floral carpeting was so paved with discarded stockings and rejected lingerie that it was like a Victoria's Secret obstacle course.

Like her sister, Page was a dedicated slob.

Shane put his finger to his lips, then paused to listen. Page and Pam were now squabbling over who Aunt Linda would have wanted to have the cobalt.

"I bought the ring for her birthday next month," Shane told me. "But she always goes through my stuff, and she found it and took it." His nose wrinkled. "See, one time I had to take one of her presents back and she'd already gone through my stuff to find out what she was getting. When the bills came in, I decided to return one gift, an emerald bracelet. She was furious and... well, you've seen how Page is when she's furious. So now, no matter how good I get at hiding stuff, she gets better at finding it, and she takes her presents, so I won't decide I've been too extravagant and return them. What she doesn't *realize* is that I've gotten better at going through *her* stuff, so—" He stopped when he saw my mouth hanging open. "What's the matter?"

"You said we needed to be quiet and quick."

Shane took long, zigzagging steps across the large room, avoiding discarded outfits as if they were piles of elephant dung. Since my legs weren't quite as long as his, I had a hard time following him.

"Here we go," Shane announced, pulling open a drawer dripping with slithery nightgowns. He groped in the back of the drawer for a silk sachet of potpourri. "This'll just take a sec," he promised.

He untied the lace drawstring of the sachet, sending bits of dried rose petals fluttering to the floor. His stealthy behavior was making me so nervous that I averted my eyes hastily and looked around the room. Four lacy bras, black, beige, white, and pink, were laid out on the chaise lounge. Clearly, Page hadn't been able to decide among them. All four were of the amply padded variety. Page Stockham may or may not have been a thief, as her sister claimed, but there was no doubt the woman stretched the truth.

"Here we go," declared Shane, as he extracted something shiny from the potpourri. More dried petals fluttered to the carpet. He handed me the ring—it was a dazzling trio of jewels: sapphire, diamond, and ruby—and told me to try it on.

"It looks like something for the Fourth of July," I commented, as I obeyed. The ring was a tad big for me. Not that it mattered, because this was collateral. I took it off and slipped it deep into my skirt pocket.

"Yeah, well," Shane muttered, as he hastily reassembled the gutted potpourri bag, tucked it back into the drawer, and picked at the dried bits at his feet. "Let's just hope she doesn't go looking for it before her birthday."

"Shane," I protested, as he hustled me down the hallway. "I really don't think this—"

"Aunt Linda never *intended* for you to have the chandelier! We specifically talked about it when I was visiting her!" Pam's voice shrilled from the living room.

"You mean, visiting her when you were *ten*?" Page shrieked back.

The doorbell rang. Peeping through the hole, Shane gasped. "It's four of my investors!" he said, trying to be heard above the yelling. "Can't you do one of those distractions you mentioned?" he begged me. The ringer bonged again: Page and Pam raised their hollering a notch. "Just do something, will you?" Shane implored desperately.

I zipped into the kitchen, where Liz was spooning out juices and melted fat from the standing rib roast pan. The roast wasn't quite done, of course, but I really needed to start on the gravy from the drippings Liz was gathering. The doorbell chimed again. OK, first things first. *When in doubt, reach for a cliché.* I nabbed a pack of matches, hopped up on a chair, teetered perilously toward a stack of bookshelves, and lit the entire pack without closing the cover before striking. Then I thrust my little conflagration up to the kitchen smoke alarm.

Within seconds, the pealing of the alarm made me think I would go prematurely deaf. But the alarm certainly had the desired effect. I heard Pam screeching to Shane for her car keys. Shane, his face stricken, appeared at the kitchen door,

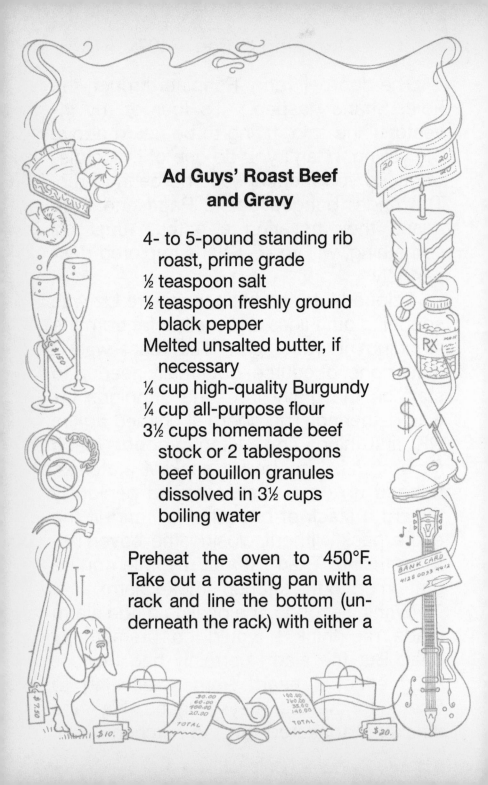

Ad Guys' Roast Beef and Gravy

4- to 5-pound standing rib roast, prime grade
½ teaspoon salt
½ teaspoon freshly ground black pepper
Melted unsalted butter, if necessary
¼ cup high-quality Burgundy
¼ cup all-purpose flour
3½ cups homemade beef stock or 2 tablespoons beef bouillon granules dissolved in 3½ cups boiling water

Preheat the oven to 450°F. Take out a roasting pan with a rack and line the bottom (underneath the rack) with either a very large piece of foil that completely covers the bottom of the pan and can be folded up over the sides or two pieces of foil that have been rolled tightly in the middle to form one large piece. The bottom of the pan should be completely covered with an airtight piece of foil.

Use a paper towel to pat the roast dry, then season the roast with the salt and pepper. Place the roast, bone side down, on the rack. Insert an instant-read digital thermometer into the roast so that the sensor is in the middle of the roast.

Place the roast in the oven and immediately reduce the oven heat to 325°. Roast until the temperature reads 115°F. (At this point the beef is quite rare, but the cooking is not done yet.) Remove the roast to another pan (even a large pie plate will do) and return it to the oven. (To obtain medium-rare, the roast should be removed when the thermometer reaches 125°F to 130°F; for medium, 135°F to 145°F.) If the thermometer reaches the desired temperature before the gravy is finished, remove the roast to a serving platter and tent it with foil.

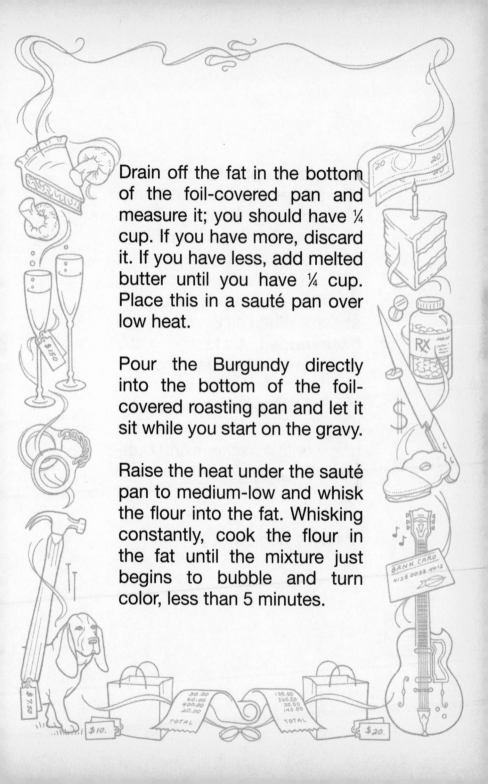

Drain off the fat in the bottom of the foil-covered pan and measure it; you should have ¼ cup. If you have more, discard it. If you have less, add melted butter until you have ¼ cup. Place this in a sauté pan over low heat.

Pour the Burgundy directly into the bottom of the foil-covered roasting pan and let it sit while you start on the gravy.

Raise the heat under the sauté pan to medium-low and whisk the flour into the fat. Whisking constantly, cook the flour in the fat until the mixture just begins to bubble and turn color, less than 5 minutes.

Using a heatproof plastic spatula, scrape the flavorful brown bits adhering to the foil into the wine. Stir this wine mixture into the cooking fat–flour mixture. Whisking constantly, add the beef stock in a slow stream. When all the stock has been added, taste the gravy and correct the seasoning.

Over medium-low to medium heat, whisk and cook the gravy until it thickens and bubbles. Serve hot with the roast beef.

Makes 4 to 6 servings

while I imitated one of the Broncos' razzle-dazzle plays by doing a one-handed toss of the keys to him, while keeping my little book of matches held high.

Over the racket Liz cried, "Goldy, what the *hell* are you doing?" Still, she had the presence of mind to slam the kitchen door shut behind Shane. We heard Pam make a noisy, stamping exit out the front door—so much for keeping the investors out of the fracas—while shouting, "I'll be back to talk about this some more! I'm not done!" Liz actually giggled.

Next Page's voice shrieked at the kitchen door, accompanied by her pounding on same. Liz cried, "Please go to a separate part of the house, Mrs. Stockham! We don't want the smoke smell to wreck your—uh—cobalt stuff! Not to worry! We've got the situation under control!"

Page stamped away. I hoped it was not in the direction of Page's Place, where she might want to try on some of her jewelry to calm herself down. But I had no time to worry about that: The chatter from arriving guests was unmistakable. My mind chattered, too, when a volume on an upper bookshelf snagged my attention. Unfortunately, it was then that the fiery matches reached my fingertips. I yelped and flung the ball of flame toward the sink. It hit the roast, landed in the pan, and ignited. Without thinking, Liz grabbed an open bottle of Burgundy and poured it over the flames, and a genuine explosion rocked the kitchen. I screamed, jumped down from the chair, nabbed an extra-large bottle of Evian, and dumped the contents on our beautiful, blazing, twenty-dollar-a-pound prime beef.

The smoke alarm was still squealing as Liz, now splashing a second bottle of Evian over the still-flaming roast, yelled, "I don't think they're going to hire us again!"

In spite of all this, the luncheon came off well. I was disappointed not to have had a chance to talk to Pam about the Barry mess, but wasn't sure I actually would have been able to. And anyway, my disappointment was allayed when *Marla* sashayed through the front door, claiming she was taking the place of someone who was sick. Because the luncheon was quite a bit smaller than Monday's party, we didn't have the opportunity to share gossip—except when she tiptoed into the kitchen to say Page and Shane had started to fight again, and that Page had stalked out. A few moments later, I saw Page's Audi—a duplicate of her sister's—whiz away.

Without his wife there to scrutinize and criticize his every move, Shane was unexpectedly brilliant. His enthusiastic pitch about The Gadget Guy On-Line reminded me of Tom Sawyer's whitewash-the-fence psychology. Only a select few were good enough to do this job, and if you wanted to be in on this opportunity to invest, you were just going to have to *get in line*! Shane's enthralled guests all beamed and asked, Was there an upper limit on how much one could invest? All, that is, except for Marla, who gave me a dramatic wink.

The food, despite our disastrous start, was out of this world, if I do say so myself. As if on cue, the snow began to flutter down again as Liz and I ferried out the steaming, fragrant bowls of soup dotted with floating dumplings. Liz stoked the fire in the dining room fireplace while I served Wild Girls' Grilled Mushroom Salad. Since Liz and I had learned one of Julia Child's lessons well—Never criticize your own food at a party—we were able to serve "Lightly Smoked Prime Rib" without batting an eye or even giggling. The investors gobbled it all up, right to the Strawberry-Rhubarb Cobbler, of which, like the investment, everyone demanded large pieces.

While we were serving the lunch, however, my curiosity began to nag. During the ring-stealing and fire-starting escapades, I'd seen a couple of things that had perplexed me, and I wanted to look into them—OK, snoop—a bit more. There were a few too many things about the Stockhams that were bothering me—the vicious way they fought, the nasty games they played, their ruthless habit of blaming others for their financial problems. All these, plus their current money mess brought on by The Gadget Guy's eviction from Westside, were making me wonder if they were more involved in the death of Barry Dean than the cops suspected. Anything to try to help Julian, I said to myself, as I scooped globes of ice cream.

While Liz handed out seconds of ice cream and cobbler, I climbed back onto the kitchen chair and turned my attention to the bookshelves. The lowest shelf contained the usual assortment of gourmet cookbooks people bought these days but

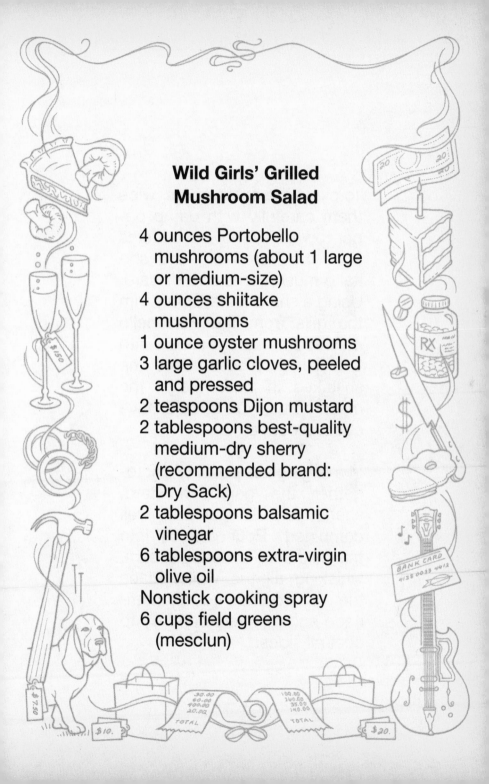

Wild Girls' Grilled Mushroom Salad

4 ounces Portobello mushrooms (about 1 large or medium-size)
4 ounces shiitake mushrooms
1 ounce oyster mushrooms
3 large garlic cloves, peeled and pressed
2 teaspoons Dijon mustard
2 tablespoons best-quality medium-dry sherry (recommended brand: Dry Sack)
2 tablespoons balsamic vinegar
6 tablespoons extra-virgin olive oil
Nonstick cooking spray
6 cups field greens (mesclun)

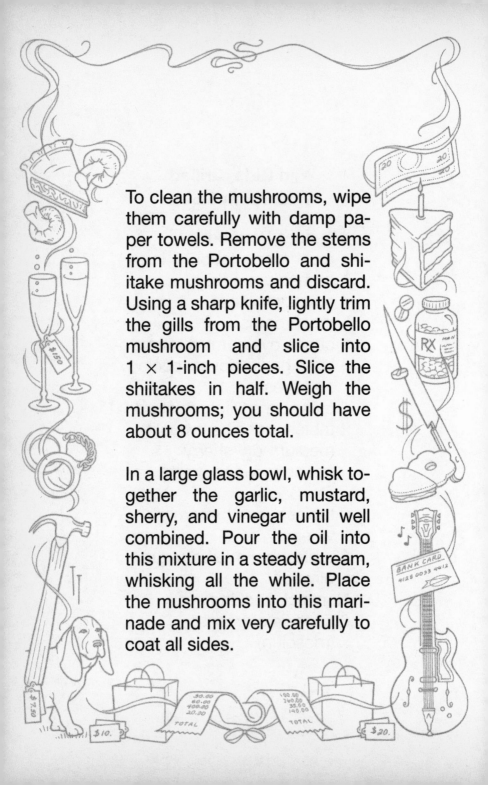

To clean the mushrooms, wipe them carefully with damp paper towels. Remove the stems from the Portobello and shiitake mushrooms and discard. Using a sharp knife, lightly trim the gills from the Portobello mushroom and slice into 1 × 1-inch pieces. Slice the shiitakes in half. Weigh the mushrooms; you should have about 8 ounces total.

In a large glass bowl, whisk together the garlic, mustard, sherry, and vinegar until well combined. Pour the oil into this mixture in a steady stream, whisking all the while. Place the mushrooms into this marinade and mix very carefully to coat all sides.

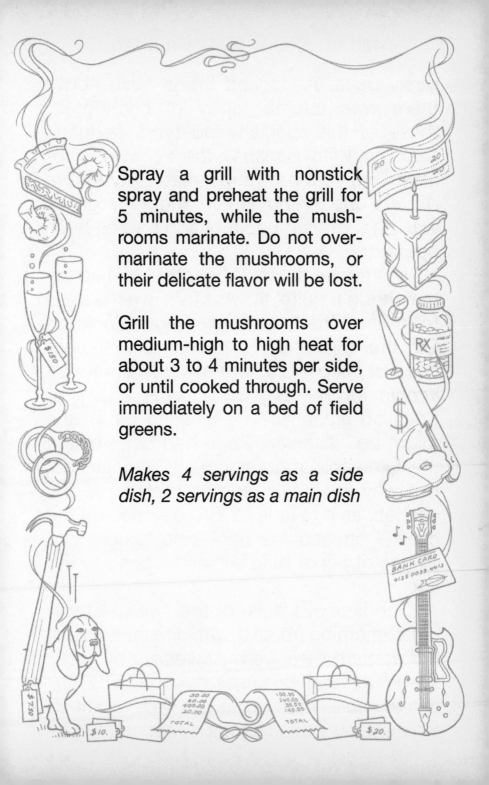

Spray a grill with nonstick spray and preheat the grill for 5 minutes, while the mushrooms marinate. Do not over-marinate the mushrooms, or their delicate flavor will be lost.

Grill the mushrooms over medium-high to high heat for about 3 to 4 minutes per side, or until cooked through. Serve immediately on a bed of field greens.

Makes 4 servings as a side dish, 2 servings as a main dish rarely used. All looked brand-new. Above them was another array of cookbooks, these of the specialty-fad type, featuring *Cooking With Bananas the Fiji Way, Creative Tofu Touches,* and *Bread Soups from Around the World* (spare me). My guess was that these books hadn't ever been opened.

But above those, I'd spotted something that hadn't quite fit. As Tom was always telling me, that's what you should look for. Off the top shelf, I pulled a well-worn copy of *Alcoholics Anonymous,* otherwise known as *The Big Book.* Was Shane or Page an alcoholic? Or thinking he or she might be? The way Page had been hitting the wine this morning might indicate so. But why keep *this* reading material in the kitchen, as if to hide it? Still perched on the chair, I opened the book and caught two pieces of paper before they fluttered to the floor.

The first was a list of the Twelve Steps, but something about it was different. I read, *We admitted we were powerless over our spending, that our lives had become unmanageable.* I turned to the second sheet. *Shopaholics Anonymous Meeting Times,* the heading announced. Hmm. I'd heard of Debtors Anonymous, but not this. Meetings were held at two times, on two days—ten o'clock in the morning and seven in the evening Mondays and Thursdays, in the—I had to read this part twice—*shoppers' lounge at Westside Mall*? Hello? Would you have an AA meeting in a liquor store?

Hearing Liz approach, I shoved the book back into its spot, then scrambled off the chair.

"Ten more coffees, two more teas," she announced, giving me a quizzical glance as I shoved the chair back into place. "Want to refill the coffeepot?"

"I already did, and it's percolating," I replied. "I'm going to the little girls' room," I added.

Liz bustled around, working on the hot drinks. Meanwhile, I sprinted down the hall, turned on the fan in the peach-colored bathroom, and, still standing in the hall, shut the door hard. Then I whipped into Page Stockham's room, aka *Page's Place*.

Unless I was very wrong, I'd glimpsed something here, too. Something—no, make that *things*—that I'd seen before, but in a wholly different context. If I was right, these items were of interest not only to me but maybe to law enforcement. I tiptoed over the clothes-strewn floor, bypassed the chaise lounge with its multicolored array of bras, and only cast a cursory glance at the armoire with its jumble of jewelry. As quietly as possible, I eased the bifold closet door to its fullest open position, then flipped on the light.

I had not been wrong. There, on Page Stockham's closet floor, was a jumbled mountain of shoes and shoeboxes. Red, pink, black, navy, beige, and white pumps spilled from cardboard and tissue. Each and every one was of the same style, featuring a cutout toe.

The last time I'd seen this style shoe, hundreds of them had been littered around the body of Barry Dean.

CHAPTER 15

Damn, I thought as I stared in astonishment down at the footwear. What exactly did this mean? That Page Stockham was the Imelda Marcos of the Rockies?

Logistics: Page hadn't physically attacked Shane; she'd acted in self-defense. She must have rejoined Marla after being hauled out of the lounge, because I knew that Marla, Ellie, and Page had been shopping together, even buying shoes, at that mammoth sale. But how could Page Stockham have bought so many of one style, and *not* seen Barry Dean Monday night? Forget seeing; could she have done something else? Was it possible that *Page* had stolen my knife, and in that corner of the shoe department that the cameras couldn't see, killed Barry herself? Maybe she hadn't quite succeeded in eliminating her husband's financial enemy, but had shoved him into the cabinet still moaning, then come back to finish the job, and bop me in the process?

I squatted down and stared at the shoes, thinking hard. What had Marla told me? That she, Page, and Ellie had left the mall together Monday evening, just before nine. I'd found Barry just after nine. In the nightmare that followed, I'd ruled each of the three women out as being the person who deserved to be behind bars, instead of Julian. Where had the women gone when they left the mall? Had they been together? I doubted the police had even questioned them, because they hadn't been in the shoe department when Julian found me. I doubted I'd find a receipt with a "time of sale" in the jumble of footwear. How long had Barry been in that Prince & Grogan shoe cabinet, anyway?

My cell phone bleated in my apron pocket. I leaped up and almost careened onto Page's chaise lounge. I grabbed the phone and turned off the power. If Page or Shane or *anybody,* for that matter, found me snooping around in a client's closet, my catering career would be over.

Strolling officiously down the hall to the kitchen, I popped back into the bathroom. There I turned the fan off. Back in the kitchen, I leaned against the side-by-side refrigerator, repowered the cell, and checked the incoming calls. Apparently, somebody at Hulsey, Jones, Macauley & Wilson wanted to talk to me in the worst way.

"Liz," I said when she came in with an empty cobbler pan, "how's it going? Sorry to have been gone so long."

"They love it." When Liz's eyes twinkled, her face seemed to light up, too. "They're demanding the recipe. With Page gone, it's a real party." She began filling the sink with soapy water, and I realized how much I appreciated one particular perk of success: being able to delegate to a trustworthy lieutenant. I said impulsively: "Liz, I'm very thankful we're working together."

She smiled. "Me, too. I haven't received any calls on my cell since we started over here. But...was that *your* cell phone I heard?" she asked, lifting one of her silvery eyebrows.

"Don't *tell* me you heard it."

"It wasn't for me, was it? I mean, just on the off-chance."

Of course, I knew what was worrying her. "No," I replied. "It wasn't about Teddy. It was...my lawyer."

"Everything's all right?"

"Oh, yeah." If it wasn't, I'd probably be the last to know. I checked my watch: one-thirty. While Liz whisked back into the dining room, I began rinsing out and packing up our containers. The window over the sink revealed that the thickening snow was coming down at an acute slant. This was a sure sign of a fast-moving storm. Liz reappeared, her eyes alight with laughter.

"Two of those widows are under Shane's spell. He looks like he's in a state of sexual ecstasy, just waiting for those checks to roll in."

I smiled. Maybe I wouldn't have to hold on to Page's ring for very long, after all. *Just don't ask me to contemplate the safety of those infatuated widows' investments.* In any event, that was beyond my control.

What I *really* needed to know was what was going on with Steve Hulsey, Esquire.

"Look, Liz. As I said, that message was from my criminal defense lawyer. Can you handle clearing while I give him a call?"

"Of course," she replied cheerfully, as she placed a stack of dirty dishes beside the sink. "I wouldn't want to miss the widows writing those checks. Fifty thou each." She glanced outside, then added, "Listen, Goldy, why don't you let me finish up *everything* here? It'll provide some distraction from obsessing about Teddy. Anyway, aren't you chaperoning a school field trip today?"

"I'm picking Arch and his pals up at their school at four." I sighed, dreading another chilly encounter with my son. "Thanks for reminding me. Maybe I better see if the attorney wants to huddle before then."

She nodded and moved back into the dining room. I dialed Steve Hulsey's number.

"He wants you to meet him at the jail as soon as possible," his secretary informed me, her voice crisp, efficient, and not at all friendly. "He needs to speak to you about Julian Teller."

"Why does he need to talk to me about Julian?"

"Mr. Hulsey has taken on his case. Mr. Hulsey is down at the jail now. Mr. Hulsey needs to see you."

I couldn't count to ten, so I counted to three. "I'm catering way up by the Aspen Meadow Wildlife Preserve." I could hear the secretary tapping away at a keyboard. Clearly, my answer wasn't worth her full attention. I raised my voice a bit. "The snow's coming down pretty *hard*. It'll take me at least half an hour to get down to the jail. Can't you please tell me what this is about? Can't I talk to Steve over the phone?"

"Mr. Hulsey will be waiting for you in the jail lobby." She disconnected before I could protest. I threw the cell phone onto the counter.

At that moment, Marla tiptoed into the kitchen, coffee cup in hand. She wore a royal blue and black wool suit, an onyx and sapphire necklace and matching earrings, and royal blue shoes. She gave me her cat-who-swallowed-the-canary look and filled her cup with coffee from the big percolator.

"So," she began, "the last time I saw you with Liz Fury, there was a *bit* of a disagreement going on. Now you two are all cozy. What happened?"

"Oh, she's having problems with her son. In case you haven't noticed, I have the same kind of problems. Listen," I rushed on, "Monday night, how did you meet up with Page after she was ejected from the lounge?"

Marla's eyes widened. "Ellie and I just had to know what had happened, so we went looking for Page at the mall's security office. The cops had just released her, so we *again* heard how much she hated and despised Barry Dean and her husband. She was really ready to shop then, so we all headed toward the shoe sale!"

"OK, but were you shopping together? I mean, the whole time in Prince and Grogan?"

Marla crinkled her nose and slurped her coffee. "We all bought a ton of shoes, if that's what you mean. Why? Does this have something to do with Julian? I'll do anything to help."

"I know Ellie went home with Elizabeth

Harrington. Did you and Page drive back to Aspen Meadow together?" I pressed.

"No, why? The cops had told Shane they'd take him home, Page said. He'd left his BMW there at the mall, so I drove Page to it. She said she was bringing it back up here."

"When was that? Eight-thirty? Eight forty-five?" I asked breathlessly.

Marla moved her wrist back and forth; the diamonds on her Rolex sparkled. "It's a nice watch, Goldy, but I feel it's gauche always to be checking it. Sorry, I don't *know* what time it was."

"How about Ellie? When did she leave?"

"For crying out loud, Goldy! She's our friend! Why do you want to know all this?"

"Just tell me!"

Marla expelled breath. "We saw an old friend, Elizabeth Harrington, at the shoe sale. You remember, the widow of Brian Harrington?"

"Right, Ellie told me she was with her."

"Elizabeth lives near Ellie, so she offered to take her home. Around nine, I guess. Why does it matter?"

"Just something else I'm trying to figure

out for Tom," I said lightly, as Liz reappeared at the kitchen door.

Marla sighed at the appearance of Liz, rolled her eyes at me, and trounced out of the kitchen.

Four minutes later, I had thanked Liz for both her hard work and her offer to clean up by writing her another check, the second one I'd given her that day. I quickly explained that I was sure old Shane wasn't going to cough up an extra gratuity. Even with all of Liz's own problems, she actually laughed. I thanked her again and hugged her.

Four additional heavy, wet inches of snow had accumulated since we'd arrived. At the end of the driveway, I looked right and left to check for traffic—there wasn't any—and glanced up into the Preserve. The curtain of flakes had thinned; maybe we were experiencing a mere flurry. Snow fell softly on millions of rows of perfectly frosted pines. It was breathtakingly beautiful, and made me feel a bit better. At least for a while.

"Julian Teller passed the second polygraph," Steve Hulsey informed me in the lobby of the jail. His voice was a deep wheeze, like a snake with bronchitis. This day, he was wearing an impeccable dark beige silk suit. "But he still will be formally charged—arraigned—on Friday morning." He loomed over me. "Second-degree murder, a heat-of-passion crime."

"What are you *talking* about?" Denial rose in my throat like a scream. The sergeant on duty, a pudgy woman with a face like a raisin cookie, watched our interchange with, I imagined, one finger on the button you use to summon officers into the lobby. But I couldn't help myself. "There's more to Barry's murder than you think!" I snapped.

Hulsey held up a hand, his face as cold and impassive as a stone statue's. I flinched. "Calm down," he commanded. "They're telling me you're not a suspect anymore. So I'm taking over on *this* case now. Please listen calmly while I tell you what's going to happen."

I bit back another protest, crossed my arms, and glared at the gleaming white tiles on the lobby wall. Couldn't they have made this place look a *bit* less like a bathroom?

"They're still developing evidence in the

case," Hulsey told me, his voice back to the bronchilian reptile. "And the county attorney's office and the detectives are going over that videotape from the party in the shoppers' lounge with a microscope. Julian is on it, having not one but *two* heated arguments with the victim. And let's not forget, the store security guard found Mr. Teller *with his hand on the murder weapon.* Friday, ten in the morning, is the time of the arraignment."

I nodded. I'd been to one of The Jerk's arraignments. There I hadn't heard justice being served; I'd heard a dispassionate declaration of war between the prosecution and the defense.

"With second-degree murder, they'll probably let Julian out," Hulsey said, a bit more gently, but with a peek at his watch. "For a price, of course. Mrs. Korman is seeing about bail."

"Mrs. Korman?" I said. Of course: *Marla.* I blinked and tried to focus. The lawyer's voice seemed far away.

"*Marla* Korman." Hulsey could not disguise his impatience. "Your friend, the other ex-wife of Dr. John Richard Korman? You're probably looking at bail of a million dollars. Bond'll be a hundred thousand." I nodded blankly. *A hundred thousand dollars.* "One more thing," Hulsey added briskly. "Since you're not a suspect anymore, you can visit Julian. That's it, then. I need to go." He handed me another one of his cards (I was accumulating quite a collection), grasped his briefcase, and sailed out the doors.

I watched Hulsey make a determined tramp through the snow to his Jag. OK, Julian was going to be arraigned. I shook my head. Our wonderful friend was suffocating behind bars. No matter what it cost, we *had* to get him out on bail.

I signed in to see Julian and was sent to the same phone-containing cubicle as before. What was I going to say to him that could possibly cheer him up? *You could be out on bail pretty soon*? Like Hulsey, I snuck a peek at my watch: almost half past two. Would Julian feel hurt when I said I could only stay for thirty minutes? Tears stung my eyes when he strolled through the door. I cemented a smile in place and sternly ordered myself to buck up. I couldn't help him if I was slobbering.

"Hey, Goldy!" Julian sang into the

phone. His face was even thinner and more haggard than before. But either he was doing a great acting job or his spirits had taken a turn for the better. "Didn't expect you here!" He pulled a torn piece of paper from his pocket and leaned forward in his chair. "Sorry if you had to wait. My lawyer just left—"

"Yeah, I heard about it—"

"And then I called Arch on his lunch hour—"

Julian's face cracked in a broad smile. He glanced down at the sheet in his hand. "This paper is my lifeline! It has the numbers of everyone I know. Arch told me to call him on his cell at certain times. So we talk three or four times a day. At his lunch hour, between his classes, like that. It's great. He told me you were taking him to the anatomy field trip. I did that at EPP. The smell of formaldehyde's really gross, by the way. Prepare yourself."

I thought of Julian's adoptive parents in Utah. Had he called them yet? I doubted it. "Yes, but—"

"And then you'll never guess whose message I just answered!" His tone was beyond bubbly; it was feverish. No talk of the arraignment. No talk of the future. I swallowed and remembered my admonition to the parents of my Sunday school kids: *Sometimes they just need you to listen.*

"Kim Fury!" Julian exclaimed. I tried not to look surprised as he continued: "Kim was a classmate of mine at EPP. We got to know each other pretty well, since we were both science kids among all the rich brats. Kim's really smart. Finished her B.S. in three years. Now she's doing graduate work at C.U. in computer science. Anyway, Kim is *really* pissed off with her brother for running away with her mom's credit cards."

I tried to look as if I understood where all this was going. But I was worried. Julian was beyond both bubbly and feverish. He was manic. How was I going to have a logical strategy-planning session with him?

"Anyway. Kim's *sure* her brother Teddy had something to do with this Dean thing, and that's why he skipped! But that's not all. She says her mother will do anything to keep Teddy from facing the consequences of his actions. Like this one time, he swiped a purse that had some car keys in it, and when he tried to start the car it jumped forward because it was still in gear—"

"Whoa, whoa, whoa. Whose car? Ellie's McNeely's?"

"I don't know," he rushed on. "But I was thinking, maybe—"

It was time to interrupt. "Julian," I said. "Please. Just take a deep breath, OK?"

Immediately the spark of hope in his eyes went out. I felt a pang of guilt.

"Sorry!" I said hastily. "But I need to take notes if I'm going to get all this down. Do you know what kind of car it was?" I dug into my purse for an index card and pencil.

"I don't know that either." His voice was barely audible.

"Did Kim have anything concrete to share about Teddy and Barry Dean? Something that might help us?"

"No."

"Well, give me her number, will you?" I scribbled the number he recited.

Julian looked up at the ceiling. "I passed the second lie detector test. Here's what's funny—it didn't matter. I had a wicked headache from caffeine withdrawal, so I've drunk about eight cups of jail coffee since the test. Stuff tastes like motor oil."

"We're going to get you out of here—"

"Yeah, yeah, yeah, I know, right, sure." He still wouldn't look at me. "Sorry to be so jazzed up. Listen, I still don't want my folks to know about this yet. I'll call down to Bluff when I'm ready, I promise." He straightened. "The formal charge on Friday will be second-degree murder. You probably heard. It's different, somehow, from that advisement on Tuesday. It all feels out of control." He shook his head. Again the sight of his thin face and unkempt hair felt like a blade in my heart. "I . . . I feel so bad about the bail money," he went on. "I feel so bad about *everything*. Seeing that knife in Mr. Dean was like noticing an electrical wire down on a wet road. You *know* you're not supposed to touch it. But your only thought is that you want to help, and then as soon as you touch it, you're either dead, in the case of the wire, or screwed, in the case of the knife—"

I leaned forward and urged, "Julian. Don't do this to yourself. As you said, all you tried to do was help, and that was the right thing to do. You are innocent of this crime. And we're going to prove it." I managed what I hoped was a courageous smile. "I promise to ask Tom to look into Kim Fury's allegation about her brother." *And to look into my own questions about the whereabouts of Ellie McNeely and Page Stockham from quarter to nine to nine, and why Page had ended up buying so many of a certain kind of shoe,* I added silently.

Julian rubbed his forehead. "I don't really want Teddy to get into trouble." He was suddenly restless. "Look, thanks for coming. Have fun at Arch's field trip." Then he hung up and walked away. He didn't look back.

Snow fell steadily as I drove up to Elk Park Prep. My muscles ached and my stomach growled. I had had nothing to eat except a reheated chocolate croissant (one of Julian's creations from the freezer) and double espresso. My mind jumped around: Page Stockham and her shoes. Liz Fury fretting over her troubled (and missing) son. Julian, alone in jail.

First things first. I punched in the phone number Julian had given me for Kim Fury in

Boulder. No answer. I left a message identifying myself and asking her to call. Then I tried Tom, who was off somewhere, and brought him up to speed on the shoes I'd found heaped in Page's closet. Had the cops checked the alibis of these two women, Page Stockham and Ellie McNeely, for the time of Barry's murder? Finally, there was Kim Fury's report of her brother stealing a car. Was he aware of any of this? I wanted to know. Had Teddy been a suspect in the theft of Barry's car? And finally, had the cops found anything at the Elk Park Prep portable toilet?

At quarter to four, I pulled off the interstate at the Aspen Meadow exit. I had to pick up my own son plus four other boys, drive back down the mountain, and endure an anatomy class. I was going to pass out if I didn't have something to eat.

To my surprise, there was no line at our little burg's drive-through espresso place. Through the thickening swirl of snowflakes, I ordered a hot croissant ham-and-Swiss sandwich for myself, plus six biscotti and six large hot chocolates. Yes, extra-hot for the cocoa, and yes, with whipped cream. *Extra* whipped cream. I accepted the treats gratefully. Times of trauma, I reflected as I bit into the delicious sandwich—flaky pastry surrounding hot, thinly sliced Danish ham, just-melted Jarlsberg, and a hint of Dijon mustard—demand comfort food. I gunned the van toward Arch's school, secure in the knowledge that when I'd finished wolfing down the sandwich, I had a cup of steaming, cream-topped cocoa waiting. Is there *any* better comfort food than chocolate? I think not.

Outside the Upper School, I pulled the van behind a line of Mercedes, Jags, Audis, four-wheel-drive Lexuses, and late-model BMW's. In the prep school big-spender environment, I knew that my van, with its emblazoned logo *Goldilocks' Catering, Where Everything Is Just Right!* gave Arch no end of anguish. The parents who did not know my son attended EPP undoubtedly thought I was there to serve gourmet hot dogs, maybe at that day's volleyball game.

Arch and a group of boys, their jackets unzipped and their wool hats askew, tumbled out of the school doors. Steam issued from their mouths as they hollered and flung quickly scooped snowballs at each other. To avoid enemy missiles, they ran and slid expertly across the snowy ice. Seeing them free and happy made me think of Julian, trapped in jail. I shuddered.

"Please say you brought us something to eat!" Arch exclaimed as he and his pals heaved their Sherpa-worthy backpacks into the van's rear. "We're starving! And freezing!"

"Hot chocolate and biscotti!" I called and received a deafening but grateful chorus of *Oh, yeah!*

"Mom, thanks," Arch murmured uncharacteristically, as he balanced his treat and surreptitiously leaned forward from the backseat, so his friends couldn't hear. Well, maybe my request for a little courtesy had hit its mark. That was two nice things he'd said to me in twenty-four hours. I glowed.

"This is how a cadaver's bone breaks," called one of the boys, as he snapped his biscotto in two.

"Oh, yeah?" my son replied. "This cocoa? It's the color of the inside of the liver."

I placed my hot chocolate firmly in the cup holder and turned my attention to the road.

During the drive, the boys joked mercilessly about the dissection and who was going to puke first. I clenched my teeth and decided not to accompany the boys inside. I had calls to make and a stomach to calm. But once in the hospital parking lot, the anatomy teacher hailed the van and said she was hoping *all* the moms could accompany the class, at least for the first ten minutes. I gulped the rest of my cocoa (for strength), hopped out carefully onto the ice, and told myself to buck up. After all, I'd seen corpses before, hadn't I?

As we filed into the small, windowless room, the odor of formaldehyde hit me like a slap. Undoubtedly kept as a sterile environment, the hospital classroom reminded me of the Furman County Morgue. A sheet draped the body, which lay on a metal table. Rows of gleaming medical instruments sat at the ready on a nearby wheeled shelf. I took a deep breath—not a smart idea, as the horrid odor flooded my lungs—and did a yoga centering exercise.

No matter how you tell yourself to detach from your feelings, it's impossible not to be apprehensive and sad when faced with a dead body. Once, the chilled flesh under this sheet had been a child, had played, and loved, and been loved. I shivered. When the teacher pulled back the sheet from the dead man's face, I squeezed my eyes shut and tried the yoga exercise again. When I reopened my eyes, the corpse's gray face and dark head of hair came into view. I slid my eyes around the group of students. Their bravado had evaporated. Instead, looks of fear, horror, and shock registered on the kids' faces. A boy and a girl bolted from the room simultaneously. When the boy threw up on the linoleum floor outside the dissection room, the girl, who was racing to the ladies', noisily followed suit.

After ten minutes of cleaning up, settling down, and comforting from the nurses and the teacher, the red-faced pair rejoined the class. Quite uncharacteristically, their classmates made no fun, but patted their peers on the back and murmured that they'd almost blown lunch, too.

Once things had calmed down, the teacher explained to the sickly-looking-but-attentive class that the subject was a middle-aged male, a diabetic with heart disease who'd died in his sleep in a small-town motel at the southwestern edge of Colorado. No family had claimed the body.

The county coroner had determined the cause and manner of death, that is, that the man had died of a heart attack. There were no signs of a struggle, no foul play was suspected, et cetera. Since the unclaimed body was of a relatively young man who hadn't been too fat, too thin, or a drug user, the Pueblo County Coroner, instead of doing an autopsy, had contacted the state anatomical board to offer the corpse as a donation for study. The board had accepted the specimen.

I steeled myself as the teacher gently peeled back the sheet. The kids gripped one another's arms and turned even more pale, but managed to keep their equilibrium. I was proud of them. After a moment, they began to study the specimen, thank God. It took courage to pull out their notebooks, turn academic attention toward the corpse, and start acting as if this really was a lab, and not hell.

The dead man had been short and stocky, with a flat abdomen and wide shoulders. Well-developed muscles had strained under skin that was now as gray as the trunk of a dead tree. Long, thin black hair curled over the cadaver's ears. An unremarkable face was distinguished by a nose that looked as if it had been broken more than once. The teacher droned on, explaining that at one point this man, an insulin-dependent diabetic, had suffered from gangrene. The effects of that disease were still visible. The class nodded, took notes, and donned surgical gloves while my eyes traveled the length of the body.

And then I gasped.

To distract the students from my gaffe, the teacher hastily murmured about how they needed to check their notebooks carefully, that they needed to follow the procedure they had been taught. I pressed my lips together and forced myself to look again at the cadaver's right foot.

Yes, this man had once been some-one's son, had loved and played. He'd also once worked as a construction manager at Westside Mall. Unless I was very much mistaken, the deceased was Lucas No-toe Holden.

CHAPTER 16

I made a hand sign to the teacher, mouthing that I'd be right back. The poor woman nodded at me distractedly as I tore out of the classroom, no doubt certain I, too, was about to be sick. In my distress, I nevertheless remembered that cell phones were prohibited in hospitals. *A phone, I thought desperately, I need a pay phone. Tom will know what to do.*

I raced at a clippety-clop down a linoleum-floored hall with echoing pastel-painted walls. The phone booth, however, boasted walls, a floor, and ceiling completely covered with carpet. It was so quiet

I felt paranoid as I whispered my frantic discovery to Tom.

"Goldy, the sheriff's department can't *touch* that body," Tom replied calmly when I'd finished. "The only person who can deal with it is the county coroner."

"But...what about the *hospital*? Can't they at least confirm this guy's identity? I mean, if it *is* Holden, that has to mean *something*. Maybe someone murdered him. Maybe the person who murdered Barry killed No-toe—"

"Hold on a sec." Tom called across to an associate, asking him to call the coroner's office and check if the cadaver now in the Lutheran Hospital teaching lab was Lucas Holden. In the distance, someone promised to get right on it. Tom returned to me.

"Miss G., the hospital's not going to know the name of the donor." He was tapping computer keys. I rubbed my forehead. Maybe I was overreacting. Maybe there were a lot of corpses with missing toes, and I was going overboard. "Yeah," Tom said, "we're still looking for Lucas Holden since it's an open case of a missing person. The coroner will talk to the anatomical board first, I can guarantee you that. He'll find out exactly how and where they got this body, then send a staff member over to the hospital. OK? But if this guy with the missing toe died of natural causes in a remote area, that really doesn't tell us much. Well, except why we haven't been able to find him."

"If it *is* Holden, he was a diabetic. If Holden had to inject insulin, he could have been given a shot of something else, something to precipitate a heart attack. Heroin, say. They didn't do an autopsy, remember."

"Miss G., *please*. The anatomical board won't accept a cadaver where there's any suspicion of foul play. And you also have to ask yourself *why* someone would want to kill this Holden. If he was an insulin-dependent diabetic with heart disease, any doctor is going to say you'd expect him to drop dead at the first opportunity. I'm not trying to be negative here. It's just the truth."

"Maybe Holden *saw* something," I insisted stubbornly. "Maybe he *knew* something. There must be a link. And you *are* being negative." My fingers drummed the vertical carpet. "Did you get anything back on the Page Stockham shoe situation? I just found out Page separated from Marla and Ellie in the parking lot that night."

He inhaled, an attempt to be patient. "The three women did tell us they were at the shoe sale, Goldy. They all agree they left just before nine. If they *hadn't* bought shoes, I'd be suspicious. But I'll mention to the guys that I think Page Stockham should be questioned again. If she doesn't have an alibi for the time Barry was killed, and if she was a bona fide enemy of his, they'll be interested. And before you ask, the Teddy Fury failed car-stealing incident involved a VW bug."

"But Kim Fury said—"

"You yourself told me that Kim the sister and Teddy the brother had an argument about one of Liz's cars on Monday. Nobody here has any idea where Teddy Fury is at the moment. My guess would be he's getting as far from that sister as possible."

I felt derailed. But I persisted. "I saw Hulsey at the jail. Any idea why they don't consider me a suspect anymore?"

"Maybe they believe you. Your story doesn't have holes. Only the guitar has holes. Should I be out looking for another present for Arch, by the way?"

Guilt thudded against my chest. "Sure," I said, and gulped. "Great. Thanks."

"No sweat. So, what about Hulsey?"

"He's representing Julian now, and says the charge at the arraignment will be second-degree murder. Bail is set at a million. Julian passed the second polygraph, by the way."

"I heard."

I thought of the seconds ticking by while the kids dissected Lucas Holden, maybe destroying valuable evidence that might free Julian. Had Tom's deputy reached the coroner? Or was I, like Julian, becoming both manic and desperate?

My thoughts whirled. Ellie's stolen Lexus had been rammed into Barry's Mercedes. That seemed like too much of a coincidence to attribute the burglary to a garden-variety car thief. Plus, somebody had tried to get rid of Ellie last night. That had not been an accident. Plus, *somebody* had been driving that dump truck on Monday. Somebody had definitely tried to kill Barry in the Westside Mall parking lot.

And, hours later, somebody had *succeeded* in killing him.

"Tom, getting back to Ellie's purse. Suppose Barry's new wannabe girlfriend, Pam Disharoon, had been watching Ellie. Pam's incredibly competitive. Say she saw her opportunity to nab the purse Teddy dumped. Could Pam have crashed Ellie's car into Barry's, picked up the cuff links, and later driven the runaway truck? All to make Ellie look bad in Barry's eyes? Then when Barry said he was sticking with Ellie, Pam stabbed him."

"Mm, I'd probably believe anything of Pam Disharoon. That woman has been difficult."

Visions of the cadaver abruptly intruded. "Tom, can you stay on top of this cadaver question? To help Julian? Please?"

Tom made his tone kind. "I promise. Don't worry, we can handle this. But I do have one thing that might interest you." I heard him shuffle papers. "A lawyer called us this morning, guy from a firm in Denver. Says his client is offering us evidence about the Barry Dean case, but only in exchange for immunity from prosecution by another governmental agency."

"You mean, immunity from a *federal* agency? As in, *Make the IRS leave me alone?*" My heart started to thump.

"Probably. Happens all the time. Only the IRS and other federal agencies don't prosecute. Not technically, anyway. They turn all their stuff over to a government attorney, who makes or doesn't make a case."

I exhaled. "What kind of evidence was this guy offering?"

"The attorney says his client will tell us why Dean had *headaches*."

"You mean, the client knows who pushed Barry down?"

"Probably. And it looks as if the guys are going to take the deal."

While he mused aloud on the immunity question, I debated about confessing to my pill-bottle-in-the-apron discovery. It was finding the Vicodin that had spurred me to get the medical records faxed to me. But I hadn't actually told Tom about the Vicodin yet. If I showed Tom the pills, was there any way I'd be able to avoid being charged with evidence-tampering? If the cops knew about Barry's headaches and their cause, would they really care so much about the painkillers themselves? I tried to remember if I'd ever seen Tom use my clarified butter, where I'd stashed the pills. I didn't think so.

"Uh, well," I stammered. "Just let me know about the coroner, will you?"

Tom paused. "You, uh, you don't know anything more about this headache deal, do you? I mean, I know you've...*reviewed* Dean's records."

I gnawed the inside of my cheek, remembering my forging exercise to get Barry's medical records. "Sorry. Listen, are you going to be home for dinner? I...have a couple of new theories about...this and that."

"I wish I didn't have to say 'I knew it.'"

"I'll explain it all later, promise. See you at six." I bade him good-bye and hung up. Sometime in the next few hours, I had to figure out how I was going to present *to* Tom all the stuff I'd kept *from* him. My own head began to hurt.

When I showed up at the classroom door, the teacher slipped out and asked if I was all right. I nodded. She informed me that the students had just started on the cadaver's spleen.

"Is there any way," I asked, "that you could wait? There could be a question from the coroner's office—"

"Wait? Wait for what? The class has waited for this trip the entire semester. If we don't proceed, we won't finish. We can't *wait*."

"Well, it's just that I... thought I might have recognized the cadaver."

The teacher's face turned as ashen as the corpse's. "Oh, dear! Mrs. Schulz, please! I really have to get back to my class. What are you going to do?"

"I'll just... go to my van," I faltered. And hope for whoever Tom's deputy could muster to put an end to this, before more evidence was destroyed. I knew I couldn't go back into the lab. Say the coroner did appear and demanded, "Which mom called about this cadaver?" Arch would never speak to me again.

Instead, I sat in my van and tried to raise Pam Disharoon on the cell. No answer. I gave up when the anatomy class rushed out the hospital doors. The five boys I'd brought squeezed into the van in high spirits. All were eager for a gross-out competition. The snow had turned to slush on the interstate, so I concentrated on my driving. It was better than listening to merrily delivered descriptions of each organ, and how it was not as bad as the dead bat they'd found on a Scouts expedition or the dead elk their dad had scraped off the Rover bumper.

To my great surprise, Tom was already home when Arch and I got there, putting the finishing touches on a cake with shiny chocolate icing. Comforted by his presence in the kitchen, I gave him a big hug, washed my hands, and got to work myself. While I defrosted stock and sautéed mushrooms, he told me he hadn't heard anything back yet on any of my inquiries. I tried to put the case out of my head as I energetically chopped vegetables for the salad I'd intended to serve at the Stockhams' lunch before changing the menu.

Because salads of chopped ingredients were all the rage among the Shop-Till-You-Drop set these days, I'd dubbed the creation Chopping Spree Salad. First I placed some hearts of palm into water to remove the brine, then assembled the rest of the ingredients. Since I was a great fan of limes for tanginess, I'd decided to feature lime in

both the grilled chicken and the dressing itself. I sliced several of the bright green cit-
rus globes and juiced them, then pounded
fresh chicken breasts between layers of
plastic wrap. After I'd whisked together a
marinade of lime juice and olive oil, I carefully placed the breasts into it. Then I rewashed my hands and set about slicing
and dicing a mountain of crisp romaine
lettuce, flavorful vine-grown tomatoes,
crunchy, barely sweet jicama, and fat scallions. Yum. While I preheated the indoor
grill, I pulverized fresh and ground herbs in
my mini food processor and whisked them
with more lime juice, a bit of mayonnaise,
and a touch of cream. Tasting the spicy
mélange, I decided to add a bit more tang
by grating in some aged Parmigiano-
Reggiano cheese. The result was a rich,
sharp ranch-style dressing that would have
sent Escoffier spinning in his grave. So
what, I thought smugly, as I toasted pine
nuts for a finishing touch. Soon the luscious scent of the grilling chicken brought
Tom and Arch clomping back into the
kitchen.

At six, Arch, Tom, and I sat down to a
meal of steaming cream of mushroom

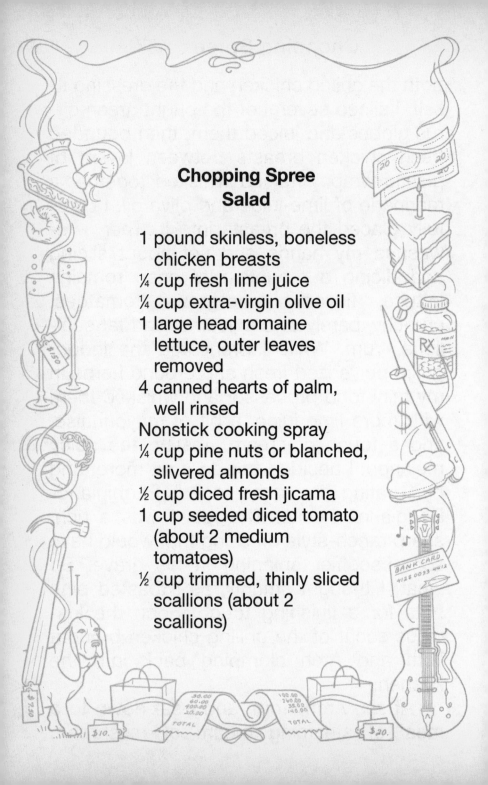

Chopping Spree
Salad

1 pound skinless, boneless
chicken breasts
¼ cup fresh lime juice
¼ cup extra-virgin olive oil
1 large head romaine
lettuce, outer leaves
removed
4 canned hearts of palm,
well rinsed
Nonstick cooking spray
¼ cup pine nuts or blanched,
slivered almonds
½ cup diced fresh jicama
1 cup seeded diced tomato
(about 2 medium
tomatoes)
½ cup trimmed, thinly sliced
scallions (about 2
scallions)

Tangy Lime Dressing (recipe follows)

Place the chicken breasts between sheets of plastic wrap and pound them with a mallet to a ⅓-inch thickness. Slice each breast in half lengthwise.

In a 9 × 13-inch glass pan, mix the juice with the oil and place the chicken into this marinade while you prepare the rest of the ingredients and dressing, about 15 to 20 minutes.

Wash the head of romaine very well, then cut an inch off the top to make an even edge. Carefully slice the rest of the head into ½-inch slices. You should have about 8 cups of romaine pieces. Rinse these well, spin them to remove any moisture, and wrap them in paper towels. Chill until you are ready to assemble the salad.

Place the rinsed hearts of palm into a bowl of cold water and allow them to soak for 5 minutes to remove the brine.

While the hearts of palm are soaking, lightly spray a small sauté pan with nonstick spray (or use a nonstick pan) and toast the pine nuts over medium-low to medium heat. Stir frequently to prevent burning. When the pine nuts are just beginning to turn golden brown (3 or 4 minutes), remove them from the heat, place on a plate to cool, and set aside until you are ready to assemble the salad.

Remove the hearts of palm from the water, pat them dry with paper towels, and cut them into ¼-inch discs. Wrap the pieces in a paper towel and chill until you are ready to assemble the salad.

Dice the jicama and tomatoes, slice the scallions, and set aside. Spray the grill with nonstick spray and preheat the grill while you prepare the Tangy Lime Dressing.

Grill the chicken over medium-high to high heat for about 4 minutes per side, or until it is cooked through but not dry. Remove the chicken to a cutting board, cool slightly, and cut into bite-sized pieces.

Place the lettuce, hearts of palm, jicama, tomatoes, scallions, and chicken in a large, attractive salad bowl. Toss with half of the dressing, then add the dressing by tablespoons until the salad is lightly dressed, not overdressed. (You may have a bit of dressing left over.) Sprinkle the toasted pine nuts on top and serve immediately.

Makes 4 large servings

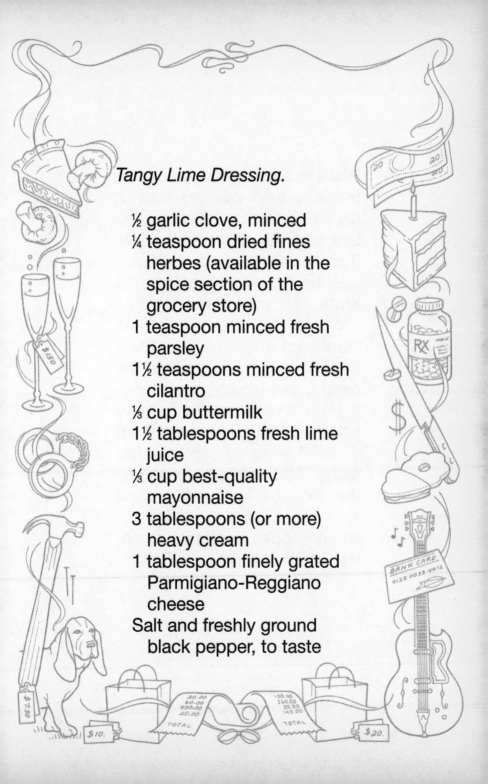

Tangy Lime Dressing.

½ garlic clove, minced

¼ teaspoon dried fines herbes (available in the spice section of the grocery store)

1 teaspoon minced fresh parsley

1½ teaspoons minced fresh cilantro

⅓ cup buttermilk

1½ tablespoons fresh lime juice

⅓ cup best-quality mayonnaise

3 tablespoons (or more) heavy cream

1 tablespoon finely grated Parmigiano-Reggiano cheese

Salt and freshly ground black pepper, to taste

Place the garlic, fines herbes, parsley, and cilantro into a miniature food processor and blend until pulverized, less than a minute. In a medium-size bowl, whisk together the buttermilk with the lime juice and mayonnaise until well combined and smooth. Whisk in the garlic-spice mixture, the cream, and the cheese, blending until smooth. Taste very carefully and add more cream if the dressing seems too tangy. Add salt judiciously, as the mayonnaise and cheese are already salty. Grind in some pepper and taste again. Use immediately.

soup, heated cornmeal rolls, and dressing-topped slices of hot grilled chicken over an enormous bed of crisp, fresh, sliced, and diced vegetables. Arch and Tom could not have cared less what the dish was named, nor did they give a hoot about it being the fad among mall-crawlers. They dug into the salad as if they hadn't eaten for days. (Come to think of it, Arch and Tom didn't care much about Escoffier, either.)

Ah, men!

Ah, food!

After supper and two pieces of Tom's melt-in-your-mouth chocolate cake, Arch announced that he had to write up the field trip.

"Did anyone come in before you left?" I couldn't help asking. "To...claim the body?"

He blinked. "Yeah, Mom. Some woman crashed through the door, grabbed the cadaver, and screamed, *'Dad! Where have you been?'*"

I shook my head while Arch and Tom exchanged grins. "Someone from the *coroner's* office, Arch."

"Oh!" Arch shook his head. "No." He dumped a third piece of cake onto his dish and disappeared upstairs.

I busied myself wrapping up the un-chopped vegetables. Tom started on the dishes. After I'd stored the leftovers in the walk-in, he asked me to sit down so we could talk. My mind reeled off an *"Uh-oh,"* and I uneasily took a seat.

"You showed me those pages you got from Dean's doctor's office," he began. He was drying the bowl I'd used for the salad. "But the guys working the case didn't find the prescription the doc made that Dean had just filled. A bottle of Vicodin Extra Strength."

I swallowed. "From what you've told me, they couldn't find a lot of things."

"The prescription was only for twenty pills," Tom went on. "If you assume Julian is innocent, then somebody followed Dean to that shoe department to kill him. Our perp saw an opportunity—customers have left, clerks gone for a moment, big cabinet to hide behind—and took it. Then when the killer was slipping out, maybe he or she saw the clerks coming back to clean up. Or maybe the killer saw you coming in with the guitar. Barry Dean was barely alive, so our perp shoved him into the cabinet. Still, Barry might tell *you* who stabbed him. So the perp panics. Whacks you with the guitar and calls nine-one-one. Julian shows up, tries to pull the knife out of Barry, and gets arrested. Hitting you and incriminating Julian were unplanned."

"So *you* think Barry's murder was premeditated. How does the sheriff's department see it? The same as you?"

"That depends," Tom mused. "At this point, they're just trying to gather enough evidence to turn this thing over to the district court." He gave me the full benefit of his ocean-green eyes. "The only thing that's going to help Julian is if our guys find out who killed Barry Dean. I don't know if they're telling me everything about the case. But I have to warn you that the trail is getting cold. It's been over forty-eight hours since you discovered the body." I *tsk*ed while Tom continued: "Our guys turned Dean's house inside out, went through his two cars and his boat. When they pulled their detail off his place, they still hadn't found much. Julian's Rover, his apartment? Nothing there, either."

I groaned. "I can just imagine the mess the cops must have made at Julian's place."

"You know how I got that chocolate icing shiny tonight?"

"How?"

He reached into his pocket, pulled out Barry Dean's Vicodin prescription, and placed it on the table. "I used an ingredient I hardly ever use. Your clarified butter. The kind you keep in the freezer."

"Tom, I was going to tell you..."

"Uh-huh."

"They...the pills, they slipped into my apron pocket somehow when I was on the shoes, you know, beside Barry.... The bottle must have fallen out of his pocket. That's how I got Barry's doctor's name."

"Goldy, you should have handed these over. With both of us handling them, there's not a hope of prints now."

"I was just trying to help Julian. How can I trust the sheriff's department, when all they're trying to do is find evidence to *convict* Julian? But I'll turn them in tomorrow, if you want."

Tom arched an eyebrow. "I'll do it," he told me gently. "Remember, I already told our guys about the shoving incident...that was in the doctor's report. They went out to the site—logical place to look for a ditch, since Barry worked at the mall. Sure enough, we found two witnesses who claim it was a woman who did the pushing. We're figuring it was one of Dean's two girl-friends. Ellie McNeely or that lady who works in lingerie."

"You're kidding!" I was incredulous. "That's it? No description?"

"That's it," he said, as he pocketed the pills and gave me a skeptical look.

"Tom, I really meant what I said about being sorry. About hiding the pills."

"Yeah, yeah, Miss G. Sorry until the next time."

"No more evidence from crime scenes. I swear it."

"Yeah, yeah."

He couldn't have been too angry. Or maybe I convinced him my contrition was sincere. I say this because a couple of hours later, once snow was again falling quietly and the house was hushed, Tom pulled me up the stairs and we made love. Afterward, wrapped in his warm arms, I drifted off, thinking that it sure would be nice if we could both take a vacation. Then, at least for a couple of weeks, we could make love all the time.

Thursday morning, I awoke feeling groggy. To my astonishment, a new five-inch blanket of snow had muted not only the traffic noise coming up from Main Street, but Arch's and Tom's getting-ready-to-go shuffling about. My body had apparently demanded, and received, its long overdue dose of sleep. I went through a slow yoga routine, showered, and dressed. This was the day of the shopaholics meeting at the mall, which I fully intended to attend. Today I also would try to talk to Pam and/or Victor, if they'd see me. Ah, but for the meeting, I needed something else....

I reached for a brown ski hat that I'd crocheted in a burst of domestic-goddess energy, back during one of Goldilocks' Catering's slow periods. In the end, the knobbles and swirls I'd crafted into the cap had made it too big and cumbersome for skiing. Now the thing looked like a twenties-era flapper's cap. Or maybe a chocolate-colored wig. But it was perfect

to disguise myself for my foray to Shopaholics Anonymous.

Tom had left me a note on the kitchen
counter.

*Miss G.: The corpse was Lucas Holden.
Found in a motel near Durango, dead of
a heart attack, no sign of struggle or
forced entry. Coroner's office is looking
into the situation, but it's going to take a
while. Sorry to say, our guys didn't find
anything up at that portable toilet. Too
much new snow. I'll pick up Arch today.
He says they're doing lacrosse drills in
the gym. See you at six. T.*

Remembering my promise to bring
cookies to Victor Wilson, the excavator-
cum-construction-manager, I removed a
batch of homemade currant-cookie dough
from the freezer and preheated the oven.
Then I pulled a double espresso, reread
Tom's note, and sipped the coffee. Even after the pop of caffeine, a weight seemed to
be pressing on my chest and dragging my
spirits netherward. I just could *not* believe
that Lucas Holden would have quit his job
at the mall in an angry huff, then conve-

niently died only days later in a motel in southwestern Colorado. Maybe Lucas was the "friend" who'd pushed Barry Dean down. Then again, he hadn't looked even remotely womanly.

I sliced the log of rich, currant-specked dough into thin disks and popped them into the oven. I set the timer and wondered about these witnesses who'd said a *woman* had pushed Barry down so that he fell into a ditch. If this included the guy who'd supposedly seen Julian driving the dump truck, then the first thing everybody at the construction site needed—after they had some cookies—was a trip to the ophthalmologist.

OK, say *Lucas* saw the person who'd pushed Barry into that ditch. And then someone had, someone had, someone had...*what?* My mind circled back to the idea of Lucas Holden being followed and injected with something lethal. With no autopsy done on an unsuspicious death that resulted in a donated cadaver, there wouldn't have been a drug or any other kind of screen.

The fragrant smell of baking cookies infused the kitchen. When the tantalizing treats were done, I carefully placed them on racks, and pulled another espresso. I munched thoughtfully on a buttery, crunchy cookie, whose texture was perfectly balanced with the sweet chewiness of the currants. I washed the cookies down with the espresso, and peered out the kitchen window at the new-fallen snow. My face in the glass reflected doubt about all the speculative roads my mind seemed bent on exploring. Then I thought of Julian waking up in jail for the third morning, and phoned Helen Keith, assistant coroner for Furman County.

Helen Keith was a fiftyish, unmarried, longtime colleague of Tom's. They were also longtime friends. He admired her professionalism; she appreciated his work ethic. Maybe she'd extend that appreciation to my attempts at amateur sleuthing. Then again, maybe not.

Helen answered on the first ring, and I genially reminded her who I was, that we'd visited at sheriff's department barbecues two summers in a row, and wasn't it great we could touch base? Not fooled, Helen politely said she was waiting for an important call. I took a deep breath and asked if we could have a quick chat. She assented.

I gave her an abbreviated version of recognizing Lucas Holden's missing-toe cadaver. In an Oh-by-the-way fashion, I asked if her office could do a standard drug screen on Holden's body.

"Goldy, I know that you have a friend in jail. But the tests aren't going to be easy, and the results certainly won't be quick," she replied, her voice matter-of-fact. "But since this corpse was connected to a crime, we'd be doing a drug screen any-way."

"Ah, well. Thanks. Any chance *I* could find out if he had any drugs in him?"

Helen Keith laughed. "Good-bye, Goldy."

I guessed that was a no.

On the way to the mall, I tried again to call Pam Disharoon. No luck. Ditto with Kim Fury. Liz Fury, however, answered her cell on the first ring—understandable for a mother who must be worried sick about her son. I told her this wasn't about catering work. Then I asked about Teddy.

"They haven't found him yet." Her con-cern crackled through the cell. "There was some activity on the credit cards, but it was all over Denver."

"All over Denver? Er, how's he getting around?"

Immediately her tone became suspicious. "Why?"

"I just...look, somebody hinted that Teddy stole Ellie McNeely's car one day at the mall," I blurted out.

"He did *not* take Ellie's car. Teddy... isn't a very good driver. He *hates* driving. He wouldn't steal a car. He has friends who drive him, most of the time....You're breaking up, Goldy. I have to go."

She disconnected before I could ask her if Teddy might like driving big trucks more than he liked driving cars.

At Westside Mall, the blanket of snow had not slowed construction. In fact, the building process seemed more frenzied than ever. I pulled the van up by a plastic fence that now prevented folks from parking in the hard-hat area and watched the flurry of activity in amazement. Workers using pickaxes broke through frozen slush— the former parking-lot drainage lake—to lay pipe. Beyond the newly smoothed sidewalk, two loaders belching black smoke chugged around the rim of a huge pit whose snow-filled bottom resembled a bowl of muddied meringue. Victor, wearing his usual day-glo orange hard hat, strode back and forth, pointing and barking orders. When he'd finished hollering at one group of workmen and yelling at a second, he hopped into a bright green golf cart and bumped over ruts to the next problem area.

"Excuse me!" I hailed him, once I'd stuffed the bag of cookies into my purse, stepped awkwardly over the plastic fence, and skirted a Porsche with the license plate DIRT GUY. Victor was scowling at the clipboard in his hands. When he turned the stare and the scowl in my direction, however, he smiled.

"The caterer!" He sounded plugged up, as if he had a bad cold. Laboring in the snow and cold wind probably didn't help. "How're you doing? Bringing us goodies?"

"You bet! If I'd known your crew was working in this weather, I would have brought you cocoa, too. Do you have a minute to talk?"

He tucked the clipboard under his arm. "Great idea. Let's go into the trailer and have some coffee."

People were always very cordial in anticipation of food you'd brought, I reflected, as I followed Victor to the construction trailer. I leaped across an area where two workers were putting in pipe, then carefully ascended the wobbly, ice-slick wooden steps to the trailer. Once through the bent aluminum door, I looked around. The trailer resembled the inside of a much-battered can. Worse, it was poorly warmed by glowing space heaters. At the desk inside the door, a bulky woman in her sixties silently thrust her formidable chin in my direction. Using a pencil, she scratched her scalp through her thinning black hair. She was watching my every move.

"Victor," she said in a low voice, "have you taken that sinus medication I gave you?"

"Not yet, Rhonda. I just need to have a bit of a visit with—"

Rhonda's fleshy jowls jiggled as she addressed me. "No reporters yet, miss. We'll have a *big* press party in six weeks, and then you can—"

"I'm not a reporter—"

"It's OK," Victor interrupted. "We'll only be a few minutes."

"Mall management said no *journalists,* Mr. Wilson," she scolded him loudly, the edginess provided for my benefit. "And I have *six* urgent messages here for you." She waved a handful of pink slips and sent another glower in my direction. Rhonda's look said *Every one of these is more important than you, bitch.*

Victor ignored Rhonda's protectiveness and handed me a foam cup of muddy coffee that he murmured might not be fresh, but was definitely hot. Huddled beside one of the space heaters, I thanked him gratefully. He gestured toward diet sweetener and nondairy creamer, non-food inventions that I wish could be relegated to kindergarten projects involving glue and construction paper. I declined and grinned in Rhonda's direction, tempted to ask for real cream. Sensing a demand, she narrowed her eyes and jutted out that scary chin.

"Let's go in my office," Victor mumbled. I followed him into a walled-off cubicle, where he shut the plywood door, removed his hard hat, and shrugged out of his filthy overcoat. Then he nodded to a metal chair on the near side of his paper-strewn desk.

"Thanks," I said again. "I really won't be

but a few minutes. Here you go," I added, pulling the zipped plastic bag of cookies out of my purse. "My thanks for helping the other day."

"No problem," he replied cheerfully as he settled into his own squeaky desk chair. He unzipped the bag, put in a hand so dirty I shuddered, and brought out half a dozen cookies. Pushing a whole one into his mouth, he nodded, mumbled gratitude, and washed the crumbs down with the coffee.

As I watched him, I wondered why I'd ever thought catering was so demanding. Construction had to be much worse. Victor's haggard cheeks glowed with grime, and his bloodshot eyes made me wonder if he was getting any sleep. After he finished a second cookie, he reached for a foil packet, probably Rhonda's sinus meds. Pulling off the foil, he popped the pills into his mouth, then washed them down with more of the dark swill in his cup. He winced and said, " 'Scuse me."

"You probably shouldn't be working if you're sick." Would my controlling-mom voice never shut up?

Victor gave me a half-grin. "Fat chance.

Listen, I never got a chance to apologize about that truck situation. We figure it was a guy from the old crew, a misfit that No-toe Holden, our former construction manager, fired. The guy's name is Jorge Sanchez. Sanchez is your standard disgruntled worker. Sometimes they come back, try to steal equipment or vehicles. Anyway, I'm really sorry about that, if you're here looking for someone to take the blame."

"No, that's not why I'm here." I smiled. "You've been on this project, what? A year?"

Victor blew on his coffee, took a sip, and let out a long breath. "From the beginning. Eleven months. Got promoted when Holden quit." He furrowed his brow. "Hey, sorry about Rhonda, too. You've got to understand we're under a *ton* of pressure here. We've got a drywall contractor refusing to send a crew out and landscapers claiming they can't put in bushes until the snow melts. Half of the interiors were painted the wrong colors. The portable toilets haven't been cleaned in two weeks, and I've got guys passing out from the stench. And that's just today."

Hey, don't talk to *me* about portable toilets. I pretended to sip some of the viscous black liquid, then set the foam cup on a grubby plastic table. "Actually, the problem is a . . . this friend of ours ended up in jail after Barry Dean was killed—"

Victor nodded and rubbed his filthy forehead. "Yeah, I know. Poor Dean. He really wanted to see this project finished." He drank more coffee, then sighed. "And I'm sorry about your friend. I know one of our guys said that the kid who was with you was driving our truck when Dean nearly got killed. I never did see who *exactly* was driving that truck. I still think it was Sanchez."

Since I was quite sure that someone, if not several people, would come forward and say that Julian had been running up the parking lot, and *not* driving the truck, I let this pass.

"You know, if I just could have more crew," Victor was explaining, "we could have had more supervision of the—"

"Victor," I said quickly, to forestall more apologies, "there's going to be something in the newspaper, probably in a few days. Lucas Holden has been found dead."

He dropped his coffee cup. "Oh, Christ!" Shaking his head, he rolled back his chair and stared at the mess at his feet in disbelief. Then he grabbed a handful of tissues from a dusty box and threw them onto the floor. "Did he kill himself?"

Now it was my turn to be surprised. Suicide was not a possibility I'd even contemplated. And Helen Keith certainly hadn't mentioned it.

"Heart attack, I think," I stammered. "But...I guess I was hoping to find out about his background. I'm thinking maybe there's something in it that could help our friend in jail."

"I'll *bet* it was suicide. No-toe was just so damned depressed," Victor continued gloomily, as if *he* were thinking of offing himself, to end his own remorse about everything. "One day, he just said, 'I quit.'" He shook his head in disgust. "Some guys just can't take the pressure of construction."

"I need to ask you about the time before Holden quit. About a month ago. Was Holden the one who pushed Barry down, so that he landed in a ditch out here on the construction site? Or did he see who pushed Barry?"

Victor's thin eyebrows rose. "No. It wasn't No-toe. But how did you hear about that?"

"Oh, you know, some gossip was reported in the paper..."

His voice turned cautious. "Well, Barry told us to keep our mouths shut about that incident. If it got out, he said, things would get worse for him. That's what he said. They're putting pipes and cables in that ditch now, but it was about seven feet deep before."

"Did *you* see who pushed him?"

"Yeah. I did." He lowered his voice. My skin crawled, and I imagined the dreaded Rhonda with one of her large ears pressed against the thin door.

"So did No-toe," Victor added, just above a whisper. I waited, heart hammering. "Dean had had a real bad fight with his girlfriend," he continued. "One of 'em, anyway. Dean was two-timing, see. But if you heard about the ditch thing, you probably heard that, too." I nodded. Victor squirmed, then finally whispered, "That girlfriend was here the day of the truck thing. Anyway, she didn't push him down so that he fell into a ditch, she pushed him *into* the ditch. Right then, Dean screamed, 'Don't! Ellie, don't!' " Victor's bloodshot eyes squinted at me. "So. Do you know this Ellie?"

CHAPTER 17

At the mention of my friend's name, I made my face blank and, shivering, tugged my coat around me. The office's little space heater suddenly seemed woefully inadequate.

"I sort of know her," I evaded.

"I found out her last name when her car got crashed into Dean's Mercedes," Victor told me. "It was in the newspaper. Mc-Neely. Wealthy woman who swears she wasn't driving." He grinned in mock defeat. "The rich never have to pay. You and I work our butts off and we get what? Hot kitchens, freezing offices, and no appreciation." He stopped to pull out a tissue. "Ever notice?"

While he blew his nose, I cleared my throat, and looked around the room again. Plans, charts, and notes were pinned to every bit of wall space. Victor was right about one thing: I'd already decided I *wouldn't* want to work in this frigid, disorganized environment.

I asked, "Did anyone besides you and Holden see Ellie McNeely push Barry into the ditch?"

"It was early in the morning," Victor replied. "Couple of guys might have been around. We were discussing delays on the project, when this woman comes running up and starts screaming at Dean about how he had a commitment to her." The phone rang and he answered it. "They are?" he said, with a glance at the clock. "OK. Just a coupla minutes more, I swear." He grinned. "Yeah, thanks. I took 'em." Clearly, the omniscient and nosy Rhonda was trying to throw her weight around.

As he hung up the phone, I stood. "Victor, I appreciate your seeing me. Did you tell the police the details of this ditch incident?"

He shook his head. "No. They asked me if Dean had any enemies, and I said I didn't know of any. He had a coupla people he didn't get along with, I told 'em, like his two girlfriends and No-toe. But I didn't want to get one girlfriend over another in trouble. Anyway, Rhonda just called to say the cops are on their way over. They've got a coupla more questions, apparently. Do you think I should tell them this McNeely lady pushed Barry?"

"That's up to you." I thanked him again, picked up the foam cup, and backed out of the tiny, icy office.

"Real sorry about your friend in jail," Victor called after me.

I ignored Rhonda's vicious glare, clomped out of the trailer, and poured the dark liquid into the ditch. Could Ellie really have pushed Barry in there, when it was seven feet deep? Was it possible she could have set up the whole portable toilet incident, just to look innocent in my eyes? I simply could not fathom it.

A sudden icy wind blasted my nostrils with a horrid stench. I gagged and stared at the stinking turquoise portable toilets. They were scribbled with racist graffiti. *Wetbacks*

Go Home!! was scrawled beneath a Spanish retort that I translated, more politely than it was written, as *We can't wait to go back to Mexico, and good luck having an incestuous relationship with your mother.* So much for racial harmony on the job site.

Near the plastic fence, a Hispanic man was hovering between my car and the Porsche. He was dressed in the garb of a construction worker, and was putting one of those bright orange ads under my windshield. Just what I needed, an encouragement to do yet *more* shopping. Before he could put an ad under the Porsche's windshield, a Furman County prowler pulled up. The ad-placer vanished as the prowler disgorged two men. They were detectives, no doubt...and maybe they would give a ticket to someone illegally distributing ads to parked cars.

The workmen hacking at the ice stopped to stare at the cop car. Bucking the wind, I ignored the detectives, and made my way toward the mall. On the way, I tossed my cup into the overflowing Dumpster with such fury that it bounced up, was caught by the wind, and sailed away.

Tampering with evidence, disobeying my lawyer, and now littering. Pretty soon my charge sheet was going to have more scribbling on it than those toilets.

Inside the mall, I ducked into a women's room and examined myself. My lips, nose, and cheeks were crimson from the cold. I reached into my bag and pulled out the crocheted cap, a small compact, and a pair of sunglasses. After doing a bit of damage control on my face, I put on the hat and glasses and emerged into the mall. I didn't know if I was incognito or not, but the sunglasses made everything *awfully dark*. I headed toward the Shopaholics Anonymous meeting, where I sincerely hoped I'd hear something useful, especially from Page Stockham, such as *I'd kill to be able to keep shopping. In fact, that's exactly what I've done!*

A handwritten sign was taped beside the entrance to the shoppers' lounge: *Private Meeting in Session*. By the time I pushed through the lounge's massive doors, the group was reciting a posted list of the Twelve Steps. As I skirted the furniture—all put back in place since the jewelry-leasing party—I focused hard through my sunglasses on the attendees, who were clustered on three long couches around a pastry-laden coffee table. No Page. At least, not that I could tell.

One member started reading aloud what sounded like a preamble. *We are not so much concerned with debt, as are our colleagues in Debtors Anonymous, as we are with shopping itself, which we use as a drug to avoid dealing with our feelings of inadequacy....*

The reader droned on as I looked around the room, where the atmosphere was palpably tense. To my surprise, the nine attendees were comprised of five men and four women. Five men! And here we women were always wondering what men were up to in those *long* trips to the hardware store. By inserting myself into the group, I created an even division between the sexes. I sat down as unobtrusively as possible and nodded at two welcoming smiles.

"I'm George, and I'm a compulsive spender," one balding man began, as he lofted an éclair. Before the woman seated beside George could introduce herself, he added, mouth full, "I got a eating problem, too."

Everyone laughed, and the edgy atmosphere vanished. At my turn, I said I was Gertrude—no lie, as this is my real name—and that I was visiting. A packet of pamphlets was pressed into my hands by George, who left chocolate smears on the top sheet. It began: *If you do nothing but shop, you WILL drop. DEAD!* Now there was a cheery thought.

"My name is Page, and I'm a compulsive shopper," someone said.

I sat up so quickly my crocheted hat wobbled and threatened to topple. Through the sunglasses, I hadn't spotted her. I slid off the sunglasses, put on my patented blank expression, then looked around. Page, who looked as if she, too, had come in disguise, was seated almost out of my range of view, at the far end of the couch. Her long blond hair was tied back in a bun that was concealed by an elaborately tied scarf. She, too, wore sunglasses—hers were of the aviator variety, and boasted pink lenses. Most atypically, she was clad in black tights and a black T-shirt, as if she'd just dropped in after ballet class. I did notice that despite the outfit, she wore a strand of large pearls—diamond clasp in front, so we'd know they were real—and a sparkly bracelet that (with my glasses off) looked like half a dozen strands of pink, yellow, and white diamonds. Why did wealthy women go out looking as if they'd just been to exercise class for hookers? Another unanswered question of the universe.

Clearly, I was losing my perspective. I reminded myself to focus, then glanced at the tray of pastries. One of the women who'd smiled at me offered me a paper plate and plastic fork.

"They're for everybody," she urged. "Food eases the pain."

Well, I couldn't disagree with that. And I do love Linzer torte, I thought as I chewed into a big bite laden with spice, ground nuts, and raspberry preserves.

A tiny woman with bobbed brown hair announced in a high voice, "My name is Carole and I'm a compulsive shopper."

Everyone murmured a greeting to Carole. Her fingers nervously pleated her skirt. "My boyfriend left at Easter last year. For a while, I didn't feel anything. I was just numb. Then a friend insisted on getting me out of the house. She took me shopping."

There was a chorus of groans.

"It was weird," Carole went on. "I felt better once I bought a new sweater. It was a cabled pink mohair, and buying it and wearing it made me feel loved again. So my friend insisted on taking me to the mall again the next weekend. With new gray slacks, plus a matching belt and purse, my feelings improved even more. I mean, I felt *alive* again! Problem was, I had to spend *more money* each time I went. One new sweater became two new sweaters. Then four new sweaters. Then ten—all on one trip!"

Carole began to sob. The group waited while one member handed her several tissues, and another put a plate with a cream puff in front of her.

"Now," Carole continued between gulps, "I'm sixteen thousand dollars in debt on four credit cards. I have, uh...Last week, I finally did a count. Six hundred and thirty-two sweaters, most of them still with the price tags on them. The worst part is that on some trips, I must have had a memory loss or blackout. Almost a dozen times, I bought the same sweater *twice*." She stopped to blow her nose. "OK, but I do have some good news. I didn't buy a single sweater this week!" The group made supportive noises. Carole snuffled and managed a shy, red-nosed smile. "It was so hard! It's *cold* outside! And ... oh, God, Talbot's just put their winter stuff on *sale*. I can barely walk by their window!"

The group burst out laughing. Carole, recognizing the laughter was affectionate, not mocking, dug into her cream puff. Murmurs of "Oh, Carole" and "You should see the stuff on sale at Saks" accompanied big grins and hands reaching for babas au rhum. I glanced around for some coffee or tea to go with the pastries, but saw only a table lined with bottles of water. Maybe caffeine stimulated shopping, blast it. When Page stood and strode over to snag a water, I quickly turned back to the group.

"So," Carole was saying, as she delicately wiped her mouth with a paper napkin, "now, instead of shopping, I'm looking forward to seeing you all, because *you* make me feel better. Not quite the way Rob my ex did, but close. And get this! On the way over here, I stopped at Goodwill, and left them *two hundred and fifty-nine sweaters!*"

The group clapped wildly. Carole, blushing and triumphant, reached for another cream puff.

"I'm Jack and I'm an image spender," a lanky fellow with gray hair offered. "Can't say I'm doing as well as Carole, sorry. Last week my ex-wife wanted to have a lunch meeting with our attorneys. This should have raised a red flag, but it didn't. I suggested we make it easygoing, you know, something modest, both lawyers and the two of us. At Duccio's." This time I gasped along with the group. Minimum tab at Duccio's on the Sixteenth Street Mall in downtown Denver, for one person having lunch, without liquor, would run about forty dollars. Add a single glass of wine, coffee, dessert, and tip, and you were looking at twice that. I had the feeling that Jack, in his gray pin-striped silk suit, Italian leather shoes, and imported tie, didn't know the concept of a modest lunch.

"Of course," Jack went on, "it turned out to be a terrible meeting, full of wrangling over child support and visitation issues. Oysters and two bottles of Château Lafitte didn't help make things jovial, either." He sighed. "I'm twenty-two thousand dollars in debt, which Gail knows but pretends not to." He gave the group a rueful grin. "Still, when the check came? I grabbed for it. I mean, I *had* to! It was like an unseen force pushed my hand to reach out for that slip of paper!" He paused. "Now I'm twenty-two thousand, four hundred and ten dollars in debt. Yesterday I went to the grocery store and bought a case of peanut butter. On sale." The group sighed. "But you all are here," Jack concluded with a wide grin. "And at least I can have free pastries on Thursdays!"

"See, that's what bothers me!" Page Stockham burst out savagely, as the group murmured encouragement to Jack. There was a collective gasp. "People always angling to get free stuff," she added, her tone hostile. An uncomfortable silence ensued, interrupted only by the sounds of pastry-eating.

"Uh, my name is George, and, Page, remember that we have a format—"

"My name is Page and I have a sister problem. I'm here because my therapist said it might help." The members squirmed. I peeked over at Page, who tilted up her chin and gazed defiantly down her nose at the group.

"My sister has always been a *taker*," Page told us bitterly. "She gets into relationships with people by adoring them. These people are *never* low-income types, I should add. As soon as they start spending money on her, she adores them even more!" Page examined her manicured fingernails. "So rich folks, mostly guys, get addicted to being loved by my sister. Then she starts freeloading. First she gives them some sob story, of course. 'I just need to borrow your car because mine's not working.' Two weeks later she's all 'Your stepson wants this car back? What am I supposed to drive? Besides, you have five cars, can't he drive one of those? Don't you care about *me*?' Then she cries and withdraws affection from the rich guy, who feels guilty and finally *gives* her his damn car. She's a horrible flirt, of course. And a slut, I should say."

For the first time in the meeting, no one was reaching for pastries. The members sat without moving, concentrating on appearing neutral, although frowns and pursed lips indicated creeping discomfort. *You need help, girl,* their expressions said. Jack, for his part, looked downright disgusted. Maybe he'd been seduced by Pam, too, and had bought her lunch at Duccio's.

"OK," Page snarled, "I probably *do* shop too much. But I *need* to. My husband used to buy me nice things, and now he takes me for granted. I *have* to buy stuff for myself. Meanwhile, my slutty sister has a new boyfriend, or she had one, anyway, and she got him to give her discounts, big ones, on all kinds of stuff." Her voice turned shrill. "Another one of her boyfriends sweet-talked the dean at... his former college, so my sister could get into a special scholarship program to go to night school for her degree. *Free!* This new guy gave her furs and jewelry from... vendors or reps or whatever they're called. And then he bought her a round-trip ticket to Hawaii for next Christmas, because he knew the travel agent here in the... well, here." Her voice ramped up a few more notches. "This boyfriend even got Pam a fifty percent discount on... a piece of jewelry. Not to buy, but...to rent. And *he* leased it for her!" Page screamed, "And *then* this same guy...*fired* my husband, so we suddenly had *no* income! I was so furious I couldn't sleep! Couldn't eat! Couldn't drive!" She leaped to her feet. "That son of a bitch ruined our lives!"

Page ran out of the room.

Silence fell over the group.

George said, "Next?"

I wanted to follow Page, but my inner voice warned me to stay put. At this juncture, she'd be in no mood to chat. So I listened sympathetically to two more people talk, or as they called it, "share." One man was a bargain-hunter with six storage sheds full of stuff he never used. He said the seller always represented his mother, who'd withheld love from him as a child. By ruthlessly bargaining, he tried to outsmart the seller, so he could "get love for free." Except he never got the affection he needed, just lots of fishing rods and motorcycle parts. The final speaker, a very large woman with a pointed chin, announced that she was a codependent spender. She fingered her plastic dark glasses and tried to straighten her very crooked curly-haired wig. She said she had a compulsion to spend money on others. By giving people huge gifts, she was hoping they would love her. The previous year, she'd won fifty thousand dollars in the lottery, now all gone on presents for which she had not received a single thank-you note. Now she had to work a crummy job that caused her no end of stress.

I squinted at her thoughtfully as the group broke up. "Why, Rhonda!" I whispered to myself, then hightailed it out of there.

In the mall, shoppers scurried or moseyed past, many of them with that hungry, pinched look that said they were rushing for a bite to eat. Monday morning, I'd bemoaned the fact that I never had time for lunch out with Marla; now I was so stuffed with pastries and water that the idea of a midday meal made my very full stomach holler in protest.

I pulled off the crocheted hat and found a chair. I needed to sit and think. Just down the staircase, the window of Westside Music displayed a painted banner: *Open Late!* With a start, I recalled that Arch's birthday was *tomorrow*. Tom had bought him a new lacrosse stick, helmet, and official-size goal, which he planned to put up in our back-yard, snow be damned. He'd also promised to look for another guitar, since the much-desired one was dented, and not done being inspected by the cops. Still, I knew Arch well enough to be sure of this: The gift he would most cherish would be to have Julian at his party. So it was in the free-Julian department that I needed to continue to bend my efforts.

I ran my fingers through my hair and reflected on the shopaholics' meeting. Page Stockham had confessed to a *sister problem,* a problem that appeared to have been very much aggravated by the presence of discount-supplying Barry Dean. My mind circled back to one of its many questions. Had Tom spurred the investigators to find out exactly where Page—and Ellie too, for that matter—had been after the two women split from Marla? Would the desires to a) have revenge on the man who evicted her husband's profitable store, and b) deprive a sibling of her ride on the gravy train, be sufficient motive to kill Barry?

There was one person I had not been able to talk to, but who, in light of the shopaholics' meeting, I now *desperately* needed to see. I headed toward Prince & Grogan. With Julian facing formal charges the next morning, I might have to buy a hundred dollars' worth of nighties from Barry Dean's onetime girlfriend. But wait— there was one detail of Page's story that I needed to check out first. I turned and quickly headed toward the mall management office.

Heather the receptionist looked quite a bit cheerier than when I'd seen her earlier in the week. She'd had her hair colored with bright pink streaks and cut in a new, spiky do. New fluorescent pink nail polish and lipstick matched her hair. She looked like an ad for pink lemonade, which she happened to be drinking from a plastic cup. When I entered the office, she set down the lemonade by her half-eaten personal pizza, which, I shuddered to see, was topped with ham and pineapple.

"The caterer!" Heather exclaimed, then

clapped her hand over her mouth. "Oops! Did I forget to call you?"

For a horrid, sinking moment, I thought Rob Eakin, the interim mall manager, might have changed his mind about the canceled prospective tenants' lunch, originally scheduled for that day. If so, and Heather Featherbrain had forgotten to notify me, then all my worry about success would be something I'd laugh about as my business went under. You simply *do not* fail to show up to cater an affair.

"First of all," she said, handing me a check, "here's a new payment for your gratuity. Rob Eakin cut another check, since the cops are keeping everything. Plus, I found what you were looking for," Heather continued brightly. She sucked noisily on her straw. "Barry did leave you something."

"Oh, Heather." I groaned, thinking of Julian's haggard face behind the jail glass. "Why didn't you call me? For crying out loud, this is about a *murder* case!"

"Look, I'm sorry, but we've been *busy*," she cried. "It's been *nuts* around here, with the crews working day and night, and Rob trying to stave off the potential tenants. Plus, somebody just called here to ask for a comment about our old construction manager turning up dead. It's like, this mess never stops."

"Just give me whatever it is, would you please? Then I need to ask you something about Barry."

"Not again!" she protested as she wedged past her desk and nabbed a manila envelope that was cantilevered off a filing cabinet. "I've got a *ton* of stuff to do!"

I didn't remark about her seeming to have time for so-called Hawaiian pizza and pink lemonade or for getting her hair done. Instead, I eyed the envelope that had a scrawled *Goldy——Dog File* across it.

"Where did you find this?" I asked.

"Barry had a file labeled 'Catering.' The cops went through it but didn't take stuff from it, it looks like." She was peering at the envelope in my hand with undisguised curiosity. "Your contracts were in the file, plus that manila envelope. What's a dog file?"

"I have no idea, and I doubt I'll find out anytime soon." I tucked the envelope under my arm. "Look, I'm sorry to be crabby but—"

"It's all right," she said, suddenly contrite. Maybe all this new cheer of hers was just her way of denying what had happened to her boss.

"A friend of ours is in jail—"

"I heard. Your assistant."

"My assistant did *not* kill Barry," I said emphatically. "And I'm trying to find out who did." When she wrinkled her nose, I persisted. "Will you help me?"

She took a sip of lemonade. She said, "I'll try," without much enthusiasm.

"What I need to know now," I told Heather earnestly, "is about discounts and gifts that Barry received. Say, from stores. Reps. Vendors. Stuff that might, you know, make people jealous."

Heather's forehead wrinkled. She didn't seem to be thinking so much as trying to find a way to say something unsavory. When I cleared my throat impatiently, she eased back into her chair. "We're supposed to have a no-gift policy. . . ."

"Supposed to?"

She took a bite of pizza and avoided my eyes. After a moment, she said, "Before Barry took over, the only discount we got was at the mall's fast food places. But when the expansion started, stores were really wild to get in here." Her hand went to her throat, where she fingered a thin gold chain. "Barry, uh, did take gifts. He gave a lot of them away, though," she added hastily. "I mean, he didn't need a woman's diamond Rolex or a monthly getaway trip to some exotic place like Maui."

I gripped the lumpy envelope. "Heather, this is terribly important. I have to know the *truth*. I need to know about *specific* things he received." In fact, that was what I'd been mulling over since Page's outburst at the meeting: *Is this true? Or is jealous Page imagining or exaggerating gifts Barry gave Pam?*

"All right, all right!" Heather cried, blushing. "Barry . . . gave me this chain, a free gift from Barton's Jewelry! And he gave my dad a case of Glenlivet. My mom asked for a Vuitton bag and he surprised her with it. That's *it,* I promise! We didn't take any other gifts from Barry and I don't know where he got the stuff. So . . . are you going to turn me in?"

I exhaled and remembered that someone with evidence about Barry's headaches had hired a lawyer to offer that evidence *in exchange for immunity from prosecution*. Would that prosecution have been for receiving gifts without paying gift or income taxes? "What did Barry give Pam Disharoon? Do you know?"

Heather's eyes widened. "Nobody knows that for sure. But lots of people wanted to."

"Like?"

"That private eye," she replied, with a dramatic wave of one hand. No question, this girl had seen too many TV crime shows. "The cops. And some tall blond woman who said she was from the IRS, but I didn't believe her for a second. She looked a lot like Pam, too. Maybe she was her cousin."

"*Do* you know exactly what Barry gave Pam?" If it was big, I thought, if it was really, really, *really* big, then maybe someone had been so angry, jealous, or *something,* that he or she had felt justified in killing Barry Dean.

Heather shrugged and popped a piece of ham into her mouth. "Barry showed me some of the jewelry. That diamond Rolex I told you about, a diamond bracelet, some emerald earrings. I asked him if he was giving pieces to Ellie, too. He said, 'Of course!

Only her taste is so conservative. And anyway, she's already got lots of jewelry.' "

"What else did Barry give Pam?"

"He . . . let her have his Audi, I think. His car got wrecked, and the Audi was in the shop, so he ended up with two problem vehicles, plus he didn't drive his BMW, usually. He only wanted one new car, the Saab, plus the Beemer racing car. Oh, and he gave Pam tickets for luxury trips, although I'm not sure they had a chance to have sexual relations anywhere but in that new car of his. Barry thought he was being followed on the weekends. Looking back, you know, I figured it was that investigator— you know, the one Ellie McNeely hired— who was following Barry."

"Barry and Pam had sex in the new *Saab*?" Was that before or after he drove me out for a latte? *Blech!* Anyway, I wasn't sure Heather was telling the truth. She was at that age when imagined sexual details made any story more fun. Come to think of it, I suppose that was any age.

"I'm *not* kidding!" she protested. "Barry told me about it, along with all the juicy details. I should have sued him for sexual harassment. 'Ever done it in a car, Heather?'

he used to ask me, after lunch. He was laughing. His clothes were all rumpled; he'd gone out with the emerald earrings and come back empty-handed, so I just *knew* he and Pam had *done* it. He said, 'The car is just the best place. You've got leather smells and risk, and then every time you drive it, you can think back to what you did in it a few hours ago.' I mean, is that sexual harassment or *what*?" She punctuated her question by taking another bite of pizza.

So much for Rufus Investigations being able to tell Ellie definitively what was going on. Whatever had been going on between Pam and Barry, it had not been a "mental affair," it had been the genuine article. No wonder he'd missed all those dates with Ellie. I felt a pang of sympathy for my old church friend. "Did Barry give Pam anything else?"

Heather folded up the pizza box and pushed it into her trash can. "Double discount coupons at all the stores, part of a promotion campaign to get mall workers to shop at the mall. He also gave her at least one mink jacket that I know of. I haven't the faintest clue how he got *that*. Oh, and he sent her lots of flowers. Denver Floral wanted to lease here *really* bad." She arched an eyebrow. "Mrs. McNeely probably got really upset when she found out about what he was doing for Pam, huh? What he was doing *to* Pam. I mean, that he was *doing* Pam."

CHAPTER 18

I thanked Heather and left. Two minutes later, I locked myself into a bathroom stall and opened the envelope. I wasn't tampering with evidence, I reasoned, because Barry had *left* this for me. Besides, Barry had always been interested in what dishes I'd be serving. Maybe it was just menus.

It was not menus. The manila envelope contained two newspaper clippings, a business-envelope-size piece of opened mail, and three cardboard boxes from the same high-end line of women's cosmetics.

First I studied the slightly tattered envelope. My name was scrawled above a typed address:

Lucas Holden
General Delivery
Prescott, Arizona 86301-9999

The envelope also bore a post-office-stamped pointy finger. I'd always thought those inked pointed forefingers looked vaguely accusatory. The reason given for the return, *Addressee Unknown/Return to Sender,* included a penned date-of-rejection, from a month before. The return address was the Westside Mall office. Inside I found Lucas Holden's paycheck, five thousand and change, plus a handwritten note:

Lucas, here's your last check. I sent it to the place you said you were going.
Please come back. I know we can work things out.

B. Dean

I put the letter on top of the toilet paper dispenser. So, I figured, that was at least one thing Barry had wanted me to figure out: what had happened to Lucas. Maybe Barry hadn't been sure; maybe he thought Lucas was on the road, or just plain sulking. But I had found out what had happened to Lucas, hadn't I? The ex-construction worker had died in a motel. Being extra cautious, though, why would Barry not have called the cops and reported Lucas as a missing person?

I knew the answer as soon as my mind posed the question. Barry's own words—*Nothing clears a mall like a security threat*—would surely have applied to a construction manager who'd quit in a huff and then turned up missing. So Barry wanted me, the amateur sleuth, to locate Lucas, because he couldn't afford any bad publicity. No doubt, the charming Mr. Dean couldn't have imagined the way I would find Lucas, any more than he would imagine the way I would stumble over his own corpse.

Unfortunately, the other items in the manila envelope were much more baffling. First was a clipped editorial from the February twenty-sixth issue of the *Mountain Journal*. The title, *Does Furman County Really Need Forty More Stores?*, was hysterically answered in the first paragraph: No way. But if Barry had been truly interested in my keeping this editorial, why had he clipped it off mid-point? The page's other side was a pastiche of ads, and included an '81 Mercedes *At a Great Price,* a lot out by the Elk Preserve where the owner would *Build to Suit,* a sale on delivered topsoil from We Got Dirt, and a heartfelt ad for homemade dog biscuits from *Caring for Canines*, which implied that if you *really* loved your pet, you wouldn't feed him those nasty treats from the grocery store.

Frowning, I reread the editorial that was missing part of its text. It was the standard stuff about the mall addition ruining the environment, encouraging big corporations to usurp state jobs, funneling profits out of state, and, horrors, contributing to the mindless growth of materialism! Maybe it was to avoid this kind of rap that Westside had offered their mall for shopaholics' meetings. But why would Barry want *me* to have a slice of *Mountain Journal* polemic?

The second clipping was another cropped article, this one entitled *Teen Held in Shopliftings*. Of course I knew all about

Teddy Fury, so I skimmed it. But I still puzzled over this clipping, because again Barry had trimmed a portion of the text, this time vertically. Had he had eye problems? The back of this sheet held more ads similar to the others. I sighed. The more evidence I collected regarding Barry's murder, the more bewildering things became.

The last three items, the fancy cosmetics boxes, were indeed all makeup. First I opened the slender rectangular box and pulled out a pale green, marbleized plastic compact, a cream foundation designated as *Honeycream*. I opened it; the compact looked as if it had been slightly used. Yuck. The next box held new red lipstick; the third was a roll-up cream blush. I checked all three for secret compartments, tiny written messages, you name it. There was nothing. No question about it—this made a *lot* of sense, as in *none*. I went back to the compact mirror, where my exhausted face squinted back. Barry wasn't the only one who had thought I needed a new look.

I stuffed all the items back in the envelope, which I slid deep into my tote. Tom would have some ideas, I reasoned. He might even know what a *dog file* was.

• • •

I was confused. I was tired. So, I was not in the best of moods when I plodded into the luxurious lingerie department of Prince & Grogan. Pam was there, holding up a lacy teddy, and shaking it from side to side, while a potential customer, a tall, distinguished-looking gentleman with silver hair, gaped. I edged over and heard her croon, "Incredibly slinky and soft against the skin," and "Oh, you'll thank me! And so will she!" and "This one's our top seller. The highest quality, of course. You have to spend money to get the best, but *you* know that."

I eased over to a table of reduced flannel pajamas and surreptitiously watched Pam go through her routine. She was good. "Don't you want something for that special weekend?" "Oh, she deserves it! *You* deserve it!" "We can't keep these in stock!" Pam was like a drug dealer for the heroin of shopping. Unlikely *she'd* ever be a guest speaker at Shopaholics Anonymous.

As Silver Hair smiled and piled items up by the cash register—black lace teddy, pink transparent nightgown, two-piece (very small pieces) nightwear, red satin bustier, feathery mules, push-up bra—he seemed to take on a glow. He told Pam jokes. Her little laugh tinkled. He tilted his silver head close to hers.

Several times, Pam announced, "Then there's one more thing you *must* buy! She is *soooo* lucky to have you."

Silver Hair beamed some more. This man was in a shopping zone. Since I'd first spotted him, he looked taller, more powerful, even happier. Which I suppose was the whole point ... while it lasted.

When he finally whipped out his credit card, I held my breath. Pam's demure voice said eight hundred and something dollars. Where was that security guard with the smelling salts? The silver-haired man beamed and said that would be fine.

"Oh, it's you," Pam said flatly when I appeared at the counter after Silver Hair had swept away triumphantly with his purchases.

"You promised you'd talk to me," I reminded her firmly.

"Yeah, yeah." She glanced around her department, probably to see if there was anyone more important than Goldy the caterer, which meant *anyone* who was willing to splurge on lingerie. "OK, make it fast," she said impatiently. "Thursday is a big noontime shopping period for us, because businessmen usually have lunch with their mistresses on Fridays. Did you know that that's why Fridays are the worst day to get a table at a romantic restaurant? The guys just can't stand the prospect of spending the weekend with their wives, and they want to reassure their girlfriends that they really care. So they buy them a sexy present for that *special* pre-weekend lunch."

"And then have sex in the car afterward? Sort of like dessert?"

Her glare was withering. I smiled innocently. "Sorry. You just hear all kinds of stuff in the catering business. I serve Friday lunches, you know. I'm always wondering what the big rush is to get out."

"Maybe it's your food." She grinned, sending the blond ponytails trembling.

I ignored that. "Pam, I just want to talk to you for a few minutes. Can't I take you to lunch?"

"I told you. I can't go to lunch because it's our busy time."

"I'll buy something." I gestured at the silken heaps around us.

"Yeah, right. I saw you pawing through the sale flannels."

"Sell me a bathrobe, then."

Her face brightened. "Lace or sheer?"

"Er, terry cloth."

"I knew it!" she said, her voice scathing. She wiggled over to a rack of sherbet-colored terry robes that I thought looked quite cozy. Then she lifted an assessing eyebrow at my short, pudgy self, moved away from the small-size robes, and pulled out three medium-size ones. I put on the first, a pale green with satin edging, and assessed myself in a mirrored column. I looked like a half-eaten lime Popsicle.

"Pam, a friend of mine has been accused of killing Barry Dean. I don't think he did it. You seemed to be Barry's friend—do you think he had any enemies the cops aren't looking at?"

Scanning her department unsuccessfully for more sugar daddies, she rolled her eyes. "I wish I knew who those *enemies* were. I'd kill 'em myself."

I unwrapped myself from the green robe and put on the blueberry-colored one. "Ellie McNeely is my friend. I've heard a lot of stuff lately about how jealous she was of you."

Pam sniffed and scowled at the blue robe. "You look like you're wearing a sleeping bag." When I reached for a lemon-colored robe, she said, "I don't know what Ellie's problem was. Barry preferred me. Maybe he would have married Ellie, but so what? I didn't want to *marry* Barry. My sister's married, and she's miserable. I just wanted to ... you know ... do stuff with him."

Like have sex in the car, I thought, but did not say. I did want to hear about Pam's sister, but I also needed to dig a bit more on the topic of Ellie. "So," I asked noncommittally, "did you read in the paper about Barry's steamy love life?"

Pam's eyes lit up. "You bet I did! That article even brought me business. *See the sexy other woman,* that kind of thing." She shook her head dismissively. "Ellie was a bitch, and she only got worse. She was *so* mad at Barry, it was scary. What's that famous quote? 'Hell hath no fury like a woman scorned. . . .' "

"Did you ever see her argue with Barry?"

"Are you going to buy a robe or not?"

"The pink, I think." I pointed to one I hadn't even tried on. Pam assumed a disgusted expression, tugged it off its hanger, and quick-stepped to the counter.

"No, I never saw or heard Ellie argue with Barry," she told me as she scanned the robe's tag. "I heard plenty about how they didn't get along, but it was all gossip."

"Oh, speaking of gossip," I said, as I handed over a wad of bills, "I heard some about your sister Page." I lowered my voice. "Something about how jealous she was of stuff Barry gave you? How she inventoried each of his gifts to you, then bought things just like them for herself, only in a bigger and more costly version? I heard she couldn't keep up, and that she *really* hated Barry, as a result."

How about that—I had undone Pam Disharoon. She stood stock-still, her cheeks vermilion, her eyes ablaze, her blond ponytails quivering. If a dozen sugar daddies had flooded into the lingerie department at that moment, I don't think she would have seen them.

She shrilled, "She *inventoried* what Barry gave me?" She cleared her throat and handed me the receipt and the bagged bathrobe. "Just leave me alone now, OK?"

I nodded to her and grasped the bag. Pam might have been convinced that Ellie was furious with Barry, but in her heart, I was pretty sure Pam now realized someone else had hated Barry even more. Someone who was family. And she couldn't face it.

Back in the van, I turned on the engine and let it idle while I reviewed what I'd learned in the mall. Barry had been a seductive, gift-giving two-timer. OK, I'd already pretty much figured that one out. Hearing more details hadn't contributed much. I was still very skeptical about the Ellie-shoving-Barry-into-a-ditch scenario, and I couldn't believe that two sisters would go to war, take no prisoners, and kill a mall manager, over the eviction of a husband and *stuff* given to the other sister.

Next: Barry had, in his weird way, sought my help in finding his missing construction manager. In addition, Barry had left me, in the cryptically named "dog file," a clumsily clipped article about Teddy Fury's thievery. Three days after Barry had been murdered, Teddy Fury was still AWOL. Barry wanted me to have the editorial decrying the mall's contribution to materialism. In the antimaterialism department, I doubted Barry's death had been staged by a group of rehabbed shopaholics.

The van's heat had not yet kicked in. I shivered from cold, from frustration, from hunger—the sugar high of pastries is woefully short-lived—and from the fact that my vow of abstention had utterly collapsed. *I hadn't had any caffeine for several hours!* Agh!

I squeezed back sudden hot tears. Try as I might, I couldn't see how any of my recently acquired information was going to help Julian.

Scolding myself aloud, I dabbed my eyes and applied some makeup—*not* from Barry's compact—to my nose and cheeks. There was at least *one* of my problems that I could solve right away. I put the van into Drive and eased out of the mall parking lot. The Westside Buzz, the espresso place that Barry had taken me to, was only a few blocks away.

As I was pulling out of the mall parking lot, a brittle flapping sound caught my attention. I made a quick turn back into a parking space; the sound ceased. I checked the backseat and found nothing. There were no loose papers, no open window...Wait a sec. A piece of folded blue paper was wedged into the right rear window. I powered down the window, which made the paper fall out. Sighing, I jumped out, rounded the van, and picked up the fallen sheet.

On one side of the turquoise-colored paper was a printed advertisement extolling the virtues of having your oil changed at Westside Lube—*While U Shop!* Virtually all the vehicles in the lot, I now noticed, had blue sheets stuck under their wipers. Then why hadn't the ad-placer put mine under one of my wipers? The answer lay on the back side of the sheet.

Someone using a black felt-tip pen had scrawled an indecipherable message in what looked like Spanish. Whoever had written it had been in a hurry, that was certain, as the tip of the pen had dragged from word to word. I raced back into the driver side of the car, locked the doors, and stared at the sheet. Of course, I realized glumly, I should be worried about finger-prints and all that. But someone had left me a note. And Julian was being arraigned the next day.

I took a pen and an index card out of my purse and tried to copy the note. It was a question, actually. It only took a few mo-ments of staring at and copying letters be-fore I was pretty sure I had the right words in front of me.

Porque tuvo dolores de cabeza?

I plugged in my not-brilliantly-remem-bered Spanish vocabulary, and eventu-ally honed in on the question as a whole—not that it made any more sense than when I'd received the anonymous phone call.

Why did he have headaches?

Oh, man, I was getting tired of this. *Why don't you just tell me?* my mind yelled back. *He was pushed and fell into a ditch. Aside from that, you're going to have to fill me in.*

My own head was beginning to ache. I needed caffeine now more than ever, so I gunned the van in reverse. The brakes squealed and sent up a cloud of dust as I raced to The Westside Buzz.

On the way over, I left a message for Tom, telling him of all the developments and asking again about the women's alibis and how Arch was doing in the gift department. I also called Marla again. She was not at home. Into her machine, I asked what time she had driven away from Westside on Monday night. Specifically, I went on, for what part of that crucial half-hour, from eight-thirty to nine P.M., had Page and Ellie been with her? Did she have any idea whether either or both of them had actually left the mall when they said they were leaving? The digital clock on the van dashboard said it was just past three o'clock. Good old Marla was probably down visiting Julian.

There was no line at The Westside Buzz. Usually by three in the afternoon, folks are trying to lay *off* caffeine. In my present state, this was definitely out of the question. I ordered an extra-hot four-shot latte made   with—decadence!—half-and-half, and two cinnamon cookies. I took a sip of the rich, creamy drink, decided the *barista* deserved a two-dollar tip for her exquisite creation, and slotted the cup into the van's plastic cup holder.

It was when I was driving away that an insight hit with such force that I slammed down on the brake. Latte slopped out on the mat. I stared at the creamy liquid and told myself I was insane.

But I didn't think I was.

I may not have completely answered the question of why Barry had crippling headaches. I certainly did not understand the meaning of the cosmetics items Barry had left for me. But I had deduced something.

I'd just figured out why Barry Dean had left me his dog.

I had to get back into Barry's house. Tom had said the department had pulled their detail off the place. Would Darlene be home next door? Would she give me a key?

I hit the accelerator again and wove through traffic. *There's something else,* I promised myself. *I know it*. If I could find whatever it was before the next morning,

Julian could be freed. I felt giddy. He'd be out for Arch's birthday! This thought, combined with greedy chugs of latte, made me speed up even more.

Thirty-five minutes later, I pulled up behind Darlene Petrucchio's old pink Cadillac, one of the consignment items she'd never been able to sell and so had bought herself. Covered with five inches of crusty snow, the Caddy looked forlorn.

"OK, here's the deal," Darlene said, once I'd reassured her I wasn't returning Barry's basset hound. She invited me into her kitchen, where I declined a beer. This day, she was clad in a crimson cashmere sweater sewn with bugle beads and a matching pleated skirt—an outfit dating from circa nineteen-fifty-six. "Barry always relied on me when he went on trips," Darlene went on. "I told the cops 'bout startin' his cars once a week, waterin' his plants, walkin' an' feedin' that dog. While the lawyers do the will, the cops axed me to watch over Barry's stuff. They said because he has no next of kin, I've got, y'know, a *proprietary interest*. Doesn't mean I get anything," she added as she lit a cigarette. "It just means the cops can't take care of the stuff, and Barry trusted me with it when he was alive, so why not now?"

"I understand," I said, then launched into a spiel I'd rehearsed mentally all the way up the mountain. "It's just that I seem to have left a computer disk full of menus over in his house. I simply *have* to *have* it. Barry loved menus, and he asked if he could borrow a bunch of mine. But now my computer's crashed, and all I have is that disk, dammit."

Darlene hesitated, and my heart sank. She pulled noisily on her cig. "You sure you don't wanna beer? 'S almost five." I shook my head ruefully. She took a long sip of hers, then, to my delight, snagged a key ring from a drawer. "I don't mind if you look in his house. Jes' don' take anythin'. The cops said they'd finished their processing. Finished their *processing*? What were they doin', smokin' hams in the livin' room?"

A moment later I was ducking long icicles hanging from the Swiss-style gingerbread on Barry's front porch. Behind me, the street was almost completely hushed, with only a slight breeze whisking the freshly fallen snow. I unlocked the front door, which featured a massive brass door knocker in the shape of a basset hound's head.

Get in and get out, I ordered myself. *You still have a birthday cake to make.* Problem was, I wasn't quite sure what I was looking for. Which was the way with scavenger hunts, wasn't it? Especially when the person who'd set the hunt up was dead.

Contrary to what I'd told Darlene, I'd never been in Barry's house. Once inside, I put the key ring in my pocket and leaned against the door, taken aback.

A decorating magazine would have entitled the living room in which I now stood *Homage to the Basset Hound.* The color scheme was entirely devoted to gold, white, and black. Gold walls were lightened with white trim and chair rail molding, in front of which Barry had placed a black lacquered liquor cabinet and long buffet. Black-, white-, and gold-upholstered sofas and chairs were grouped between black lacquered tables and around black braided oval rugs. Wide, narrow, rectangular, and round needlepoint pillows graced the couches and chairs. Every one of them pictured a basset hound.

As I looked for the kitchen, I noticed a

faint but pleasant smell of dog still hanging in the air. The scent made me unaccountably sad. When I finally found the kitchen, it was a small, plain oak-and-tile affair that didn't look as if it had been used much.

"Latte," I said aloud. "So, Barry, where'd you put your coffee stuff?" I began opening cupboards.

Because that was what it had to be, I'd suddenly realized at the espresso place. After the attempted-murder-by-truck, Barry had realized he was in terrible danger. So that was why he'd raced back to his office—to call his neighbor and finish setting up a trail of clues, a scavenger hunt of crime, in case he didn't make it.

Why would he do that? my mind demanded. Why not go directly to the cops? Or at least to the mall owners? But I thought I knew the answer to that one, too. Barry had bent the rules for himself and his own appetites, the likes of which I'd seen with the sexy, gift-greedy Pam Disharoon. Any kind of official investigation would have unearthed the fact that Barry had obtained goodies from vendors, reps, and who knew who else. If he made it home, and the truck driver was arrested, he'd be OK. If not, he'd

left a scavenger hunt for me, his old coffee pal, to figure out what was what. Maybe he'd been planning to leave the state, or even the country.

Anyway, he'd called Darlene. He said if he didn't show up after work, she was to give his dog to me. He'd told Darlene how to spell the dog's "new" name, and instructed her to tape the coffee moniker onto the canine food dishes. In her world of beer, cigarettes, and old Caddies, Darlene did not know from espresso drinks: She'd simply thought Barry had misspelled *Late*.

But the word *Latte* had meaning for yours truly. Correction: It had meaning for *us,* Barry and me. But what exactly was that meaning? We'd drunk the dark stuff together in college; we'd had some together in the last month. And somewhere in that common experience, I was absolutely convinced, he'd pounced on a detail that he now wanted me to ferret out.

I located a pair of scissors and a white plate, which I put on the counter before retrieving a fresh trash sack from under the sink. I opened the sack, set it aside, and pulled out every bag of coffee beans I could find, from the cupboards, two canis-

ters, and the freezer. These I methodically cut open and dumped onto the plate. I was looking for anything remarkable, anything out of place, and most importantly, anything that would somehow clear Julian. After sorting through the beans, I tossed each examined lot into the trash. Eight bags of coffee later, I gave up.

His computer, I thought. Maybe he had a special "latte" or even another "dog" file with information. I pushed open the door to Barry's study, which felt much colder than the rest of the house. I booted his PC, but wasn't blessed with any luck in that department, either. Lots of files on 1st Quarter Profit Projections, Advertising Budget Break-down, Lease Schedules, and the like, but no dog or latte file.

"Something to put the latte into!" I cried, and zipped back to the kitchen. Reopening cupboards, I laid eyes on too-high shelves of cups, saucers, and mugs. I dragged over a chair, climbed up, and took down one after another—the man must have owned fifty mugs and cups—and examined each one, inside and out. On about mug number forty, I began to feel disheartened. But when I came to the last row of five, my heart leaped. The logo on the orange mug said *Thanks a latte*. The cup clanked when I picked it up, and I thanked God with all my heart.

Inside the mug was...a key? A Saab key? I had a key to Barry's Saab on the ring Darlene had given me. I scrambled down from the chair, pulled the key ring out of my pocket, and held both car keys up to the light. They were identical.

"This isn't making sense, Barry!" I protested aloud. Startled by my own voice, I slammed through the door out into the cold, and headed grimly toward his garage.

CHAPTER 19

Behind the garage, Barry's pontoon boat was parked at a slight tilt. It was covered with a canvas sheet now frosted with snow, and spoke of a summer that felt more than three months away. I turned to the garage door. It boasted a hefty new padlock.

The padlock must be an addition from Darlene, I figured. After the cops had processed Barry's Saab, previously parked in the Westside Mall lot, they would have delivered the Saab to Darlene, as the one with the so-called *proprietary interest*. But I was willing to bet that Darlene's own garage was filled to the brim with consignment stuff. I could imagine her insisting the Saab go back into Barry's garage, with her promise that that was where it would stay.

As my chilled fingers fumbled for the padlock's keyhole, I wished desperately for my gloves. I thanked all the heavenly angels when the smallest key on the ring Darlene had given me slid into the padlock and turned. The lock gave; I removed it and pushed through the wooden door.

Barry's silvery-green Saab, glazed with ice like the padlock, was parked next to a black M-6, his BMW racing car. My footsteps scrunched over garage-floor grit as I headed to the Saab. I unlocked the driver-side door—Barry had probably either lost the remote opener, or hidden it in the bottom of a uranium mine—and pulled the lever to open the trunk. You had to start somewhere, I thought grimly.

Carpeted with black fuzzy stuff, the trunk was a disappointment. It held nothing but a pristine spare tire in its well. I'd heard once of people hiding money in the well, though, so I hefted out the tire, which was as cold and heavy as a frigid boulder. For all my effort, the wheel well was empty.

I slammed the trunk shut and slid into the Saab's driver's seat.

I should have guessed the upholstery would be cold, but the icy, hardened leather still sent a chill down my spine. My breath clouded the inside of the car as I poked around, looking in every crevice. I was careful, though. After hearing Heather's story of her boss's lunchtime activities, I didn't want to examine the seats themselves too closely.

At least the cops had not left a mess. The car interior was spotless. On the backseat floor, a thick rumpled towel indicated Barry had probably taken Latte on rides the way he had taken his beloved Honey years ago. Other than that, there were no newspapers, no clothes, no sporting equipment, no clutter of any kind. I groped gingerly under the seats and again came up empty.

The glove compartment yielded the proof of insurance and manual, period. I slammed it shut, frustrated. Then, remembering a trick I'd seen in a movie, I turned the Saab key one click in the ignition, so as to run the accessories. Then I deftly punched the Eject button on both the CD and cassette players. They were empty.

"Dammit!" I yelled, creating another big cloud of verbal steam. Barry had been so proud of this car. The perforated leather seats were ventilated with fans, the turbo kicked in with a blast of power, and he had shown me all its zippy bells and whistles when he'd taken me out for . . .

Coffee. I smiled. Bells and whistles, indeed. Those inventive Swedes had designed a particularly cool gizmo for holding your coffee. Barry himself had pressed the button that brought down a vertical plastic cylinder that automatically turned ninety degrees to hold my . . . latte.

Breathing another prayer, I pushed the button. It didn't move. I cursed silently and pressed it again. The vertical panel squeaked out and opened sideways. Inside the empty circle where my latte had once sat was a key, stuck under plastic tape.

With my frigid fingers barely able to move, I scraped and ripped at the tape until I'd pulled that sucker of a key out of the cup holder. As I stomped back to the house, key ring and new key in hand, I tried to stay calm.

You think this is fun, *Barry?* my mind growled. *Did you ever spend time in jail?*

Have any of your friends been stuck behind bars? Next time, leave typed instructions with your lawyer. It'll be easier on both of us.

I ransacked his office, looking for a file cabinet that needed a key. Nothing. Every drawer was unlocked.

Dog File, Barry had written beside my name on the manila envelope. Maybe if I again spread out everything that was in that packet, I'd see a common element that would lead me to the dog file.

I jammed all the keys into my pocket, slammed out the front door, and traipsed over the ice to my van. It was getting late. I was tired, frustrated, and upset. But it was unlikely Darlene, much less the cops, would ever let me into Barry's house again to look for an imaginary disk. Not only that, but I was running out of time. At my van, I pulled out the manila envelope, then crunched through the packed ice back to Barry's chalet.

Packet in hand, I settled onto the scratchy, black braided rug in the living room. At eye level, I was surrounded by the mournful faces of needlepointed, painted, and lacquered basset hounds.

"Yeah, yeah," I muttered to them. "How come your master had to make everything so difficult?"

On the floor, I laid everything out: the compact, lipstick, and blush; the editorial decrying the mall addition; the article on Teddy; the paycheck to Lucas Holden that had been returned by the post office. Next to them, I placed the manila envelope itself, with its scrawled *Goldy* and *Dog File* notations written in different colored inks, probably penned at different times. My guess was that the *Goldy* reminder had come later, once Barry decided after the truck incident to send me on a wild-goose chase, in case he took a powder.

I surveyed the stuff. Some people enjoy creating a tangle for others, so that only the most determined folks will try to figure out the solution. Clearly, Barry was that kind of person. On the day he died, he'd bequeathed his newly named basset hound to me; he'd also assembled some articles and stuffed them in a manila envelope labeled with my name and a reference to an enigmatic dog file. Less than an hour before he'd been murdered, he'd written me a note saying he had a "tip" for me. Since

Barry had mentioned both a check *and* a tip in his note, I had to assume that that "tip" was verbal in nature, and would have explained everything.

"But the risk, Barry," I said aloud, thinking hard, "is that when you leave too many clues, no one, not even a caterer-turned-sleuth-with-a-friend-in-jail, *no one* will be able to figure out what the *hell* you were trying to say."

All around the room, the basset hounds looked sadder than ever. I ignored their canine countenances and picked up each item from the floor, examined it again, then set it down.

Nothing.

My back ached. I eased myself up to a chair, propped my feet up on an ottoman, and again surveyed the pattern of items. Still, no ideas popped. If I were an old-fashioned deductive English detective, I reflected, I'd have a nice glass of sherry and ponder. I surveyed the living room. Along one wall, the black lacquered cabinet—complete with a family of basset hounds painted on the front—held a silver tray of crystal sherry glasses and, bless me, a bottle of Dry Sack.

I heaved myself up, crossed the room,

uncorked the opened bottle, and poured myself a very small dose. I recorked the bottle and downed a lovely sip. Barry the showman undoubtedly would have pre- ferred offering me a rare wine, and I proba- bly should have checked to see if he had any, but I wasn't choosy, I thought, as I took another sip. Besides, I thought as I peered downward, the liquor cabinet was . . . oh, God.

Locked.

I was so startled I turned too fast and sent the sherry bottle flying. I grabbed for it and missed. The bottle didn't break, thank goodness, but rolled across the living room rug. In trying to catch the bottle, though, I did drop my glass, which crashed and shattered. Exhaling, I stepped over the splinters of glass and the puddle of sherry, tiptoed to Barry's keys, and nabbed the one I'd extracted from the Saab cup holder. With my heart thundering, I inserted it into the cabinet keyhole.

The heavy door opened easily. Inside were not the bottles of expensive wine I had expected, but a stack of files about three inches high. I grabbed them. Why had the cops not taken the cabinet? I wondered. I could hear what they would say. *Because it was extremely heavy, because it was in the living room, because it was a liquor cabinet, because it was locked*. As the ace investigator in the department, Tom would have taken it, of course, and broken into it. But he'd been off the case from the beginning.

I danced back across the room and opened up the files.

Inside the first file was a bulkily folded blueprint. I spread it out, stared at it, and finally figured out that the *Existing Structure* was Westside Mall. Numbers dotted the plan for the addition and lot, but what did that tell me? Not a thing. Someone—Barry?—had penned x's in three different spots. Barry had been trained as an architect; he'd known what the diagram meant. For me, it might just as well have been in Swahili.

Next in the pile was a banded packet of Polaroids and folded sketches. I laid the sketches—there were three of them—out in front of me like cards. The Polaroids were not of Pam or Ellie, but of concrete and dirt photographed from what appeared to be different angles. At the bottom of each photo were penned dates, all in February. The sketches were in Barry's hand, and resembled a cross-section of an archeological dig. *Where footings should be,* he'd written, beside a set of lines. *Where they are,* he'd written to the left of another diagram, and then added: CHECK PHOTOS!

O-kay. I took a thoughtful breath and plowed on. Next was a sheet: *Siblings & Incomes,* with two names typed and annotated.

1. Lawrence. Criminal defense attorney; partner in firm. Annual income: 5 million ++++.
2. Bachman. Orthopedic surgeon; operates on world-class athletes. Annual income: 3 million ++++.

At the bottom was another Barry-scribbled note. *Amount he's borrowed to build custom home: $520,000. Approximate profit from sale of topsoil from this site: $1,600,000.*

And last, there were two more newspaper clippings. One was a piece on a new playground in Aspen Meadow, the other covered the rise in traffic stops for reckless driving. Mystified, I turned them over. Both of them, like the flipped clippings on the floor, included ads for topsoil from We Got Dirt.

OK, so Barry had been on to something. But what? I went back to the Siblings & Income sheet. Did I know either Lawrence or Bachman? With a sinking feeling, I pulled out one of the cards that my—and now Julian's—lawyer had handed me. Underneath Hulsey's name was the listing of the firm's partners.

"Oh, Lord," I breathed. I scurried over to a lacquered end table that held a phone and directory. Flipping through the Aspen Meadow section, I looked for the name and address I'd seen right near the Stockhams' gorgeous place. Brother Bachman, too, had done very well, moving into one of the ritziest areas of Aspen Meadow. And he'd dated Marla!

This was just like Pam and Page, I thought, as I punched buttons. Like Kim and Teddy. One sibling can't stand having less than the other. And then he or she just can't stop competing for stuff, no matter what gets in the way. *No matter what*.

Tom's number had not connected before a large hand closed around my neck. In a split second, another hand wrenched the phone away, and pulled it so hard the cord snapped. The phone went flying. I twisted away from the choke hold with all the energy I could muster. The second hand closed around my throat. I gasped for breath and kicked backward instinctively with first one, then the other foot. Black clouds formed in front of my eyes as a distant voice reminded me, *The abusive husband always tries to silence the wife, to make sure she has no voice. . . .*

With a surge of furious energy, I simultaneously clamped my own hands onto the choker's, turned my head, and bit as hard as I could into my attacker's palm. The choker screeched with pain as blood spurted into my mouth. I yanked myself free and dived toward the front door. Two fists banged into my back, and I reeled onto the couch.

Above me, Victor Wilson tried to hit me again, but I rolled away, scrambled to my feet, and screamed bloody murder as I raced the other way, toward the back door.

"Hey!" he bellowed, sprinting after me. "Get back here!"

I slammed into the back door and fumbled frantically for the doorknob. Victor crashed into me, grabbed handfuls of my hair, and jerked me so brutally that I almost passed out.

"You aren't going anywhere!" he snarled as he flung me down. I staggered sideways into the liquor cabinet and bounced off it onto the floor, the breath utterly knocked out of me.

"Stay there! And shut up!" Victor yelled, as he kicked me viciously in the back.

Again black spots spiraled in front of my eyes. I whimpered and panted for breath.

"You're a thief," I gasped. Victor placed his booted foot on my thigh. He was pressing hard as he looked for something. Pain ratcheted into every cell of my body. "You followed me here!"

"Shut *up,* you nosy bitch! Or I'll smack you again!" He was groping, I realized dimly, through a filthy sack.

Not for a knife, I prayed. *Please, not for another knife.*

"You killed Lucas Holden! And Barry, too!" Talking might slow him down, might give time for Darlene to figure out that the racket she was hearing next door was not the noise from some TV show.

"Shut *up*!"

Squirming, I looked around desperately for something—anything—to distract him. His boot pressed down firmly, pinning me to the floor. *Where in the hell was my cell phone?*

I wheezed, "And . . . and you were going to let our friend Julian, or Ellie McNeely, take the rap. Ellie never crashed her car into Barry's, *you* did. What'd you do, pull her purse with the jewelry receipt and car keys out of the Dumpster where Teddy threw them? Ellie never pushed anyone into a ditch. She never killed anyone. What were you going to do after you trapped her in the toilet tank, kill her and dump her body under some cement at your construction site?"

Victor, still rummaging for something, grunted, "Something like that. Now shut up before I choke you again!" He pushed down harder on my thigh. I winced. There was a lot more to say, but I knew now it wouldn't help. They teach you in self-protection classes to talk to criminals if they attack you. You're supposed to call them by name, you're supposed to appeal to their soft side. Crap to that. Talking doesn't change the mind of a greedy, vicious man.

Victor finally found what he was looking for in the huge bag: a long coil of thick rope.

"What's that for?" I gasped.

"I'm gonna bury *you* under the foundation for our last store," he said matter-of-factly.

My adrenaline soared and I desperately scanned the room. How could I get away from him? Applying more pressure to my leg, he leaned over me. Double crap.

"Victor," I screamed, "I know about your brothers! I know what you're doing! And I brought you *cookies,* you bastard!"

This took him back for a millisecond. And in that millisecond, I kicked away his boot with my free leg, and crab-scrambled a yard away. With an angry roar, he vaulted after me. But by that time I had something in my right hand. When he pounced around the corner of the couch, I hit him square in the face with the Dry Sack bottle.

He squealed and reeled backward, his face a bloody mess of glass shards, liquor, and torn flesh. While he howled, I scooted over to Barry's door and snatched up the doorstop with its needlepoint picture of a basset hound. Under the decoration, thank God, was a heavy brick. While Victor screamed, "You bitch! You *bitch*!" I slammed it into his stomach with all the strength I possessed. He wheeled forward, bellowing with pain, spun around, and landed hard on top of all the papers Barry had meticulously assembled to prove his excavator's wrongdoing. Then, because I'd learned about this in self-defense and because I didn't want to risk Victor waking up before I could get the cops here, I hit him once more, very, very hard. With the brick.

Where it really hurts.

CHAPTER 20

"It's called overexcavating," Tom informed me, as he broke eggs carefully into a bowl late the next morning. "Most of the builders in the Denver area are honest. But there are some crooks, and they love to brag. That's probably how Victor Wilson heard about the way to do it."

It was Arch's birthday. Tom had taken the day off, he said, so he could take care of me *and* bake Arch's cake. After my violent struggle with Victor Wilson, I was definitely out of cooking for the next couple of days. Tom was happily taking over so I could recuperate. And I was determined to let myself rest and heal. I'd even handed my next client over to Liz Fury.

Meanwhile, Arch—otherwise known as the Birthday Boy, which we of course could *not* call him to his face—was ecstatic that Elk Park had another in-service. My son was sleeping in.

"*Over*excavating?" I asked Tom, as I chased four ibuprofen with a double espresso. Every part of my body ached. I was determined to think about, to talk about, anything except how I was feeling.

Tom measured sugar, then dumped it into the whirling mixer. "Works like this. Guy either is or is not in cahoots with the soil and building inspectors. Sometimes inspectors are just stupid, which is what we had with the Westside Mall addition."

"Oh, great."

Tom checked the bittersweet chocolate he was melting in the top of our double boiler. "Remember you told me about that lake of drainage water by the back entrance?" he asked.

"You mean, the one that Victor was so helpful bringing my boxes across?"

"The very one," Tom replied with a grin.

He lifted the pan with its pool of melted chocolate off the heat.

"OK. So there's a lake of drainage water by the mall's back door. How is that so important?"

"Drainage problems, which that project had in the worst way, often come from improper grading. With overexcavation, your crook is going to sell over a *million dollars* of extra dirt. The grading is never going to fix the problem. Lotta rain, lotta snow? That water's gotta go *somewhere*. It can't drain back into the earth, because the impervious surface of a parking lot won't let it. So it just becomes a puddle, a pond, or one of the Great Lakes."

"How much had Victor overexcavated?"

" 'Bout six or eight inches. Over that huge expanse of land, you're talking a lot of dirt. He sold it all through those little We Got Dirt ads, and he made about a million and a half. He had his crew helping him out, too, for cash."

"So...how do we reconstruct the whole thing?" I puzzled.

Tom tilted his head and considered. "It's complicated. Victor Wilson was not only very greedy, he was a very mean, very smart guy."

But he acted nice, my mind automatically supplied. The creep.

Tom went on: "Say Lucas No-toe Holden, the former construction manager, discovered the drainage problem and accused his excavator of overexcavating and selling off the dirt. Maybe Lucas wanted to alert Barry but Victor intercepted him. By the way, you want to hear about everybody's favorite cadaver?"

"Is this going to destroy my appetite?"

"Hope not. We got back the drug screen. Holden had been injected with cocaine, and that, we think, caused the heart attack. Again, it was probably Victor, but I doubt we'll ever be able to prove that. Our theory is that after Victor Wilson intercepted Lucas Holden and used the hypodermic on him, Victor quickly drove— through the night—to a motel where he could wear Lucas's sweatshirt and ball cap to check in *as* Lucas. Then Victor set up a scene so that it looked as if Lucas died of natural causes, and left the body."

"And the coroner out there didn't test for drugs because..."

Tom stood to make me another espresso. Except for bruise marks around my neck, I was in pretty good shape. I liked being pampered, though. In fact, I loved it.

"Because Lucas Holden was a diabetic with heart disease, Goldy," Tom explained, as velvety dark coffee spiraled into a new English china espresso cup. Tom had bought it for me and hidden it until an appropriate occasion presented itself. He figured catching Victor Wilson qualified. "There was no *obvious* drug use," he went on. "So they didn't run a screen. That kind of case, the medical examiner probably wouldn't get involved. Remember, a coroner can be a nurse whose husband is a rancher, say. Her only job is to determine the cause and manner of death. And with no foul play, no obvious drug use, the corpse in pretty good shape, then the coroner thinks, Bingo! Donation."

"But how did Ellie become involved?" I wondered aloud, as I gratefully accepted the crema-loaded espresso.

"First you gotta look at what happened with Barry and Victor. Again, our theory is that Victor typed up a note, supposedly from Lucas Holden, saying 'I quit! I'm going to Arizona. Send my check there.' '*Where in Arizona?*' Barry probably asked Victor, and Victor said 'Prescott' because it came into his head. While Barry was out at the site, though, he saw that something was wrong with the footings. They were even with the surface level of the dirt, instead of below it. Barry had an architecture degree, so—"

"So he acted on his own," I interrupted, "and got the plans from the county. And took pictures. And confronted Victor?"

Tom sighed. "We think so. But that's not all Barry confronted him about."

I sipped the coffee and ran my fingers along my throbbing neck. "When was all this?"

"We're guessing a month ago. That's when Barry first confronted Victor with the overexcavation, and the returned check from Arizona. Where was Lucas? Barry wanted to know. Why hadn't Lucas ended up where you said he was going? And, what the hell are we going to do about this drainage problem you've created?"

"Good Lord."

"We figure Victor pushed Barry into the ditch when they had this confrontation. Unknown to Victor at that time, two illegal Mexican immigrants who worked for him, Jorge and Raoul Sanchez, were watching. Jorge and Raoul speak great English. And they worked their butts off for Victor, who sometimes paid them and sometimes didn't. One day, the two brothers came early for their money, and overheard the whole thing. Barry probably asked Victor one question too many. *Hey, by the way, how come these concrete footings are even with the topsoil, instead of being eight inches lower than the soil?*"

I sighed and shook my head. "So Jorge and Raoul saw Victor push Barry Dean into the ditch? And knew why, after that, Barry complained about headaches?"

"Yup. Jorge and Raoul, chewed out, unpaid, and maybe just a little scared of how violent Victor could become, walked off the job. Victor, instead of being afraid of Jorge and Raoul ratting him out, called them up and said, 'One of you needs to come over here and drive this truck into Barry Dean or I'm going to turn all of you into the INS. Then you two and your mother and all your

little illegal family will be bused straight
back to Mexico.' "

"That *bastard*."

"Victor made Jorge and Raoul swear
the person who had pushed Barry into the
ditch was a woman. Using the same blackmail technique, he forced Raoul to phone in
an anonymous tip that Julian had driven
the truck that almost killed Barry and you.
But they both felt guilty, which is why
they called you anonymously to tip you off
about the headaches. And left you that
note in Spanish, too."

"And I brought the bastard cookies! But
I still don't understand about the cuff links,
and Ellie, and all that."

"After the ditch incident, Victor must
have been real worried about what Barry
would do. In particular, he might have worried about how much Barry had told his
very public girlfriend, Ellie. So before Barry
could do anything, Victor probably decided
to kill Barry and frame Ellie. He followed Ellie around, saw Teddy Fury nab her purse.
Teddy kept the purse and the cash, but
tossed the rest of the purse's contents—including Ellie's car keys and the cuff links receipt—into the Dumpster. Victor fished that

stuff out and laid his plans. First he'd crash Ellie's car into Barry's, to establish the jealousy. Then he planted the cuff links in the dump truck, so it would look as if Ellie tried to kill Barry because he was having something on the side with Pam. But the truck scheme to kill Barry failed."

"And I lost a box of shrimp rolls," I commented.

"At that point, Victor was probably desperate," Tom went on. "He stole your Henckels knife, stalked Barry, and stabbed him in an area invisible to security cameras, behind the P and G shoe cabinet. When the clerks approached to do the cleanup, he shoved Barry *into* the cabinet. But as he was leaving the store, he saw *you* coming in with Arch's guitar. You were asking one clerk after another where the shoe department was. He waited, watched you discover Barry, and whacked you with the guitar."

"Then when Julian was arrested, that worked for him, too," I concluded glumly. "He just blackmailed—who was it? Raoul the construction worker?—to say Julian was driving the truck! That son of a bitch!

He didn't succeed in getting Jorge and Raoul into trouble, did he?"

"Don't worry," Tom reassured me. "Jorge's lawyer got the INS deal he wanted, and both Jorge and Raoul are cooperating fully in the investigation."

"Raoul and Jorge," I murmured. "Two siblings who *really* care about each other."

"Oh! And speaking of siblings! Kim Fury finally called. Apologized profusely for not getting back earlier, but she had gone out looking for her brother, whom she still seems to be constantly ticked off at. But at least she found him. Teddy wasn't holed up studying quantum mechanics, either, sorry to say, or doing volunteer work in the ghetto. But they're probably going to close the strip bar where he'd been living in the basement."

"Ah." I frowned at the dregs in my demitasse. "What was Teddy doing there?"

"Busboy. Got free rent and meals, made good tips, and he got to see the shows for free." He perused his cake recipe and began assembling ingredients.

"All right," I said finally. "Before we get into the whole Pam and Page thing, tell me why Barry didn't just *fire* Victor when he discovered what he was doing."

Tom turned to me. "Goldy, you yourself gave us the answer to that. First of all, as mall manager, Barry didn't have the power to fire Victor. Pennybaker International would have had to do that. And why didn't Barry contact Pennybaker?"

"Because he was afraid of negative publicity," I answered grimly. "Because he was afraid all his borderline-legal antics with giving the vendors' goods away would be discovered. Because if Pennybaker swooped in with their analysts and managers, Barry would be blamed, somehow, for the delay in the mall construction. Maybe they'd discover he was blackmailing Shane Stockham over the rent issue. And...maybe they'd even get wind of his affair with Pam Disharoon. So Barry figured, 'I'll hire my old college pal Goldy, the caterer who solves crimes. She'll help me to find out what happened to Lucas No-toe Holden.'"

"You did great on this," Tom reassured me. "The guys did check out those alibis for Ellie and Page, by the way. The women did go straight home, Ellie with Mrs. Harrington, Page in Shane's car. Shane called a former employee of The Gadget Guy to drive him back up to the Stockham place. He didn't want to risk driving with his wife after they'd almost killed each other at the party. Oh... and our guy who checked out Page's alibi also asked her about all those suspicious shoes. Page never saw Barry in the shoe department. She said she bought so much footwear because that was the best way to get revenge on her stingy old husband."

I shook my head. Tom folded sifted cocoa and sugar into the melted butter and chocolate mixture, then folded in yolks, then creamy, beaten whites. Even as much as my neck now was beginning to ache, I had to appreciate his skill. Tom regarded me with concern. "You look like you're in pain."

"I've had worse pain, please don't worry," I assured him.

He scraped the bowl's luscious dark contents into a springform pan and slipped the pan into the oven. Then he came over and murmured, "Let me rub where it hurts."

Tom's warm hands eased along my upper back. Meanwhile, because it was not a catering day and because Tom had sworn to disinfect the kitchen over the weekend, the dogs were enjoying an unusual foray into the kitchen. Jake the bloodhound and Latte the basset hound pressed in next to me for pats. Like Tom, they also appeared worried about me. Scout the cat, however, was still in hiding. And someone else was missing, too.

"You know what's bothering me most," I said. "Julian—"

"OK, look. Hulsey told me to tell you that neither of us should go down to the jail. It's an embarrassing situation for his firm, and they don't want you or me around just yet."

"Bad publicity?"

"You bet," Tom replied. "Hulsey, Jones, Macauley and Wilson is the best-known criminal defense firm in the state. One partner represents a murder case's initial suspect, you. Then he works with a second suspect, Julian Teller. Later, when a much more credible suspect gets apprehended and hit in the groin by a cop's wife"—I shrugged modestly—"and it turns out the guy now hitting the high notes is the *brother* of the Wilson in Hulsey, Jones,

Macauley and Wilson, they've got a damage-control problem on their hands. They're worried sick the press will be all over them."

"Yeah, yeah," I muttered. Another sibling problem.

"Julian will be all right," Tom reassured me. "And there's something else," he added. "Minor by comparison to all this. Shane Stockham called. Before he could say why he was phoning, I blasted him on his claims about the payoffs to Barry on the rent issue. I told Stockham if he didn't tell me the truth, he'd go straight to jail. Scared the guy to death. He admitted Barry hadn't demanded anything from him. He just made that up so he wouldn't be blamed for holding back on his rent. His lawyer was already dealing with Pennybaker."

"You must have put the fear of God into him."

"That's my job. Anyway, Shane turned all ingratiating after his admission, as if he were the best friend a cop could ever hope to have. He also said he signed up all the investors he wanted. He really needs to get some ring back from you, though. He'll exchange it for the check he owes you." Tom stopped his wonderful massage. "A ruby, sapphire, and diamond ring? Please, please, Miss G.—tell me it's not *stolen*."

I laughed, then promised him I would call Shane. At that moment, the doorbell rang, and the dogs went berserk.

A moment later, Tom was ushering in Ellie McNeely. I tried not to look disappointed that it wasn't Julian. Ellie was carrying a handsome flower arrangement of dark blue iris, daffodils, and white stock, set not in a basket, but on a base topped with a... lacrosse helmet?

"It's for Arch," she said, her tone apologetic. "For his birthday. I told the florist I needed the most masculine thing possible, with a lacrosse theme."

"They're gorgeous," I said, deeply touched.

"Oh," she added, pulling an envelope out of her pocket, "and here's an Abercrombie and Fitch gift certificate for him, too, just so he won't think I'm *totally* square."

"This is so unnecessary, Ellie."

"Goldy," she said earnestly, "I didn't really come here because of Arch's birthday. I came because I wanted to thank you, because I *needed* to thank you." Before I could protest and say, *It's nothing,* she hurried on: "You found out what happened to Barry, and got half choked to death in the process, I heard. You've been great."

We invited her into the kitchen, where we all had more espresso and kept watch over the cake through the oven window. At length, Arch, clad in the sweatsuit he'd slept in, made one of his silent floating appearances.

"It's the Birthday B—!" I stopped instantly when I registered my son's threatening countenance. Laboriously, I got to my feet and shuffled in his direction, hoping for a birthday hug.

"Mom, don't." Arch drew back and gave me a pained look: *Can't you ever treat me as if I were older than three?* "What's that?" he asked, frowning at the flowers.

"They're from Mrs. McNeely," I said. "They're for you. For your birthday."

"Thanks," he mumbled, and nodded in Ellie's direction. "Thanks a lot." He looked from Tom to me. "So my party's going to be now? Is Julian out yet?"

"Don't know," said Tom. "But breakfast

definitely won't be the end of today's party-
ing."

"They really are nice flowers," Arch said
to Ellie, with a sincere smile and brief nod.

"There's a gift certificate, too," Ellie
said, "for A and F." She pointed to the envelope she'd placed on the table.

At that, Arch brightened a bit more.
"Well, gee. Thanks!"

Tom removed the cake from the oven,
set it on a rack, then rummaged through
the freezer for the last batch of Julian-made
chocolate-filled croissants. I set the table
and poured orange juice.

When we were digging into the flaky
croissants a few minutes later, Ellie said
suddenly, "I guess I'll never know if Barry
meant to get engaged or not. It doesn't
matter." Her lovely, wet eyes regarded me
earnestly. "He was two-timing me, but he
wanted to get married, Goldy. He told me
so at the jewelry-leasing event. He said, 'All
these arrangements we're making today
are for the temporary wearing of stones.
But ours will symbolize a lifelong promise.'" I knew she was looking at me for
affirmation. I nodded, thinking only that

Barry had a gift for communication, not necessarily one for commitment.

"Who's ready for another croissant?" Tom cried jovially.

Arch raised his hand. Ellie, still preoccupied, burst out with, "If only I could have figured out that riddle!"

Arch cut his eyes at me. I lifted my eyebrows and gave him a knowing grin. My son had always been an expert at riddles, codes, and puzzles, and he knew how much I appreciated his talent. Arch then glanced at Tom, too, who nodded almost imperceptibly. But before Arch said anything, he unexpectedly looked back at me. His eyes held such tenderness that I was undone. Maybe in that split second, my son realized, as he hadn't in a while, how much my appreciation of him meant that I loved him. I swallowed; my eyes flooded with tears. And then the moment was over.

My son put down his pastry and said, "I know a lot about codes, Mrs. McNeely. If it's that kind of thing."

"It's not a code, it's about sex," Ellie explained.

Arch beamed. Well, he *was* turning fifteen. He said, "Fire away."

Ellie demurred. "Oh, I've taken up too much of your party time. I'm sorry. I'm just preoccupied with my own problems."

"So what's the code?" Arch persisted.

" *'When we fight, and then we* BLANK, *when you do it alone, you'll find your ring.'* " Ellie wrinkled her nose. "You see, whenever we fought, we . . . made love afterward. I sure don't want to know what he meant by 'do it alone,' for crying out loud."

Arch shook his head. A huge grin creased his face. "I *don't* think it's about sex, Mrs. McNeely. When you fight with somebody"—and here he gave me that affectionate expression again—"you do other things. You . . . apologize. You get something for 'em. You . . . make up." Ellie let out breath, still bewildered. "Look, Mrs. McNeely," Arch went on, "Barry meant when you *make up,* get it? Then later you put on *makeup,* you know? Don't you get that?"

Oh Lord, I thought. I bolted from our table as swiftly as a person with a sore shoulder and bruised neck can bolt. From my tote, I retrieved the manila envelope Barry had left for me, that I had remembered to bring home from his place.

When Tom eyed it skeptically, I said,

"Look, I left all the clues to Victor's wrong-doing there in the cabin, OK? This is separate. It's not withholding evidence." Tom shook his head and rolled his eyes, but said nothing. I opened the envelope and shook out the lipstick and blush, both new.

And the compact, slightly used. I grabbed a clean table knife, put a paper towel under the compact, then pried up a corner of the makeup. Bits of creamy chalklike stuff broke, splintered upward, and spilled over the top of the compact. I tried again. And again. When I reached the edge of an object in the middle of the makeup, everyone leaned in. I levered out a thin, delicate cylinder.

And then I held up the ring Barry had intended to surprise Ellie with.

Ellie burst into tears.

For reasons I could not understand, I felt happy for Ellie. The good side of Barry, the side that didn't want to philander, that side of him had left her a promise for what their life together could have been. Maybe some women would have sold that ring faster than you could say *money-back guarantee,* but I knew that, for Ellie, it represented something else. A love—imperfect, to be sure—but still precious, still something to be treasured.

And wasn't it treasure all the players from our drama of this week had been looking for? I checked to see if the cake had cooled as Ellie, Tom, and Arch fed too many homemade dog biscuits to our spoiled hounds. Barry had used *stuff*—not always legally his to give, mind you—to buy admiration and love. Shane, Page, Pam, and most tragically of all, Victor, had wanted material goods to assuage feelings of inferiority, sadness, and loss. Living in resentment, Page spent enormous sums to rent jewelry and buy cars that equaled Pam's. Shane, driven to please his wife, always lived on the brink of financial disaster. Pam and Page competed instead of enjoying each other's company; the two sisters drained their financial resources where they could have just spent time together.

Nor was I immune. For months, I had worried that my son would stop loving me if I failed to buy him a hugely expensive birthday present. But that wasn't what success as a mother was about, was it? Now, seeing him bask in Tom and Ellie's appreciation of his riddle-solving ability, I didn't even think he cared about the darn guitar.

Over the din of dogs and happy chatter, Marla's voice rose shrill and loud from beyond the front door. "Open up!" she shouted. "You can't have this party without me!" She kicked at the door. The dogs howled and raced toward the hall. "What does it *take* to get one of those *pastries* I know you're gobbling *up* in there?" my friend shrieked.

We all tumbled out from the kitchen, people falling over dogs and one another, and pulled open the front door. Marla, grinning triumphantly, was balancing *another* cake, plus a bulging bag of gifts.

"Hey!" she crowed. "Where do you think I've been these last few days? *Shopping* for Arch! Now somebody take this cake! I'm gonna drop it!" Ellie reached through the door, relieved Marla of the pastry box, and lofted it above the dogs' leaping attempts to get it.

From beside the door, Marla then produced a black-and-red guitar that looked about twice as expensive as the one I'd originally bought Arch. Arch cried out with joy.

Then, like a magician, Marla sashayed sideways. She cried, *"Ta-da!" From behind her, Julian appeared.

"I'm here!" he hollered. "Happy birthday!"

He didn't even make it into the hall. I suppose that to the neighbors, we—Arch, Tom, Ellie, yours truly, and both dogs—looked like a football team. How else could a group of people and hounds surge forward in such a perfect wave? Nor would the neighbors have understood why we were yelling and carrying on. This was April the fifteenth, for crying out loud. Nobody was happy on tax day.

But we were. After I hugged Julian, and Arch had given him a cool high five, Arch turned to me.

"Hey, Mom," he said, "I love you." He gave me a tight, firm hug.

"Happy birthday," I said. And I hugged my son back.